'Raven and Sarah . . . make a formidable team, much like Brookmyre and Haetzman, whose first collaboration in fiction is a resounding success'
THE HERALD

'I adored this atmospheric, enthralling novel. Victorian Edinburgh comes thrillingly to life'
JENNY COLGAN

'This menacing, cleverly plotted tale set in 1840s Edinburgh . . . heralds the dawn of a new collaboration between Christopher Brookmyre and his wife Dr Marisa Haetzman'
SUNDAY POST

'A terrific read – Victorian Edinburgh's medical world resurrected, and brought vividly to life'
GAVIN FRANCIS

'*The Way of All Flesh* is a fine tonic, and Ambrose Parry a welcome fresh voice'
SCOTLAND ON SUNDAY

'A great read. Fascinating, informative and intriguing. Old Edinburgh brought to life, and death, within these pages'
LIN ANDERSON

Also by Ambrose Parry

The Art of Dying

THE WAY OF
ALL FLESH

AMBROSE PARRY

CANONGATE

This paperback edition published in 2019 by Canongate Books

First published in Great Britain and the USA in 2018 by Canongate Books Ltd,
14 High Street, Edinburgh EH1 1TE

Distributed in the USA by Publishers Group West

canongate.co.uk

3

Copyright © Christopher Brookmyre and Marisa Haetzman, 2018
Extract from *The Art of Dying* © Christopher Brookmyre and Marisa
Haetzman, 2019

The moral right of the authors has been asserted

British Library Cataloguing-in-Publication Data
A catalogue record for this book is available on
request from the British Library

ISBN 978 1 78689 380 2

Typeset in Van Dijck by Palimpsest Book Production Ltd,
Falkirk, Stirlingshire

Printed and bound in Great Britain by Clays Ltd, Elcograf S.p.A.

MIX
Paper from
responsible sources
FSC® C018072

For Natalie

ONE

o decent story ought to begin with a dead prostitute, and for that, apologies, for it is not something upon which respectable persons would desire to dwell. However, it was the very assumption that the gentle folk of Edinburgh would shy from such a thing that set Will Raven upon his fateful path during the winter of 1847. Raven would not have wished anyone to consider the discovery of poor Evie Lawson as the beginning of his own story, but what truly motivated him was the determination that neither would it be the end of hers.

He found her four flights up on the Canongate, in a cold and crooked wee garret. The place was reeking of drink and sweat, barely tempered by a merciful note of something more perfumed: a womanly musk to be sure, if cheap and redolent only of a woman who sold herself. With these scents in his nostrils, if he closed his eyes he could imagine she was still there, about to haul herself down to the street for maybe the third or fourth time in as many hours. But his eyes were open, and he didn't have to feel for the absence of a pulse to know otherwise.

Raven had seen enough death to understand that her passing from this life into the next had not been an easy one. The sheets on the bed were swirled up around her, testament to more writhing than she ever feigned in her counterfeit passion, and he feared it lasted longer than any of her customers ever did. Her body, far from lying in repose, was in a state of contortion, as though the pain that had carried her off was still with her and there had been no release in death. Her brows remained contracted, her lips drawn apart. There were collections of froth at the corners of her mouth.

Raven laid a hand on her arm and quickly withdrew it. The cold was a shock, though it shouldn't have been. He was no stranger to handling a corpse, but seldom one whose touch he had known when warm. In this moment of contact, something ancient in him was moved by how she had gone from a person to a thing.

Many before him had seen her transformed in this room: from the sum of their desires to a wretched vessel for their unwanted seed, adored and then despised in the moment they spilled it.

Not him, though. Whenever they had lain together, the only transformation he contemplated was the desire to elevate her above this. He was not merely another customer. They were friends. Weren't they? That was why she shared with him her hopes that she might find a position as a maid in a respectable house, and why he had promised to make enquiries on her behalf, once he began to move in the right circles.

That was why she came to him for help.

She wouldn't tell him what the money was for, only that it was urgent. Raven guessed she owed somebody, but it was pointless trying to prevail upon her to reveal who. Evie was too practised a deceiver for that. She had seemed mightily relieved and tearfully grateful that he had got it, though. He didn't tell her from where, concealing a concern that he might have put himself in hock to the self-same money-lender, effectively transferring Evie's debt to him.

It was two guineas, as much as he might expect to live on for several weeks, and thus a sum he had no immediate means of paying back. He hadn't cared, though. He wanted to help. Raven knew there were those who would scoff at the notion, but if Evie believed she could reinvent herself as a housemaid, then he had been prepared to believe it twice as hard on her behalf.

The money had not saved her, however, and now there would be no escape.

He looked around the room. The stumps of two candles were guttering in the necks of gin bottles, a third long ago melted down to nothing. In the tiny grate, the embers were barely glowing in a fire she would otherwise have sparingly replenished hours ago from the coals in a nearby scuttle. By the bed was a shallow basin of water, wet rags draped over its rim and a ewer alongside. It was what she used to clean herself afterwards. Close by it on the floor lay an upended gin bottle, a modest puddle testifying to there being little left inside when it tumbled.

There was no label on the bottle, its provenance unknown and therefore suspect. It would not be the first time some back-alley gut-rot distiller had inadvertently brewed up a lethal draught. Complicating this thesis was the sight of a bottle of brandy on the windowsill, still half full. It must have been a client who brought it.

Raven wondered if the same individual witnessed Evie's throes and left it behind in his hurry to escape the aftermath. If so, why didn't he call for help? Possibly because to some, being found with a sick hoor was no better than being found with a dead one, so why draw attention to yourself? That was Edinburgh for you: public decorum and private sin, city of a thousand secret selves.

Aye. Sometimes they didn't even need to spill their seed for the vessel to be transformed.

He looked once more upon the glassy hollowness in her eyes, the contorted mask that was a mockery of her face. He had to swallow back the lump in his throat. Raven had first set eyes upon her four years ago when he was but a schoolboy, boarding at George Heriot's. He recalled the whispers behind hands of the older boys who knew the truth of what they were looking at when they spied her walking along the Cowgate. They were full of that curious mix of lustful fascination and fearful scorn, wary of what their own instincts were making them feel. They wanted her as they hated her, even then. Nothing changed.

At that age, the future seemed unattainable even as he was hurtling towards it. To Raven, she appeared an emissary of a world he was not yet permitted to inhabit. For that reason, he regarded her as someone above him, even after he discovered that the future was unavoidably here, and learned how easily certain things *were* attainable.

She seemed so much older, so much more worldly, until he came to understand that she had seen only a small, grim part of the world, and far more of that than any woman should. Woman? Girl. He later learned that she was younger than him by almost a year. She must have been fourteen when he saw her on the Cowgate. How she had grown in his mind between that moment and the first time he had her: a promise of true womanhood and all he dreamed it had to offer.

Her world had been small and squalid. She deserved to see a wider one, a better one. That was why he gave her the money. Now it was gone and so was she, and Raven was none the wiser as to what his debt had paid for.

For a moment he felt as though tears were about to come, but a vigilant instinct cautioned him that he must get out of this place before he was seen.

He left the room on quiet feet, closing the door softly. He felt like a thief and a coward as he crept down the stairs, abandoning her to preserve his own reputation. From elsewhere in the close he could hear the sounds of copulation, the exaggerated cries of a young woman feigning her ecstasy to hasten the end.

Raven wondered who would find Evie now. Her landlady most likely: the redoubtably sleekit Effie Peake. Though she preferred to pretend ignorance when it suited her, she missed little that went on under her roof unless she had already succumbed to the gin for the night. Raven felt sure the hour was yet too early for that, hence the softness of his tread.

He left out the back way and through the middens, emerging from an alleyway onto the Canongate a good forty yards west of Evie's close. Beneath the black sky, the air felt cold but far from fresh. The smells of ordure were inescapable around here, so many lives piled one upon the other in the foetid labyrinth that was the Old Town, like Bruegel's *Tower of Babel* or Botticelli's *Map of Hell*.

Raven knew he should repair to his cold and joyless wee room in Bakehouse Close for one last night. He had a whole new beginning ahead of him the next day, and he ought to rest himself ahead of it. But he also knew sleep was unlikely to come after what he had just witnessed. It was not a night for solitude, or for sobriety.

The only antidote to being confronted with death was the hearty embrace of life, even if that embrace was smelly, sweaty and rough.

TWO

itken's tavern was a morass of bodies, a thunderous noise of male voices ever rising to be heard over each other, and all enveloped in a thick fog of pipe smoke. Raven did not partake of it himself but enjoyed its sweetness in his nose, all the more in an establishment such as this for what it covered up.

He stood at the gantry sipping ale, talking to nobody in particular, alone but not lonely. It was a warm place to lose oneself, the greater cacophony better than silence as a backdrop for his thoughts, but he also enjoyed the diversions afforded by homing in on individual conversations, as if each of them were tiny vignettes playing out for his entertainment. There was talk of the new Caledonian Railway Station being built at the end of Princes Street, fears expressed about the possibility of hordes of starving Irishmen finding their way along the track from Glasgow.

Any time he turned his head he saw faces he recognised, some from long before he was permitted inside an establishment such as this. The Old Town teemed with thousands of people, glimpsed upon the street and never seen again, and yet at the same time it could feel like a village. There were always familiar faces anywhere you looked – and always familiar eyes upon you.

He noticed a man in a tattered and ancient hat glance his way more than once. Raven didn't recognise him, but he seemed to recognise Raven, and there was little affection in his gaze. Someone he had gotten into a brawl with, no doubt, though the same draught that precipitated the fight had also blurred the memory. From the sour look on his face, Tattered-hat must have taken second prize.

In truth, mere drink might not have been the cause, on Raven's part at least. There was a dark want in him sometimes, one he was learning to be wary of, though not enough to be the master of it. He felt a stirring of it tonight inside that gloomy garret, and could not in honesty say whether he had come here to drown it or to feed it.

He met Tattered-hat's gaze once more, whereupon the man scurried towards the door. He moved more purposefully than most men might exit a tavern, casting a final glance Raven's way before disappearing into the night.

Raven returned to his ale and put him from his mind.

As he raised the tankard again, he felt a slap on his back, the hand remaining to grip his shoulder. Instinctively he pivoted on a heel, fist formed tight and his elbow drawn back to strike.

'Hold, Raven. That's no way to treat a colleague. At least not one who still has coins in his pocket to match his drouth.'

It was his friend Henry, whom he must have missed in the throng.

'My apologies,' he replied. 'One cannot be too careful in Aitken's these days, for standards have slipped and I'm told they're even letting surgeons in.'

'I didn't think to see a man of your prospects still patronising an Old Town hostelry. Aren't you moving on to fresh pastures? It won't make for the perfect start should you present yourself to your new employer having had a bellyful of ale the night before.'

Raven knew Henry wasn't serious, but it was nonetheless a timely reminder not to push things too far. One or two would be adequate to help him sleep, but now that he had company, one or two was unlikely to be the whole of it.

'And what of you?' Raven batted back. 'Have you not duties of your own in the morning?'

'Indeed, but as I expected my old friend Will Raven to be indisposed, I sought the ministrations of another associate, Mr John Barleycorn, to soothe the woes cast by my duties today.'

Henry handed over some coins and their tankards were refreshed. Raven thanked him and watched Henry take a long pull at the beer.

'A taxing shift, was it?' Raven asked.

'Bashed-in heads, broken bones and another death from peritonitis. Another young woman, poor thing. Nothing we could do for her. Professor Syme could not discern the cause, which drove him to a state of high dudgeon, and which of course was everyone else's fault.'

'There'll be a post-mortem, then.'

'Yes. A pity you are not free to attend. I'm sure you could offer greater insight than our current pathologist. Half the time he's as pickled as the specimens in his laboratory.'

'A young woman, you say?' Raven asked, thinking of the one he just left. Evie would be afforded no such attention once she was found.

'Yes, why?'

'No reason.'

Henry took a long swallow and eyed Raven thoughtfully. He knew he was under exacting scrutiny. Henry was quite the diagnostician, and not merely of what ailed the body.

'Are you well enough, Raven?' he asked, his tone sincere.

'I'll be better once I've got this down me,' he replied, making an effort to sound cheerier. Henry was not so easily fooled, though.

'It's just that . . . you have a look about you, of which I have long since learned to be wary. I don't share your perverse appetite for mayhem and nor do I wish to find myself treating your wounds when I ought to be resting.'

Raven knew he had no grounds for protest. All charges were true, including the glimmer of that dark want he feared was in him tonight. Fortunately, given Henry's company, on this occasion he felt sure the ale would quench it.

You've the devil in you, his mother used to tell him when he was a child. Sometimes it was meant in humour, but sometimes it was not.

'I am a man of prospects now, Henry,' he assured him, proffering payment and gesturing for two refills, 'and have no wish to jeopardise them.'

'A man of prospects indeed,' Henry replied. 'Though why the esteemed Professor of Midwifery should award such a coveted position to a reprobate such as yourself remains a mystery to me.'

Reluctant as he was to admit it, it was a question that gave Raven pause too. He had worked hard to win the professor's approval, but there had been several equally diligent and committed candidates for the apprenticeship. He had no solid notion of why he had been given the nod ahead of the rest, and did not like to dwell upon the precariousness of such caprice.

'The professor hails from humble stock,' was as much as he could offer, an answer unlikely to satisfy Henry any more than it satisfied Raven. 'Perhaps he believes that such opportunities should not be the sole preserve of the high-born.'

'Or perhaps he lost a wager, and you are the forfeit.'

The drink flowed, and with it old tales. It helped. The image of Evie flickered in and out of his vision like the guttering candles in her room. But listening to Henry, Raven was reminded of the world Evie did not get to see, reminded of the opportunity waiting for him across the North Bridge. A little of his love for this place and for the Old Town in general had died tonight. It was time to leave it all behind, and if anyone was a believer in new beginnings, it was Will Raven. He had reinvented himself once before and was about to do so again.

Several tankards later they stood outside Aitken's watching their breath turn to steam in the chill of the night air.

'It's been good to see you,' Henry said. 'But I'd best be getting my head down. Syme's operating tomorrow, and he's all the pricklier when he can smell last night's tobacco and beer on his assistants.'

'Aye, "prickly" is the word for Syme,' Raven replied. 'With emphasis on the first part. Meanwhile I'm back to Mrs Cherry's for one last night.'

'Bet you'll miss her and her lumpy porridge,' Henry called out as he turned onto South Bridge in the direction of the Infirmary. 'Not to mention her effervescent personality.'

'For sure, she and Syme would make a fine match,' Raven called back, crossing the road and heading east in the direction of his lodgings.

Raven knew there were elements of his time here that he might one day regard with nostalgic fondness or regret, but his accommodations were not among them. Ma Cherry was a cantankerous old crone who resembled her name only in that she was round and reddened, for there was certainly nothing sweet about her. She was as sour as earwax and as desiccated as a corpse in the desert, but she kept a lodging house that was among the cheapest in the town; just above the workhouse in terms of comfort and cleanliness.

A smir of cold rain blew about him as he headed down the High Street towards Netherbow. Clouds had gathered and the moonlight disappeared since he made his way to Aitken's. He noticed that some of the street lights remained unlit, making it almost impossible to avoid the piles of muck on the pavement. He inwardly cursed the lamplighter who had failed to do what Raven considered to be a straightforward job. If he himself was as incompetent, lives would be lost.

Lighting fell within the responsibility of the police office, as did keeping the gutters clear. Their main priority, however, was the investigation and recovery of stolen property. If they observed that as well as their other duties, Raven thought, then every thief in the Lothians could sleep easy.

As he approached Bakehouse Close he stepped on something soft and his left shoe began to fill with water; at least he hoped it was water. He hopped for a couple of yards, trying to shake off whatever was clinging to his sole. Then he became aware that a figure had emerged from a doorway and was loitering in front of him. He wondered what the fellow was waiting for, and why he would be lingering with the rain becoming heavier. Then Raven drew close enough to see his face, which in the gathering darkness was also close enough to smell the rancid decay from his carious teeth.

Raven did not know his name, but he had seen him before: one of Flint's men. Raven had christened him the Weasel, after his furtive manner and rodent-like features. The Weasel did not strike him as the type to chance confronting Raven alone, which meant he was bound to have an accomplice nearby. Probably that slow-witted fellow he was with the last time: Peg, Raven had named him, for the sole tooth standing amid his ruin of a mouth. Raven had probably passed him without realising a few moments ago. He would be hiding in another doorway ready to cut him off if he ran.

This encounter was not mere happenstance, he realised. He remembered the man who had been staring at him and then departed so purposefully from the tavern.

'Mr Raven, you're not trying to avoid me, are you?'

'As I can think of nothing that would commend your company, then my general intention *would* be to avoid you, but I was not aware I was being sought.'

'Anyone who owes Mr Flint will always be sought. But you can guarantee my absence just as soon as you make good on your debt.'

'Make good on it? I have barely owed it a fortnight. So how about you sub me an advance on that absence and get out of my way.'

Raven brushed past him and resumed walking. The Weasel did not seek to apprehend him, and nor did he immediately follow. He would be waiting for his accomplice to catch up. He and Peg were used to breaking the bones of already broken men, and some craven instinct perhaps detected that Raven had a greater stomach for the fight. The ale might have doused what burned in him before, but the sight of this sphincter-blossom was reigniting it.

Raven walked slowly, aware of the footsteps behind him. He was searching in the gloom for a weapon. Anything could be turned to such a purpose: you simply needed to know how best to use it. His foot happened upon something wooden and he bent to lift it. It was a splintered length, but solid enough.

Raven turned around and rose in one movement, the stick drawn back in his right hand, then something exploded inside his head. There was light everywhere and a whiplash movement, as though his inert body was being hauled like a dead weight by the momentum of his head. He hit the wet cobbles with a rattle of bones, too fast to make any attempt to cushion his fall.

He opened his dazed eyes and looked up. The blow had rendered him insensible, he reasoned, for he was having visions. There was a monster above him. A giant.

Raven was dragged from the street into the dark of an alley by a creature that had to be seven feet tall. His head alone was twice the size of any man's, his forehead impossibly overgrown like an outcrop of rocks at a cliff-edge. Raven was paralysed by pain and shock, unable to react as he saw this Gargantua rear up before him and bring down a heel. The sound of his own cry echoed off the walls as pain erupted inside him. He flailed in response, curling his limbs tight about him, then felt another post-holer of a blow drive down through the huge trunk of his assailant's leg.

Gargantua crouched to sit astride him, pinning his arms to the floor with the sheer weight of his thighs. Everything about this brute seemed stretched and disproportionate, as though certain parts of him had just kept growing and left the rest behind. When he opened his mouth, there were even gaps between his teeth indicating that his gums had kept spreading out around them.

The pain was indescribable, worsened by the knowledge that Gargantua's fists were free to rain down more damage. No amount of alcohol would have been sufficient to dull his senses through this, else the operating theatres would be going through more whisky than Aitken's.

His mind was a storm, coherent thought nigh impossible amidst such agony and confusion, but one thing seemed clear: there was no prospect of putting up any kind of fight. If this monster wished to kill him, then he was going to die here in this alley.

Gargantua's face was a compellingly grotesque vision, more fierce and distorted than any gargoyle clinging to the walls of a church, but it was his thick, sausage-like fingers that drew Raven's gaze in the gloom. With his own hands helplessly restrained, he was entirely at the mercy of whatever these outsize pommels might wreak.

Raven felt relief when they were directed to rifling through his pockets, but this was short-lived as he remembered that there was little to be found there. Gargantua held what few coins Raven had left in the palm of his hand, which was when the Weasel emerged from the shadows, pocketing the money and crouching down alongside the monster.

'Aye, not so free with your mouth now, are you, Mr Raven?'

The Weasel produced a knife from his pocket and held it up in what little light was to be found in the alley, making sure Raven could see it. It was about four inches long, the blade thin, a bloodstained rag wrapped around the wooden handle for a surer grip.

Raven silently prayed for a quick end to his ordeal. Perhaps a stab upwards under his ribs. His pericardium would fill with blood, his heart would stop beating and it would all be over.

'So now that I have your attention, let us properly address the issue of your debt to Mr Flint.'

Raven could barely find the breath to speak, with the weight of the monster crushing him and the pain still gripping his trunk. The Weasel seemed to notice and ordered the hulk to raise himself just enough for Raven to be able to issue a whisper.

'See, it seems you were keeping your light under a bushel. Since lending you the sum, we have learned that you are the son of a well-to-do lawyer in St Andrews. So having re-evaluated your status, Mr Flint has brought forward the expected date of redemption.'

Raven felt a new weight upon him, though Gargantua had eased himself off. It was the burden of a lie returned to its teller, in accordance with the law of unforeseen consequences.

'My father is long dead,' he wheezed out. 'Do you think if I could have borrowed from him, I would be seeking out cut-throat usurers?'

'That's as may be, but the son of a lawyer must have other connections, in time of need.'

'I don't. But as I told Flint when he lent me, I have prospects. When I begin to earn, I will be able to pay, with interest.'

The Weasel leaned closer, the stink from his mouth worse than anything in the gutter.

'Oh, there will be interest. But for an educated man, you don't seem to understand this very well. Mr Flint doesn't wait for prospects. When you owe him money, you find a way to get it.'

The Weasel pressed the knife against Raven's left cheek.

'And just so you know, us usurers don't only cut throats.'

He drew the blade across, slow and deep, all the time looking Raven in the eye.

'A wee something to remind you of your new priorities,' he said.

The Weasel slapped Gargantua on the shoulder by way of telling him they were done. He climbed to his feet, freeing Raven to put a hand to his face. Blood was welling through his fingers as they tenderly probed the wound.

The Weasel then pivoted on a heel and kicked Raven in the stomach where he lay.

'You find the money,' he said. 'Or next time it's an eye.'

THREE

aven lay in the dark for a while and concentrated solely on breathing. With his assailants gone, he felt relief flood through him, an uncontainable elation that he was not dead. Unfortunately this manifested itself in an unexpected urge to laugh, which proved far more containable under protest from his ribs. Were they broken, he wondered. How much damage had been done? Were any of his organs contused? He could imagine blood dribbling between the layers of the pleura, putting pressure on his bruised lung, constricting its expansion even now that the brute had removed himself.

He put the image from his mind. All that mattered was that he was still breathing, for now, and while that remained true, his prospects were good.

He put his hand to his cheek again. It was wet with blood and mushy, like a bruised peach. The wound was deep and wide. There was no option to return to Mrs Cherry's without this being seen to.

Raven dragged himself to Infirmary Street, where he decided it would be best to avoid the porter's lodge and the stern questions his appearance would surely prompt. Instead he made his way along the wall to the section most favoured by the house surgeons for climbing over. Henry and his peers used this means of ingress when they did not wish to draw attention to late-night excursions, as such behaviour might see them called in front of the hospital board. It took several attempts in his enfeebled state, but Raven eventually hauled himself over the wall before climbing in through a low window that was always left unlatched for this specific purpose.

He shambled along the corridor, leaning against the wall when his breathing became too laboured and painful. He crept past the surgical ward without incident, hearing loud snoring emanating from just behind the door. The noise was likely coming from the night nurses, who frequently imbibed the wines and spirits supplied for the benefit of the patients in order to ensure for themselves a good night's sleep.

Raven made it to Henry's door and knocked repeatedly on it, every second it remained unanswered adding to the fear that his friend was in a post-tavern stupor. Eventually, the door swung inward and Henry's bleary and tousled visage appeared around it. His initial response was one of horror at what creature had visited him in the night, then came recognition.

'Gods, Raven. What the bloody hell has happened to you?'

'Someone took exception to the fact that I had nothing worth stealing.'

'We'd better get you downstairs. That's going to need stitching.'

'I diagnosed that much myself,' Raven said. 'Do you know a competent surgeon?'

Henry fixed him with a look. 'Don't test me.'

Raven lay back on the bed and attempted to relax, but this was not easy given that Henry was approaching his lacerated face with a large suture needle. He was trying to recount just how many times Henry's tankard had been refilled, calculating the implications for how neatly he would be capable of stitching. Drunk or sober, no quality of needlework was going to spare him a scar, which would be the first thing anyone noticed about him in the future. This was likely to have ramifications for his career, but he could not afford to think about that right then. Most immediately his priority was to remain still, but the pains racking him and the prospect of Henry's needle were militating against that.

'I realise that it's difficult, but I must ask you to refrain from writhing, and when I commence, from flinching. Part of the wound is close to your eye and if I get the stitching wrong it will droop.'

'Then I will have to be rechristened Isaiah,' he replied.

'Why?' Henry asked; then it came to him. 'Mother of God, Raven.'

Henry's expression was funnier than the joke, but any relief it gave Raven came at a sharp cost to his ribs.

Raven lay still and attempted to transport himself from the here and now, so that he was less conscious of the procedure. Unfortunately, his first destination, quite involuntarily, was Evie's room, the sight of her twisted body appearing in his mind just as Henry's needle first penetrated his cheek. He felt it push through the skin and into the soft layer below, could not but picture the curve of it bridging the sides of the wound before re-emerging, which was when he felt the tug of the cat-gut through his already ravaged face. It hurt far more than the Weasel's knife, that being over in a couple of seconds.

He put up a hand as Henry was about to commence the second stitch.

'Have you any ether?' he asked.

Henry looked at him disapprovingly. 'No. You'll just need to tolerate it. It's not as though you're having a leg off.'

'That's easy for you to say. Have you ever had your face stitched?'

'No, and that good fortune might be related to the fact that nor do I have an inclination to bark at the moon and pick fights with Old Town ne'er-do-wells.'

'I did not pick any— ow!'

'Stop talking,' Henry warned, having recommenced. 'I can't do this if your cheek is not still.'

Raven fixed him with an ungrateful glare.

'The ether doesn't always seem to work anyway,' Henry told him, tugging the cat-gut tight on the second loop. 'Syme has just about given up on it, and with someone dying of the stuff recently, I think that will nail down the lid.'

'Someone died of it?'

'Yes. Down in England somewhere. Coroner said it was a direct result of the ether but Simpson continues to champion it.' Henry paused in what he was doing. 'You can ask the man about it yourself when you start your apprenticeship with him in the morning.'

Henry continued with his needlework, his head bent low over Raven's face. He was close enough that Raven could smell the beer on his breath. Nonetheless, his hand was steady, and Raven got used to a rhythm of penetration and tug. No stitch was any less painful than its predecessor, but nor were any of them more painful than the ache in his ribs.

Henry stepped back to examine his handiwork. 'Not bad,' he declared. 'Maybe I should conduct all my surgery after a bellyful at Aitken's.'

Henry soaked a piece of lint in cold water and applied it to the wound. The coolness of the material was surprisingly soothing, the only pleasant sensation Raven had felt since his last swallow of ale.

'I can't send you back into the arms of Mrs Cherry looking like that,' Henry said. 'I'll give you a dose of laudanum and put you in my bed. I'll sleep on the floor for what's left of the night.'

'I'm indebted, Henry, truly. But please don't allude to Mrs Cherry's arms again. In my current state, the image is liable to make me spew.'

Henry fixed him with one of his scrutinising stares, but there was mischief in his tone.

'You know she provides extra services for a small additional fee, don't you?' he said. 'I gather many of her young lodgers have sought comfort in those arms. She's a widow and needs the money. There's no shame in it. I mean, between the scar and the droopy eye, you may have to begin revising your standards.'

Henry led Raven to his bed, where he lay down delicately. He hurt in more places simultaneously than he had ever hurt in individually. His face was full of cat-gut and, joking aside, he really might have to alter his expectations with regard to his marriage prospects. But it could all have been so much worse. He was still alive, and tomorrow was a new beginning.

'Right,' said Henry, 'let's get you that laudanum. And if you are going to be sick, please remember that I'm on the floor beside you and aim for my feet rather than my head.'

FOUR

arah was tarrying in the professor's study when the bell rang, an unwelcome but inevitable interruption to a moment of tranquillity. She was taking time and care about her duties as she loved being in this room. It was a sanctuary of calm insulated from the chaos in the rest of the house, but her opportunities for asylum were infrequent and usually short-lived.

She had taken some trouble over the laying of the fire, ensuring that there was a plentiful mound of coal piled in the grate. The fire was lit winter and summer to ensure the comfort of the patients the doctor saw here, but it was a particularly cold day and it was taking some time for the air in the room to thaw. A small amount of ice had formed on the inside of the window beside the doctor's desk, a delicate pattern of fern-like fronds that disappeared when she breathed on it. She wiped the resulting moisture away with a cloth and took a moment to admire the view. On a clear day such as this you could see all the way to Fife. At least that is what she had been told. She had never ventured much beyond the outskirts of Edinburgh herself.

The desk beside the window was piled high with books and manuscripts that Sarah had to clean around without disturbing. She had over time perfected her technique, a skill acquired through painful trial and error and the rescuing of errant scraps of paper from the fireplace.

The room had not always seemed so welcoming. When she first came into Dr Simpson's service, she had been quite terrified by what confronted her in here. Against one wall stood a tall cabinet upon several shelves of which sat jars of anatomical specimens: all manner of human organs immersed in yellowing fluid. More troubling still was that many of them were damaged, diseased or malformed, as though their very presence was not unsettling enough.

In time she had come to be fascinated by all of it, even the jar that contained two tiny babes, face-to-face, joined together along the length of the breastbone. When she had first seen it, Sarah had been gripped by questions regarding where such a thing had come from and how it had been procured. She also wondered about the propriety of keeping such a specimen, preserving what was quite clearly human remains instead of burying them. Was it right that such a thing be displayed? Was it somehow wrong to look at it?

Beneath the shelves was a cupboard housing the doctor's teaching materials for his midwifery class. Sarah was unsure whether exploration of the cupboard's contents was permitted, but as it had not been specifically prohibited she had indulged her curiosity on the few occasions when time allowed. It contained an odd collection of pelvic bones and obstetric instruments, the use of which she could only guess at. There were forceps, of course, with which Sarah was familiar, but there were other more mysterious implements, labelled as cephalotribes, cranioclasts and perforators. Their names alone suggested something brutal and Sarah could not imagine what place they had in the delivery of a child.

In keeping with its curator, there was a distinct want of method in the organisation of the study in general and of the library in particular, which Sarah would have remedied had she the time to do so. Books seemed to be randomly allocated a position on the shelf. For instance, there was a red-leather-bound compendium of Shakespeare sandwiched between the family Bible and the *Edinburgh Pharmacopoeia*, and she recalled how a list of the family's pets had for some reason been inscribed within the cover.

Her finger reverentially touched each spine in turn as she read the titles: Paley's *Natural Theology*, *The Anatomy and Physiology of the Human Body*, Adam's *Antiquities*, Syme's *Principles of Surgery*. Then Jarvis popped his head round the door.

'Miss Grindlay is calling for you,' he said, rolling his eyes as he withdrew.

Sarah allowed the tips of her fingers to linger for a few more moments on the spines of the leather-bound volumes. It was one of the great frustrations of her position: ready access to an eclectic collection of books but very limited opportunities to read them. Her hand came to rest on a book she had not seen before. She removed it from the shelf and slipped it into her pocket.

As she left the room and headed for the stairs she became caught up in a storm of newsprint precipitating from the upper floors. The doctor was evidently on his way down. He liked to read the daily papers – the *Scotsman* and the *Caledonian Mercury* – in their entirety before getting out of bed, and thought it entertaining to drop them over the banister on his way down the stairs. This was much appreciated by the two elder children, David and Walter, who liked to ball up the paper and throw it at each other and the staff; less so by Jarvis who had to clear it all away. Sarah manoeuvred her way around falling newspaper, excitable children and grumbling butler and ascended the stairs.

She entered Aunt Mina's room on the third floor and was confronted by the usual chaos. The entire contents of Miss Mina Grindlay's wardrobe appeared to have been scattered about the room, dresses and petticoats strewn over every available surface, bed, chair and floor. Mina herself was still in her nightclothes, holding up a dress in front of the mirror before discarding it with all the others.

'There you are, Sarah. Where on earth have you been?'

Sarah assumed the question to be rhetorical and so remained silent. Mina seemed to be continually frustrated at Sarah having to perform other duties around the house, oblivious to the fact that, being the only housemaid, if she didn't lay the fires, bring the tea, clean the rooms and serve the meals there was no one else who would do so. Mrs Lyndsay seldom left the kitchen and Jarvis, butler, valet and general factotum, had his hands full tending to the doctor.

'How many times have I said,' Mina continued, 'that a woman in my position should have a lady's maid?'

Almost every time I come in here, thought Sarah.

'I can't be expected to dress myself.'

'Mrs Simpson seems to manage it,' Sarah suggested.

Mina's eyes flashed and Sarah immediately knew she had spoken out of turn. She was about to apologise, but Mina had begun to speak and it would compound her transgression to interrupt.

'My sister is a married woman and in mourning to boot. Her choice of attire is an entirely straightforward matter.'

Sarah thought of Mrs Simpson in the heavy black bombazine she had been wearing for months, pale and wan from prolonged time spent indoors.

'But Sarah, you really must refrain from giving voice to your every thought. Your opinions, unless specifically requested, should be kept to yourself. I was indulgent of this when you were new to the position, but I might have done you a disservice by not reining you in. I fear you will misspeak before someone less understanding and find you have talked yourself onto the street.'

'Yes, ma'am,' Sarah replied, casting her eyes down in contrition.

'There is much to commend the simple discipline of holding one's tongue. I have to do so often enough when I disagree with how my sister wishes to run her household. I am merely a guest here, and grateful for that, as you should be grateful for your position. We each have our duties, and dressing well is an essential one for a woman of my station.'

Mina gestured towards the mountain of clothes on the bed, indicating that she required Sarah to help her choose what she should wear.

'What about this?' Sarah held up a modest grey silk dress with a lace collar which she had starched and pressed only the day before.

Mina looked at it for a few minutes, assessing its suitability.

'Oh, it will have to do,' she said, 'although I fear it is a little too plain to have men reaching for their pens in order to write me a sonnet.'

Sarah glanced in response towards Mina's writing table. As always there was a letter in progress, and beside it a novel.

'What are you reading?' Sarah asked, knowing the subject of literature would reliably serve to put her recent impertinence from her mistress's mind.

'A novel called *Jane Eyre*, by Currer Bell. I have just finished it. I was not previously familiar with the writer.'

'Did you enjoy it?'

'That is a complex question in this case. I would prefer to discuss it with an informed party, so please feel free to take it for yourself.'

'Thank you, ma'am.'

Sarah slipped the book into her pocket alongside the other slim volume she had just procured from the library.

Now that an acceptable gown had been selected, Mina stepped into her corset and stood with her hands on her hips as Sarah grabbed the laces and pulled.

'Tighter,' Mina demanded.

'You'll be unable to breathe,' Sarah said as she hauled on the laces again.

'Nonsense,' said Mina. 'I haven't fainted yet, despite the fact that all the ladies of my acquaintance swoon with great regularity. Sometimes with an element of stagecraft,' she added, a hint of a smile playing upon her lips.

Once Mina was suitably clothed Sarah then had to style her hair. This took considerably longer than tying a corset. A starch bandoline had to be applied to ensure that the hair, once wrestled into place, would remain there throughout the course of the day. The hair was then parted in the centre at the front, braided and looped round the ears. A second parting was made across the top of the head, from ear to ear, and the hair swept up in a tight bun at the back. The task required patience and precision, two qualities when it came to styling hair that Sarah seemed to lack.

'This is why I need a lady's maid,' Mina said to her reflection, her lips pursing at Sarah's efforts. 'I know that you do your best, Sarah, but I will never attract a husband without the right kind of help.'

'I could not agree more, Miss Grindlay,' Sarah replied, gratefully laying down brush, comb and hair pins.

'The problem is that good, reliable help is so hard to come by. Look at the difficulties Mrs Simpson has had trying to find a suitable nurse for the children.'

The rapid turnover of nursery nurses was no mystery to Sarah. The Simpsons had three children: David, Walter and baby James. David and Walter were rarely confined to the nursery at the top of the house, their natural curiosity at all times indulged, and previous incumbents had baulked at the behaviour that was not just permitted but encouraged. Another factor was that Mrs Simpson seemed reluctant to fully hand over responsibility for her children to anyone else, presumably as a consequence of having already lost two at a young age.

'The Sheldrakes have just lost one of their housemaids,' Mina continued, turning in her chair to address Sarah directly.

'Which one?'

'I think her name was Rose. Do you know her?'

'Only in passing. I know the other housemaid, Milly, a little better. What happened?'

'Absconded. Just like that. Though there are rumours that she was seeing a young man. Actually the rumours are that she was seeing several.'

Mina turned back to the mirror and applied a little rouge to her cheeks. Sarah made it for her using rectified spirit, water and cochineal powder. She wondered why it should be considered so wrong for a housemaid to court male attention when it seemed to be Mina's predominant purpose.

'I met her just last week,' Sarah said. 'Outside Kennington and Jenner's.'

'How did she seem?' Mina asked, turning in her chair again.

'Fine,' Sarah replied, ever aware that duty obliged her to give a neutral answer.

In truth Rose would have seemed fine to anyone who had never met her before, but Sarah had been struck by the sullenness of her demeanour. She had come upon Rose and her mistress as they were exiting the shop on Princes Street. Mrs Sheldrake stopped to exchange pleasantries with an acquaintance, allowing Sarah and Rose to do the same, albeit more awkwardly. As Sarah had told Mina, she was more familiar with Rose's colleague Milly, and was easier in her company. Rose was 'vivacious', according to Milly, a politer way of describing a girl Sarah regarded as flighty and full of herself, and of whom she was instinctively wary.

Rose had seemed uncharacteristically reserved that day, as though weighed down by a heavier burden than the packages she was carrying. She was pale, her eyes puffy, and she said little in response to Sarah's gentle enquiries as to her health.

Sarah had glanced across at Rose's mistress, a heavy-set woman around the same age as Mrs Simpson but who seemed considerably older. This was partly due to her physical appearance, about which she did not seem to take the greatest care, and partly because of her austere countenance. Sarah wondered uncharitably what her husband must look like, never having seen Mr Sheldrake.

It was well known that Mrs Sheldrake had a temper, of which the young women in her employ frequently bore the brunt. Rose was doubtless on the receiving end more than most, but this lifeless despondency seemed more than the result of a hearty dressing down. Perhaps it was cumulative, Sarah had thought gloomily, worrying for her own future. If life in service could dull the light in someone like Rose, what might it do to her?

'Well, don't just stand there, Sarah,' Mina said, the subject of Rose's disappearance quickly forgotten. 'I'm sure you must have other things to attend to.'

Thus dismissed, Sarah left the room and made her way downstairs, thinking about the many duties she could have completed in the time it took to squeeze Mina into a dress and subdue her hair. As usual there were more things to be done than hours in which they could be accomplished, and today there was the additional task of airing one of the spare bedrooms for the arrival of the doctor's new apprentice.

Sarah wondered if he could be prevailed upon to take an interest in Mina. At least that would make the extra work his presence generated worthwhile.

FIVE

gust of wind whipped about Raven as he crossed the North Bridge, causing him to reach up with one hand to secure his hat. Its sting made the warmth of August seem a memory of a forgotten age, and within it he felt the harsh and certain promise of winter. There were other promises in that wind, however. The blast was cold but fresh, blowing away the pervasive reek that had surrounded him these past years. Here on the other side of the bridge lay quite another Edinburgh.

He turned onto Princes Street and passed Duncan and Flockhart's, where he caught sight of himself in the druggist's window. In the glass he was reminded that though the Old Town's stink could be blown away, its mark would be upon him for life. The left side of his face was swollen and bruised, the stitches sitting up prominently along the contused curve of his cheek. Beneath his hat his hair was sticking out at odd angles, matted together in places with dried blood. When he arrived at Queen Street, Dr Simpson was as likely to send him abed as a patient as to welcome him into his practice.

The pavement was broader here, the crowds thinner. The people he passed were straight-backed and assured in their gait, strolling in a manner that was purposeful and yet unhurried as they browsed the shopfronts. By contrast, the Old Town was a hill of ants, its inhabitants bowed and scuttling as they hastened about its twisted byways. Even the road seemed to lack the mud and ordure that piled up relentlessly within the narrow alleyways of the Canongate.

As he turned onto Queen Street, a brougham carriage drawn by two lively steeds pulled to a halt just ahead, prompting Raven to wonder absently if the coachman had trained his beasts to void themselves only in the poorer parts of town.

No. 52 was one of the largest houses in that part of the street, spread out over five levels if the basement was included. Broad steps, clean and recently swept, led up from the pavement to a large front entrance framed by two pillars on each side. Even the railings appeared to have been freshly painted, giving the impression that cleanliness and order would be found inside. This caused him to think of how late he was, due to Henry's laudanum. He considered what he might say by way of explaining himself. Perhaps his face would be excuse enough. And perhaps he would be told the offer of apprenticeship was void given that he had not shown sufficient decorum as to at least be prompt on his first day.

Raven straightened his hat and tried not to contemplate the condition of his clothes as he reached for the brass knocker. Before he could grasp it, the door began to open and a great beast of a dog bounded through the gap, almost bowling him to the floor. It continued towards the waiting brougham, where the coachman held open the door as though the hound itself had summoned the carriage.

The dog was followed by a figure clad in a voluminous black coat and top hat. Professor James Simpson seemed equally intent upon the carriage until his attention was taken by the waif reeling on his threshold.

Raven's new employer stopped and looked him up and down. He seemed momentarily confused before one eyebrow shot up, signalling that some form of deduction had taken place.

'Mr Raven. Not a moment too soon, yet within a moment of being too late.'

Simpson indicated with a sweeping gesture that his new apprentice should follow the dog into the carriage.

'We have an urgent case to attend – if you feel you are able,' he added archly.

Raven smiled, or at least attempted to. It was hard to know exactly what his damaged face was doing. He hauled himself aboard the carriage and attempted to squeeze in beside the dog, which seemed reluctant to surrender any part of his position on the seat to the newcomer.

No sooner had he gained a small piece of the upholstery for himself than Dr Simpson took his position opposite and called to the driver to proceed. The carriage took off at impressive speed and the dog immediately hung its head over the edge of the window, tongue lolling as it panted with delight.

Raven did not share its joy. He winced as they rattled over the cobbles, pain shooting through him as though the wheels were running over his ribs. The doctor did not fail to notice, and was intently scrutinising his damaged face. He wondered if he should try to concoct some more palatable explanation for his injuries, or whether he would be storing up greater trouble by lying to his employer on his first day.

'I should perhaps have left you in the care of our housemaid, Sarah,' Simpson said reflectively.

'Your housemaid?' Raven asked, his discomfort rendering him unable to moderate an ungracious tone. He wondered if this was Simpson's subtle way of conveying displeasure at his tardiness, downplaying his afflictions by implying that they required no greater ministration than a hot cup of tea.

'She is rather more than that,' Simpson replied. 'She helps out with the patients: dressings, bandages and so on. Quite a capable young woman.'

'I'm sure I'll manage,' Raven said, though his ribs were telling him otherwise. He hoped that the patient they were going to see could be dealt with quickly.

'What happened to you?'

'If you don't mind, I'd rather not revisit the subject,' he replied, which was honest at least. 'Suffice it to say I am glad to have left the Old Town behind me.'

The brougham turned left onto Castle Street, prompting Raven to wonder where their destination might lie: Charlotte Square, perhaps, or one of the fine townhouses on Randolph Crescent. On the bench opposite, Dr Simpson was looking through his bag, an expression upon his face indicating concern that he may have forgotten some vital piece of equipment in his hurried departure.

'To where might we be bound, professor?'

'To assist a Mrs Fraser. Elspeth, if I recall her name correctly. I haven't had the pleasure of a formal introduction.'

'A fine lady?' Raven ventured, the promise of moving in more rarefied circles like a balm to his wounds.

'No doubt, though we are unlikely to find her at her best.'

At the foot of the hill, the carriage turned left again, proceeding east away from the castle. Raven speculated that perhaps Mrs Fraser was staying at one of the impressive hotels along Princes Street. He had heard tell that wealthy ladies would often travel from the country so that physicians of Simpson's calibre might attend them.

The brougham did not stop at any of them, however, instead continuing the very length of Princes Street before turning right onto the North Bridge and taking him straight back to the very place he thought he had left behind.

The carriage drew to a stop outside a shabby building only yards from where he had found Evie last night, and just around the corner from his own lodgings. As he climbed down from the brougham he wondered if Mrs Cherry might be in the process of tossing all his belongings into the street, as he was moving out today and should already have been back to collect them this morning. He wondered too if Evie had been found yet. If not, she would be before long. The smell would become obvious soon enough, even in that squalid close.

Simpson stepped from the carriage followed by the dog. He searched the doorways and shopfronts momentarily, then set off up a narrow and dimly lit close, the dog scampering after him.

Confusion reigned in Raven's aching head. What was a man of Dr Simpson's stature and reputation doing in the Canongate? Where were the rich ladies of the New Town that he had been led to expect? What of the grand houses wherein lay the sweet-smelling wives and daughters of the quality?

Raven followed his new chief into the passageway and was confronted by a familiar ammoniacal aroma, like cabbage boiled in urine. Clearly Mrs Cherry had been sharing recipes around the neighbourhood. They climbed three storeys up a dark staircase, Simpson's pace remaining steady throughout the ascent even as Raven felt the strain grow in his thighs and an ache pound in his battered chest.

'It's always the top,' the professor observed, with gratingly good cheer.

The door was opened by a typical male inhabitant of these parts, unshaven and missing his front teeth. It always amazed Raven that he could live so close to people and yet never have seen them before, or at least not noticed them any more than the cursory assessment of whether they might be a threat. The sight of this one would ordinarily be enough for Raven to check his pockets were secure, but there was no need, they having already been emptied by the Weasel and Gargantua.

Despite his unkempt appearance, the man did not smell too bad, which came as a small relief. The same could not be said for the chamber they were shown into. The stench hit him full in the face, an ungodly combination of blood, sweat and faecal matter. He observed the merest wave of discomfort on Simpson's visage, before the doctor masked his response behind a calm veil of politeness.

The man of the house hovered at the threshold a mere moment before absenting himself with visible relief.

Mrs Fraser was lying within a tangle of visibly soiled sheets, her face contorted with pain. Raven banished an image of Evie in the throes she endured alone and confined himself to the here and now, though this was scarcely more pleasant. The patient was evidently in labour and making heavy weather of it, drenched in sweat with her face an unnaturally purple colour. She was scrawny and malnourished, similar to many of his erstwhile neighbours and almost all of the patients he had encountered both in his dispensary work and in walking the wards of the Royal Infirmary.

Simpson seemed unfazed by his surroundings, which did not bode well as far as Raven was concerned. He really did not wish to spend his time ministering to the poor when there was money to be made among the wealthy, particularly with his eye under threat should he not soon make good on what he owed.

Simpson whipped off his great black coat and rolled up his sleeves.

'Let's see what's what, then,' he said, as he made his initial examination.

A few moments later he reported that the cervix had not yet fully dilated and declared himself content to await events. He installed himself on a chair beside the only window, where he began to read his book. The dog curled itself up beside him on the floor, indicating that the beast was sufficiently versed in its master's habits to know they were in for a long haul.

'I like to make use of bits and pieces of time,' Simpson said, indicating the volume on his lap. 'Some of my best papers have been written at the bedside of my patients.'

Raven took in the only other seat in the room, a three-legged stool, liable to put skelfs in his arse. He lowered himself reluctantly onto it, thinking he would have ideally preferred to wait out the time in a nearby hostelry, which prompted him to remember that he had no money on him, and precious little back at Mrs Cherry's either. He would have little option but to develop more abstemious habits. Would that he had done so one day sooner.

Lacking any reading material by way of diversion, time seemed to slow. Raven reached instinctively for his watch and remembered that it was gone. Gargantua had been through his pockets and found the one thing of value that Raven possessed. In truth, the old timepiece was of modest monetary worth and would do little to reduce the sum that he owed even if it was passed on to Flint, which he doubted. But its absence was felt keenly, because his father had given him that watch. It was thus a valuable keepsake inasmuch as it was a constant reminder that the old wretch had given him nothing else worth having.

With some difficulty he got up and moved the stool into a corner of the room, hoping that by doing so he might rest his head on the wall and perhaps sleep for a while. He changed his mind when he saw the damp and peeling plaster, seemingly held together by clumps of black mould. He had to make do with sitting upright and letting his head fall forward onto his chest.

He must have drifted off at some point because he was suddenly hauled from oblivion's gentle respite by a scream from the patient. The laudanum which had been liberally applied to Mrs Fraser by a local midwife prior to their arrival had evidently worn off. There was a young, worried-looking girl – when did she arrive? he wondered – filling a bowl with water from a jug.

Simpson looked over at his new apprentice as he washed his hands.

'Ah, Mr Raven. You are awake. It is time to re-examine the patient and decide upon the best course of action.'

Raven rinsed his own hands in the bowl and watched as Simpson performed the examination, but there was little he could see. A blanket had been draped across the woman's knees, obscuring the view. The doctor then turned to face him.

'Would you care to make an examination yourself?'

Raven could think of little he would like less right then, but it was not an invitation. He steeled himself and took a moment to remember how hard he had worked to put himself in this position.

He reached beneath the blanket, closing his eyes as he attempted to work out the position of the infant's head relative to the maternal pelvis. With only touch to guide him, his inexperienced hands were not so gentle as the doctor's, and the woman grunted in her discomfort, occasionally eyeing him with a resentment bordering on violence. He was increasingly tempted to toss the blanket aside. If he was to learn anything from these encounters, it would be better, would it not, if he could at least see a little of what he was doing.

'What are your findings?' Simpson asked, his voice calm and quiet. Raven was uncertain whether this tone was intended to reassure him or the patient, but it served to remind him that he was not the one who ought to be feeling the greater stress.

'The infant's head is sitting at the pelvic brim,' he stated, surprised at his own conviction. 'It has not descended as it should have done.'

Simpson nodded, eyeing him thoughtfully. 'How should we proceed?'

'Forceps?' Raven ventured, a question rather than a statement of fact.

The mere mention of the dreaded instrument drew a loud moan from Mrs Fraser, while the young girl diligently mopping her brow stopped what she was doing and began to weep.

'Fear not,' the doctor told her, his tone still as measured. 'Bear with us just a bit longer and we shall have the little one delivered safe.'

Simpson then turned to Raven, his voice deliberately quieter, inaudible to the others above the cries and moans.

'The head has not yet entered the brim of the pelvis, so it is too high even for the long forceps. In this case I think turning would be the better option.'

The doctor picked up his bag and rooted around in it, eventually removing a piece of paper and a stubby pencil. Leaning on the wax-spattered table, he drew a cone shape and pointed at it as though it explained everything. Raven's incomprehension proved legible enough upon his expression for Simpson to add some arrows as he attempted to clarify what his diagram represented.

'The whole child can be considered cone-shaped, the apex or narrowest part being the feet. The skull can also be thought of as a cone, the narrowest part of which is the base. By turning the child in the womb, the feet can be pulled through the pelvis first, distending the maternal passages for the transit of the larger part. The feet are first brought down then used to pull through the body and the partially compressible head.'

Raven grasped the notion only vaguely but nodded vigorously to forestall any further explanation. The screams were rattling his aching head and he wanted the whole thing to be over almost as much as Mrs Fraser.

Simpson then removed an amber-coloured bottle from his bag.

'This is an ideal case for ether,' he said, holding up the vessel as evidence of his intentions.

Raven had seen ether used before in the operating theatre. The patient had complained vigorously about its lack of effect while oblivious to the fact that his gangrenous foot was being removed even as he spoke. Raven was amazed, but there were those who argued it had only been partially successful, inasmuch as they thought the very purpose of the anaesthetic was to render the patient insensible and therefore altogether less troublesome.

He had inhaled it himself at a meeting of the Edinburgh Medico-Chirurgical Society, shortly after its anaesthetic effects had been discovered. It produced an unpleasant dizziness resulting in much staggering about. This caused some short-lived hilarity but he had not fallen asleep as others had done. He had wondered if perhaps he was resistant to its effects in some way.

Raven watched as Simpson poured some of the fluid onto a

piece of sponge. The air was immediately filled with a pungent aroma, which was welcome in that it partially masked the other odours still permeating the place. The sponge was then held over the patient's nose and mouth. She recoiled initially at the fumes, before the young girl said gently: 'It's the ether, Ellie, like Moira had.'

The agent's reputation evidently preceding it, she breathed in the vapour eagerly now, before passing quickly and easily into sleep.

'It is important to administer a narcotising dose,' the doctor said, 'thereby avoiding the potentially troublesome primary stage of exhilaration.'

He spoke of ether with knowledge and enthusiasm, just as Henry had implied. There were those who were already dismissing it as a passing novelty, but clearly Simpson was not among them.

He indicated that Raven should take command of the soporific sponge while he busied himself at the other end.

'Ether is most helpful when turning or using instruments,' he said as he reached his hand into the patient's uterus. The lack of response from Mrs Fraser, in contrast to her previous tortured writhing, convincingly bore this out.

'I've found a knee,' the professor reported, smiling.

With Simpson's activities largely obscured by the blanket, Raven looked down at the sleeping woman; except she wasn't sleeping. She lay completely still, almost as though she was suspended in some realm between life and death. She had become an effigy of herself, a figure cast in wax. Raven found it hard to believe that she would ever wake up, and with alarm recalled Henry's mention of a recent death from the stuff.

A few minutes later Simpson announced that the feet and legs had been delivered. The body and head soon followed in a gush of blood and amniotic fluid which formed a puddle at the doctor's feet.

Simpson produced the infant from beneath the blanket, rather like a stage magician revealing a dove from an upturned hat. It was a boy. The child began to cry, lustily. The ether evidently had little effect on him.

The baby was swaddled and handed to the young girl, who had been standing statuesque and wide-eyed while the delivery was in progress. She stirred herself now and began singing softly to the child, seeking to soothe its angry bawling.

The mother slept on while the placenta was removed and the baby cleaned and dried. Then she woke as if from a natural sleep and seemed surprised to the point of confusion to find that her ordeal was over.

As the child was placed in the delighted mother's arms, the young girl went to summon the new father. Mr Fraser stepped tentatively into the room at first, almost in a state of disbelief. He looked to Simpson as though for permission, before approaching closer and placing a hand gently onto the head of his newborn son.

Raven was surprised to see tears welling in Mr Fraser's eyes. He hadn't thought him the sort. That said, there had to be a great well of relief gushing through him, as the outcome in cases of obstructed labour was always far from certain. Raven was more surprised to feel tears well up in his own eyes. Maybe it was an effect of all that had happened last night, but he felt this dank and squalid place transformed briefly into one of hope and happiness.

Mr Fraser wiped his eyes on his grubby sleeve then turned to shake the doctor's hand while fumbling in his pocket for the fee that was due. Raven caught a glimpse of the modest specie in the man's dirt-smeared palm. It seemed a paltry sum to offer a man of Dr Simpson's reputation, particularly as he had performed the delivery himself.

Simpson also appeared to be examining the proffered coins. Clearly it wasn't enough, and Raven was bracing himself for an awkward exchange. Instead the doctor reached out and gently closed Mr Fraser's fingers around the money.

'Naw, naw. Away with ye,' he said, smiling.

He picked up his bag, waving to Mrs Fraser who was now nursing her infant son, and led Raven from the room.

They stepped out into the Canongate, Raven enjoying the feel of a cool breeze upon his face. He imagined it blowing away all that had adhered to him in the preceding hours, feeling as though he had been confined inside Mrs Fraser's womb itself.

Simpson was looking about for his carriage, which was not where they left it, the coachman having perhaps decided to take a turn to relieve the monotony during the many hours they were inside. Raven cast an eye about the street also, which was when he noticed a small gathering outside a close across the road. Evie's close.

He drifted nearer, as though conveyed there by an involuntary compulsion. There were two men carrying out a body swathed in a shroud, a cart waiting by the roadside. The shroud was grey and tattered at the edges, one that had been used many times before. Nothing fine, nothing new to clothe poor Evie, even in death.

There were several familiar faces standing on the pavement, other prostitutes. Some he had known through Evie, and some he had merely known. Evie's landlady was there too, Effie Peake. Raven kept his head down. He did not wish to be recognised, and even less to be hailed.

There was an officer of the police standing at the mouth of the close, watching the corpse being loaded onto the cart. Raven overheard someone ask him what had happened. 'Just another deid hoor,' the officer replied neutrally, not even a note of regret in his voice. 'Killed herself with the drink, looks like.'

The words echoed and echoed around Raven's head. He felt a hollow open up inside him, something deeper than shame.

Just another deid hoor.

That was not the woman he knew. Evie deserved to be more than that.

SIX

arah surveyed the waiting room and observed with a frown that there were a good many patients still to be seen. Dr Simpson's sudden departure had resulted in an inevitable delay as Dr George Keith, his assistant, was left to deal alone with all those who remained. Sarah liked George, but he was slow and had a tendency to lecture the patients, which she didn't care for. She wondered if she should request that Dr Duncan come and help but decided it was unlikely he would. He was always too busy with his experiments, though this was perhaps no bad thing. He had the coldest of manner and seemed better suited to dealing with chemicals than with people.

She much preferred watching Dr Simpson work, but that was a relatively rare occurrence. He mostly saw the well-to-do patients upstairs, where Jarvis had the equivalent to Sarah's role. To be fair, Jarvis was better equipped to deal with the clientele up above, being seldom cowed by their complaints. He exhibited a healthy disregard for their position in society and as a result was seldom intimidated, browbeaten or lost for words.

Jarvis was a tall man, which made it difficult for others to physically look down on him. He was also very particular about his appearance, carrying himself with great elegance and dignity, and was confidently articulate. Sarah often thought that with a different set of clothes Jarvis could easily pass for a member of the upper orders himself. On one occasion she had seen a gentleman approach the butler, waving a rolled-up newspaper in a rather threatening manner. 'I have been waiting to see Dr Simpson for more than an hour,' he had said, 'which I find to be quite unacceptable. I have come all the way from Jedburgh.'

'Is that so?' Jarvis had replied witheringly. 'The last patient was from Japan.'

Sarah looked again at the sorry assembly littering the downstairs waiting room that was her domain. They were poor-looking souls suffering a variety of maladies that Sarah could often diagnose merely by looking at them. Scrofula, consumption, ringworm and scabies were all frequently in evidence. The sound of coughing and expectoration was so commonplace that she was no longer aware of it, although it was always there.

She sighed as she noticed the time on the clock above the fireplace. There was always so much work to be done and so little time for the pleasures that others took for granted. She patted the books still weighing down her pocket and wondered if she would have the opportunity to open them today.

She was shaken from her musings by the sound of someone coming down the stairs. She looked up, expecting to see Jarvis, but it was Mina.

'Sarah, I have been ringing the bell in the drawing room repeatedly and no one has answered.'

'Mrs Lyndsay doesn't always hear the bell when she's in the scullery, ma'am.'

That was certainly what Mrs Lyndsay claimed to be the case. The cook insisted that she was deaf in one ear, which was why the bell sometimes went unanswered, but Sarah suspected otherwise. Mrs Lyndsay resented being interrupted when she was cooking.

'I am in need of tea. I have been struggling with the same piece of embroidery for the past hour. Such a difficult pattern.'

'Wouldn't it calm your spirits to be reading a book instead?' Sarah suggested.

Mina's expression indicated that this was a notion so self-evident as to be stupid, and was about to explain why.

'Of course I would rather be reading. I would spend all my days reading if I could. But for reasons passing understanding, embroidery is considered a desirable accomplishment in a prospective wife, and therefore it is incumbent upon me to master it, such is my lot. So for pity's sake, bring tea or I shall run mad.'

Sarah looked again at the waiting patients. She was unlikely to be called upon to escort any of them to the consulting room soon, as a dependably garrulous old woman had only recently been shown in.

'I shall bring up some tea directly,' Sarah said as Mina retreated swiftly back up the stairs with her handkerchief at her nose, evidently having caught a whiff of the waiting room.

Sarah plodded down to the kitchen, wondering if she should ask Mrs Lyndsay about Rose, the Sheldrakes' missing housemaid. In her time at Queen Street, Sarah had developed a degree of scepticism about the veracity of Mina's accounts of things. Her stories always contained a kernel of truth but this was frequently obscured by the embellishments she so liberally applied.

The cook was bent over a large pot on the range. The kitchen was filled with a rich, meaty aroma and Sarah's stomach rumbled in response to it.

'Game pie, is it, Mrs Lyndsay?'

Sarah liked to guess what was on the menu by the smell of it. She had a good nose and was usually correct in interpreting what it told her.

'The doctor delivered the heir to a great estate last week and received a brace of pheasants and some rabbits for his efforts. Is her ladyship wanting tea?' Mrs Lyndsay looked towards the ceiling as she said this, indicating that she had indeed heard the bell.

'Yes. She's doing battle with a troublesome bit of sewing,' Sarah said as she filled the kettle.

Mrs Lyndsay chortled, the laughter rippling through her large frame. 'Still busy upstairs?'

'There seems to be no end to it today.'

'Having the new apprentice should help. And then perhaps you will be able to concentrate upon the job you're actually employed to do.'

'But I like helping out with the patients,' Sarah said. 'It's the best part of my duties.'

'That's as may be, Sarah, but the floors won't wash themselves. The medical work should be left to those who have been trained to do it. Don't you think?'

Sarah could see no point in arguing. 'Yes, Mrs Lyndsay,' she said with a sigh.

As she placed the teapot and cups on a tray she thought she might risk bringing up the subject of Rose Campbell. As a general rule Mrs Lyndsay disliked gossip, but would often divulge small pieces of information if asked directly.

'Miss Grindlay says that the Sheldrakes' housemaid has run away.'

'Apparently so.'

'Why would she do such a thing? The Sheldrakes are good people, are they not?'

'Who is to say what happens when the doors are closed and the world's not watching.'

Sarah waited for elaboration but there was none. Mrs Lyndsay's aversion to gossip often meant things were referred to rather elliptically.

Any request for further information was curtailed by a very insistent ringing of the drawing-room bell.

'Best take that up,' the cook said, indicating the tea tray.

Sarah lifted it and left the kitchen before anything further could be ascertained.

She entered the drawing room, happy that she had managed

to navigate stairs and door without any spillage. Mina was propped up on a chaise-longue reading a book, her embroidery discarded on the floor beside her. Mrs Simpson was in an armchair by the window staring at the view outside. She looked pale and tired, her fatigue exacerbated by the black she was obliged to wear.

'Are there any ginger biscuits?' Mrs Simpson asked.

'Yes,' said Sarah. She was happy that she had anticipated this need – Mrs Simpson frequently suffered with her digestion – though she began to fear she hadn't brought enough as Mina was already hovering above the tray.

'Sarah, I wish to go shopping tomorrow,' Mina said, biting into a biscuit before her tea was even poured.

Sarah groaned inwardly at the prospect. Shopping with Mina was usually a prolonged affair. There was likely to be no time for books today and there certainly would be no time tomorrow.

She had just finished pouring when another bell sounded, the front door this time. She excused herself and exited in time to see Jarvis escorting one of the upstairs ladies into the consulting room.

Sarah trudged down the stairs feeling increasingly irritated. On her way through the hall she passed the lower waiting room, where the same patients (to her mind suffering from more pressing complaints than the ones upstairs) sat listlessly, staring at their shoes.

Sarah opened the door and what little patience she still possessed drained from her. She was confronted by two women who were, without doubt, of the upstairs variety. They were extravagantly dressed in what Sarah assumed to be the latest fashion: ermine-trimmed coats, kid gloves, boots with no mud on them (how did they manage that?), and elaborate hats perched precariously upon their coiffured heads. Compared to those already waiting they seemed to be in robust good health, though one kept dipping her head as if attempting to hide her face beneath her hat. Large, perfectly formed ringlets dipped down below the border of her bonnet. Her hair was the most remarkable shade of red.

'Is the doctor at home? We should like to consult him,' said the one with the bigger hat, the less retiring of the two. Her companion's gloved hand was resting in the crook of her arm and she gave it a reassuring pat as she spoke. Sarah was momentarily distracted by the huge piece of millinery balanced at an improbable angle on her head. There was a profusion of feathers, brightly coloured ribbon and lace. Sarah could imagine magpies nesting in it.

The lady looked at Sarah with disdain, as though she had expected the doctor to answer the door himself and was disgruntled at having to deal with an intermediary. Her gaze was so disapproving that Sarah initially thought she must have something unseemly on her apron to cause such offence. But there had been no contact with pus or blood that morning and a quick look confirmed that her apron was in fact quite clean.

'I'm afraid the doctor is from home. An urgent visit,' she said, hoping that this explanation would suffice.

The lady in the bigger hat sighed and turned to her companion. 'Shall we wait, dear? I think that we shall wait.'

Her companion did not respond.

Sarah took a deep breath and explained that there were already more patients waiting than could reasonably be seen upon Dr Simpson's return, thinking while she did so that she might have been better fetching Jarvis to deal with this.

Both ladies now looked at her as though she was being deliberately obstructive. Did they think she was lying about the doctor's absence and the waiting patients?

The lady with the large hat looked down her aquiline nose and spoke firmly. 'My dear girl, I am sure we can be admitted. Take my name. Dr Simpson knows me!'

Sarah looked back at the accumulated mass of human misery already installed in the waiting room. There were almost as many upstairs too.

'Madam, Dr Simpson knows the Queen,' she said, then closed the door.

SEVEN

r Simpson's coachman had brought the brougham around after only a few minutes, the dog taking its preferred seat with proprietorial speed before Raven could climb aboard. Raven settled himself back against the red leather upholstery and closed his eyes. He hoped Dr Simpson would return to the book he had been reading all afternoon, but he was to be disappointed.

'Where do you hail from, Mr Raven?' the doctor said as the coach set off.

Raven tried to sit up more erectly in his seat.

'I was born in Edinburgh, sir.'

'And what does your father do?'

'He is no longer with us,' he replied. 'But he was a lawyer.'

Rehearsing this lie brought him back to last night in that alley not a hundred yards from here. It would have to serve once again, however. The truth was for another time, once Raven had enjoyed the chance to cultivate a reputation based upon his deeds rather than his provenance.

'In Edinburgh?'

'Originally. But lately in St Andrews.'

This at least had a modicum of truth to it. His mother lived there now, reliant upon the generosity of her brother. He truly was a lawyer, and a miserable, pious and self-righteous one at that.

'I once contemplated studying the law,' Simpson mused wistfully.

'Really? For how long?' Raven asked, wondering how the man could possibly have accommodated more than one field of study given his relative youth and famously prodigious career.

'Oh, at least the length of a day. An early encounter with the operating theatre had me racing off to Parliament House to seek employment as a clerk.'

Raven responded with a smile, no doubt a lopsided one given the burden on his cheek. He too had little love of the operating theatre. Much as he had admiration for the swift and steady hand of the surgeon, he had no wish to spend his time excising tumours and hacking off limbs. The barbarity of it appalled him, for no surgeon was as steady and swift as to spare the patient unimaginable torment.

'What brought you back?' Raven asked with genuine curiosity.

'The desire to alleviate pain and suffering, and the belief that one day we will find a means of achieving it.'

'And are you of the belief that ether has done that?'

'It is a step in the right direction but I believe we can do more. Now we understand that the inhaling of certain chemical compounds can produce a reversible insensibility, I am sure that if we experiment we will find something better than ether. It was one of the reasons I decided to take on an apprentice again this year. I need as many hands as possible to assist me in my search.'

This was not Raven's primary interest in working with the professor but he quickly warmed to the idea. If he was involved in the discovery of a new anaesthetic agent, his success in the profession would be assured. A share in the patent, aye, that would be the keys to a fortune.

'And do you believe you can succeed?' Raven asked, the prospect of such riches prompting a cautious scepticism.

The professor leaned forward in his seat. 'I believe that with a passionate desire and an unwearied will, we can achieve impossibilities.'

The door to 52 Queen Street opened the moment the doctor's carriage pulled up outside the house. A young woman in a starched cap stood in the doorway adjusting her apron as Raven stepped down onto the pavement. She recoiled momentarily at the sight of him and a sadness fell upon Raven as he realised that this was something he would have to get used to.

The dog ran into the house first, followed by the professor, who shrugged off his coat and handed it to a male servant who had materialised behind the young woman as though from thin air. He was tall, clean-shaven and immaculately dressed, which only served to emphasise Raven's state of dishevelment. The man stared down at this unkempt new arrival with unguarded disapproval.

'Jarvis, I'll take tea in my study,' Simpson said.

'Very good, sir,' he replied, before nodding at Raven, who was still loitering on the threshold. 'And what would you like me to do with that?'

The doctor laughed. 'This is Mr Raven, my new apprentice. He won't be joining us for dinner as I believe he's in need of his bed.'

Simpson met Raven's eye with a knowing look. Raven endured a moment of concern regarding just *what* the doctor knew, but mainly what he felt was relief.

'Show him up please, Sarah.'

The doctor proceeded along the corridor towards the back of the house. 'Jarvis will arrange to have your belongings collected,' he said over his shoulder.

'That is assuming you have any belongings worth collecting,' the butler said, closing the door.

Raven followed the housemaid up the stairs to a bedroom on

the third floor, the ascent sapping the last of his energy so much that he feared she might have to grab his lapels and drag him up the final flight. She breezed fussily ahead of him into the room and placed a towel onto a chair before he could sit on it, any concerns about offending him apparently trumped by the state of his clothes.

'We'll need to draw you a bath,' she said, evidently deeming his current condition an affront to the crisp white sheets adorning the bed. Raven hadn't seen linen so clean in a long time. He could think of little he wanted more right then than to crawl underneath it, but was too weak to argue. He sat holding his head in his hands, only vaguely aware of the bustle around him.

When he raised his head once more, he saw that a hip bath had been placed before the fire and filled with warm water. The butler helped him off with his clothes and offered an arm to steady himself as Raven climbed over the side. There appeared to be petals and twigs floating in the water, which caused him to pause with one foot in.

'Camomile, rosemary and lavender,' Jarvis offered by way of explanation. 'Sarah says it will help with the bruising. And the smell.'

Raven sat down in the warm, fragrant water and felt his aching muscles begin to relax. He could not remember having a bath quite like this. At Ma Cherry's, an old tin tub would be grudgingly filled with tepid water, just enough to cover the buttocks and feet. He could still hear the old sow's sighing and tutting as she hauled in the cans, as though bathing was some strange and alien practice he was inexplicably insisting upon. From the smell of her, it was certainly strange and alien to Mrs Cherry.

A sponge and a bar of soap had been left just within reach, but Raven felt disinclined to move. He allowed his good eye to close and time to drift. He heard the tread of footsteps in and out of the room a couple of times but he chose to ignore them. He then felt the sponge move across the tops of his shoulders.

He knew there was further insult implicit in Jarvis letting him know he did not trust Raven to clean himself properly, but he was too exhausted to object. He kept his eyes closed, however, as he had no desire to see the distasteful look on the butler's face while he performed this task.

'You'll have to lean forward so I can rinse your hair.'

It was a female voice that spoke. Raven lurched upright and opened his good eye. The housemaid Sarah was standing in front of him, holding a large ewer in both hands.

'What do you think you're doing?' he asked, thrusting his hands down to cover himself.

She smirked. 'Helping you get cleaned up,' she said. 'No need to be bashful. I'm as much nurse as housemaid in this place, so whatever you've got, I've seen it before.'

Raven hadn't the will to do anything but submit, though he kept one hand in place.

Sarah was very gentle, perhaps because of his obvious injuries – he seemed to have bruising from sternum to pubic bone. She smelled of tea and lavender and freshly laundered linen. Clean smells, healthy smells. New Town smells.

His hair was duly rinsed, after which Sarah offered to help him get out of the tub.

'I'm not an invalid,' he objected, a little more harshly than the girl deserved.

She gathered up his clothes. 'I've left a nightshirt on the bed for you,' she said, leaving him to perform the last of his ablutions alone.

When he did attempt to stand, he was almost toppled by a sudden onset of vertigo. He sat down again and waited for the spinning to stop. Given the impression he had made on the household staff thus far, he did not wish to be found prostrate on the floor with his arse in the air.

Rising more cautiously, he managed to get himself dried and into bed before Sarah entered again, this time carrying a tray.

'Beef tea, bread and butter.'

She put the tray down and took a small tin from her pocket.

'I'm going to put some salve on your wound. It's looking a bit red.'

Without waiting for his consent, she began applying some strange-smelling ointment to his cheek. With her eyes intent upon the work of her hands, he allowed himself to gaze upon her face: the freckles on her nose, the curl of her lashes.

For a moment he pictured Evie before him, dressed like that, a housemaid in the New Town. He could not sustain the image, though, and it was rapidly replaced by his memory of her contorted body.

Another deid hoor.

As Sarah put the liniment tin back in her pocket and bent to pick up his wet towel, Raven hoped she appreciated how fortunate she was.

EIGHT

onsciousness came at Raven like an ambush, sudden and without mercy. For the second successive morning he had woken in an unfamiliar bed, but on this occasion it was not his new surroundings that disoriented him so much as what he had left behind in sleep. He had been with Evie, the essence of her suffusing a dream so vivid that upon waking he felt the enormity of her loss all over again. How could she be gone when she still felt so real to him? It seemed as though he could walk to her lodging this very morning and find that it was her death that was the dream.

Raven looked at frost on the room's tiny window and was instantly transported to a freezing cold day they had spent together in her room, sharing a dry loaf and washing it down with wine, only leaving her bed to use the privy. It was not the physical intimacies that echoed now, but the warmth of friendship, of being in the company of someone with whom he could let the hours drift. He recalled how he had talked about his ambitions, and his promises to help her as soon as he was in a position of any influence.

He had caught her staring at him, that inscrutable look upon her face. It felt good to be stared at by her, to be the subject of her fascination, though he had no notion what she was thinking, what observations and secrets she was keeping to herself. Perhaps she heard such promises all the time. When he spoke this way, Evie seemed to accept that he was sincere, but that wasn't the same as believing him.

'You're always looking to take up cudgels for a noble cause, aren't you, Will?' she had said, lying with her head propped up on one hand, gently stroking his back with the other. She sounded amused but sympathetic. 'Always in search of a battle to fight.'

His instinct was to deny it, as people always do when someone has shown that they know them better than they find comfortable. However, to Evie such a denial would be as good as an admission, so he said nothing.

'Was there a particular one you lost, that you're ever after trying to make up for?'

'No,' he had replied, grateful he had his back to her. His answer was the truth, yet nonetheless a deliberate deceit.

Sometimes it was a fight you won that proved hardest to bear.

Raven got out of bed and examined his face in the mirror above the washstand. He was pleased to discover that he could open both eyes. He gently prodded along his cheek, which was coloured by purple bruising that extended almost to his chin. The wound remained tender but looked clean, without any signs of impending infection around the stitches. The salve that Sarah applied appeared to have been quite effective. If it was a remedy of her own making, she should patent it, he thought. Or perhaps *he* could, once he had qualified and could put his imprimatur upon the product as an Edinburgh doctor. He would ask her about it later. Obtaining the patent on a popular new medicine could prove highly lucrative, especially if it actually worked.

He recalled his conversation with Simpson the day before regarding the search for an alternative to ether. The alleviation of all pain and suffering was certainly a lofty ambition, but Raven doubted if such a thing was possible, even with an unwearied will and a passionate desire or whatever pieties Simpson had been spouting. However, anything that offered a way out of his chronic penury was worth pursuing, particularly with Flint's debt to be considered. Simpson would find him a willing participant in whatever experiments he proposed.

His bags had arrived from Mrs Cherry's, a clean shirt and trousers making him look and feel instantly more respectable. His clothes from yesterday seemed to have disappeared. He wondered if the butler had burned them.

Raven rubbed a hand across his chin. At nineteen years old, his face was not quick to bristle, but stubble was beginning to form a shadow as he hadn't shaved in two days. He had never pictured himself with a beard, but looking at Henry's needlework, it struck him that growing whiskers may prove a necessity, as they would cover up the scar.

He descended to the dining room, finding it empty, though the fire had been lit and the table laid, suggesting he would not have long to wait for breakfast. It was a large room dominated by an expansive table and a mahogany sideboard. A richly patterned paper decorated the walls and a pair of heavy brocade curtains in a complementary colour hung either side of the windows. A cage containing a large grey parrot was situated before the glass, presumably so that the bird could enjoy a view of the street and the gardens beyond. The parrot's interest was primarily taken right then by a Raven, which it was eyeing with the same mixture of curiosity and distrust as its housemate Jarvis.

On top of the sideboard a selection of serving dishes were waiting to be filled. Raven picked up a pepper shaker, turning it upside down to look for a hallmark. This resulted in a streak of pepper spilling onto the sideboard which he hurriedly swept up in his hand and then sprinkled onto the carpet. The parrot squawked loudly, as though in rebuke.

Placing the shaker carefully back down, he noticed that one of the sideboard doors was ajar, and he bent to satisfy his curiosity. As well as a stack of crockery and a large soup tureen, he spied several piles of papers with barely legible notes scribbled upon them, as though scrawled in a hurry. More intriguingly he also observed a selection of glass bottles containing a variety of clear liquids. These were labelled in a contrastingly precise hand, though some of them were smudged, presumably from repeated handling. Nitric ether, benzine, chloride of hydrocarbon. To Raven, who had been a middling chemistry student at best, the names didn't mean much. He removed the stopper from the bottle of benzine and took a sniff. It had a pungent aroma and caused a slight dizziness. Given his recent infirmity, he decided that further investigation was best avoided at present.

He had just returned the bottle to the cupboard when the dining-room door opened and the entire household seemed to pour through it.

'Mr Raven. What a pleasure it is to meet you.'

The woman who greeted him had a pleasant, open countenance but appeared exceedingly pale, as though she hadn't been outdoors for some time. She was dressed in black, evidently in mourning. Raven wondered for whom.

'I am Mrs Simpson and this is my sister, Miss Wilhelmina Grindlay.'

'Delighted to make your acquaintance,' Raven replied.

Miss Grindlay looked momentarily taken aback by his appearance but regained her composure to offer him a smile.

'You may call me Mina,' she said.

Mina was slightly taller and thinner than her sister, making her features seem pinched in comparison. She was beyond the first flush of youth but still pleasing to the eye. Raven wondered why she was not yet married.

The ladies were followed by the domestic staff, who lined up along one wall. Raven allowed himself a glance at Sarah, but averted his gaze as a matter of reflex when she met his eye. It was his understanding that servants were specifically not supposed to do this. He wondered whether the Simpson household afforded greater leeway to those below stairs or whether this meant that his status was not considered to be above.

His attention was taken by the arrival of a fellow surely not much older than him, but who carried himself with a great deal more certainty and poise (not to mention within a suit of far finer tailoring). He had the gait of someone comfortable in his surroundings and enjoying great confidence in his purpose. He did not introduce himself, instead taking position behind a chair as they awaited the master of the house.

Dr Simpson entered last of all, bade everyone good morning and took his seat at the head of the table. He opened a grand leather-bound Bible and read something from Psalms. Everyone then bowed their heads for a few minutes of silent prayer. To Raven's empty stomach, this represented an unwelcome delay, rendered all the more frustrating by his never having been much inclined towards the church. He was not even sure whether he believed in God. (The devil was quite another matter.)

Eventually the doctor said amen and the domestic staff left the room, Raven hoped as a prelude to their imminent return bearing food. When the door opened once more, however, it was the dog that entered, followed by two small boys who proceeded to chase it round the table, and from whose giggling entreaties he learned that its name was Glen.

He heard an approaching thump of hurried footsteps and had to suppress a smile at the harassed appearance of their nanny, who looked mortified that they had escaped her charge. Raven felt guilty for his amusement as he braced himself for the rebuke that would surely be handed down, reckoning that whether the boys or the nanny got the worst of it would be a revealing detail. However, Simpson responded instead with raucous laughter, to which almost everyone reacted with similar mirth, prompting the dog to bark with excitement before even the bloody parrot joined in.

Almost everyone, mark you. There was an exception. The

smartly dressed young man merely issued a tired sigh, while presenting a token smile as thin as Ma Cherry's porridge.

Simpson quieted the dog with an affectionate hand upon its head, the tail wagging like a metronome. Then the squealing boys were similarly calmed by the tender ministrations of their father's hands before being led away meekly by their grateful governess. The sight piqued something bittersweet in Raven, but before he could dwell upon it, his senses were busied with the arrival of platters piled high with sausages, eggs, kippers and freshly baked bread.

Raven eyed it all longingly, awaiting Simpson tucking in as his cue to commence. The doctor was reaching for a sausage with a fork when he suddenly paused and put it down again.

'But I am forgetting myself. Introductions! James, this is my new apprentice, Will Raven. Will, this is Dr James Duncan, recently arrived from Paris.'

Raven was about to extend a hand but noticed that Duncan's remained fixed by his side. He wasn't sure he was on the right side of the etiquette, but he was quite sure Dr James Duncan saw him as an inferior, and by 'saw him', he meant much as in the way one sees a fellow by using a telescope.

If Raven was the type to feel slighted, then the sting would have been drawn by Simpson finally signalling that everyone should eat. For appearance's sake, he did not pile his plate conspicuously, but even then it was probably more food than he had faced at a sitting since last he visited his mother, and he was sure it would taste so much the better without his uncle reminding everyone who had paid for it.

'Dr Duncan, I meant to ask but I kept forgetting,' ventured Miss Grindlay, peering across the table. 'Are you any relation to Mr Duncan of Duncan and Flockhart on Princes Street?'

Duncan gave her a look indicating that he considered this a self-evidently stupid question.

'No. Though I understand they're doing a fairly brisk trade

in ether since its discovery.' This latter he addressed towards Simpson, by way of moving the subject on.

Raven decided to move it right back again.

'Any relation to Mr Duncan the surgeon at the Infirmary, then?'

For this he earned a sour look, one of which Raven was sure Duncan had a varied repertoire.

'Again, no. There appears to be a surfeit of Duncans in Edinburgh at the moment. I am considering adding my mother's maiden name to mine to distinguish myself.'

'And what will your name become?' asked Mina.

'James Matthews Duncan.'

'That does sound most distinguished,' said Mrs Simpson. 'You'll have to make some notable contribution to medicine now, in order to be worthy of it.'

'I intend to,' he replied flatly.

Raven thought this was another pass at shutting down irrelevant contributions from the distaff side, but it was in fact merely an overture. Once Duncan had gobbled down the solitary boiled egg he had abstemiously selected from the cornucopia before him, he proceeded to lay down his credentials, at the end of which Raven had a stark perspective upon just how powerful that telescope would have to be.

Duncan had studied medicine in Aberdeen and Edinburgh, gaining his MD last year at the tender age of twenty, which required some form of special dispensation. He had travelled to Paris to further his studies, and while there had made extensive pathological examinations of women who had died in childbirth, considering himself to be something of an expert upon inflammatory conditions of the female pelvis. He spoke fluent German and French, and had translated Dr Simpson's 'Notes on the Inhalation of Sulphuric Ether' into the latter, which had naturally flattered their host and no doubt played a part in his being offered a position as an assistant to the professor.

'I have come here to find a better drowsy syrup than ether,' he declared, which put a stopper in it as far as Raven was concerned, as he had only just begun entertaining the notion that this might be his own route to success.

James Matthews Duncan, he decided, was going to be insufferable. He had the bearing of a young man who had never been punched full in the face for an unguarded remark, and Raven instinctively felt he might be the one to remedy that.

The gathering was soon joined by another gentleman, who apologised for being late (having come on foot from his home on Howe Street) and insisted nobody should rise. He looked a few years older than Raven, tall and neatly dressed, with a receding hairline and a full beard. He was evidently well known to the family, as he sat down at the table without waiting for an invitation and was promptly served a cup of tea by Sarah.

'This is my associate, Dr George Keith,' Simpson explained, before completing the introduction.

Dr Keith reached across the table to shake Raven's hand, pausing momentarily as he took in his appearance.

'What the devil has happened to you?' Keith asked, not restrained by the same delicacy as the ladies around the table.

'I was set upon by thieves in the Old Town,' Raven said. 'They came at me late at night and dragged me into an alley. I tried to fight them off, but that proved a mistake. They took every penny I had on me, which was quite a sum, as well as my watch. So as well as being battered and bruised, I am out of pocket and out of time.'

He laughed a little at his own polite joke, as though trivialising his condition. Nobody joined in.

'How awful for you,' Mina said, looking genuinely distraught at his misfortune.

'Are you quite out of funds, then?' Simpson asked. 'I'm sure that I could assist.'

'Oh, not at all. I couldn't possibly,' he replied.

The words spilled from his lips before Raven was aware of

saying them. He knew immediately that his refusal of Simpson's offer would come at a cost. Living here he would have bed and board, but beyond that he had only a small sum of money left among the belongings delivered from Mrs Cherry's. Certainly not enough to keep Flint and his creatures at bay.

However, having turned up bloodied and bruised, he did not wish his hosts to know also that he was impoverished. If you wished to be accorded respect by those who had money, it was imperative that they believed you had money too. It was a deception at which he had become practised, but it was easy to disguise your penury when you were a student living among your peers.

'Well, at the very least allow me to lend you a spare timepiece until you can replace your own,' Simpson insisted.

'You are most kind, sir. I thank you.'

Raven was contemplating a second serving of everything and wondering how much he could make selling stolen sausages when George Keith placed a hand upon his shoulder.

'I think it's about time we got started, don't you? They were spilling out of the waiting room already as I came through.'

'Who were?' Raven asked.

'The patients,' Keith replied, holding open the door. 'Our consulting rooms are this way.'

Raven obediently took his cue, though not without noticing that Duncan remained where he sat, the remains of his miserably ascetic breakfast still in front of him as he continued to converse with Simpson.

'Dr Duncan's duties are confined to the area of research,' Keith explained. 'You will be required to assist him, but mornings are for clinics.'

Raven followed Keith out and past the stairs, where a woman wrapped in a dirty shawl was sitting nursing a grubby infant.

'Dr Simpson sees the patients here, in his home?' he asked.

'Yes. They turn up every morning and draw lots to determine who is seen first. That is unless a case is conspicuously urgent.'

'There is no appointment book?'

Keith pointed to his temple. 'Dr Simpson insists that he can retain all important appointments and visits in his head.'

'And can he?'

Keith smiled. '*Most* of the time,' he replied. 'And when he forgets, the patients usually forgive him.'

'But why see them here?' Raven thought that if he were ever to own a house such as this he would not permit the great unwashed to parade through his downstairs hallway.

'Convenience, I suppose. The professor is not unique in having consulting rooms where he resides, although many of his colleagues choose to keep their patients at a distance. Professor Syme, for one, lives out at Morningside, far away from the patients that he sees.'

Raven was shown into a small room containing a desk and a couple of chairs.

'When you're ready, call for a patient and Sarah will show them in. I'm just next door. If you see anything strange or unusual let me know. Dr Simpson likes to see the rare stuff himself. He'll be seeing the upstairs patients. The ones who pay the large fees.'

'So what kind of fees do the ones we'll be seeing pay?' Raven asked, reckoning it would at least be better than nothing.

'The invisible kind.'

Raven saw a variety of complaints, mainly in women and children: sore throats, painful ears, coughs, sprains and skin diseases. He had hoped that Dr Keith would be on-hand to supervise his diagnoses and prescribed remedies, but it quickly became apparent that there was no time for such doubling of duties. He was unsure just what Sarah's contribution in all this was supposed to be, particularly given that each time he emerged, he found her perched on a chair outside the door reading a book.

'What are you doing?' he asked.

She looked up from the volume, her expression suggesting she was suppressing any number of impertinent replies.

'Reading a novel.' She flicked back to the title page. 'By someone named Currer Bell.'

'A novel?'

'Yes. It's called *Jane Eyre*. Have you read it?'

Raven was exasperated. 'Do you think a man has time to read fiction when he is training to be a doctor?'

'I'm rather sure Dr Simpson did.'

She put the book in her pocket and got up from her chair.

'I'll bring the next patient, shall I?'

Raven was speechless as she summoned a bald-headed man suffering from the most distressingly livid rash. This was not how he imagined household staff ought to behave. His uncle certainly wouldn't tolerate it, but this thought gave him pause. If he was using Miserly Malcolm as the compass for his behaviour, then he would soon be lost.

He returned to his consulting room and sat down with the next patient, the poor fellow concerned that his rash might soon be the death of him. Raven diagnosed it as a psoriatic eruption and dispensed a soothing ointment to calm its angry heat. Without even having applied it, the man appeared to experience some relief, merely at his suffering having been given a name. Raven suspected this effect might not be so efficacious if the man knew how little experience his 'doctor' had, but was satisfied to be of assistance.

He showed the man from his consulting room and stepped back into the waiting area, where the numbers appeared to have grown. So, quite considerably, had the volume of noise. Alerted by his appearance, he was dismayed to spot Sarah slipping the novel into her pocket again as she got to her feet. If she wasn't even paying attention, he didn't see what need there was for her to select the next patient when he was perfectly capable of assessing such things for himself.

To wit, his attention was immediately drawn to a shabbily dressed man convulsed by bouts of coughing, a rattletrap undertaking which he was directing into a singularly gruesome handkerchief. This bark might ordinarily have shaken the room, but at that moment it was all but drowned out by the sounds of three nearby children, two of whom were bawling while a third shrieked in on-going delight merely at the volume she had discovered her voice might achieve.

Mindful of the possibility of consumption, and keen to put at least a door between his ears and these intolerable howls, Raven bid the man follow.

Sarah stepped between them, signalling to the man to remain seated.

'Mr Raven, this woman here ought to be your next patient,' she told him, while to Raven's growing chagrin, the coughing man retreated in obedience.

'What is your name?' he asked, almost breathless in his incredulity.

'It is Sarah,' she replied, her words barely discernible over the sound of the screaming children.

'Yes, I know that part. Your surname.'

'Fisher.'

'And you are a housemaid, Miss Fisher, are you not?'

'Yes, sir.'

'Then by what rationale do you see fit to gainsay my instruction as to which patient should be seen next?'

'It is my duty to assess those waiting and to recommend the order of urgency by which they ought to be admitted.'

She had to raise her voice to be heard, which Raven was aware did not make for a fitting spectacle in front of the patients. Nonetheless, some lessons were best learned in public.

'You may *recommend* an order, but if I call for a particular patient, then you ought to remember that my knowledge of such matters considerably trumps your own.'

Summoned by the altercation, Dr Keith appeared in the waiting area and stepped closer to enquire after the dispute.

'I wish to attend to this man suffering from what may prove to be a serious ailment of the chest,' Raven explained, almost shouting over the clamour of tiny but disproportionately loud voices that was filling the hallway. 'However, the housemaid evidently believes she has a sharper diagnostic eye than mine and is insisting I prioritise that woman there, who appears to be suffering from nothing more troubling than having too many children in her care.'

Dr Keith turned to look at Sarah, then back at Raven.

'Do you mean the woman accompanied by her three bairns over whom we are fighting to make ourselves heard?'

'Indeed.'

'And whose subsequent absence would make the waiting areas considerably quieter and more agreeable?'

Raven felt a sudden heat in his cheeks as the manifold elements of his humiliation compounded. He looked like a fool, an arrogant fool at that, and had been made so foolish by a household servant in front of Dr Keith. It could only have been worse had it been the professor himself.

NINE

arah tramped along Princes Street several paces behind Mina, giving her an uninterrupted view of the dirt that was becoming attached to Mina's skirt. She was effectively sweeping the pavement with her numerous petticoats. Sarah added the cleaning of these to the perpetually lengthening list of chores that she would be expected to complete by the end of the day. She thought of Sisyphus and his giant boulder, condemned for all eternity to engage in an ultimately pointless task.

Mina had dressed with particular care that morning, most likely for the benefit of the doctor's new apprentice, but was perhaps now regretting her efforts given that the man in question bore a closer resemblance to a street urchin than a practitioner of the healing arts. Mina was no doubt disappointed, seeing another opportunity to escape her suffocating spinsterhood evaporate into the ether.

Mina had questioned Sarah about Raven that morning before breakfast, and she had been tempted to give her a detailed physical appraisal, afforded by having helped him bathe. Having studied Dr Simpson's anatomy textbooks, Sarah could have traced out various muscle groups on Raven's lean frame: pectoralis major, latissimus dorsi, gluteus maximus. He was a fine specimen of a man in the anatomical sense. His personality was another matter.

The short time she had known him had been enough to identify Raven as typical of his kind: self-regarding and prone to pomposity, believing his education elevated him above those who had been more limited in their opportunities. She thought of his arrogant dismissal of her advice at the clinic. He would soon learn that she made a better friend than an adversary, but she was prepared to be either – it all depended on him.

His behaviour may have been typical, but his appearance had definitely fallen short of expectations. When he arrived on the doorstep it looked as though he had been mauled by a rabid dog. Mrs Lyndsay and Jarvis could offer no explanations as to why the professor would employ such a man, let alone allow him to live with them. Sarah imagined that, whether she knew the reason or not, Mina would likely have an opinion on the matter, and so ventured a question.

'Is it usual for the professor to take on an apprentice like Mr Raven?'

Mina stopped walking. 'To take on an apprentice, yes. Like Mr Raven, no.'

'Why do you think he has done so?' she asked as Mina resumed her progress. 'Mr Raven seems rather . . .' Sarah paused for a moment searching for an appropriate word. 'Disreputable.'

'Rather a strong sentiment to be voiced by a housemaid, Sarah. But on this occasion, I find that I am in agreement. It may be that my brother-in-law has taken it upon himself to save this young man, rescue him from his circumstances. It is perhaps an expression of grief.'

'Grief? How so?'

'One of the greatest physicians in Edinburgh has lost two of his children, powerless in the face of infectious fevers. If he could not save them, with all his knowledge and accomplishments, perhaps there is some solace to be found in the salvation of someone else.'

Sarah paused for a moment to rearrange some of the packages she was carrying. Mina's explanation certainly seemed plausible enough, though it was not one she had considered herself. Had the doctor seen something in Raven worthy of salvation? If that was the case, she would perhaps be forced to search for the attributes that commended him to the professor but had so far been hidden from her.

Sarah shifted some of her load from one arm to the other. None of the parcels was particularly heavy but together they were cumbersome. She was weighed down with life's necessities wrapped in brown paper: reams of fabric, lace and embroidery thread. Sarah vastly preferred shopping trips in the company of Mrs Simpson. They occurred infrequently and were limited to a few establishments as Mrs Simpson was an efficient shopper with little time for dallying over ribbons and frills.

They had already been to the dressmaker, the milliner, and of course Gianetti and Son on George Street, perfumers to the Queen. Mina rarely purchased anything there but was a frequent visitor, trying scents and exchanging gossip with Mr Gianetti. Today's conversation had centred upon a murder and scandal reported in that day's newspaper. 'A gentleman in Glasgow has been found guilty of killing his wife,' Mina said. 'And what drove him, it turns out, was that he had entered into a relationship with one of the servants. Further, it is speculated the gentleman had previously murdered a housemaid because she bore his child. It seems the girl died in a fire, her room locked from the outside.'

Sarah did not think the word 'gentle' ought to be appended to such a creature, but from her tone, it appeared Mina regarded his consorting with the help to be the real affront to decent values.

Mina spent her usual half an hour trying various scents before deciding against such an expensive purchase because her allowance would not stretch to such luxuries. She would have to make do, she complained to Sarah as they left the shop, with her usual brand of eau de cologne and handkerchief water from Duncan and Flockhart's, where Dr Simpson had an account.

'I long for the day when I have control of my own household,' Mina said. 'In my present state I am but a burden to my relatives.'

As they resumed their progress along Princes Street, Mina beckoned Sarah walk alongside for a spell, which meant there was something she wished to discuss.

'Have you finished reading *Jane Eyre*?' she asked.

'No, ma'am,' Sarah replied, bracing herself for Mina's disappointment. There was so little time, particularly during daylight, and she was still annoyed by Raven's response to finding her reading between cases.

'But you have made some progress?'

'Yes. About half.'

This seemed satisfactory enough, and her mistress proceeded to probe her for her impressions. Sarah liked this about Mina. She was extraordinarily well-read and had a keen mind for analysis of books and poetry, yet she was always hungry for Sarah's perspective. Sarah suspected this was because she lacked a suitable companion with whom to discuss such things. Mina socialised a great deal, but understandably considered many of the women she visited to be intellectually inferior, concerned only with talk of husbands and children – in each case both real and prospective.

'I find the heroine courageous and impressively strong in her will,' Sarah said.

From her expression she could tell Mina did not share this opinion.

'I found her rather frustrating,' Mina observed. 'But upon reflection I realise that this frustration was born of recognising that I share certain of her traits. And what might seem strong-willed decisions to a younger woman appear more like follies with the wisdom of experience.'

'What do you consider follies, ma'am?'

'I feared she was being too exacting in what she sought in a husband, with the consequential danger that she may end up with no one. It ends well enough for her, as it only can in the realm of novels, but the real world is usually less forgiving.'

Sarah knew that Mina had been romantically disappointed on more than one occasion; promises made and then broken. She knew also that there had been suitors Mina considered beneath her expectations, something Sarah admired in her.

'I have not finished the story, but is it not better for a woman to remain alone than to be married to someone unsuitable? Someone who does not meet whatever standards she sets?'

'That is a question I ask myself ever more frequently as the years pile one upon the other. I would not consider an unsuitable man, but I would admit that what I consider suitable has changed. I have long since discarded the foolish notions of my youth. I think there is much to commend a companionate marriage: a man I respect, whose work I admire and whose household I would be proud to run. I confess that in this I am envious towards my sister. She has all of this with a man she truly loves, and who truly loves her.'

Sarah was always flattered to be the recipient of such candour, but the feeling only ever lasted until she remembered that Mina felt free to be so open with her because she didn't count. She would never be so candid with anyone of status.

Following a detour into Kennington and Jenner's to examine their silks, they arrived outside the druggist's. It was a premises with which Sarah was very familiar and more than a little fond. She was frequently sent there on errands, Dr Simpson's practice always having a need for items such as dressings, plasters, ointments and unguents.

Mr Flockhart was a surgeon as well as a druggist, and both he and his partner Mr Duncan had many friends among the medical practitioners of the city. They were intelligent and innovative gentlemen: excellent practical chemists who could turn their hand to the production of any medicinal product, and according to Dr Simpson, the results were always of the highest standard. Sarah was in no position to judge such matters, but she had found Mr Duncan to be a kindly man, always willing to share his expertise regarding the healing properties of certain medicinal plants which he grew in his herb garden, just outside the city.

As she pushed open the door the little bell above it tinkled and she smiled to herself. This was one of her favourite places in Edinburgh.

The shop was dominated by a marble-topped counter, behind which shelves containing rows of glass bottles stretched all the way to the ceiling. The bottles held powders, liquids and oils with exotic-sounding names. Some she was familiar with – ipecac, glycerine, camphor – while others were labelled with abbreviated Latin terms she could not decipher.

When they entered, the druggist's assistant was carefully weighing out a powder on a set of brass scales. He looked up and winked at Sarah, his expression at once lecherous and self-satisfied. Sarah hated having to deal with this one. His lasciviousness was matched only by his stupidity. She wasn't sure what effect he believed his wink to have: whether she was supposed to be intimidated by his worldliness or weak-kneed in delight.

'Good afternoon, Master Ingram,' she said, flashing him a smile that was as broad and confident as it was insincere.

Master Ingram rapidly lost his concentration and the powder he was measuring spilled across the counter. He stopped what he was doing and rushed through to the dispensing room at the back of the shop, presumably to find someone more competent to help him. Mr Flockhart duly emerged.

'Ladies,' he said, opening his arms as if he was planning to embrace them. 'How may I be of assistance?'

Mr Flockhart was a tall man, as effervescent as the stomach powders he sold. He was a great enthusiast for social gatherings and functions, and as such he always had stories to tell and gossip to impart. Mina made straight for him.

Meanwhile, Mr Duncan emerged from the back, presumably to tidy up the mess left by his assistant.

'Are you in need of anything today, Sarah?' he asked as she approached the counter.

'Not today, thank you.'

Mr Duncan took in her weary face and suggested she place her parcels upon a chair in the corner of the shop. He glanced over at Mina, who was enthusiastically engaged in conversation with Mr Flockhart.

'You could be here for some time.'

Once she had divested herself of her packages, Mr Duncan told her: 'I have something for you to try. I have been experimenting with a new confection made with icing sugar and flavoured with lemon and rosewater.'

He held out a piece of wax paper bearing two round comfits, one pink and one yellow, each with a little heart-shaped pattern imprinted on one side. Sarah tasted each in turn. They fizzed on her tongue and flooded her mouth with sweetness. She closed her eyes briefly. When she opened them, Mr Duncan was smiling at her.

'They're wonderful!' she said. 'What are they called?'

'Haven't decided yet,' he said, wrapping a few more for her to take home.

Sarah took the proffered paper parcel and quickly put it in her pocket, reasoning that if Mina saw it, she might object. She had rules of etiquette which defied any rational explanation and which she applied with equal measures of vigour and caprice. The only consistent element appeared to be that they interfered with whatever Sarah happened to be doing or saying at any given time.

The junior assistant had still to reappear and Sarah wondered if he was being punished somewhere – perhaps being forced to make a large batch of a particularly pungent and malodorous ointment. She hoped so. She watched as Mr Duncan cleaned up the mess on the counter. He transferred a quantity of the powder from the scales to a mortar and began to grind it.

'What do you look for when taking on a new assistant?' she asked, thinking about the daft lad who had already gained a position there.

Mr Duncan paused before answering and looked towards the back of the shop as though trying to remind himself.

'We require someone who can read and write well,' he said, continuing to pound away with his pestle. 'They must have a good grasp of mathematics in order to accurately calculate totals on bills of sale. They must be industrious and well presented.'

He paused again and smiled.

'An ability to decipher hieroglyphics is also useful. Some of our customers write their requirements on slips of paper and their command of the written word is not always their greatest strength.'

He pushed a soot-soiled scrap of paper towards Sarah. On it was written in childish script: 'Dull water for eye cups'.

Sarah could make nothing of it. She looked at Mr Duncan and shrugged.

'Dill water for hiccups,' he said, laughing. 'Why do you ask about the job of assistant? Do you know someone who might be interested in a position here? A brother or a cousin perhaps?'

Sarah thought for a minute about her own abilities. She had a neat hand, a good head for numbers (she always checked Mrs Lyndsay's account books before they were presented to Mrs Simpson and they were seldom in error) and was already familiar with a host of herbal remedies. She looked over at Mina, who was testing out a hand cream and was oblivious to Sarah's conversation. She thought about the drudgery of much of the work at Queen Street and Mrs Lyndsay's determination to limit her involvement with the more interesting parts of her job.

'I was thinking about myself,' she said.

'You?'

Sarah straightened her back and lifted her chin.

'Yes, me. Why not?'

Mr Duncan gave her an apologetic look.

'Sarah,' he said, 'our assistants must inspire confidence in our customers. For that, only a man will do.'

TEN

n a few short days, Raven had become accustomed to journeying to the Old Town in Dr Simpson's carriage, a luxury which spared him from (or perhaps merely deferred) the anxiety besetting him now. His duties as Simpson's apprentice also involved assisting with the professor's lectures at the university, and on this occasion he was having to make his way there in advance, in order to prepare a practical demonstration while the doctor attended a case out in Balerno.

His fear was all the more unsettling for being an unfamiliar sensation in entirely familiar surroundings. These streets had been his home for almost seven years: he well knew their dangers but that was not the same as being afraid. He had never felt scared here before.

Raven had first come here at the age of thirteen, when he was enrolled in George Heriot's, a school 'for poor fatherless boys'. It was an educational opportunity that would previously have been far beyond his means, an unforeseen consolation accruing from the tragedy that had otherwise so reduced his family's circumstances. The significance was not lost on Raven that dying was the most substantial contribution his father ever made towards providing him with a future.

He recalled how tentative his early ventures out to the surrounding neighbourhood had been, haunted by the stories the older boys told to frighten their juniors. But Raven had always been drawn to explore that which he feared, not to mention that which might seem forbidden. By the time he was a student at the university (the requisite fees extracted with difficulty from and following prolonged negotiation with his parsimonious uncle) he felt like a native of the Old Town, if not entirely at home there.

Up ahead, the sanctuary of the university's courtyard beckoned him in the murk. He felt he would be safe within its walls, particularly as it was daylight; or daytime, at least. The whole city remained shrouded in a choking fog that refused to lift though it was already after noon.

From the moment he crossed the North Bridge, he had been looking over his shoulder for the Weasel and Gargantua, though together with Peg, these were the only associates of Flint that he even knew to be on the lookout for. Gargantua at least he should be able to see coming, perhaps the most conspicuous creature in Edinburgh. What gruesome disorder had blighted the fellow? Given the nature of their only encounter, Raven was disinclined to be sympathetic towards the monster's plight, but as a medical man he recognised that the man was surely afflicted. He wasn't merely large: parts of him had kept growing when they ought to have stopped, and that didn't augur well for his prospects. Unfortunately he was unlikely to die soon enough to save Raven, and even then Flint would not be short of a replacement.

He had tried to steady himself by considering his situation rationally. It had only been a matter of days since the Weasel braced him: surely they wouldn't expect his financial situation to have sufficiently improved as to be able to redeem the debt? But then he realised that making rational assumptions was a dangerous mistake. He had to stop thinking of them as reasonable people. They were demanding he got them their money by any means necessary, under the threat of mutilation. It wouldn't stop with an eye, either.

Meanwhile, the longer he went without seeing them, the more they would expect him to pay when they caught up to him again.

The archway to the courtyard was mere yards away, and Raven's stride grew apace the closer he got. His view was fixed upon it, eyes dead ahead, when he heard someone call his name.

A shudder ran through him. More than a shudder, for a shudder passes quickly. It was a tremor, accompanied by the threat of tears and a sharp twinge in his cheek as though he could feel the slice of Weasel's blade again. It happened every time he was startled, whether by a sudden noise or a phantom in the dark as he waited for sleep. It had even happened at dinner two nights ago, when Simpson raised a carving knife and the gleam of the blade caught his eye.

He came close to breaking into a sprint, before the voice resumed and he was able to recognise it.

'Slow down, man. You're walking like the wolves are at your back.'

It was Henry, jogging to catch up, and Raven was able to disguise his relief as pleasure.

'We New Town residents walk as quickly as we can through the poorer districts, don't you know.'

'I don't doubt it. How are you finding the estimable Professor Simpson and his household?'

'I'm not sure what I expected, but I can say that it wasn't what I found. It's a menagerie, Henry. Dogs, children, chaotic clinics. I may need some time to adjust.'

'And what of colleagues?'

'There is a Dr George Keith, who lives nearby. He is a decent sort. And there is a James Duncan, who if he was made of chocolate would surely eat himself, were his appetites not so abstemious.'

'James Duncan? I think I may have encountered him. Studied here, and at Aberdeen before that? An uncommonly young graduate?'

'That's right.'

'Yes. Gifted of mind but an altogether odd creature. Set upon an ostensibly humanitarian undertaking and yet giving off as much warmth as a dying penguin's last fart.'

'Sadly not unique among our peers. Impeccable in his conduct but a singularly joyless soul.'

'Never trust a man who has no apparent vices. The concealed ones are apt to be disgusting. And what of the staff at Queen Street? Any pretty housemaids to delight your eye?'

The image of Sarah leapt unbidden into his head, but whether she delighted his eye was moot, because he could not picture her without reliving the incident at his first clinic. The very thought of her made Raven feel awkward and embarrassed. For all his years of diligent study, a mere girl had been able to make him feel like he had learned nothing of practical worth. That she was worldly and he a schoolboy.

'Unfortunately not,' he said, hoping that Henry read nothing in his expression that encouraged him to press the subject.

Henry's scrutinising eye was upon him, but fortunately focused on something more superficial.

'Your swelling is going down nicely,' he remarked, words that put Sarah right back into Raven's mind. He had to get off the subject.

'Evidence of a deft hand,' he said. 'So what business occupies those deft hands today?'

Henry's gaze returned to the courtyard widening before them, students traversing the flagstones in all directions, flitting in and out of vision like ghosts in this stubborn fog.

'I am in search of a butcher,' he replied.

'Then I may be able to assist, now that I am widening my circle of acquaintance. Mrs Lyndsay, the Simpsons' cook, buys her meat from Hardie's, on Cockburn Street. He would have to be a fine butcher, as her standards are exacting.'

'I am not looking for a fine butcher. I am looking for an unconscionable one.'

Henry had a singularity about his expression, his thoughts finely focused.

'You recall that death from peritonitis that was so vexing Professor Syme? When we carried out the post-mortem we discovered that her uterus had been perforated, as had a loop of small intestine.'

'A butcher indeed,' Raven said.

'She wasn't the last, either. We've had another case since, also fatal. Similar injuries.'

'Have the authorities been informed?'

'Yes, but they won't act. No one is going to admit that they know anything about it, and more importantly it hasn't affected the right class of people. You know how it is. There's no way of knowing for sure it's the same culprit, but I fear somebody has set up to trade.'

'An amateur?' Raven asked.

'Impossible to be sure. It's certainly not the worst I've seen in my time.'

'When it comes to this, nobody truly knows what they're doing,' Raven stated. 'But nonetheless, a level of medical knowledge is necessary to even know where to begin.'

'I wouldn't speak those words too loudly, my friend, and nor would I wish to be the first to suggest adding it to the curriculum. But you speak the truth. It is disappointing to think of someone offering what they know to be literally a stab in the dark, butchering women in their greed for fast cash.'

Raven thought of Weasel's blade and understood how quickly one's ethics might be abandoned given a powerful enough motivation.

'We can only hope that his technique improves quickly,' he suggested. 'Else these two won't be his last victims.'

'Can we say for certain it is a he?' Henry asked.

'I suppose not,' Raven admitted. 'There are always unscrupulous midwives ready with a sharp knitting needle if the price is right, and I have heard it suggested that women feel easier about approaching someone of their own sex when soliciting such illicit services.'

'Not merely for illicit services,' Henry replied. 'I have heard tell that there is a French midwife working in the city, eagerly sought after by ladies who would rather not be treated by a man.'

Raven thought of the needless encumbrance of the bedsheets that prevented him and Dr Simpson seeing what they were doing. He wondered if the preservation of modesty was less of an issue when the practitioner was female.

'French, you say?'

'A graduate of the Hôtel Dieu, no less, if the accounts are to be believed.'

'Then you don't need to worry about her being this butcher,' Raven said. 'A graduate of the Hôtel Dieu would know well enough what she was about.'

'Then perhaps it's not I who ought to worry about her. You're the one she's competing with.'

'I'll start worrying when they start training women to be doctors.'

Henry laughed.

'So who were they?' Raven asked. 'The victims?'

'One of them was a tavern maid, the other a prostitute.'

Another deid hoor, Raven thought.

'We don't get fine ladies washing up at the Infirmary,' Henry went on. 'The quality can afford a home visit from the likes of Dr Simpson.'

'I don't believe this is a service that he offers,' Raven said, though it struck him that he had no means of knowing.

'No, and nor was that what I was suggesting. Though I

sometimes wonder what they do over in the New Town when there is an inconvenient issue.'

'They simply have the babies,' Raven supposed, thinking of the household staff commanded by Mrs Simpson, reputedly modest by some standards. 'Then pass them off to nurses and nannies. It is always different when there is money. These young women must resort to desperate measures because they feel they have no alternative.'

Henry nodded solemnly, slowing his stride as they reached the entrance where their routes would diverge.

'More desperate than anyone might believe,' he said ruefully. 'I'm told an infant's leg was found in a gutter by a scavenger rooting in an alley near the Royal Exchange. The authorities are looking into that one, at least.'

As they parted ways, Raven was left with a profound sense of sadness over the fates of these women, though he had not known them, nor even seen them. He knew that it was down to a sense of guilt over Evie, whose death scene he had run from like he had something to hide.

Raven wondered what he might have missed. Had he been so startled by the discovery that she was dead and the danger of being found in there with the body that he hadn't looked properly – hadn't seen things he might otherwise have noticed?

Though Flint's men were on the prowl, he knew he had no choice. He would have to go back.

ELEVEN

he waiting rooms always filled up quickest on a Monday morning, there being no clinic on the Sabbath. Sarah took a moment to catch her breath and rapidly assessed the assembly: old and young, male and female; a chest infection here, a fever there; swellings, rashes, sweats, shivers. There was a general, low hubbub of muted conversation, punctuated at irregular intervals by spluttering coughs and ill-contained sneezes.

One young woman sat with a small child on her knee, his cheeks lividly flushed and two rivulets of greenish mucus escaping from his nostrils to form a small lake on his top lip. He appeared far from content with his circumstances and Sarah knew the threat of voluble crying was never far away. However, his mother proved herself resourceful in having come equipped with a means of soothing her fractious charge. Every now and then her hand would disappear into a pocket and then emerge with a small piece of confectionary, which would be popped between his lips to buy a few more minutes of silence.

Sarah watched this from her position at the door and groaned inwardly at the thought of the threads of stickiness his little fingers were likely to leave behind. There was also a trail of muddy footprints leading from the door to the fireplace. As much as she enjoyed helping out at the doctor's clinic, the daily congregation of patients fairly added to her workload.

She noticed that the fire was beginning to die down, so she crossed the room, knelt down at the grate and shovelled in some more coal. As she poked at the fire, Will Raven emerged from his consulting room. He took a moment to spot her, crouched by the hearth, but she knew he would not proceed until he had her attention. She stood up and indicated a man cradling his right hand, which was wrapped in a particularly grotty cloth. Sarah had no inkling what was beneath it, but the smell had made it a priority, and not merely because the source might prove serious.

Sarah watched Raven lead the man away, still holding his forearm as though bearing a dead weight. She remained unsure quite what to make of the professor's new student apprentice. He lacked the confidence and self-assurance she was used to in the gentlemen who called to the house, and even allowing for his comparative youth, Raven's manner was in marked contrast to that of his predecessor, Thomas Keith. Dr Keith's younger brother had seemed altogether more comfortable in his position, although she ought to consider that when Thomas first arrived, Sarah was new too, and not merely to the household, but to her job.

She had the impression Raven was out of practice in dealing with domestic staff, most likely resultant of his time spent in lodgings whilst attending the university. This perhaps also accounted for the fact that he seemed rather thin and not nearly as well-nourished as she would have expected. Sarah had heard tell of how driven young men could become obsessive in the pursuit of their studies, and consequently neglectful of their worldly needs. This struck her as ironic in one studying medicine, training to look after bodily health, but for Raven to have secured such a coveted position with the professor, she supposed he might have been just so single-minded.

If there was one thing she had to give him credit for, it was that he was always kind and solicitous towards the patients, listening attentively and never talking down to them. Once again, it might seem ironic that such a trait should be remarkable in a supposedly caring profession, but Sarah had come to recognise a particular haughtiness common among medical men. Perhaps Raven hadn't yet acquired it, or perhaps it was this aspect of his manner that had won him Dr Simpson's approval.

Sarah occasionally amused herself by dwelling on the notion of herself as a student: what her days would have been like and which subjects she might have liked to study. She had an interest in botany and horticulture, as well as in the traditional healing arts, inherited from her family background. Any time spent in the professor's study caused her to marvel at all of the myriad disciplines and fields of knowledge one might explore, and the idea of spending whole years doing precisely that seemed heavenly. However, this was a distraction that came at a price, for although it was pleasant to indulge such fantasies, they also forced her to confront the harsh truth. She had not the means to attend university nor any prospect of ever acquiring them. Being female was also an obstacle that she could not easily overcome.

Mrs Lyndsay told her she would only enjoy contentment once she came to accept her station, but Sarah could not imagine anything quelling this restless want, and nor could she imagine ever feeling a genuine desire to do so. To numb her curiosity would be to cut off a part of herself.

Sarah did not consider it a coincidence that since that conversation, she had been permitted to assist at the morning clinic on fewer occasions. Mrs Lyndsay would assign her extra chores, or find fault with the tasks she had already carried out, and as a result declare she could not be spared. Nor did she consider it a coincidence that the clinics she missed appeared to be even more noisy and disorderly than usual.

From behind her, Sarah heard an explosive bout of coughing, ending in a loud and voluminous expectoration which prompted her to hope this individual was in possession of a handkerchief, as those without had been known to spit upon the floor. As she resumed poking at the fire she noticed how red and sore her hands looked, the skin beginning to split across the knuckles. This was a result of the recent cold weather and she hoped that she still had enough of her oatmeal ointment left to treat them, as she had not the time to make another batch.

Climbing once more to her feet, she heard a panic-stricken voice call out: 'Jamie! What on earth is the matter with you?'

Sarah turned to see the young woman with the catarrhal child grip her son by the arms, shaking him as though he was refusing to heed her instructions. Drawing closer, Sarah could see that the child was frantically struggling against her grasp, his eyes wide with fright. The boy's growing terror was mirrored in the face of his mother, who began loudly appealing to the room for assistance.

'I don't know what's wrong with him,' she squealed, shrill in her desperation. 'For the love of God, please, someone help him!'

The boy seemed unable to draw breath, his lips turning blue. Sarah could tell that the fight was beginning to drain from him, his movements becoming languid. She looked at his helpless, flailing arm and recalled the sticky fingers that had so recently concerned her. Suddenly, she knew what was wrong.

Sarah grabbed the child from the woman and bent him over her forearm. With her other hand she slapped his back sharply between the shoulder blades: once, twice. On the third attempt, something hit the carpet at her feet, whereupon the boy drew in an enormous breath and then began to cry.

The child's mother took him back onto her knee to comfort him as Sarah stood motionless, staring at the small, orange, sticky lump that was now firmly imbedded in the pile of the carpet.

The commotion had alerted the rest of the house. Dr Keith and Will Raven were quickly in the room, Dr Simpson arriving at the door moments later.

'Whatever is the cause of this?' Raven demanded.

Sarah pointed at the floor.

'Barley sugar,' she answered.

Whatever fortitude had guided Sarah's vital intervention quickly
deserted her once the danger had passed, and she found herself
suddenly tremulous and unsteady on her feet in the aftermath.
At the professor's bidding, she was escorted to his study, where
she was furnished with a strong cup of tea. Mrs Lyndsay had
great faith in its restorative powers, but as Sarah sat on the couch
and slowly sipped, she reflected that perhaps simply enjoying the
peace and time to drink it was the brew's most efficacious property. The pounding in her chest gradually subsided and her
breathing, which had been for a while rapid and shallow, returned
to its usual rate and depth.

There was a gentle rap at the door and Dr Simpson entered.

'How are you feeling now, Sarah?' he asked.

'Much better, thank you, sir.'

'I must congratulate you. You showed great presence of mind
in dealing with that situation. You saved that wee fellow's life,
and no mistake. I am immensely proud of you. But I am also most
curious as to just how you knew what to do.'

Sarah cleared her throat. '*Buchan's Domestic Medicine*, sir. We
didn't have a great many books at home, only that one and the
Bible. As a result, I must have read it through a number of times.'

'Indeed?' asked Dr Simpson, smiling. Something about her
answer appeared to have amused him. She felt that she ought to
explain further.

'My grandmother was the village howdie. A midwife and a
healer. That is probably why I developed an interest in such matters.
I know a little about herbal remedies. What she taught me.'

Dr Simpson smiled again. 'Hence your efforts in cultivating
a little herb garden at the back of the house. I hope you're not
planning to go into competition with me as a healer.'

'No, sir,' she answered bashfully.

'My grandfather too was a healer of some repute,' Dr Simpson told her. 'Mainly of livestock but he set a few bones in his time. He was, however, prone to indulging in country superstitions. He once buried a cow alive in an attempt to halt the progression of cattle plague, the image of which stayed with my father and haunted him to his dying day.

'Fortunately, there is no place in modern medicine for such nonsense. Health and disease is not a straightforward business. It would seem that the more we know, the more there is to know. Always be suspicious of those who claim to have simple answers to complex problems. Beware the foul waters of quackery.'

Sarah had heard similar speeches before and was well aware of the less-than-scrupulous travelling salesmen with their cure-all mixtures. While it was certainly true that country folk could still be a little credulous, being far removed as they were from great seats of learning, Sarah understood that when there was a dearth of knowledge and education, people – no matter their origins – were inclined to believe just about anything communicated to them with sufficient confidence and authority. However, Sarah also knew from personal experience that when all hope was lost, when all else had failed, people were willing to try almost anything to save those that they loved.

'Surely botanicals cannot be considered quackery?'

'Most definitely not,' the doctor replied. 'Nature has provided us with many useful remedies, but it is chemistry that will unlock her secrets. As a result of chemistry, we now know that it is quinine in Jesuit's bark that makes it useful in tertian fever and morphine that gives the opium poppy its power.'

Dr Simpson went to his bookcase and began searching the spines.

'I have the most informative book on the subject: *Outlines of Chemistry, for the Use of Students*, by my colleague Professor William Gregory. Would you be interested in learning more about it?'

Sarah smiled, put down her teacup and held out her hand.

TWELVE

aven entered the lecture theatre alongside the
professor, loaded down by a stack of notes which
Simpson typically ignored. The lecture room was full
and the students unusually attentive. Raven had been
on those same benches in the preceding two years, and it had
been Simpson's passion and clarity on his subject that had drawn
him towards the field of midwifery.

On this occasion the lecture was about the parturient with a
contracted pelvis. As always the professor was a warm and
engaging speaker, seldom taking his audience's attention for
granted, and illustrating his points through reference to relevant
clinical examples. These were detailed in the case notes Raven
had looked out and hefted into the room at Simpson's request,
but he never had need to refer to them.

Looking at the packed theatre and comparing it to some of
the sparsely attended meanderings he had sat through in the same
venue, Raven considered how much the professor would make
from the fees of this class alone. By his calculations it was a
significant amount. Perhaps one day he might lecture here himself,
or in the short term at least, now that he had been over the
course, he could offer personal tuition to some of the rich students
lining the benches. These were pleasant enough daydreams, but

even if they were to come to fruition, it would not be soon enough for Flint.

Towards the end of the lecture a messenger appeared at the door, sweaty and breathless from running, and clutching a soiled piece of paper. Raven intercepted him in the corridor outside before he could disrupt the doctor's concluding remarks.

'The professor is urgently requested to attend at a house in the Grassmarket, sir,' he panted, thrusting the paper into Raven's hand.

'By whom?' Raven asked, opening the note, the penmanship of which was illegible.

'By the doctor who is already there.'

'And did he write this with his feet?'

'No, his left hand. He was using his right to stop the bleeding.'

The doctor's carriage sped them through the narrow streets, avoiding carts, barrows and the odd heedless pedestrian seemingly intent upon self-murder. The dog would have loved this, thought Raven, though he was not sorry that on this occasion the beast had been left at home.

They pulled up outside a building on the south side of the Grassmarket and were directed by the messenger to an upper apartment. Simpson for once was panting due to the urgency of his ascent, unable to spare the breath to again observe 'always the top'.

Inside they found a young woman in labour, deathly pale and covered in a sheen of perspiration. Standing useless against the wall was a terrified-looking midwife who had some hours ago realised she was out of her depth.

In this, she was not alone.

The young doctor who had written the left-handed note looked besieged by his circumstances, crouching at the foot of the bed, blood spattering his face and his clothes. He had clearly been there for some time, and looked up with a bright expression of relief upon seeing Simpson, betraying that he had not been sure the professor would respond.

Raven took hold of the woman's wrist while Simpson shed his coat. Her pulse was rapid and thready. With the professor stepping in to intervene, the young doctor moved aside and climbed to his feet. He was shorter than Raven and slight of build, with something boyish about his countenance. He was expensively tailored, however, the clothes sitting elegantly upon his neat frame even as blood and sweat stuck the shirt to his chest.

'Tell me what we have here,' Simpson bade him.

Raven had expected an anxious voice befitting the circumstances and his physical stature, but the young doctor explained the details of the case in a calm, clear register, his account as lucid as his note had been illegible.

'Liquor amnii discharged early, ineffectual pains, two doses of ergot of rye given. There was considerable vomiting after the first dose, and after the second the patient said that she felt "something give" inside. The infant's head remained high, and so I employed long forceps but to no avail. Considerable haemorrhage followed the attempt at delivery, whereupon I dispatched my urgent note requesting your assistance.'

Raven was impressed as much by this display of professional detachment as by the contents of his description. He knew well enough how flustered one could become in the face of mounting trauma, sufficient that the maelstrom inside his head could pour out as babble from his mouth.

'Name?' Simpson asked.

'Beattie, sir. Dr John Beattie.'

'Of the patient,' he clarified.

'Oh. Williams, I think. Or was it Williamson. I can't quite recall. It has been a long day.'

Dr Simpson examined the patient, looked at Raven and beckoned him closer. His face was grim.

'The infant's head is at the upper aperture of the pelvis and is fairly wedged there,' he whispered. 'It is not sufficiently far down in the pelvis for a forceps delivery to have any chance of success and I am worried that the uterus itself might have ruptured. We must deliver the infant without delay – it is the mother's only chance of survival.'

As Simpson began fishing about inside his bag, Raven wondered what implement might be in there that could succeed where the forceps had failed. Simpson withdrew what Raven recognised as a perforator, and immediately he understood what was about to happen. He should have known already, but his faith in the professor as some kind of miracle-worker had caused him to misread the possibilities. He was going to perform a procedure known as a craniotomy.

Simpson took the bottle of ether from his bag. At least she wouldn't have to be awake during this.

'She shouldn't need much,' he said, looking at Raven.

'Mrs Williamson won't be having any of that,' the midwife objected. 'We're of the same church and the minister says it's not right to use it.'

Raven looked at her in confusion and disbelief.

She responded by thrusting a pamphlet at him, a diatribe penned by one Reverend Malachy Grissom.

Raven glanced at it and then looked to Simpson, who responded with a weary expression. He had clearly encountered this form of resistance before.

'The primeval curse,' he said by way of explanation. 'Genesis. "In sorrow thou shalt bring forth children." Some consider it to be anti-scriptural to remove the pain associated with labour.'

Raven thought that this sounded like needless stupidity, a description that fitted many words and deeds he had witnessed on the part of churchmen. Why a so-called man of God would deny a woman pain relief, especially given what was about to happen, made no sense to him.

'Perhaps Mrs Williamson should be permitted to make that decision for herself,' Raven suggested, earning himself a scolding look from the midwife.

The woman herself could not be persuaded, however.

'I'll not risk eternal damnation for the sake of delivering a child,' she replied weakly.

The midwife nodded with undisguised satisfaction, her eyes fixed on Raven, and so Dr Simpson proceeded without the aid of a soporific.

For once Raven was grateful for the sheet that was shrouding the woman's legs and genital area. He knew what was happening, he had seen it before and he had no desire to see it again today. He could more or less recite Dr Simpson's lecture on the subject anyway:

Many children can be brought into the world by the use of forceps and turning, but there are cases where the infant's head is too large and the maternal passages too small to admit the delivery of the child alive without bringing the life of the mother into the most imminent danger. In such circumstances, we can save the life of the mother by sacrificing that of her pregnancy. By opening the head of the infant by means of perforating instruments, we can remove the contents of the cranium and then break down the vault of the skull, bringing away the fragments until only the base of the cranium and the bones of the face remain to be extracted by means of the crochet.

Even in her weakened state, Mrs Williamson writhed a great deal as the various instruments were inserted to break down the infant's head and haul it out. Raven felt turmoil watching her and thinking of the tiny life that was being snuffed out before it had a chance to take a single breath. This was the thing that most caused him to fear he was not made of the right stuff to be a doctor. He knew for sure it was why he couldn't be a surgeon.

His mother always said he had the devil in him, but she simply meant he had a keen sense of mischief, the imp of the perverse. The human in him had a tendency to feel other people's pain too keenly.

After the infant was delivered – what was left of it – the placenta followed without delay, but the uterus would not contract. The patient continued to bleed despite the binder tightly wound round her abdomen. Raven knew this was a serious complication. He also knew there was nothing more they could do.

The cleaning and tidying away of instruments was performed in near silence. Dr Simpson spoke to the midwife, giving instructions that she should see to her patient's every comfort, vowing to return later in the day to check on her progress.

He shook his head as he left the room.

THIRTEEN

he medical men, all of them now dishevelled and blood-spattered, emerged onto the Grassmarket, which was busy with carters and street-traders going about their business. It seemed incredible that the rest of the world could carry on as if nothing had happened: small-scale horror and tragedy swallowed up by the day-to-day affairs of the city.

Simpson suggested that they repair to a local hostelry for a restorative to raise their spirits, nominating an establishment he had frequented as a medical student.

Baxter's tavern sat rather incongruously beside Cranston's Teetotal Coffee House, which Raven noted with some satisfaction had little in the way of customers. Given the nature of the afternoon's proceedings, he had no doubt which he would rather patronise but did have his concerns regarding who he might see in the alehouse, or more pertinently who might see him.

Entering at the professor's back, he scanned the room from the doorway, ready for a sharp departure. Simpson seemed to be on friendly terms with both proprietor and clientele. He ordered a round of Edinburgh ales, which he took an age to bring across due to how many conversations he struck up between the gantry and their table. Raven drank deeply, thirstier than he realised and in need of the comforts alcohol could offer.

Beattie seemed altogether less traumatised by the outcome of the case. Perhaps this was because he had been a participant throughout rather than merely an impotent witness, and perhaps his greater experience of such things had inured him to the emotional effluent. He seemed unperturbed by the spit and sawdust of the pub, despite his expensive outfit suggesting he might be used to more salubrious surroundings. There was an awkwardness about his gait in keeping with a pronounced quickness to all his physical movements that reminded Raven of a small bird: fleet but restless, as though wary of predators.

Up close and in clearer light, Raven enjoyed a closer appreciation of his boyish visage, which revealed the man to be not so youthful as he first appeared. Initially he believed he had encountered another prodigy like James Duncan (though hopefully not such an obnoxious one), but he could now see the lines around his eyes, suggesting Beattie might be in his late twenties.

Simpson asked Beattie a little about his background, beginning with the seemingly inevitable question regarding his father's occupation.

'My father is dead, sir,' Beattie replied. 'Indeed, I lost both my parents when I was twelve. However, I am fortunate in having a benefactor in the form of my uncle, a Mr Charles Latimer, who is a man of some property in Canaan Lands on the Morningside.'

Raven hoped Beattie's uncle wore his largesse more lightly than Miserly Malcolm, who turned every penny spent on his nephew into a token of his sister's failure and poor judgment in her choice of matrimonial partner.

'You don't sound as though you hail from these parts,' Simpson suggested.

'No. I was schooled in the south of England, but my mother grew up here. I attended university in Edinburgh to be closer to my uncle, who has become frailer over the years.'

In the manner peculiar to all medical men, Simpson ignored all reference to finance and property and asked for details regarding the uncle's debility.

'He suffers from a severe form of rheumatism which causes him much pain. He has tried all manner of therapies in his attempts to find relief. He most recently embarked upon a trip to Austria to try a water treatment promoted by a fellow named Priessnitz. Runs a therapeutic establishment somewhere in the mountains.'

'Did your uncle find any of this helpful?'

'He found his pain to be somewhat improved but his spirits more so. It makes me think that there may be something in it – cold baths, simple diet and the withdrawal of all internal medicines. His response to these therapies – and more pertinently the sum he paid for them – leads me to envisage that there might be a lucrative market for hydropathic treatments.'

Simpson rubbed his chin, fixing Beattie with a thoughtful gaze.

'It could perhaps be argued that it was the withdrawal of his usual medicaments which resulted in his improvement, and not the regular soaking with cold water. We are perhaps too ready to dose our patients with powerful purges and bleed them to the point of depletion, don't you think? My friend and colleague Dr George Keith is a great believer in Nature's Method and the idea of masterly inactivity on the part of the physician.'

'*Primum non nocere*,' nodded Beattie in agreement.

Do no harm: the Hippocratic injunction.

Simpson took a gulp from his ale by way of toasting the sentiment, draining the last of it.

'Forgive me, Dr Beattie, I have just spied a good friend at another table. But before I go, let me say I have very much enjoyed meeting you this afternoon. You must come to dinner at Queen Street.'

'I would be honoured,' Beattie replied with a quiet grace.

Raven could only imagine how he might have spluttered his

response had someone so feted extended such an offer. This together with his fine garb suggested it was not the first time Beattie had been invited to dine in estimable company.

They watched the professor stride across the tavern and loudly hail a fellow on the other side of the room.

'The professor is a man of broad acquaintance,' Beattie said, as though this was in some way amusing. 'I wouldn't have thought him comfortable in a place like this these days. He is reputedly much in demand among the ladies of the aristocracy.'

Though I am yet to see much evidence of it, Raven thought.

'He is of humble origins, though,' Raven said. This was another of the factors that had drawn him to the professor. If Simpson could rise to such stature and wealth from ordinary beginnings, he had reasoned, then perhaps a keen apprentice might learn to follow his path.

'The son of a village baker,' Beattie stated. 'A seventh son and the last of eight.'

This was more than Raven knew, and it showed.

Beattie flashed him a self-conscious smile. 'It is always wise to learn as much as you can about the great names in your field, in case fate should throw you into their company. Though being found blood-spattered and helpless at the foot of a patient's bed – a patient I failed – is not the best first impression I could have hoped to make upon the man.'

'Well, it can't have been so bad if he invited you to Queen Street. And frankly, I was amazed at how calm you seemed amidst it all. I can't keep my mind from returning to that room and of thinking about how it is likely to go for Mrs Williamson.'

Beattie supped from his beer, an equanimity about him that further belied Raven's early impression of his youth.

'I very much doubt she will live,' he said. 'Even despite the attentions of Dr Simpson.' His tone was even, as though discussing something third-hand rather than a woman whose blood even now daubed his shirt.

'Does it get easier, then?' Raven asked.

'Does what?'

'Dealing with such suffering. When I witness a case such as we just left, it holds me in its grip long after, and I fear the cumulative burden. Yet you were reasoned amidst it all and seem unaffected now.'

Beattie regarded Raven for a moment, giving some thought to his answer.

'Each man only has so much pity to give, and in our profession we encounter every day some tragedy upon which one might spend a large portion of it.'

'Are you saying that in time I will become numb to this? For I am not sure I would wish that either.'

'It is not so much a process of becoming numb, but of a perspective that is harshly learned through your own wounds rather than those you might treat. When you have known true sorrow, the plight of a patient, no matter how pitiful, will not hurt you like you have felt hurt before.'

Raven thought he had known sorrow enough, but if he was still so vulnerable to the sufferings of others, then perhaps he had not known as much as Beattie. He said he had lost both his parents at the age of twelve, but something about the man suggested there was more than that. He was curious to know, but did not feel it his place to press.

'And if I have not yet felt true sorrow?' Raven asked.

'Be grateful, and do not wallow in the misery of others. I am sincere in this. The patients require a distance from you, that you may exercise your judgment and skill undistracted by your emotions.'

Raven knew this was right, though it was not easy to hear. He knew there was much he could learn from a doctor such as Beattie, but equally, seeing how he conducted himself was a stark reminder of how far he had to go.

'So you're set on a career in midwifery yourself?' Beattie asked, this change of subject accompanied by a lightening in the tone of his voice.

'Yes. I had thought of surgery, but it is decidedly not for me.'

'Good choice. There is a brighter future in this profession than among the sawbones. Financially speaking, I mean.'

Raven took in Beattie's expensive garments and wondered whether these had been paid for by his uncle or by his earnings.

'I have not seen much evidence of that so far,' he confessed. 'Unless some day I can be the one delivering those aristocratic ladies, but that seems likely to be a long way off.'

Beattie had an impish grin, the lines around his eyes more distinct as he smiled.

'This is a wider field than you understand, one that is even now opening up to new and lucrative possibilities. You need to think beyond babies and more about the women who bear them. There are all manner of new and exotic treatments for the various maladies the fairer sex seem prone to. Galvanism, uterine manipulation – scientific treatments for that perennial female affliction, hysteria. There is much money to be made from unhappy women and their exasperated husbands.'

Raven made no reply, causing Beattie to continue in a similar vein.

'Success is all about identifying opportunity,' Beattie told him. 'Talking of which, this ether stuff is promising, is it not? Think of what a price patients would put upon the oblivion you can provide during a procedure.'

'Those who don't have a religious objection,' Raven muttered.

'It's potentially a gold mine,' Beattie went on, paying no heed. 'I gather the dentists in this town can't get enough of it. You must be getting rather adept at its administration, working with Simpson.'

'He has been training me in its use, yes. When it's a complicated case, that is often the only thing he lets me do myself.'

'Don't complain. I'm sure it will prove a valuable skill.'

'Though maybe not as valuable as dousing rich people in cold water,' Raven replied.

Beattie laughed, and suggested they have another ale. Raven would have dearly loved to. This was an acquaintance he would do well to cultivate, but he had other business to attend, and he would need all his wits about him for it.

FOURTEEN

t was dark as Raven made his way down the Canongate, bound for Evie's lodgings. The lamps seemed almost futile in their efforts to penetrate the blackness and the fog, but he quietened his fear with the knowledge that if he could not make out his enemies amidst such gloom, then neither could they.

He entered Evie's close with a soft tread, but did not make it as far as the stairs before a familiar figure blocked his path. She had emerged from her lair on the ground floor, beyond which a mouse could seldom pass unnoticed unless this fearsome sentinel was already well in her cups.

Evie always described Effie Peake as her landlady, but she didn't own the place. She merely collected rent and kept a close eye on behalf of whoever did, for which she presumably got her own lodgings at a short rate. The woman was the nature of Edinburgh in microcosm, adept to the point of self-deception at compartmentalising her public and private faces. She insisted on being addressed as Mrs Peake, but this was rumoured to be an affectation, as according to Evie there had never been a Mr Peake. She reacted with outrage at any suggestion she was aware immoral conduct might be taking place upon her premises. But in truth, very little business escaped her notice: 'Not when she's taking a slice of every storm of heaves that happens beneath her roof,' as Evie had put it.

So she knew who came here, and who they saw. Raven had no doubt that as well as the local clientele, those visitors included men of high standing, of impeccable moral repute, of power and of influence. He also had no doubt that neither Effie's word nor the word of any woman here would be worth a fig against such men should an accusation be made. Nonetheless, Raven suspected Mrs Peake might prove a rich fount of information, if anyone could find the right means of tapping it.

She was short and stout, as though having developed her shape specifically to block this passageway. Despite her girth there was something narrow about her features, pale and pinched, suggesting that should she ever smile it would unravel the tight bun her hair was scraped into at the back. 'If you're looking for Evie, she's not here,' she said. An interesting choice of words, not least because it reassured him that she did not know he had been in the building that night.

Raven opted therefore to play along.

'Where is she?'

'Gone.'

'Gone where? Will she be back soon?'

Effie sighed, a weary look coming over her. 'I'm only telling you this because I recognise your face and I know Evie had a fondness for you. Evie is dead.'

Raven feigned shock and hurt, a task assisted by what Effie had just said about Evie having a fondness for him. It was also the first time he had heard anyone talk about her death beyond those callous words that had spilled from the mouth of that policeman.

'What happened?'

'Found her that way. Four, no five days ago.'

'Where is she now?'

She looked at him as though he was a simpleton. 'Buried. Where else would she be?'

'I merely wondered, given that her death had been so sudden, whether it might have prompted an investigation of some kind. A post-mortem perhaps?'

'A post what?'

'An examination of the body, to determine the cause of death.'

'Doctor from the dispensary determined it simply enough. Said it was the drink. Signed the certificate to that effect. Didn't need much time to work that out.'

Raven pictured the body being carried out to the cart in that tattered and filthy shroud. Never mind a post-mortem, the doctor from the dispensary would have barely looked at her. Sometimes they didn't even enter the house.

'Where was she taken?'

'How should I know? Some pauper's grave, as there was no one to pay for anything else. Anyway, that's all I can tell you, so you ought to be on your way.'

She folded her arms, her posture unmistakably defensive. She wanted him gone.

'Could I see her room?'

'Why? Are you some kind of ghoul?'

'No, I'm a man of medicine.'

Effie allowed herself a scornful smirk. 'You don't look like a *man* of anything to me.'

Raven ignored this. 'I would like to see if there is anything there that might help me deduce what became of her.'

'I've already rented it. Can't afford to keep good lodgings empty.'

'Was there anyone with her before she died?'

'I wouldn't know. I respect my tenants' privacy.'

Like her folded arms, this mutually understood lie was an indication that she was putting up the shutters. She would tell him nothing more, which served only to make him wonder what she wished to conceal.

Raven heard a door open above, saw a female face peering over the stairwell to investigate what she had overheard. The face disappeared again following a sharp look from Effie.

'And what of Evie's possessions?' Raven enquired.

'Sold. To cover expenses. Not that you get much for a couple of dresses and a pair of jet earrings.'

'What about the brandy?' he asked, wondering whether it and not the gut-rot might have proven toxic.

'What brandy?' she asked, but she had betrayed herself with her transparent surprise that he should know about it.

'The bottle I saw in her room when last I visited.'

Effie's face took on a defiant expression. 'That's long gone too,' she said. 'I drank it.'

'In that case, I have reason to thank you.'

This truly confused her. 'Thank me?'

'For performing the most basic but reliable form of toxico-logical analysis. I had a concern that Evie's death might have been attributable to drinking something that proved poisonous. By virtue of the fact that you are standing in front of me, I can deduce that it could not have been the brandy.'

With that, Raven departed back into the gloom.

He had barely traversed the breadth of the building when he heard footsteps at his back, approaching at speed. He turned, bracing himself to attack or to flee, but found himself confronted by the young woman who had been peering down the stairs some moments ago. It was difficult to be sure in the paltry light that fell here between two street lamps, but he thought she seemed familiar.

'It's Will, isn't it?' she asked.

'Yes.'

'Aye. I saw you with Evie sometimes. She talked about you. I'm Peggy.'

'I recognise you. Can I help?'

'I overheard. You were asking if Evie had anyone with her the night she died. She did. I'm in the next room.'

'You saw who came and went?' he asked, suddenly fearing where this might be going.

'I never saw. I heard them, though.'

This came both as relief and disappointment. She hadn't seen Raven, but nor would she be able to identify the visitor.

'I don't suppose his voice was familiar to you?'

'No, but see, that's the thing. It was a woman's voice I heard.'

FIFTEEN

or all Raven had told Henry that it would take some adjustment in getting used to his new accommodations, he could not deny he felt a sense of sanctuary as he crossed the threshold. He hoped the Simpson family appreciated how privileged they were to live in this place, safe not only from cold and hunger, but from the world of danger, anxiety and suspicion that he had grown used to. Here on Queen Street, he no longer had to be in a state of constant alertness, concerned for his possessions, his safety, or, in the cramped confines of Ma Cherry's, his privacy.

He remained conscious of being a guest in another family's home, but equally he was aware of their efforts to make him feel welcome. It was true Jarvis still regarded him with less respect than Glen the dog, and of course there was Sarah, who did not accord him as much as that, but on the whole, he was beginning to feel comfortable at No. 52.

He walked quickly towards the stairs with the intention of warming himself before he got cleaned up for dinner. A fire was always lit in one of the large public rooms on the first floor at this time of day, particularly welcome after the cold breeze that had chilled him on his walk back from Effie Peake's place.

As he began to ascend, something shot past his head, an

improvised missile that served as warning that Walter and David were on the loose. Raven heard the roar of a war cry as David chased his younger brother down the stairs, excited giggles and screams accompanying their progress as usual. They disappeared into a room below with the inevitable slam of a door, after which the ensuing moment of silence seemed all the more pronounced by contrast.

It was broken by voices from his intended destination, Mrs Simpson and Mina continuing what sounded like a fraught conversation. The door was ajar and from the unguarded nature of their discussion, he deduced they were heedless of his approach because his tread upon the stairs had been masked by the noise of the children.

It was Mina he heard first, her tone soft but adamant, as though concerned about being overheard. He felt trapped, conscious that were he to continue his progress, he would be heard and his eavesdropping discovered. Even if it was by accident, people did not readily forgive it when they knew you had happened upon their secrets.

'I think you have become so used to the status Dr Simpson's good name confers, that you forget how precarious reputations can be when there is scandal in the offing.'

'It is blethers, Mina. Nothing more.'

'You should consider that it's not just his reputation that is at stake. It's yours too. He is paying out twelve pounds a year to another woman. Isn't the obvious question: why?'

'It is an act of charity. Surely no one can cast aspersions over something so noble.'

'In my experience people are happy to cast aspersions over anything when the morality of an action can be called into question. You would be naive if you didn't anticipate the conclusions that are likely to be drawn. In your interpretation, it is an act of charity. To someone else, it might imply a guilty conscience.'

'That is absurd, Mina. There is nothing of any substance for rumours to attach to.'

'Jessie, James is a man much admired by the ladies of this town, and you shut away in mourning all this time. They rain upon him compliments and affection. Is it so difficult to imagine where that might lead?'

'I have no control over gossip. What is important is that I know the truth of it.'

'Do you?'

'I would warn you, Mina, to remember beneath whose roof you reside.'

A door flew open downstairs and the boys exploded from it once again. Raven seized the opportunity to proceed unnoticed to his bedroom. They were joyfully oblivious of the complex ways of adults, and he had been almost as naive. Cut beneath the epidermis in any household and you would surely find that life there was not as harmonious as it appeared on the surface.

He had only heard a brief exchange, but he recognised what was going on. Mina was trying to gently coax her sister into seeing what was obvious to her and therefore to others. Raven was only too familiar with the spectacle of a wife seeking every possible interpretation that might allow her to escape the most painful of conclusions. He recalled his own mother, a bright and intelligent woman, making herself seem foolish in her desperation to elude the inevitable truth. Her husband had been a drunk and a philanderer. She couldn't deny the former, for she was confronted with the fact of it in her household almost every night. But it was the nights on which she was spared by his absence about which she had persistently deluded herself.

Could Raven believe this of Dr Simpson? Unlike his own father, he seemed the perfectly contented family man, available and affectionate around his children where so many others were aloof and distant. But Raven had always to remember that this was Edinburgh, the city whose crest ought to be the head of the Janus: one face for polite society, another behind closed doors.

SIXTEEN

arah picked up the shirt, pinching a small amount of the filthy material between the tip of her index finger and thumb. She wished she had a pair of tongs for the job. It looked like Raven had been washing floors or cleaning the grate with it.

As if.

The thin cotton, which she presumed had at one point been white, was now grey in colour and streaked with dirt. There were dark splotches on both sleeves that she recognised as blood. One of the sleeves was attempting to part company from the rest of the garment, a tear at the seam having been ineptly repaired at some point.

'I hope he can stitch wounds better than that,' she mused as she dropped the offensive item into a basket by the door. The notion brought to mind the nasty cut on Raven's cheek, about which she suspected he was being less than truthful. He claimed he had been randomly set upon, but her instinct was that he must have played some part in precipitating the attack. She recognised something restless in him. Ambitious and driven, yes, but not at peace with himself.

He struck her as impetuous, desperate to prove himself, though to whom would be an interesting question. Since he got here, he had been trying too hard to look like he was in control, over-compensating for the fear that he was in over his head. Recalling her own first steps and missteps as a housemaid, Sarah well understood how difficult it could be when you were new to a situation. However, her sympathy was limited by the fact that his was a privileged problem to have. She would have loved to be negotiating his new situation rather than that of a domestic servant, who could be cast out onto the street for speaking out of turn.

Sarah had come into service here at Queen Street following the deaths of her parents, the local minister finding this position for her as he was an old friend of Dr Simpson. Her premature departure from the parish school had no doubt been a relief to her schoolmaster, who was becoming increasingly wearied by her arguments regarding her exclusion from subjects deemed suited only to boys, such as Classics and mathematics. He was convinced that her grasp of reading, writing and arithmetic was sufficient for a girl of her station, insisting that knitting and sewing would be of more use to her and would open up the possibility of industrial work in the future. As though a factory job or work in a mill should be the culmination of all her ambition. If one was capable of carrying out a task or learning a body of knowledge, then why should it matter whether one be male or female? Her fury at this injustice had cooled little since.

She turned to take in the rest of the room, wondering what other horrors might be lurking there. To be fair it was not as messy as Mina's chaotic fiefdom but it was far from tidy. Open books and papers were scattered across the small writing desk in one corner, spilling onto the floor in a wide circle. A black coat – mucky cuffs, threadbare around the collar – was hanging from the back of a chair and muddy boots had trailed clumps of dirt across the carpet from doorway to fireplace. Sarah sighed. This was going to take a bit of time to sort out.

In order to see more of the carpet so that she could put some tea leaves down and sweep it, she decided to start at the desk, or at least the floor surrounding the desk. As she stooped to pick up some of the discarded papers she found herself next to the battered trunk that had followed Raven from his previous accommodation. It was open, some of the papers having landed inside. The trunk mostly contained books, presumably not deemed of immediate necessity, as there were plenty of those piled elsewhere.

She recalled his high-handed conduct on the morning of his first clinic.

Do you think a man has time to read fiction when he is training to be a doctor?

Evidently, he had time to read fiction once, for there were several piled up inside the box. She picked up the topmost one, *The Luck of Barry Lyndon* by William Makepeace Thackeray. Beneath it was *The Last of the Mohicans* by James Fenimore Cooper, and below that three works by Walter Scott.

Sarah turned the Thackeray book in her hand. She was sure Mina had a copy. She opened it, noting that the inside of the cover had been proprietorially inscribed with a handwritten name: Thomas Cunningham. A gift? A theft? Sarah examined the Cooper, noting the same name inside. Second-hand, then. A job lot, purchased from a fellow student.

She gathered up the papers and attempted to order them. Some dealt with what looked like injuries sustained during childbirth, others concerning a procedure known as a craniotomy, the illustrations for which she was sure she must be misreading. Sarah winced and picked up another, which turned out to be a letter. Upon discovering this, she turned it over and put it back down, but not without observing that it was from Raven's mother, and more intriguingly that she had addressed him neither as Will nor William.

She smiled at this discovery, moving the letter to one side so that it did not get lost among the piles of notes. That was when she encountered an open journal, her eyes drawn by the contrast between two pages. On one side were dense paragraphs of Raven's neat handwriting, a cursory glance at which revealed them to be detailing the procedure for administering ether. On the opposite folio, there were but two words in impatiently scrawled capitals:

EVIE POISONED?

Sarah heard the tread of footsteps too late. She had been seen.

'What the devil do you think you're doing?' Raven asked. He snatched the journal from where it lay upon the desk, slamming it closed with a force that caused several of the papers she had gathered to drift from their piles. He seemed disproportionate in his vehemence, making her wonder at the significance of whatever he feared she might have read.

'There is no need for temper,' she responded, keeping her voice even in the hope that it would calm his ire. A complaint from the professor's apprentice would give Mrs Lyndsay all the reason she needed to curtail Sarah's clinic duties. 'I am merely attempting to tidy up.'

'You were not merely tidying up, you were going through my private things, which I will not tolerate. There is nothing among these papers that concerns you, and still less that you would even understand.'

Despite the precariousness of her situation, Sarah could not prevent Raven's words from raising her hackles. She knew she should retreat, but an uncontainable instinct urged her to advance instead. She could just about tolerate bowing and scraping to the upstairs patients, but not to this scruffy youth.

'Who is Evie?' she asked.

He seemed flabbergasted, which had the unintended effect of spiking his bluster by putting him on the back foot.

'She is . . . no business of yours.'

Sarah decided to press her advantage. 'How did you really get that cut on your face, *Wilberforce*?'

His eyes flashed, but she could see a hint of anxiety beneath the outrage. Raven had secrets, and that was the real reason for this display of indignation.

'You read a letter from my *mother*?'

'I would not so intrude. I merely saw the addressee. I have heard Mrs Simpson address you as William several times and you've never corrected her. Why would that be? Does Dr Simpson know your real name is Wilberforce?'

Raven's face flushed. 'You would do well to remember your position. You seem to forget that you are a servant. What kind of house is this where such behaviour is not reined in?'

Sarah gazed down at the trunk and then to her basket. 'Are you used to greater deference from those below stairs, *sir*?' she enquired.

He did not answer. He looked worried now more than angry. He was afraid of what she might know, and he was right to be. It appeared there was someone in the household with an even more tenuous grip upon his position than she had.

'Who is Thomas Cunningham?'

'I don't know.'

'Yes, you do. He was the previous owner of the second-hand books in your trunk. Mrs Simpson said your late father was a lawyer in St Andrews, but I'd wager you're no higher born than I am.'

She lifted up the soiled and threadbare shirt from the laundry basket.

'There is little you can conceal from the woman who does your laundry.'

Raven looked at the shirt, his indignation spent, his demeanour meek, even vulnerable. It was as though her seeing the state of the garment was a greater trespass than the reading of his notes.

'What are you doing with that?' he asked meekly.

'Your shirt is soiled. It needs to be cleaned and is in sorry need of repair. I was going to soak the stains out of it and stitch the hole in the shoulder seam.'

Raven took a step towards her, fire returning to his eyes.

'I will thank you not to touch my things,' he said.

Sarah held his gaze.

'As you wish.'

She dropped the shirt onto the floor, turned on her heel and left the room.

SEVENTEEN

he brougham was fairly bouncing on its springs as it raced down the hill past Gayfield Square. The day was young but not bright, relentless fine drizzle falling from low skies. Raven was grateful for the early hour and the shelter of the carriage. From his schooldays he recalled a classmate remarking that the further one traversed down Leith Walk on foot after dark, the more likely one was to end up with, as this boy had put it, 'a burst mooth'.

'I used to have this two-wheeled claret curricle,' Simpson told him. 'If you think this swift, you ought to have seen how that contraption clattered over the cobbles. Mrs Simpson insisted that I change it for something more weatherproof.'

There was a joyous twinkle in his eye as he spoke, but the professor's enthusiasm proved less infectious than usual because Raven could not help recalling Mina's conversation with Jessie the night before. Who was this woman Simpson was paying money to, and for what? Raven knew that Mina could be wrong, and equally that without the full context he might have misunderstood the brief exchange he had overheard. Nonetheless, the scars left by his father ran deeper than the one upon his cheek, and therefore he could not look upon the professor without suspicion.

He attempted to put it from his thoughts, but the other

matters he turned to offered little respite. The sad fate of Evie was seldom far from his mind, but was all the more prominent since his conversation with the evasive Mrs Peake. And then there was his most recent encounter with Sarah.

The girl had seen through him, her gifts of deduction as sharp as her inquisitiveness was impertinent. And though nobody else in the house was likely to reach the same conclusions, it was in her power to help them see the truth too. He just hoped that her appetite for novels had not led her to read the Thackeray she had spied, for it was about someone from a fallen family attempting to pass as a member of the upper orders.

He had felt such a stab of fear when she asked him about Thomas Cunningham. Fortunately she had wrongly inferred the significance of finding his name written inside Raven's books, so she maybe wasn't quite as clever as she imagined. Nonetheless, clever she undoubtedly was, and he appeared to have made an enemy of her.

Why did she despise him so? He hadn't done anything to harm her. Obviously there had been that incident at the first clinic, but she had shown disdain for him before that – almost from the moment he walked in the door.

He would simply have to endure it. His time at Heriot's had taught him that sometimes people could take an instinctive or irrational dislike to you, as you could to them. In such instances, there was nothing you could do to change that, and it proved a fool's errand to try.

Similar difficulty attended his relationship with James Duncan, although in that case the cause of dislike wasn't instinctive or irrational. Duncan seemed to regard him not so much as a subordinate as an affront, a burden Dr Simpson had foisted upon him rather than a potentially valuable assistant. Although Duncan was content enough to assign him menial and unpleasant tasks, he behaved as though he resented Raven working alongside him even in the capacity of dogsbody. Raven suspected that this was because he did not wish anyone to have even a partial claim of contribution to anything that he was to discover. The young doctor was brilliant no doubt, but at the same time lacking in any grace, humour or humility.

The carriage swung around, Raven sliding in his seat as it turned at speed onto Great Junction Street, heading for the port. The professor had not said what it was they were rushing to attend. Someone had come to the house, as was often the case, requesting his urgent presence. As always, a part of Raven was surprised and admiring that someone of Simpson's stature should answer these calls with no promise of a commensurate payment, far less a guarantee that it was worth the time of one so eminent. He suspected the professor enjoyed the thrill of the urgency, and of being needed. For who would not?

Raven became conscious of a growing hubbub beneath the constant ululation of seagulls, the sound increasing as they drew nearer its source. He leaned out of the window to see a crowd gathered at the edge of the Water of Leith, the numbers thick enough that should someone trip, he might send a dozen of them tumbling over the edge. Over their heads he could see a forest of masts stretching into the middle distance, as though the ships in the dock were also craning to see whatever had attracted this gathering.

A cry went up as soon as Simpson stuck his head out of the carriage.

'It is Dr Simpson. Clear a way, clear a way.'

The sea of people parted before him as Simpson stepped down into the street, Raven tight in his wake lest the crowd close before him again. At the end of this human channel there were three policemen, two standing to the left of a smartly dressed fellow Raven took to be their superior. This was confirmed when Simpson hailed him.

'Mr McLevy, sir. May I be of assistance?'

Raven felt an involuntary tightening in his chest, reminiscent of those times at George Heriot's when the headmaster would enter his classroom unannounced. The policeman in charge was no less than the famous James McLevy. Raven had never seen the man in person but knew him by his reputation – the nature of which tended to alter depending on which side of Princes Street you stood. Among the respectable citizens of the New Town, he was a dogged and resourceful detective, peerless in his recovery of stolen property and indefatigable in the lengths to which he would go to get his man. Over in the Old Town, however, he was feared for the brutality and ruthlessness of his methods, and while legendary for always closing his cases, rumour was that this didn't necessarily mean the true perpetrator was the one brought to justice.

He did not look so fearsome right then, for there was a look of sorrow and regret upon his face.

'It's too late for even your skilled hands, Dr Simpson,' he replied, his accent pegging him from the north of Ireland.

At McLevy's prompting, the other officers stood aside and Raven was able to see a sheet upon the flagstones, damp soaking through it from the rain.

'Drowned?' Simpson asked.

'I suspect so. But I think she may have had some kind of seizure that caused her to fall in.'

McLevy briefly tugged the sheet back and a chill engulfed Raven as though he had been plunged into the cold, black waters below. Beneath the sheet was a young woman, blue-lipped and grey of skin. She had been dead in the water for some time. But what gripped Raven was her twisted expression and the contorted posture of her body.

He only glimpsed her for a moment, and then the sheet was replaced.

'May I see?' Raven asked.

Simpson put an arm on his shoulder. 'No, we must away. This is not what we were summoned for and time is of the essence. There is another young woman whose life we may yet be able to save.'

The patient turned out to be the labouring wife of a mariner, her husband having recently left the port of Leith on a voyage to

Stromness. She was in a state of visible distress and exhaustion, to Raven's eyes resembling a wrung-out cloth as she lay almost lifeless upon the bed.

'Mrs Alford has an extremely contracted pelvis,' said the worried-looking gentleman who was her usual medical attendant, a Mr Angus Figg. He was a grey-whiskered and fidgety old soul who introduced himself with great deference to Dr Simpson. He spoke to them in hushed tones, away from the bed.

'This led to a previous confinement lasting four days. In that instance, delivery by forceps was unsuccessful and eventually the infant had to be drawn out in pieces.'

He glanced back at the patient.

'She was advised about the hazards of risking another pregnancy,' he went on. 'I was not made aware of her condition until earlier today when she was already at full term and in labour.'

Raven looked to Mrs Alford and found her gazing back, weak but anxiously awaiting the results of their council. He understood that her torment was not merely from the pain she was experiencing but in anticipation of what was to come.

Simpson examined her, Mrs Alford's eyes permanently upon him.

'Am I going to die?' she asked rather matter-of-factly, as though she had been preparing herself for such an outcome.

'Not if I can help it,' Simpson replied.

He announced that he would attempt podalic version, or turning, and instructed Raven to administer ether.

'That is if you have no objection to it?' Raven asked her, dousing the sponge in readiness.

Mrs Alford looked at him as though she didn't understand the question, which struck him as the correct answer.

She breathed in the vapour with some alacrity and soon slipped into a state of unconsciousness. Raven found the rapidity of the transition somewhat alarming but her breathing remained regular and her pulse rate, which had been elevated, began to decline to a more acceptable level.

With the patient in this relaxed state, the child was turned easily, the feet, legs and trunk pulled down without much effort. The extraction of the head proved to be more difficult. Simpson applied the forceps and some considerable exertion was required on his part before the infant's head would pass through the woman's misshapen pelvis. Difficult as it was, the delivery was completed in less than twenty minutes.

The infant was handed to Raven while the afterbirth was delivered. It gasped several times but would not breathe, its head having been flattened and compressed, the parietal bone indented on one side. He wrapped the child in the blanket which had been laid out for this purpose and looked around the small room for a place to put it. There were several tallow candles lit around the bed and Mr Figg held an oil lamp, but the corners of the room remained in darkness. As no appropriate receptacle presented itself, he placed the small, pale, lifeless bundle beside the still sleeping mother. The child was pale, tinged with blue.

At this point Raven realised that he hadn't noticed the sex of the baby; he wouldn't be able to tell the mother when she woke up whether the child was a boy or a girl. He hoped that she wouldn't ask.

When the patient did come around, she seemed to be primarily concerned that her ordeal was over. She had evidently not expected a live child to result from this confinement. She showed no emotion when the infant was presented to her, but expressed relief that she had not suffered this time as she had before.

Simpson promised to return in a day or two to see how she was.

'You would do well to heed Mr Figg's advice and take pains to avoid another pregnancy,' he told her softly.

'Best tell that to my husband,' she said in reply.

EIGHTEEN

he sounds of disputation once again greeted Raven's approach to the drawing room as he ascended the stairs, though on this occasion the voices were male. He paused on the threshold, keen to gather what was being discussed by way of forearming himself. He could make out Duncan's assured tones, sounding as always like he was carrying the Ten Commandments. Raven was in no mood to be lectured to and was thinking about beating a retreat when he heard someone clear their throat behind him. He turned to see Sarah carrying a tray bearing a decanter and glasses.

'Open the door, if you please, Mr Raven,' she said, smiling, evidently amused at catching him eavesdropping.

She haunts my very shadow, he thought.

Raven did as he was bid, allowing her to proceed into the room before him. Mrs Simpson and Mina were sitting beside each other on a sofa while the men, Drs Simpson, Duncan and Keith, were gathered round the fireplace.

'Raven!' said Duncan, with unaccustomed brightness. 'Come and join the fray.'

'What is the subject?' he replied, wary that Duncan was about to seize an opportunity to make him look uninformed.

'We are discussing Hahnemann's theories of *similia similibus curantur* and infinitesimal doses,' Duncan chimed.

Like cures like. Duncan would have to try harder than that to catch him out.

'Homeopathy,' he replied.

He looked over to where Sarah was pouring out measures of sherry into glasses, hoping that she had witnessed this small triumph. She seemed intent on her task and failed to raise her eyes from the decanter.

'And what is your impression of it?' Duncan pressed him, this time with one eyebrow raised, as though waiting for Raven to position himself squarely on the wrong side of this debate.

'The doctrine that like cures like makes little sense to me,' Raven said. 'And as for the notion that repeated dilutions paradoxically increase the efficacy of a solution, I believe my former landlady Mrs Cherry must have been a firm advocate. Her soup often contained only an infinitesimal trace of meat, which according to Hahnemann would provide greater nourishment than a juicy steak.'

Simpson laughed and thumped Raven heartily on the back. He was never at risk of being on the wrong side of this argument, as the professor had made his views clear to his class on many occasions. He liked to recount the story of receiving a box of homeopathic remedies from a friend and giving them to his sons to play with, which of course had led to the medicines being mixed up. The same box had then been passed on to an enthusiastic practitioner, who later reported that he employed them with great success.

'Some homeopathic remedies are not even taken internally but applied using the technique of olfaction,' Simpson said, demonstrating by taking a theatrical sniff from his sherry glass. 'I heard tell of a lady who was subjected to the process,' he went on. 'When it came time to settle the bill with her practitioner, she passed the fee before his nose and then put it back into her pocket.'

The professor's joke was greeted with laughter by everyone,

with the familiar exception of Duncan. He looked thin-lipped and impatient for the moment to pass, which was his response to every interruption for laughter. It was as though his mind did not understand the very mechanism of humour, or perhaps saw no need for it.

'Though at least the consolation of a medicine without effect is that it has no ill effects either,' suggested George Keith. 'For there are some utterly abhorrent concoctions foisted upon unwary patients every day. Mercury, for one, is a pestilent and entirely pernicious drug. And Syme is sceptical about almost every internal medicine with the exception of rhubarb and soda.'

At that moment, the door opened and John Beattie strode into the room with his over-eager birdlike gait, bringing with him a scent of tobacco and a far stronger smell of cologne.

'Gregory's powders,' he said, responding to Keith's last remark as though he had been present the whole time. 'I prescribe it frequently. But then I hardly ever leave the bedside of a patient without providing a new bottle or prescription of some sort. Dr Simpson, good evening.'

Simpson got to his feet and introduced his guest, who shook each offered hand with accustomed grace.

Raven was impressed with the assuredness of Beattie's manner. Though he was not the tallest of fellows, he thrust himself into company in contrast to Raven's instinct, which was to shrink against the side-lines. Raven noted the curiosity and instinctive suspicion in Duncan's expression at this unheralded interloper and felt all the warmer towards Beattie as a result. The man had looked smart enough even spattered with blood and in his day clothes, but dressed for dinner, Beattie in his dandified pomp was a sight to behold. As Raven's mother might have put it, he was wearing the clothes; the clothes weren't wearing him.

The effect was not lost on Mina, who rose from the sofa and approached him, her hand extended. Beattie bowed and kissed the offered fingers.

'I find the scent of your cologne to be quite divine,' Mina said. 'Did you purchase it from Gianetti's? In George Street?'

'I did not. This scent is Farina's original eau de cologne, imported from Europe. Bergamot and sandalwood with top notes of citrus.'

'How exotic,' said Mina, clearly impressed.

'The sense of smell is the one most closely related to memory,' he added with a smile. 'One always hopes to be remembered.'

Raven cast another glance at Duncan, who looked unsettled, as though the new arrival represented a threat to his supremacy. His brow furrowed as Beattie accepted a glass of sherry from Sarah.

'I *intend* to be remembered,' Duncan said, raising his glass in a toast, 'for something more significant and more popular than even Gregory's powders. To memorable contributions.'

'To being remembered,' Beattie replied, raising his own glass and draining it. He turned to face Mina again, denying Duncan the opportunity to elaborate on his grand plans. 'I cannot recall the last time I encountered so many beautiful women in one room,' he said, taking in all of the ladies present.

Mrs Simpson smiled, Sarah snorted and Mina demurely lowered her eyes to the hem of her dress, etiquette precluding any direct acknowledgement of the compliment.

Raven watched their charmed reactions and realised with a certain sadness that though he might learn much from Beattie as a doctor, there were certain talents that simply could not be taught.

Beattie sat beside Mina at dinner, which surprised Raven. He had thought their new guest might wish to seize the opportunity to make a direct impression upon Dr Simpson. It had not occurred to him that Beattie might take a genuine interest in the professor's sister-in-law, who was on the edge of spinsterhood, but perhaps her age liberated Beattie from concerns that his attention might be misconstrued. They spoke freely and at length, Beattie seeking her opinions on everything from women's fashions to literature and poetry.

He had perhaps sought to impress her with his wide-ranging knowledge of the latter only to find that Mina had a familiarity with Byron and Shelley which easily surpassed his own. And rather than withdraw from the conversation now that his superiority had been challenged, Beattie seemed to relish it all the more, and the two discussed the relative merits of the romantic poets as though they were alone at the table and had been intimates for some time.

Beattie interrupted their conversation only briefly to express his admiration for the Simpsons' cook. 'Sublime!' he pronounced as he cleared his plate.

Raven did not feel he was in a position to make an informed contribution, given the measly portion he had been served. He could identify but two chunks of mutton amongst the carrots on his plate. This amount of food would be insufficient for the parrot, never mind a fully grown man. Raven noticed that everyone else had received a more generous portion than he, and tried to catch Sarah's eye as she passed between sideboard and table with various dishes, but she seemed intent on ignoring him.

During the serving of dessert (of which again Raven received a homeopathic helping), Mina continued to hold Beattie's attention until his host intervened and dragged him back into the general conversation.

'Dr Beattie here was previously availing me of his ambitions for opening a hydropathic spa,' Simpson announced, a familiar spark of mischief in his eye. 'Before you arrived, we were deep in discussion about unregulated practices and I was wondering where you might draw the line between physic and quackery.'

'I remain unconvinced about the benefits of homeopathy,' Beattie replied, which made Raven wonder if he too had paused outside to eavesdrop before making his entrance. 'It seems to be based upon a somewhat flimsy premise and yet it has proven to be quite popular.'

'I know many who swear by it,' said Mina, in support of this last statement.

'Indeed,' Beattie said, turning back to her. 'And that is why it would be premature to dismiss it entirely, Miss Grindlay.'

'Professor Christison refers to homeopathic remedies as "drops of nothingness, powders of nonentity",' Duncan added, his tone as tactlessly dismissive as Beattie's had been polite.

Mina looked at him as though he had just blasphemed in some way. Raven could imagine Dr Duncan being struck off Mina's mental list of potential suitors, Beattie's name being added instead, and perhaps underlined. Several times.

'What about phrenology?' Simpson asked.

'That the shape of the skull can provide information regarding the personality? I think that there may be something to it,' Beattie replied. 'There are many medical men who support it, Professor Gregory among them.'

'I'm not sure that the belief of others makes for a convincing argument,' Simpson chided gently. 'While it is true that many eminent medical men are members of the phrenological society, that in itself does not convince me.'

'Quite so,' said Duncan. 'No absurdity is ever too groundless to find supporters.'

Beattie looked momentarily at a loss, as though slighted by the harshness of Duncan's rebuttal. Then his countenance cleared and his smile returned, his equanimity restored.

'Whoever determines to deceive the world may be sure of finding people to be deceived,' he said.

Duncan smiled thinly in reply, satisfied that this served as some form of surrender.

Raven drank more of his wine. He had consumed several glasses of the doctor's claret by this point (and not that much to eat) and was beginning to enjoy himself.

'The waters of quackery may be foul,' he said, 'but there's money to be made if you're prepared to swim.'

His contribution was not so much in support of Beattie as in solidarity against a common foe.

'You would risk drowning, my boy,' said Simpson. 'A reputation thus tarnished could never be recovered.'

At this point Sarah entered the room with a pot of coffee and bent slightly to pour. Raven found that his eye was drawn to her head, although any detail of its shape was hidden by her white cap. What would an examination of her skull reveal? Combativeness? Lack of propriety?

As she turned to leave the room, he noticed that a small ringlet of honey-coloured hair had escaped the confines of her cap and was delicately hovering at the nape of her neck. He wondered absently what her hair would smell like, and realised, perhaps for the first time, how young she must be.

Raven took his coffee and stood by the window, mindful of the parrot, which was eyeing him suspiciously from its perch. Beattie appeared at his side, ostensibly examining the flamboyant but cantankerous bird, clearly wishing to talk away from the rest of the room.

'It's easy for him to say,' Beattie stated quietly.

'What is?'

'Pontificating about how a doctor might make money. There is little sacrifice in taking the moral high ground when your coffers are overflowing.'

Raven wondered if Beattie had guessed about the parlous state of his own finances.

'I admit,' Raven replied, 'I might find it difficult to remain noble to my principles should some rich and credulous lady offer to reward me for harmless but useless therapy. And if it made her feel better purely because she believed it efficacious, then was the therapy truly useless? Perhaps that question would be enough to salve my conscience.'

'I have a proposition that would require you to broach no such ethical dilemmas,' Beattie stated. 'A patient who requires a certain procedure but is reluctant to submit without the benefit of ether. I told her I had found someone who could administer it.'

'Me?' Raven asked, barely daring to believe it.

'Of course. As an associate of the great Dr Simpson, your services would attract a handsome fee.'

'A junior associate and hardly an expert.'

'I'm sure you are proficient enough. What is there to lose?'

Raven caught sight of his reflection in the black of the window. The wound on his cheek tingled as if to remind him what indeed he had to lose.

'How handsome?' he asked.

NINETEEN

he following day Raven was granted respite from the chaos of the morning clinic, as part of his apprenticeship was to include regular duties at the Royal Maternity Hospital. Unfortunately, it would have taken a higher power than Dr Simpson to offer him respite from the piercing headache that was plaguing his every step. He would admit he had drunk of the professor's claret with uncommon gusto in celebration of Beattie's offer and the imminent prospect of making back the money he owed to Flint. However, the tolerable ill effects of this indulgence had been brutally compounded after breakfast, when Duncan compelled Raven's assistance in his researches.

Raven was initially curious about Duncan shedding his reluctance to involve him directly in his work, and wondered whether his contributions the previous night had raised him in the young prodigy's estimations. Then he discovered that Duncan had assembled a fresh batch of potential anaesthetic agents, and Raven's role was little above that of poison taster; or poison sniffer, to be strictly accurate. Duncan had wafted various vapours beneath his nose, none of which precipitated any effect greater than mild dizziness and a cumulative pounding in his brain.

The Maternity Hospital was situated within Milton House

on the Canongate, a Georgian mansion that had either seen better days or had been built with the intention of warning off unwanted visitors with the threat of impending collapse. He was due to meet Dr Ziegler, the hospital's surgeon, and given the pounding in Raven's head, he hoped the man was more a Simpson than a Syme.

The door was answered by a tall woman in a starched cap, who, on looking him up and down, gave the impression she was about to fetch a stick with which to chase him off. Clearly his beard was not growing thick or fast enough to effect the transformation he had hoped for.

'Mr Will Raven. For Dr Ziegler. I'm Dr Simpson's apprentice. I believe I am expected.'

Raven hoped that the mention of his employer would smooth his passage into the hospital, past its sullen gatekeeper. The woman made no reply but let her eyes drift downwards, where her gaze remained. Raven felt compelled to do the same and found himself examining his own footwear. His boots looked as they usually did, a thin layer of mud clinging to the sides: unsurprising as he had made the journey from Queen Street on foot.

'Mrs Stevenson. Matron,' she said. 'I'll thank you to wipe your feet before you come in.'

Raven wagered that she wasn't the type to thank anyone for much else. She stood with her arms folded, watching as he applied his feet to the boot scraper at the door. Once satisfied with his efforts, she stood aside and let him enter.

'Dr Ziegler is in the ward, making his rounds.'

She indicated a door to the left, then disappeared into a room on the right, closing the door to leave Raven alone in the hallway. He proceeded as directed, becoming aware of the faint aroma of lemons mixed with something earthier. It was a considerable improvement upon the foetid stink he associated with the wards of the Royal Infirmary.

A strong breeze was gusting through as all of the windows

were open – an attempt to blow away the spectre of puerperal fever perhaps, the scourge of any such institution – and consequently the fireplace at the end of the room had a good fire going, helping to take the chill out of the wind. There was a row of beds against one wall and a large table in the centre of the room where a small, dark, spectacled man was writing in a ledger. Without lifting his eyes from the volume, he raised a palm as he heard Raven approach, by way of telling him to wait.

Raven complied silently, the question of a Simpson or a Syme now tipping towards the latter.

Ziegler finished what he was writing and looked up, a brightness about his features. 'Keeping the casebook up to date,' he said, closing the ledger and placing his hand reverentially upon it. 'Every delivery must be entered. Accurate information is the key to unlocking many a mystery. Now, would you care to take a tour, Mr Raven?'

Ziegler proceeded to show Raven around, evidently proud of the small hospital and its collection of expectant or recently delivered mothers. To a woman they were poor souls whose personal circumstances made a home confinement impossible.

'We do good work here,' Ziegler said as he showed Raven into the empty delivery room, 'but our funding is precarious. Charitable giving is frequently inhibited by moral concerns.'

'Moral concerns?'

Raven was reminded of the pamphlet penned by the Reverend Grissom denouncing the use of ether in labour, but Ziegler was referring to a more general anxiety regarding the hospital's attendees.

'Our policy of admitting unmarried mothers provokes a deep discomfort in many a Christian breast. Some believe that it encourages immoral behaviour.'

'What is the alternative?' Raven asked.

'A worthy question, young sir. In my opinion it is illogical to withhold care from someone who needs it merely because you disagree with the manner in which they conduct themselves. Judge not lest ye be judged.'

'Quite so,' Raven agreed, thinking again about Evie and the manner in which her death had been dismissed.

Another deid hoor.

'I believe it is important to provide the best possible care for patients regardless of the manner in which they got themselves into their present predicament,' Ziegler continued. 'Desperate people are often driven to do desperate things. I have known young women to take their own lives because they could not face the consequences of being with child; and some because they could not face their families discovering it. Sometimes one has to contemplate which is the lesser of two evils.'

Ziegler fixed Raven with a piercing look. Raven sensed that he would be evaluated according to his response, beginning with whether he even understood what Ziegler was talking about.

'You mean abortion?'

Ziegler nodded solemnly. Raven hoped he had passed.

'Abortion, infanticide. These things happen more frequently than we would like to admit. When no records are kept, there is no way of knowing with any degree of certainty.'

'There have been two cases recently at the Infirmary. Perforated uterus and peritonitis in each instance.'

'Fatal?'

'Yes. Tantamount to murder.'

'When you deliberately inflict such damage and are only interested in the fee, then it *is* murder, plain and simple. And the culprit?'

'Hasn't been identified.'

'That doesn't surprise me. It is a relatively easy thing, getting away with murder, especially when the victims are deemed to be of no consequence.'

'Do you know anything about it?' Raven asked.

'Me?' Ziegler replied, his curious look making Raven fear for a moment that the man thought he was being impugned.

'I only mean that the women must talk about such things. Perhaps you have heard something.'

'I can't say that I have. The women don't tend to confide in me and I disregard anything I hear from them during labour. Perhaps matron might have heard something, though. Women seem to be more at ease discussing such things with each other.'

Ziegler led the way back to the small room Mrs Stevenson had retreated to after letting Raven in. Given his introduction to the woman, he was sceptical as to whether an interview with the gatekeeper would yield much. The matron was seated behind a desk, totting up a column of figures in an account book when they entered.

'Dr Ziegler,' she said, smiling as she looked up from her calculations, her affection for the little man quite evident.

'Mr Raven tells me that someone's practising the dark arts again,' Ziegler said, sitting on the edge of her desk.

Mrs Stevenson sighed and put down her pen.

'Heard any tales?' he asked.

Raven was surprised at the ease with which such a delicate subject was raised.

'About the dark arts, no,' she said. 'Though I have heard talk about some new secret remedy to "restore regularity".'

Raven did not follow. 'A laxative?'

'To the monthly cycle,' Ziegler explained.

Raven smiled at his own misapprehension, but the grave expression on Ziegler's face told him he was still missing something.

'A euphemism,' Raven acknowledged.

'Indeed. Sometimes such remedies are advertised as "for the relief of obstruction", but it is the same thing.'

'And is this new secret remedy reputed to be successful?'

'As successful as any before it,' Mrs Stevenson said, by which she meant not at all. 'We deliver the obstructions here all the time, whereupon the monthly cycle is restored to regularity.'

'There has long been a trade in such quackery,' Ziegler explained. 'Pills and potions with no effect. Cheap tricks and empty promises.'

'Oh, they're never cheap,' the matron stated, 'for that's the hook. The more expensive the remedy, the more a desperate woman is likely to believe the rumours of its efficacy and part with her coin.'

'Rumours no doubt sown by the same rogue who is rolling the pills,' Ziegler added.

Raven thought of the discussions the previous evening. The principle was the same, but there was a greater dishonesty here, for the patient's belief that the medicine was working would make no difference in this case.

'Charlatanry,' he observed.

'Aye, though there is worse,' said Mrs Stevenson. 'More dangerous than the mere charlatans are those attempting to concoct genuine medicines. I've seen girls become horribly sick after taking such remedies, without any relief of the "obstruction" they were intended to remove. Racked with pain, they were. God only knows what they ingested, believing it would lift their burdens.'

Her words called up Evie's contorted posture, her agonised expression, as well as the brief glimpse he had been afforded of the woman pulled from the water yesterday. But there was more than the usual regret and anxiety attending his memory of finding Evie. Her urgent need of money and her reluctance to say what for might finally have an explanation.

For the first time, it struck him that she might have been pregnant.

Raven was turning this new possibility over in his mind as he made his way back along the Canongate in the gathering darkness, trying to calculate the implications and reliving some of the last conversations he had had with Evie. Belatedly he realised that if she had been pregnant, then she must have known there was no future for her in a job as a maid, even if there was a house that would have her. She had been stringing him along, knowing it couldn't happen. Raven had always been a little blind when it came to her, willingly so. This dream of her raising herself up had been no more than that: a dream, a fantasy. And he understood now that it had been a fantasy to entertain him rather than one genuinely held by her.

So lost was he in this reverie that he failed to notice a distinctive shape approaching him until it was almost too late. The unmistakable silhouette of Gargantua was emerging through the fog, lumbering down the hill from the High Street.

At this distance, in the gloom of the narrow channel, Raven could not be sure whether he had been seen. There was little chance of passing Gargantua unnoticed, however. Raven had no option but to duck through the doors of the nearest tavern and hope for the best.

The place was crowded, which was a blessing, its warmth welcome on a chill evening. The fug of smoke and the smell of spilled ale instantly wrapped around him like an old friend's embrace. He only wished his pockets were not so empty.

Raven made his way towards a dark corner to wait it out. He had barely pulled up a stool when he saw the doors swing and the giant thrust himself through them, bowing down so that his head would not strike the lintel.

Raven pressed himself against the wall as Gargantua approached, the monster's gaze fixed intently upon him. Raven looked about the room but saw no faces he recognised, no stalwarts who might come to his aid. He had no friends here, but realised strangers might still be his salvation, for surely the man would not carry out an attack in front of so many witnesses.

The comfort of this thought lasted as long as it took to wonder how many men might be prepared to stand and testify against this creature in court.

'I will have money for you soon,' Raven pleaded, feeling the scar upon his cheek tingle afresh as the giant drew within feet of where he stood.

'Sit,' Gargantua ordered.

Raven complied, though it pinned him in a corner with Gargantua blocking the route to the door. He was a conspicuous sight, and yet he drew few direct looks, Raven noticed: only stolen glances. They wanted to gawp at him, but not to meet his gaze.

'I will be carrying out well-paid medical work in a few days with a wealthy patient of the New Town,' Raven told him, quickly and quietly. 'I am apprentice to Professor Simpson, training to be a doctor, and—'

Gargantua held up a huge hand by way of silencing him. His face was all the more disturbing now that Raven could see it in indoor light. Its proportions were wrong, the flesh loose in places, stretched in others. He was sweaty despite the cold outside, a sickly pallor about his skin.

'I know what you are training to be. That's why I followed you in here.'

Raven saw a glimmer of hope and struck out for it. 'Is there something I can assist you with?' he asked as brightly as his fear would allow.

Gargantua's expression darkened. 'You misunderstand. I wanted you to know that I despise your profession.'

Raven could barely find the breath, but somehow managed to reply, as he felt the question was being invited.

'Why?'

'Because of your attitude to people like me. Freaks of nature.'

'I assure you, we only wish to understand any unusual medical condition, and by that understanding to assist those afflicted.'

'Tell that to Charles Byrne,' Gargantua said, the words grumbling across the table like thunder at the head of a storm. 'Have you heard of him?'

Raven nodded. Much had just become clear, none of it good.

'A man like me. Even bigger, though. The Irish Giant, they called him. He came here to Edinburgh once. Lit his pipe from one of the lamps on the North Bridge without even standing on his toes. Aye, you medical men all wanted him, but not to "understand", or to "assist". The shameless maggots were offering him money for his corpse while he was still alive.'

Raven knew the story, as any medical man would. Byrne had refused their advances, no matter how much coin was offered. He believed in the resurrection, that the Lord was going to raise him up when Judgment Day came, and for that he would need his body. But the anatomists had plans for their own resurrection, and when Byrne died in June of 1783, they were fighting each other for the spoils, heedless of the man's own wishes.

Byrne's friends rallied to protect his corpse. They exhibited his outsize coffin to help raise funds to charter a boat and saw that he was buried at sea in accordance with his will. But with a vast bounty being offered for the body, there was always a danger of treachery, and unbeknownst to the burial party, it was a coffin full of stones that they tipped into the water. Somewhere on the way to Margate, a switch had been made and the body stolen. Inevitably, it found its way into the possession of the man who had prized it most, the esteemed surgeon and anatomist John Hunter.

News of the theft made the papers and raised a scandal, which was why Hunter never dissected the body as he planned, instead swiftly chopping it up and boiling it down to bones. He kept his possession of the remains secret for several years, but in time reassembled the skeleton and put it on display. Perhaps the worst of it was that Hunter thus learned nothing from the corpse. He spent a great sum to acquire not a crucial specimen but a mere trophy, like an organ in a jar.

Gargantua's eyes flashed and he leaned forward, gripping Raven's neck and pulling their foreheads together, the giant's foul breath engulfing his face.

'Eight hundred guineas, Hunter paid. Do you think Charles Byrne earned a fraction of that his whole life? Men like you see men like me as worth more dead than alive. And that is why, should Mr Flint give the command, it will not merely be my duty to rip you apart, but my pleasure.'

Gargantua let go and stood up, the throng parting before him as he walked to the door.

Raven sat there trembling, his mouth as dry as he could ever remember, his drouth all the more a mockery for him sitting here in a tavern.

Charles Byrne died at the age of twenty-two. Raven wondered if Gargantua understood the implications for himself. He had not seemed well, and was unlikely to live long, but he might yet outlast Raven.

Beattie's commission was now a matter of life and death.

TWENTY

arah was sweeping out the downstairs hall, pondering just how many pairs of feet had tramped through it during that morning's clinic, when Jarvis materialised silently at her side and placed a hand upon her broom.

'You are to report to the kitchen. Mrs Lyndsay would like to speak to you.'

Sarah's insides turned to stone. She knew from the wording and the tone – as well as the fact that Mrs Lyndsay had not summoned her directly by a shout or a bell – that she was in trouble. There was a degree of theatre to it that she had learned to recognise, and she knew what it was about too. She had seen the woman head up the stairs earlier that morning, shooting her a scowl as she passed. It took her but a moment to deduce why her sour face seemed familiar.

Sarah walked down the stairs slowly, dreading what might await her at the bottom. She tried to convince herself that it was not what she assumed: perhaps merely another harangue about her duties at the clinic interfering with the rest of her workload. Mrs Lyndsay had always been opposed to this secondary draw upon her labour, but from Jarvis's summons she knew this must be regarding a matter as serious as it was specific, and there was only one thing it could be.

Mrs Lyndsay was standing with her back to the range, gripping a wooden spoon tightly in both hands. It being some time since she last provoked this formal level of ire, Sarah had thought that she was no longer afraid of the cook. One look at her stern expression told her otherwise, bringing back all the fear she had felt every time she faced Mrs Lyndsay's wrath.

When she first started working here, she had to be thoroughly trained in her tasks, in the rules of the house and in all manner of arcane etiquette. Any lapse, misstep or failure to meet the required standards would lead to a dressing down in the kitchen and often some form of disciplinary measure. Sarah was always diligent and didn't find any of her duties difficult to master, so it was seldom the quality of her work that was at issue. Rather, it was the way she comported herself that most frequently provoked the cook's disapproval. 'Overstepping the mark' was the most common citation, a phrase she had learned to both dread and detest, along with 'you have ideas above your station, girl'. This one stung the more because it was true, and Mrs Lyndsay's job was to hammer home what Sarah's station was.

'There has been a complaint of quite disgraceful conduct towards one of Dr Simpson's patients,' Mrs Lyndsay said. Her tone was even but spoke of a controlled anger she could unleash at will.

Sarah's reaction was one of cold fear. Deep down, she had known these consequences would find her. Even as she closed the door that day, she knew it was the beginning rather than the end of the matter. The sour-faced woman on the stairs was one of the pair for whom she had refused to make special accommodations on a day when the clinic was particularly busy and Dr Simpson was from home.

'A Mrs Noble, who had travelled here from Trinity, said that not only were you unspeakably rude and disrespectful, but that you refused to admit her and then slammed the front door in her face.'

Sarah gaped. 'I did not slam the—'

'Are you compounding this by calling Mrs Noble a liar?'

Sarah averted her gaze, staring at the floor and feeling her cheeks begin to burn. She knew from experience that further explanation would not assist her case. A housemaid's account of such an exchange did not matter. And besides, the force with which she closed the door was not the issue, but that Mrs Noble was on the wrong side of it at the time.

It was the remark about the Queen that had really torn it. It had felt satisfying in the moment, but her satisfaction had turned almost instantly to regret. She had wounded the woman's pride, and that would never go unanswered.

'No, ma'am. But the clinic was especially busy that morning and I merely—'

Mrs Lyndsay silenced her by simply raising the spoon.

'The details are immaterial, and I doubt this woman is in the habit of making up complaints to amuse herself. Your conduct caused her gross offence and this in turn has caused embarrassment for the entire household. Mrs Noble has demanded your dismissal.'

Mrs Lyndsay let her words hang there, allowing Sarah time to contemplate what this would mean. She felt tears well up and was a moment from begging.

'If you ask me, it is only because Mrs Simpson does not take well to being told how to run her own house that you are to be retained. Nonetheless, she has asked that I deal with it. I think this business of assisting at the morning clinics has been giving you ideas above your station.'

There it was, and what hurt the most was that she had brought it upon herself. Again. Why could she not learn to control her mouth? Master, as Mina had recently told her, the commendable art of holding her tongue?

'You will not be spared to assist any more, at least until you have better learned your place.'

'But I am needed at clinic,' she protested, thinking not so much of what she was losing but of the chaos in the hall every morning, and her role in managing the crowds.

Mrs Lyndsay scoffed at this. 'Needed? Do you know how easy it is to replace a housemaid? That's what you have to understand. I don't want to see you on the street. Do you know what it is to be dismissed without character?'

Sarah nodded silently. It meant being dismissed without letters of reference vouching for one's worthiness to a prospective employer. Without those, it would be impossible to find a position in another house.

'Because that is the danger for a girl who is disrespectful, who brings disgrace upon her place of employment. I have worked in many houses and I have seen it happen many a time. But what is worse is I have seen what became of those girls, when they had no other means to make a living.'

Mrs Lyndsay prodded Sarah in the chest with the spoon, lifting her chin with it so that she met her eye.

'Selling themselves: that's how they ended up. Didn't know they had a good life until it was gone, same as will happen to that one who ran off from the Sheldrake house. I wouldn't want that happening to you. Is this not a good house to work in?'

'Yes, ma'am.'

'Are you not grateful for your position here?'

'Yes, ma'am.'

'Then remember that, for you are on your final warning. Keep your head down and think only of your duties, nothing else. Otherwise you will *have* no duties to keep you under this roof.'

TWENTY-ONE

obody knew her name.

This was the third tavern Raven had visited in Leith, insinuating himself into company and conversation so that he might turn the subject to the young woman whose body he so briefly glimpsed on the quayside. A few people had heard about the discovery, but that was as far as it went.

He thought of James Duncan, so quick to state his ambitions when he sensed a rival in Beattie. It was in the gift of caprice to decide whom history would remember, but it struck Raven as a particularly sad fate to die unknown, nobody to miss you, to remember you.

'I'll tell you what I did hear,' said a ruddy-faced docker with salt-blasted skin and the roughest hands Raven had ever seen. 'That she was twisted up and tied in knots.'

Raven was in an ancient establishment called the King's Wark, close to where the girl had been recovered the day before, and was seated at the gantry, where he thought himself best positioned to pick up on what was being said. The landlord had noticed this and regarded him with a modicum of suspicion, but as long as he was buying ale, Raven knew he would be tolerated.

Raven had not learned what he came for, but he was enjoying

the opportunity to sit in a tavern without fear of who he might run into, emboldened by the promise of Beattie's paying work. If he encountered the Weasel, he would be able to tell him that his debt would be redeemed very soon, but only if he remained corporeally intact to carry out work for which he would be hand-somely rewarded. His men might be vicious, but Raven was confident that a man such as Flint would not wish to dole out punishment that reduced his chances of being paid.

'That's the devil's work,' said another, a wiry fellow with eyes so narrow it was a wonder he could see out of them.

'A bad business, for sure,' said the docker.

'No, I mean the work of Satan and his worshippers. That's a sign of possession, when a body is all twisted like that.'

'Or a seizure,' Raven suggested.

'If that were the case, the body would straighten again in the water,' Gimlet-eyes insisted, which Raven would have to concede was a fair point. He didn't know how long she had been floating. 'She was bewitched, I'm telling you. Could be she flung herself to her death because it was the only way to be rid of the demon inside her.'

'There are Satanists abroad,' another man agreed, nodding sagely as though no reasonable fellow might dispute it. 'I've heard they gather on Calton Hill.'

'There's no end of strange and godless types come off the ships down here,' the docker said. 'From all manner of dark and far-flung lands.'

'There are devils enough come over from Ireland,' another drinker averred, drawing murmurs of agreement from all around. 'Glasgow is over-run with them, and soon Edinburgh will be too.'

'They eat their babies,' said a yellow-skinned old goat, clinging on to a table as though he would otherwise be spun off. 'So who knows what other abominations they commit.'

'Aye, when Ireland sends its people, they're not sending their best.'

'There was a bairn's leg found in a gutter last week.'

'The savage Erse bastards.'

'I don't imagine an Irishman was responsible for that,' Raven argued.

'And why not?' demanded Yellow Skin.

'Well, if what you say is true, he would hardly waste good eating.'

This drew a gale of laughter, but Raven knew there was nothing to be learned from this gathering. He took in the room to estimate whether anyone else might be worth talking to. This was when he appreciated how profoundly his medical studies had changed him. No longer could he enter a place without assessing the pathology presented there, of which there was usually a plentiful supply. The wheezily obese barmaid currently pouring whisky at the end of the gantry sported a sizable goitre; a fellow headed for the door was demonstrating the wide-based, stamping gait of *tabes dorsalis*, an advanced stage of syphilis; and a man in the corner was exhibiting great difficulty in getting his glass to his mouth without considerable spillage as a result of a shaking palsy. It seemed that once such knowledge had been acquired there was no respite from it.

A sudden shout from the corner of the room caused Raven to look up just as a tankard sailed over his head and hit the soot-blackened wall behind him. A scuffle broke out but the combatants were too far gone to land many punches on one another. The landlord ejected the pair without difficulty. He was a tall, muscular specimen with a domed, bald head, no hair upon his brow either. Upon disposing of his unruly customers, he bent down to retrieve the discarded tankard, which had landed close to Raven's feet.

'You're not from round here, are you,' he said, a statement rather than an enquiry. Evidently Raven's scar did not have the same impact upon everybody.

'No, I live in the town.'

'I heard you talking about that lassie they found. How come you know about that?'

There was an unmistakable note of suspicion in his voice.

'I happened to be passing yesterday when she was laid out on the quayside. Did you see it?'

'Too busy in here. I've heard all the blethers, though. Eejits. If you ask me, she probably fell from a ship – or was tossed from it. In which case the poor soul could have come from anywhere.'

'From her clothes, she didn't look at all far-travelled. Too pale of skin also.'

The landlord trained a scrutinising gaze upon him. Raven guessed that in his line of work he was an accomplished reader of men, and wondered what he saw in the one before him. Someone out of his element, for sure, and quite possibly out of his depth. But maybe, if he could truly peer beneath the surface, he saw something darker.

'So what do *you* reckon happened to her?' the landlord asked.

'I have a medical background,' Raven said, by way of establishing some measure of credentials. 'I have a suspicion she may have been poisoned before she went into the water.'

'Why would someone poison her and *then* throw her into the drink? Surely the villain who murders with poison wishes to disguise his intentions, so that it may look like she died in her sleep?'

'I don't know,' Raven conceded. 'Maybe it didn't work as swiftly as intended. It makes more sense than the notion that it was the work of Satan.'

'Don't you believe in the devil?' the landlord asked, his countenance darkening. 'You would if you lived round here.'

Raven didn't answer. He looked down into the last of his drink. He heard his mother's voice. *You've the devil in you*. Said in humour, said in reproach.

Many was the time Raven had witnessed demons seize a man and transform him. They had seized him too, as Henry could attest. It usually began with a mischievous tongue when he knew the wiser path lay in remaining circumspect. But he chose the reckless path because something in him sought 'mayhem', as Henry described it: inner torments demanding their external manifestation.

And then there was the night that Thomas Cunningham died.

Raven was condemned for ever to see himself standing over the body of the man he had just killed, while his wife cowered on the floor beside him, weeping.

Yes, he believed in the devil.

Raven felt altogether less emboldened about who he might encounter as he made his way home in the blackness of the night. His eyes searched beyond the shallow pools of light beneath the lamps, probing into the shadows for shapes and movement that might signal danger.

He made it past Great Junction Street without having to negotiate anything more hazardous than a few drunks and beggars, but as he began his ascent towards the town, he soon became convinced there were footsteps behind him. When he stopped so did they. And when he turned, there was nobody to be seen.

He felt reassured when a coach passed upon the road, for it meant potential witnesses and people he could call out to for help. But when the clip of hooves faded, he was even more conscious of his isolation. There was greater light where buildings stood, particularly at the junctions, but between these were stretches of foreboding gloom, hedgerows bordering fields shrouded in utter blackness. If he wished to do a man harm unseen by any witness, this would be where to strike.

He hurried his pace towards Pilrig Street. Still he heard the footsteps, and again they stopped when he did. He glanced back, and this time spied a darting movement on the edge of the light.

He was not deluding himself. He truly was being followed.

Should he run? He thought of how he had been blindsided

by Gargantua when his attention was fixed upon the Weasel. He had no way of knowing what he might be running into.

Raven slowed beneath the lamps where Pilrig Street met Leith Walk. Buildings stood upon each corner of the crossroads, gaslight and shadows flickering behind the windows. There was comparative safety here, but Raven could hardly loiter all night. He looked at the climb still ahead, the New Town a dim glow in the distance. That was when he realised that the darkness was his ally.

He passed into the space between two lamps, softening his tread. Then he veered sharply from the path and hopped over a hedgerow, where he concealed himself behind the dual trunks of a great tree in the field beyond. There he waited, drawing shallow breaths and listening for his pursuer. Sure enough, he soon heard footsteps, quickening presumably for fear that they had lost their quarry.

Raven watched him pass beneath the next lamp, approaching Haddington Place. With his back to Raven there was no way to see his face, not that he would have been able to see much at this distance. However, even in the gloom he could make out a domed, bald head atop a tall, powerful frame.

It was the landlord from the King's Wark.

TWENTY-TWO

aven shifted in his seat, putting down his finished cup of tea upon the silver tray with a loud finality that he hoped would be the cue to move things along. Beattie did not seem to notice, but his patient started a little at the sound, and from that Raven suspected she was as nervous about the planned procedure's commencement as he was about further procrastination. Only Beattie seemed relaxed, though on this occasion his confident manner was not proving as infectious as usual.

They sat in a drawing room on Danube Street. It was Raven's first venture behind the grand doors of the New Town in any kind of a professional capacity. Everywhere wealth was ostentatiously displayed. A gilt-edged mirror spanned the width of the fireplace, emphasising the height of the ceiling, while vast landscape paintings lined the walls. From the ceiling hung two matching glass chandeliers, each large enough to kill a man should they fall, and Raven gauged that if the furniture was pushed back there would be enough room to perform an eightsome reel.

Raven told himself he was anxious to get started, but in truth he was just anxious. This in itself was annoying him, as such anxiety was needless. He had administered ether at least a dozen times now, with no ill effects, and though Henry's report of a

death in England preyed on his mind, Simpson was adamant that
the case had been mismanaged and the agent itself was safe.

Nonetheless, a nagging voice kept asking why, if there was
no risk attached, he had not told Simpson he was doing this. The
stark answer was that he needed the money more than he needed
the professor's permission. Perhaps if there had been a salary
attached to his position he might have felt differently, but right
now he feared Flint's ire more than that of his employer.

The maid who answered the door to them had given Raven
a disdainful look when she saw him. He had felt the sting of the
slight, thinking that his problems with housemaids were becoming
more general – did they communicate with each other? Was Sarah
part of a coven of like-minded insurgents? – until he remembered
that his face was still conspicuously bruised. The swelling had
gone and his features had regained their usual symmetry but the
purple on his cheek had transmuted into an array of yellow, green
and brown which he had to admit was far from attractive. His
nascent beard could only be expected to cover so much.

Beattie greeted the mistress of the house, Mrs Caroline
Graseby, with an easy familiarity more akin to friend than physician and Raven wondered how long he had known her. She gazed
upon the man as though eager for his approval, which seemed
odd for a woman of her stature and wealth.

Raven had heard Mina talk about how certain women would
fuss over Simpson, hungry for his attention. Beattie could not
boast Simpson's accomplishments, but given his fine dress and
youthful countenance, it was possible to imagine rich and bored
ladies manufacturing complaints in order that he might minister
to them – with their husbands footing the bill.

Beattie had warned Raven that she was extremely nervous
about medical matters, and to this end asked him to call him only
by his first name. 'A certain informality puts her at ease, as would
the avoidance of the word "doctor".'

They had all sat down and taken tea together, which Raven

thought an odd prelude to any form of surgical procedure. Mrs
Graseby sat by the fire sipping her Darjeeling. Beattie, Raven
noticed, sat in close proximity to his patient and touched her
hand frequently when speaking. He enquired after her health and
made conversation about the weather and acquaintances they had
in common. She did not address him as Dr Beattie, rather as
'Johnnie', which sounded not merely informal but a pet name.
Given the nature of what Beattie was about to do, Raven wondered
how this sat with the professional detachment Beattie had previously espoused. Perhaps how Beattie behaved and what he
genuinely felt were two different matters; certainly there was
little doubt the man knew how to present a version of himself
appropriate to the company before him.

Raven was beginning to wonder whether this visit would turn
out to be a mere prelude to carrying out the procedure at a later
date, when Beattie put down his cup and declared: 'I think we
had best be about our business.'

At this point Mrs Graseby visibly paled and dabbed her lips
repeatedly with her handkerchief. 'I suppose we must,' she said,
rising from her chair. She looked to Raven with apprehension, as
though he might step in and call a halt. 'The room has been
prepared,' she added quietly.

She led them from the drawing room towards the back of the
house, past a portrait of an austere-looking individual with an
ostentatious moustache. She noticed Raven studying it.

'My husband,' she said. Raven had assumed it was her father,
given their respective ages.

They entered a smaller chamber at the back of the house
which appeared to have been cleared of all furniture with the
exception of a daybed and a small side table. Beattie asked for a
larger one to be brought in so that he could lay out his instruments, and there ensued a degree of fuss as a servant searched
upstairs for a table of suitable size before manoeuvring it into
the room.

Raven was still unclear as to the precise nature of the procedure that Beattie intended to perform, and had initially been told little about the patient herself apart from the fact that she was young and in good health. He had pressed Beattie for more details as they made their way to the house, but the only thing he had been forthcoming about was the reason for his reticence.

'If this procedure is successful – and I have every confidence that it will be – then there will be demand for it, and I will only profit fully from my innovation if I am the sole doctor who can offer it.'

'I am not going to be able to replicate your technique if I can't see it,' Raven had argued. 'All my business is at the other end, so you could at least tell me the generalities of what you are attempting.'

'A fair point,' he conceded with a sigh. 'I will be performing a manipulation to correct a retroverted uterus, which I have assured Mrs Graseby will increase her chances of conception. Her husband is keen for a son and heir, and is frankly becoming impatient with what he considers a failing on his wife's part.'

'And will Mr Graseby be present?' Raven had asked, thinking he could do without the pressure.

'Gods, no. He is overseas. America, I think.'

Raven watched as Beattie laid out a selection of probes and a uterine sound. How this manipulation was supposed to assist with conception he wasn't entirely sure, but whatever was intended did not seem unduly complicated and was therefore likely to be achieved quickly.

Raven removed a bottle of ether and a sponge from his bag, Simpson's voice sounding in his head as he did so. *The only difference between a medicine and a poison is the dosage.*

Mrs Graseby lay down on the daybed and placed her handkerchief across her eyes. Her respiration was shallow and rapid and Raven could see small beads of perspiration on her top lip. He realised, perhaps a little belatedly, that she was unlike anyone he had anaesthetised before. For one thing, she had not been in labour for several hours and she was considerably more nervous than her predecessors. In many cases they had been so desperate for oblivion that they had forcibly pulled Raven's hand towards their own faces. Mrs Graseby, by contrast, initially turned away as the sponge was brought near, whimpering into her pillow.

'Now, Caroline,' Beattie said in a firm tone. 'You know this must be done.'

Mrs Graseby swallowed then nodded. She took a couple of breaths of the ether but then attempted to move Raven's hand away. Speaking to her in a calm tone, as he had seen Simpson do, he brought the sponge in closer to her nose and mouth, and within a few minutes she appeared to succumb.

Beattie began the procedure and Raven felt for the pulse at the wrist. All was well.

'I notice there is no painting of her,' Raven said quietly.

'No,' Beattie replied. 'It's an expensive business, so they often don't commission one of the wife until she has brought forth an heir. And survived it.'

'Unless it's a love match,' Raven suggested, deducing that this was most probably not.

'One should never assume in such matters,' Beattie replied. 'But no, I suspect not in this case.'

'She certainly seems taken with you,' Raven ventured, injecting a note of humour into his tone.

Beattie seemed bemused in his response. 'It is a double-edged sword,' he said. 'Women tend to think my appearance boyish and their maternal instinct draws them to me. It is therefore easy to strike up a rapport but there is a danger they may misinterpret my intentions.'

'And is such attention so unwelcome?' Raven asked, curious at Beattie's thin-lipped expression and, he would admit, a little envious.

'When a woman is attracted to my boyishness, that often goes with a tendency to regard me as junior, as trivial. Even worse is when the woman is young and trivial herself and thinks me an ideal match. You might imagine such attentions flattering, but I have quite had my fill of flirtations.'

Raven thought of how Beattie had talked so long with Mina at dinner, and suddenly saw their conversation in a different light.

His reverie was interrupted as Mrs Graseby uttered a moan and her hand shot up in apparent response to something Beattie was doing. It caught Raven on the left side of his face and he shouted out, more in surprise than pain, the noise causing Beattie to drop the instrument he was holding.

'For God's sake, Raven. Keep her still, will you.'

Raven quickly poured more of the ether onto the sponge and pushed it roughly onto the writhing woman's face. Within a few breaths she had quietened again. Beattie looked up at Raven as though he would like to stab him with the implement he had retrieved from the floor.

'I shouldn't be much longer here but I am at a critical point in the procedure. Please ensure that she does not move again.'

Beattie's face was flushed and Raven decided not to argue with him. He merely nodded and continued to feel for the pulse. He noticed that it had become quite rapid, much as his own in the last few minutes, but even as his calmed, Mrs Graseby's continued to increase.

'Is everything all right down there?' Raven asked. 'There isn't any bleeding, is there?'

'There is but a little,' Beattie replied, a little testily.

A few minutes later he threw his instruments down on the table and wiped his brow.

'I am done,' he declared.

'I am worried about the pulse rate,' Raven told him. 'It is very high.'

'It is the ether. You must have given her too much.'

'I don't think so,' he argued, though in truth he knew he couldn't be sure.

They looked at each other as Beattie wiped his hands. 'There is no bleeding,' Beattie said again. 'We must simply wait for her to recover.'

The next few hours were among the worst that Raven had ever known. Mrs Graseby remained drowsy, never fully regaining her senses. Her pulse rate remained high and her pallor corpse-like.

'All will be well,' Beattie assured him, no more flustered than had she been suffering a nosebleed. 'Time and patience are all that is required. You should leave her in my care and get yourself home.'

Raven had no intention of abandoning her in this condition, and steadfastly refused to move from her bed. Finally, however, her pulse began to slow, which he reported to Beattie with some relief.

'She will rally now,' Beattie insisted. 'Go back to Queen Street and get yourself some rest. You look quite spent.'

'I would rather wait until she is fully awake.'

'Your work is done, Will. But I will send for you as soon as she opens her eyes.'

Raven did as he was bid, feeling the burden begin to lift as he made the short walk back to Queen Street. He suspected that his anxiety had been magnified because he was working for the first time without Simpson's supervision, but perhaps taking difficult steps on your own was the only way to learn. Nonetheless, he knew he would not feel entirely secure about it until he had returned to Danube Street and seen Mrs Graseby fully conscious again.

He ate little at dinner, which piqued the unwanted interest of Mina.

'Are you troubled by indigestion? You might care to try one of my stomach powders. I got them from Duncan and Flockhart and they work very efficiently indeed.'

Raven respectfully declined and excused himself as soon as he deemed polite, unable to concentrate on the conversation. He retreated to his room, waiting impatiently for word and emerging to disappointment twice when the doorbell rang with messages for the professor.

The longer he waited, the more he began to fear, as it did not augur well if it was taking this long for Mrs Graseby to recover. That said, it was possible Beattie had been tardy about remembering his promise, and was engaged in further flirty conversation with his patient.

Finally, at about ten o'clock, there was a third ring on the doorbell. A few moments later Jarvis knocked on Raven's door.

'Dr Beattie is here to see you,' he said quietly. Raven wondered anxiously what he might infer from the butler's soft tone, but told himself his quiet delivery was more a reflection of the hour. Nonetheless, he hurried down the stairs and found Beattie awaiting him in the half light of the hallway.

He was clutching his hat. Raven's stomach turned instantly to lead.

Beattie waited until they were alone, and when he spoke, his words were barely above a whisper.

'She did not recover.'

'Dear God. How?'

'I fear it was the ether.'

Raven felt himself shrink, the darkness around threatening to swallow him. 'I am finished. I will have to tell Dr Simpson.'

Beattie gripped his arm and whispered into his ear. 'You will tell no one. I brought you into this. I will see you are not blamed.'

With this, Beattie walked to the door and closed it quietly behind him. As Raven watched him withdraw, he felt an undeserving gratitude, but no relief and absolutely no comfort.

TWENTY-THREE

aven was engulfed by the bleakest misery, confined within a prison of his own making, and what made it harder still was that he had to conceal his pain from everyone around him. He had to conduct himself as though nothing was amiss, there being no option to withdraw and hide away, as the following day had been hectically busy.

It had begun with a typically rumbustious morning clinic, at which he was besieged by unwary souls to whom he felt he ought to admit to being a dangerous fraud. He felt nervous and under-confident in his diagnoses and the advice he dispensed. Consequently, several patients left him with the impression that they were not convinced by what he told them, and therefore less likely to take the steps he recommended.

He thought of the homeopaths and the benefits their patients experienced due solely to the confidence they had in their doctors. If there was an opposite effect, then he was surely generating it.

Nonetheless, there was one case in which he had no doubt regarding his diagnosis, though his confidence did not provide for any better an outcome. The patient was a Mrs Gallagher, who had presented with what she initially described as a stomach complaint. Raven had palpated her stomach to little response, but when he put the merest pressure against her ribs, she winced and withdrew. He instantly recognised what he was looking at, just as he recognised her reluctance to lift her chemise and show him her sides.

'I need to check for a particular kind of rash that may be infectious,' he lied, by way of convincing her to cooperate.

He found the bruising where he expected, extensive but easily concealed.

'Your husband did this,' he stated.

She looked hunted, afraid even that Raven had said this aloud.

'It was my ain fault. I burnt the scones and there was nae mair flour. He had a tiring day and I should have been paying mair heed.'

'Where might I speak with Mr Gallagher?' Raven asked, but she was already on her way to the door.

She departed rapidly, leaving him with the impression that he had made matters worse, or at least frightened her into leaving before he was able to do anything for her.

This miserable morning had been followed by the usual diet of assisting at lectures and home visits. Adding insult to injury, one of the latter marked the first time he had accompanied Simpson to a rich client in the New Town, where inevitably he had been required to administer ether. When Simpson suggested it, Raven had looked around in the hope that he might see one of the Reverend Grissom's pamphlets, but he was not so blessed.

How his hands had shaken as he fumbled for the bottle, Simpson asking with a mixture of concern and irritation if he was all right.

The final trial was dinner, when once again he had to conceal his torment lest someone enquire as to what was troubling him. The hardest thing about this burden was that he absolutely could not share it with anybody.

Raven had seldom felt so isolated, so lonely, but at least his efforts at such concealment appeared to be successful. Following last night's solicitations and attendant offer of stomach powders, Mina's attention was notably not upon him this evening. She seemed distracted by some hidden excitation. She had news she was impatient to share, but had to await her moment.

Raven suspected Simpson had divined this, as he seemed to draw out saying grace as though intent upon frustrating her. Ordinarily this would have frustrated Raven also, with his meal having been placed before him, but he was lacking in appetite.

His head bowed, Raven observed that he had been given a larger portion than anyone else. He glanced up, caught Sarah's eye, and saw a conciliatory expression upon her face which told him his true condition had not gone entirely unnoticed. She could have no idea what was wrong, only that he was suffering.

He offered her a tiny nod of acknowledgment. He just hoped she wouldn't misinterpret if he failed to clear his plate.

The formalities concluded, Mina did not pause to eat before making her contribution.

'I learned the most dreadful news today,' she said. 'Truly dreadful and most tragic.'

Raven felt his insides turn to ice as it struck him that she was about to reveal the death of Mrs Graseby, right here before Dr Simpson.

'You will remember the Sheldrake family's housemaid, the one who had run away?'

'Sheldrake?' asked James Duncan with a sour curiosity, by way of emphasising that he had not been party to the previous discussion to which Mina was alluding.

'Mr Sheldrake is a dentist,' Mrs Simpson informed him, 'with a very successful practice. One of his housemaids absconded recently.'

'Rose Campbell,' said Mina. 'She was found dead, and there is a rumour that it was murder. Pulled from the dockside down in Leith. It's thought the man she ran off with must have done for her.'

'How awful for the Sheldrakes,' said Mrs Simpson. 'And for the staff who knew her.'

'It is thought that her own behaviour might have contributed to her demise,' Mina went on. 'She was reputedly free with her favours.'

Mina shook her head as though the relevance of this last statement was self-evident. Raven wondered at this sense of natural justice people seemed to draw from such judgments, as though any carnal knowledge of which they did not approve must inevitably lead to the direst of consequences. Perhaps they embraced this by way of reassurance that they could never meet a similar fate because of the morality they observed.

He sometimes felt sorry for Mina in that she appeared to have no greater purpose in life than to get herself married off, and was making scant progress in this endeavour. Vicarious excitement and scandal were therefore of disproportionate significance to her, and she was a busy conduit for all manner of gossip. Mina spoke with ill-disguised fascination about this poor girl's gruesome fate, as though she were reading from a penny dreadful.

Raven's eyes lit briefly upon Sarah. She was upset and attempting to conceal it. Her efforts were precisely as successful as his had been, in that only one person had seen through to the truth.

Sarah knew the girl.

Mina's reverie was cut off by the professor, who had heard enough.

'This kind of speculation is not appropriate for the dinner table, Mina,' he stated firmly. 'And it is no more than blethers. I happened to run into McLevy the police detective today, and he said nothing about murder.'

'What did he tell you?' Mina asked.

'The details are not for sharing in gentle company,' Simpson replied, which closed the matter for the duration of the meal.

Raven made a point of seeking out the professor on his own

once dinner was concluded. He intercepted him on his way to the stairs, before he could disappear into his study.

'What did McLevy tell you, sir?'

Simpson looked at him as though surprised at his interest, then a dawning passed over his expression as he remembered that Raven had been there at the quayside.

'He is awaiting the results of a post-mortem by the police surgeon,' Simpson said, his voice low. There was nobody in earshot, but he was perhaps concerned that a door might open nearby at any moment. 'I implied to Mina that there was no murder, but the truth is McLevy has not ruled anything out until he knows more.'

'So was there anything specific to suggest foul play?'

'He was very guarded. Between you and me, McLevy sometimes says more than his prayers. He likes to exaggerate the enormity of what he is up against so that it reflects the greater upon his achievement when he gets his man. But on this occasion, I do not believe that to be the case. He asked for my discretion, which you understand I would therefore expect of you also.'

'Unquestioningly, sir.'

'With a young woman found dead like that, he does not want word to spread that there may be some monster at large.'

Raven recalled the absurd talk of devils and Satanists that he had overheard. He well understood the hysteria that might ensue, not to mention the accusations. He recalled also the landlord, who had been keen to know the nature of Raven's interest, and who had followed him later. He might even have discovered where Raven lived, had he not managed to give him the slip.

'Had McLevy any suspicion as to what might have happened?'

'As Mina has said, Rose Campbell was rumoured to have been seeing a number of men, and possibly to have run away with one of them.'

'When we saw her by the quay, her posture was strangely contorted. What of that?'

'McLevy made no mention of it. But as we have no notion how long she was in the water, that might have been the result of rigor mortis. Why do you ask?'

What could Raven tell him? *Because a whore of my acquaintance, and of whom I have occasionally had knowledge, died in a similarly twisted posture and I crept away like a coward in order to protect my own reputation.*

'I am simply curious as to what might have caused it.'

He watched the doctor slip away quietly into his study. There was nothing further to be learned from him, but there was one person in the house who might know more.

Raven waited until he knew her duties were complete and she would have retired to her quarters. He ascended the stairs to the topmost floor and knocked softly upon the door.

'Yes, come in?'

Despite the invitation, Raven opened the door but remained in place, not considering it appropriate to proceed fully inside. He knew that he was not who Sarah was expecting when she called out her reply. She was sitting upon the bed, a book open on her lap.

She wore a familiarly implacable expression: a mixture of defiance and disapproval, though on this occasion missing the usual note of amusement bordering on scorn. Her face nonetheless failed to conceal that she was surprised to see him.

She closed the book and got to her feet.

The room smelled like fresh linen: clean and crisp. Sarah herself had a scent of cooked meat, smells that had adhered to her clothes from working in Mrs Lyndsay's kitchen.

'How may I help you, Mr Raven?'

So, not Wilberforce today. She was caught off-guard and using formality to shore up a barrier. There was a redness about her eyes to indicate that she had recently wept.

Raven was struck by how small and bare her room was. He had imagined it must be at least the same size as his, his position being temporary while hers was long-term. He realised with private embarrassment that this had been a baseless and indeed foolish assumption. It seemed so drab, so inadequate, and yet this was her lot.

The furnishings consisted of a small bed, a trestle table, and a chest of drawers atop which sat a sewing basket and a washing bowl. There were no pictures on the narrow walls, no shelves full of books. He had imagined she would have a collection of novels at least, but understood now that she must borrow them from Dr Simpson's library.

Behind her on the bed was the volume she had just closed, an illustrated work concerning the cultivation of herbs and other plants. He recalled seeing her tending a particular patch of garden at the back of the house. On the trestle table sat *Outlines of Chemistry, for the Use of Students*, by Professor William Gregory, who taught at the university. Raven was intrigued as to what she could possibly be wanting with that. He had found it challenging enough, so what chance did she have of comprehending anything from it?

'What are you reading?' he asked.

'I am interested in the healing properties of herbs,' she replied, an impatience to her tone clearly not welcoming further discussion.

'And what about the Gregory?'

She glanced towards the volume that had once so tormented him.

'Chemistry is the key to identifying the properties of individual plants which provoke specific effects. But as you had no way of knowing these books were here, I can deduce that this is not what you have come to enquire about.'

'No, it is not,' he admitted. 'May I come inside?'

Sarah nodded, though she folded her arms and took a step back – not that there was much space to put between them in this small chamber.

'Rose Campbell, the young lady who was found. You knew her, didn't you?'

Sarah glanced down for a moment, a darkening in her expression.

'Only a little. I knew her mainly through a mutual friend, Milly Conville. We sometimes meet when we are out in the town on errands.'

'She and this Milly were maids in the same house?'

'Yes. I believe Mr Sheldrake has the richest dental practice in the city, his clientele drawn primarily from here in the New Town. He has a household staff to match. What of it?'

'It was rumoured that Rose had run away with someone. Had you heard anything about this?'

Sarah's eyes narrowed. 'Why do you wish to know?'

'I am simply curious.'

'Enough to venture forth into the uncharted territory of the top landing and knock on this door. That is not an idle curiosity, Mr Raven. Something else must be driving it, so you ought to do me the courtesy of disclosing what.'

Raven had no such intention, but he had to step lightly. If she knew nothing, she would have simply told him that.

'When Miss Grindlay said that she was dead, I observed that you appeared distressed by the news. I was concerned that you might be upset.'

Sarah looked him in the eye, nodding to herself. 'That would be most solicitous of you, Mr Raven, if it were the truth.'

'It is the truth,' he insisted. 'I was aware you may not have anybody you could talk to about it, so I sought you out.'

'I mean the whole of the truth. You have described a mere pretext. What is the real nature of your interest?'

Raven searched for somewhere else to cast his gaze. There was but one small window, and nothing to be seen through it at night time.

'It concerns matters that would not be appropriate to share with someone of your standing.'

Sarah's eyes flashed with anger. 'My standing? Do you mean as a housemaid or as a woman? How little you must think of me that you would come here seeking information, but with no intention of reciprocating even if it might assist in what I could tell you.'

Raven withstood her ire, for in it she had betrayed what he suspected.

'So you do know more?'

'I am answering no more questions until you answer some of mine. Such as why you have seemed so burdened these past couple of days. Is that related to your interest in poor Rose?'

'No. I have merely been suffering the trials of my apprenticeship and of being new to certain duties.'

Sarah scoffed, that scornful look putting in its first appearance. 'I don't believe you. If you were struggling with your duties, I would discern it in Dr Simpson's manner. Something more specific is troubling you. Is it to do with this Evie, whose name you wrote down in your journal? Who is she?'

Raven felt something tighten inside him, an instinct drawing him to fold his arms too.

'That is absolutely no business of yours.'

'Indeed it is not,' she replied. 'And as I have absolutely no interest in your business, I will bid you goodnight.' She stepped past him to hold open the door. 'Though before you go, Mr Raven, I would suggest that you might seek out my friend Milly at the Sheldrakes' house. See if she wants to speak frankly and openly about this raw and painful loss. I can imagine no impediment. After all, you have already established such great rapport with me, so I see no reason why that should not be reprised with a complete stranger.'

Raven got the message. He could vividly imagine how such an approach was likely to go.

'Very well,' he said. 'Evie was a friend who lived in the Canongate, close to my former lodgings.'

'Was? Lived? So she is no more?'

He spent a moment calculating what he could disclose, attempting to anticipate the ramifications within ramifications. It was impossible. He could not tell her anything without telling her everything. If he really wanted to find out more, he would have to commit, holding nothing back.

'If I am to tell you this, I must have your absolute confidence. I need to know I can trust you.'

Sarah seemed momentarily taken aback. 'I guarantee my discretion. Your words will not pass these walls.'

'They will not have to. Your hearing it will be enough. Once I have told you what I must, you are not going to like me, Miss Fisher. That is, you are going to like me even less than you do already.'

Sarah looked at him almost pityingly. 'I do not dislike you, Mr Raven. You have misinterpreted. You see, I am in the household to serve, but that does not mean you may automatically command my respect or my affection; or even, though many would be satisfied with it, a pretence of either. But you can have my trust.'

Raven saw a sincerity in her face that he had not observed before, having seldom witnessed anything other than studied neutrality, practised detachment and outright hostility.

'Evie was a prostitute,' he said quietly.

Sarah considered this a moment. 'One you used?'

He sighed, battling his own resistance. 'I had . . . knowledge of her, yes. But it was what she did, how she made her money. I did not judge her for—'

'One you used,' she repeated. Her tone was not bitter, but it was insistent and inescapable.

Raven felt the shame of it now, of what he had done, of the vulnerability he had exploited. The lies he once told himself about the nature of it were now crumbling.

'Yes,' he admitted. 'I was younger then, curious. Tempted. She seemed far above me, something unknowable and forbidden

– and yet attainable. I was troubled then, given to bouts of . . . abandon. But yes, I used her. At first. Then we became friends.'

'Close friends? Or merely a prostitute and a former client who might yet be a client again?'

'I thought we were close friends, but I accept now that I will never know. When you lead a life such as Evie did, you cannot afford the luxury of trust, or of becoming close to anybody, though you may become adept at feigning it.'

Raven paused, picturing Evie how she once was, wondering whether her friendship was as illusory as her bedroom intimacies.

'She asked me for money,' he said. 'She wouldn't say why, only that her need was urgent. I gave her it. Then I visited her on the night before I came to live here, hoping to hear that her troubles were dealt with. Instead I found her . . . no more, her body twisted in agonised contortions. When I glimpsed Rose Campbell lying upon the quayside, she was in a similar condition.'

'Did you tell anyone what you had found? Or about this similarity?'

'I could not. On the night I found Evie, I had to leave unseen, lest anyone thought I was responsible for what happened to her.'

Sarah's reaction mirrored everything he felt about it himself.

'Oh, I think it would only be fair to conclude that you were not *responsible*.'

'I am not proud of what I did, but I panicked. What if I was thought a murderer?'

'So you believe she was killed?'

'I suspect she was poisoned, yes. And it is possible Rose was too, by the same means if not by the same hand.'

'Was any investigation prompted by Evie's discovery?'

'No. It was assumed she had died from alcohol.'

'Even though she was found as you describe?'

'Nobody looks closely when it's "another deid hoor", as I heard a policeman call her.'

'Rose was no hoor. They will investigate her, surely. You must tell McLevy what you know.'

As soon as the words had fallen from her mouth, it was clear Sarah understood how this could not be so.

'Except that you cannot, in case he thinks you were involved,' she stated.

'They say McLevy always gets his man, but living in the Old Town, I heard it different. Over there, they say he gets *a* man, then doesn't worry so much about whether it is the right one as long as the story fits and the jury convicts.'

Raven swallowed, looking her in the eye. 'I want to find out what happened to Evie, which is why I want to know more about Rose. Will you help me?'

Sarah returned his look, contemplating, evaluating. She appeared to arrive at a verdict.

'My assistance comes at a price, Mr Raven.'

'As you so accurately deduced, I have very little money.'

'Not that kind of price. I would ask the same thing you asked of me. Trust. You will keep nothing from me, and in this endeavour you will at all times treat me as your equal.'

'I give you my word. It is agreed then?'

'Not yet. Those were merely my conditions. The price I will tell you when I am good and ready.'

TWENTY-FOUR

arah found herself repeatedly falling into step a few paces behind Raven as they made their way along the Cowgate. A pattern had emerged whereby Raven would slow down in response, only for her to drift into the rear again soon after. Eventually he stopped dead and turned to her with a querulous expression.

'Why are you dawdling? Are you trying to make us late?'

It took his saying this for her to understand what she was doing. She had an impulse to apologise but she swallowed it.

'I was not dawdling,' she replied. 'I am more used to accompanying Miss Grindlay or occasionally Mrs Simpson, servants not being expected or indeed permitted to walk alongside their employers. It is a matter of habit rather than a reflection of your perceived status,' she added.

Raven's ignorance of the everyday practicalities of her station was proving a source of frustration to himself and of teeth-grating irritation to Sarah. In the ensuing couple of days following their late-night discussion, he kept appearing in the kitchen or intercepting her in hallways with the same question.

'Have you had opportunity?' he would ask.

After a good half-dozen replies in the negative, she laid it out for him.

'My duties do not allow much time for social visits; certainly not during hours that are safe or appropriate for a young woman to be out upon the streets. Besides, it is not as though I can simply knock upon the Sheldrakes' kitchen door and start asking questions. It would be best if it appeared a casual encounter.'

'You said you know this girl. When do you normally see her?'

'My opportunities to converse with Milly in the past have generally been in the gift of happenstance. As I said before, we would sometimes meet when we were both on errands, such as to the haberdasher's or occasionally Duncan and Flockhart.'

'You were out in the town only today,' he pointed out.

'I was with Miss Grindlay,' she responded.

Raven looked exasperated. 'Then the Lord knows how long I might be waiting.'

Sarah was about to give him a broadside by explaining that the only free time she got was on Sundays, when she realised that she knew precisely where and when she would find Milly and indeed the entire Sheldrake household.

'You will be waiting until the Lord's day,' she said. 'I can speak to Milly after Sunday worship.'

'The Sheldrakes attend the same church as we do?'

'No,' she confessed, immediately seeing where her plan would fall down. The Simpson household all had to attend Sunday worship together at St John's, Dr Simpson favouring Thomas Guthrie's sermons above all others. Milly would be in attendance elsewhere. 'Though perhaps you could suggest to Dr Simpson you have heard that the minister in a particular church is an interesting speaker and that we are both curious to find out his perspective upon certain matters.'

Raven had looked less than hopeful in response to this notion. They both knew it would sound an odd and unlikely thing to suggest to the professor.

'Do you even know the name of this minister whose church the Sheldrakes attend?'

'I *only* know his name,' Sarah admitted. 'Not where his church is. He is the Reverend Malachy Grissom.'

At this, Raven's eyes bulged. 'You know, I think we just might be able to convince Dr Simpson of my curiosity after all.'

It was for this reason that they were now walking along the Cowgate, Raven having discovered the location they sought. It was a bright, if cold, Sunday morning and yet he seemed to be permanently looking about himself, as though wandering here in the dead of night. This state of anxious vigilance was perhaps why he was so irritated at having to slow down for her.

'What are you looking for?' she asked. 'Anyone would think you were avoiding someone.'

'I am. Some former acquaintances with whom I'd rather not be reunited.'

'Why not? Who are they?'

'They don't concern you, for which you ought to be grateful.'

'I thought we agreed you would keep nothing from me.'

'Only in matters pertaining to this endeavour.'

'And how am I to know you are telling the truth regarding what matters do or don't pertain to it?'

'I was attacked and I had my face slashed, remember? I am apprehensive of running into the culprits again.'

'But why did they do it? Don't say you were robbed at random, because I don't believe you.'

Raven sighed. 'Because I owe them money, and I don't have it. Is that clear enough for you?'

It was not. Sarah had plenty more she might ask, not least *why* he owed them money, but she knew when to leave well alone.

Sarah had been speaking the truth when she said she didn't dislike him, but she did dislike his presumption of superiority over her, as she disliked it in all young men. Given the same chance, she was confident she would excel over any of them, so it stung when all they saw was a housemaid. Out of necessity,

Raven was looking beyond that. Or at least she was offering him the occasion to. She hoped he didn't disappoint.

'Why were you so confident that Dr Simpson would sanction this absence from our normal Sunday worship?' she asked as they passed beneath George IV Bridge.

'The Reverend Grissom has been campaigning against the use of ether in childbirth. He has been distributing pamphlets about it all over the city.'

'Why on earth would he want to do that?'

'Not why on earth. Why in heaven. There is a Bible verse stating that "in sorrow thou shalt bring forth children". He believes that the pain of childbirth is in some way sacred.'

'What arrant stupidity. And we are to listen to this man?'

'I anticipated that Dr Simpson would be curious – or at least amused – to know what else he might have to say. The Bible also states that when you are committing a charitable act, the right hand should not know what the left hand is doing. Given that surgery could be described as a charitable act, perhaps the Reverend might suggest the surgeon be blindfolded, or have one hand tied behind his back out of sight.'

Raven found this notion more amusing than Sarah, but that was because he was missing something rather obvious.

'He would suggest no such thing, for I doubt it a coincidence that he has chosen to object to the relief of a pain he is certain never to endure. If Grissom had a dose of the toothache, I can't imagine him finding a theological justification why Mr Sheldrake should not use ether in his dental extractions.'

Raven indicated that the place they sought was just ahead, its congregation already filing through a set of doors on the south side of the Cowgate. It appeared to be a modest meeting hall, and not a church as anyone might ordinarily recognise one.

'I expected somewhere grander,' Sarah admitted.

'Not all ministers of the Free Church were as fortunate as

the Reverend Guthrie in retaining their premises following the Disruption,' Raven told her. 'Many have had to make do with whatever halls and meeting places can be found.'

Sarah had heard mention of the Disruption, but paid little attention to matters involving pious old men bickering with each other. As she understood it, the schism had come down to the right of patronage, which allowed the state and wealthy land-owners to appoint a minister to a parish over and above the wishes of the parishioners. Those who broke with the main Church four years ago had consequently needed to form their own ministries, with the support of those in the laity who wished to follow them. Hence the ad-hoc nature of this place of worship.

She and Raven slipped inside, taking their seats towards the back. Sarah had seldom found churches to be joyful or inspiring places, but this one seemed particularly drab, and yet very well attended. A few minutes later, she watched the Sheldrake house-hold file in close to the front, their position perhaps reflecting the dentist's contributions to the new parish's coffers. Mr Sheldrake walked in at the head of the line, his wife, son and two daughters taking their seats alongside him as Milly and the rest of the household staff slipped into the row behind.

Sheldrake struck Sarah as an unlikely match for his dowdy and grim-faced wife. He was a tall, smartly dressed fellow, slim of build and clean-shaven. In the same way that it was said of certain women that they were handsome, Sheldrake could be said to be pretty: a feminine quality not only to his features, but also in the way he carried himself. His clothes were modern and fash-ionable to the point that there seemed something incongruously rakish about him, though perhaps any note of finery seemed out of place in this dour setting.

She glimpsed Milly momentarily between the rows of heads. She looked numb and shocked, trying to suppress tears. Milly would have known for some days about Rose's death, but Sarah understood from experience that being back in a familiar place for the first time could serve to bring it all home, another reminder of death's finality.

The room fell silent as the Reverend Grissom entered and took his place behind the lectern that served as his pulpit. He was a small man with the proud gait of one who believed himself to be at least a foot taller. Fine grey hair hung lank around his crown as though draped from a circular pelmet, his pate bald but for a few wispy tufts that Sarah felt the constant urge to ascend the stage and shave. Beneath it his face was dominated by a nose so large and pointed that when he turned his head it was as though he were indicating the direction in which he imminently intended to leave.

Unfortunately, he did not leave for quite some time. He preached at considerable length, though had nothing to say about ether. He talked much of humility whilst his tone, demeanour and indeed every physical gesture emanated self-importance, his permanently serious expression admitting no hint of levity.

Sarah thought it must be exhausting to be constantly dismayed by so many things.

'Pride makes men fools,' he said, his voice surprisingly loud for a small man. 'Vanity makes them seek glory in their own reflection, and they do not seek that reflection merely in the looking glass, but in the admiration of others. How they wish to see it in the faces of their peers, but worst is how they crave to see it in the faces of *women*.'

His voice dropped as he said this, as though the word itself were obscene.

'And in this, the worst of women are complicit, for they are the tauntresses. *Their* pride is served by this. *Their* pride escalates that of men. They paint themselves, they dress themselves, these jezebels. Not only the fallen ones upon the night-time streets, but in their husbands' homes too. The proud man seeks their approval. And he seeks that approval manifest in physical knowledge. That is why the greatest sin of a woman is to feed this pride in men, to encourage it. For to do so is to be the occasion of another's sin, to lead another into temptation.

'The good wife is modest. The good woman is modest in her appearance and in her manner. It is modesty that I commend, modesty to which I entreat you. As the Lord's mother was modest.'

Raven leaned towards Sarah and spoke softly as the service ended and the congregation began to disperse.

'And yet Jesus chose the company of prostitutes over that of preachers.'

Sarah had to stifle a gasp, concerned that his remark might be overheard. However, she suspected that to shock her had been his intention, so she decided to respond in kind, albeit more quietly.

'I don't believe your own such dalliances put you closer to the Lord. Was it the sin of pride that made you seek out a woman of the night?'

'As I recall, the sin of lust was adequate to the task. I cannot pretend to the Reverend Grissom's modesty, but perhaps he has greater reason to be modest than I.'

Sarah made her way smartly out onto the Cowgate, where worshippers were gathering to trade their Sunday greetings. She and Raven stood close to the doors, the ideal vantage point for interception.

'You had best keep your distance,' Sarah told him, watching Mr Sheldrake lead his family down the aisle towards the vestibule. 'Milly is not going to be very candid with a stranger in our company.'

Raven's attention appeared to have been taken by something else in any case.

'Yes, certainly. I'll meet you back here,' he said, swiftly departing through the crowd.

Sarah saw Mr and Mrs Sheldrake stop in the vestibule to talk to Reverend Grissom, Milly continuing towards the exit. She stepped into her path and offered a conciliatory smile.

'Sarah!' Milly said, surprise in her voice. She sounded meeker than usual, her tones more nasal. Sarah could tell she had cried a great deal in recent days. 'What are you doing here?'

'I got permission from Dr Simpson to worship here today. I wanted to see you and to tell you how sorry I was to hear about Rose.'

Milly swallowed, looking as though her eyes might fill again. She nodded. 'Thank you. It has been difficult.'

'I can't begin to imagine. I felt so guilty.'

'Guilty? Why?'

'Because when I was told she had absconded, I was envious, imagining some exciting life she might have escaped to. I had heard rumours she was seeing someone and had run away with him. Was this true?'

Milly cast an eye to the side, towards the Sheldrakes. It was innocent enough for her to be talking to Sarah, a fellow housemaid, but she was clearly concerned not to be overheard. For the moment, they were not in earshot.

'I couldn't say,' Milly replied. 'Rose had secrets, and there was a man involved. That much was inescapable.'

Sarah thought this an odd choice of word.

'Inescapable how?'

Milly glanced again at her employers. She looked afraid she had given something away.

'I shouldn't speak further. I've said too much as it is.'

'You can trust me, Milly,' Sarah implored.

'I do. But it's not you I've said too much to.'

Sarah placed a hand on her shoulder. The poor girl looked like a hollowed-out shell where once there had been so much more.

'You must let me know about the funeral,' Sarah said, trying to keep her talking.

This seemed to burden her even more, tears threatening again.

'I do not know that there will even be a funeral. And it is my fault.'

'How can that be?'

'A policeman came to the house to ask us questions. An Irishman, McLevy. I was only trying to be honest, but because of what I told him, he is of a mind that Rose killed herself.'

'For what reason would Rose possibly take her own life?'

Milly's eyes swept to the side again. The Sheldrakes had finished speaking with the Reverend Grissom and were moving towards the door.

'She was sure she would be dismissed, and she did not know what else she could do.'

Sarah gripped Milly's arm in case she should walk away.

'Dismissed for what reason?'

With Mr Sheldrake imminently in earshot, Milly's last words were but a breath.

'She was with child.'

TWENTY-FIVE

aven had just been told to keep his distance when his eye was drawn to something on the other side of the Cowgate. At first he couldn't be sure because he only glimpsed them through the departing congregation, but as he moved beyond the crowd and the pair drew close, there could be no mistake. Walking westward towards the Grassmarket was the woman who had recently come to him with such horrific bruising, accompanied by a scowling and ruddy-faced man.

They were both dressed for church, heading home from worship. Her head was bowed low, as though reluctant to meet anyone's eye, while he walked with his chin thrust forward, his peering eyes seeming to challenge the world around him to explain itself. It was Sunday morning, but Saturday night was still etched across his visage, a drinker's face with pudgy pink skin and a bulbous nose. These were the only parts of him that appeared soft. The rest of the man resembled a coiled spring.

They had passed by the time Raven made it across the road. 'Mr Gallagher!' Raven hailed him, making sure he had the right person.

The man turned around, his expression conveying irritated curiosity when he failed to recognise who had called him. His

wife, by contrast, had a look of fear as she immediately identified the man approaching them. She was evidently terrified of
the repercussions should her husband learn what Raven had
deduced, or maybe even the mere fact that she had visited a
doctor.

'What do you want?' he asked, looking Raven up and down.
There was evident disdain at being summarily apprehended by
some young upstart, though Raven noted that his eye lingered a
moment upon the scar.

'I need to speak to you.'

'Then speak.'

Mrs Gallagher's head remained down. Raven was sure she was
trembling.

'It concerns a delicate matter, inappropriate for discussion in
front of your good lady wife.'

Mr Gallagher looked confused and dismissive, instantly rele-
gating anything Raven might say in terms of its potential
relevance.

'Please, I'm sure what I have to impart will be greatly to your
benefit. Let us step somewhere close by where we might enjoy
some privacy.'

Raven led him off the Cowgate into a narrow close between
two buildings, the hubbub from the Free Church congregation
immediately softer.

'Well,' Gallagher said impatiently, 'out with it.'

'I am your wife's medical practitioner. I thought we ought to
discuss a chronic condition that has been afflicting her.'

His suspicious eyes narrowed further. 'What condition is that?'

'Please do me the courtesy of not thinking me a fool. She
endeavoured to conceal the source of her injuries for fear of more.
But I understood what I was looking at all too well.'

Gallagher looked outraged at Raven's impertinence. 'She
doesn't pay attention. She gets distracted. A man works all day,
then comes home to find the last of the flour's been ruined. What

business is it of yours how a man runs his house or disciplines his wife?'

'Oh, we're talking about discipline? Is that the same mettle you require to say no to another whisky when you've already drunk your fill and spent the wages your wife needs to live on?'

'Who the hell do you think you're addressing, boy?'

'I am acting in my patient's interest.'

'No, you're sticking your neb where it ill belongs. So you should mind it doesn't come to some harm.'

Raven noticed Gallagher ball his right hand into a fist. It hadn't taken much. He knew a thing or two about men like this.

Raven put up his palms in a placatory gesture. 'Very well, Mr Gallagher. It is your business how you discipline your wife. Just as it is my business how I treat her affliction. And having identified that affliction as the lump of shite standing in front of me, I hereby prescribe a remedy. I am going to ask her to come and see me regularly, and if I see further evidence of your hands upon her, I will find you and I will knock seven bells out of you. That way you get to handle your business and I get to handle mine.'

Rage built up in Gallagher, but he did not move. Yet.

'I'll do what I will with these hands, son, including beating you to a pulp if you ever cross me again.' Gallagher made another fist. He was getting there, but something was holding him back: the very fact that Raven was not afraid.

'Why wait? I'm in front of you right now. Come now, you've shown great vigour in hitting a woman. Why don't you show me how you hit a man?'

'I won't do this on the Sabbath.'

Raven put his hands by his sides, leaving himself open. 'Does that mean your wife can burn the scones with impunity today?'

That was the tipping point, the moment Gallagher's rage overcame his cowardice. He swung for all he was worth, launching his fist towards Raven's face. But Raven was quick; quick enough for a drunk like him. He moved his head in a twinkling and Gallagher punched the wall, with all his weight behind the blow.

Gallagher dropped to his knees, letting out a guttural moan as he looked in horror at the mangled fingers, broken, bloody and raw. The only thing he had beaten to a pulp was his own hand.

Raven stood over him and held his chin, forcing him to look up.

'Remember I did this without even touching you. Strike her again and that will change.'

TWENTY-SIX

arah looked about for Raven, unable to find him in the throng that had spilled out of the Reverend Grissom's service. The Sheldrakes had gathered their staff and were proceeding in the direction of Blair Street, Milly walking with her head bowed. She did not glance back.

Sarah located him emerging from a close across the street, his countenance a grim contrast to the departing worshippers'. Their expressions befitted those who believed they had just communed with the Lord, while Raven's intimated dealings altogether less holy.

Sarah felt vindicated in her instinctive impression that there was something restless and impetuous in Raven. She estimated that both of these traits had played their part in whatever had led to his face being wounded, but she also doubted he would tell her the truth about it. There was a swirling fog of dark secrets behind his hazel eyes.

She would admit that there was undoubtedly something kinder in there too, though at Queen Street anyone might seem warm next to Dr James Duncan – or Dr James Matthews Duncan as he was now insisting upon. That one was restless and impetuous also, but driven entirely by ambition and the desire to make a name for himself, as evidenced by his concern that his name itself should be distinct.

Raven, by contrast, was striving on behalf of a woman who was too dead to thank him for it. Perhaps he was trying to atone for not having helped enough to keep her alive. Sarah knew to be wary of such motives, noble as they may seem. They said the road to Hell was paved with good intentions, and she suspected Raven had the recklessness to take her there with him if she did not step carefully.

'Did you speak with her?' he asked.

'Rose was pregnant,' Sarah told him. 'She feared she would be dismissed as soon as it was discovered. Milly told McLevy as much, and now he is apt to conclude she drowned herself.'

Raven took a moment to absorb this.

'I have a suspicion Evie might have been pregnant too.'

'How do you know?' Sarah asked, before realising what the question might imply.

'It would not have been mine,' he answered evenly. 'I told you, I was no longer using her in that way.'

'Then what makes you think . . .?'

'I don't know. It just fits. But what does not is the idea that Rose drowned herself. That would not explain the contortions, similar to Evie's.'

'You said you suspected they both might have been poisoned. Is it not possible that they took a poison to kill themselves?'

Raven considered it. 'Theoretically, yes. But the same one? And one that appears to have racked them with pain? Why choose to die in such a horrible manner?'

'Perhaps they were misled into believing it would ease their passing, like opium.'

'I find it too hard to accept that Evie would end her own life. Why would she need money so urgently if she planned to kill herself?'

'I find it difficult to believe the same of Rose, but how can anyone know what they might do in a position of utter desperation?

To be with child but having no means of supporting it or herself once she was dismissed.'

'Professor Ziegler at the Maternity Hospital did say he had known young women to kill themselves,' Raven admitted, his voice taking on an apologetic tone. 'In some cases they could not even face the prospect of their families discovering their condition. It seems such a resort of final despair, though.'

'What other resort would be open to a girl like Rose?'

Raven gave her a look that said she already knew the answer to that question; and knew also that it could not be spoken aloud in the hearing of strangers.

They increased their pace, putting some distance between themselves and the departing worshippers.

'Desperate women explore all manner of options before self-murder,' he said. 'There was a newborn's leg found recently in a gutter near the Royal Exchange. I suspect the poor mite was done away with by its mother.'

It was not the first time Sarah had heard of such a thing.

'The mother must have been able to keep her condition secret, though,' she said. 'I doubt that would have been an option for Rose. She feared she would be dismissed long before such a horrible course would even have been open to her.'

'There are other desperate measures,' Raven said. His voice was low even though there was no one close by. It was an invitation to complicity.

'Indeed,' Sarah replied, by way of accepting.

'Though if they had chosen to go down that route, it might have ended just the same for them. My friend Henry recently encountered two cases of young women who died from attempted abortions.'

Sarah was trying to imagine the fear and hopelessness Rose must have felt, asking herself what she might do in the same situation. She suspected there was nothing she would not consider. That was when an idea struck her.

'What if they took a poison not in order to kill themselves, but believing it would purge the burden they carried?'

Raven turned in response. She could tell the notion was not outlandish.

'Women have taken all manner of concoctions in the hope that they might induce a premature labour,' he agreed. 'Thus far they have either been utterly without effect or harmful only to the mother.'

'Nonetheless, one could charge a great deal for a pill or a draught that promised to solve such a problem, as long as the buyer believed in it. Could this have been what Evie needed the money for?'

'Evie was no gullible fool. But desperation is often the mother of misplaced faith. I think you could be right.'

Raven gazed up towards the grey skies, as though answers might be hidden behind the canopy of clouds.

'I just wish we knew what manner of poison she might have taken.'

TWENTY-SEVEN

aven came to in the darkness, his half-waking disorientation suddenly sharpened into alert consciousness as he observed that there was a figure standing
at the end of his bed holding a lamp. In his startled
state and in the poor light, it took him a moment to recognise
the intruder as Jarvis, the butler.

'What the devil are you doing?'

'I came to rouse you, Mr Raven.'

'Then why are you looming there like a bloody phantom? Why
didn't you call my name?'

'I have called your name three times, and before that spent
some time knocking upon your door, all to no avail. My next
resort would have been to fetch a cup of water to throw over
you, but happily we have not reached such an eventuality.'

As always, Jarvis's voice was calm and implacable, answering
questions with patience and yet nonetheless conveying the impression that merely speaking to Raven was somehow beneath him.
He hoped he was making some headway in breaking down Sarah's
antipathy, but suspected Jarvis's disdain would remain a permanent fixture.

'What is the hour?'

'It is a quarter after four. Dr Simpson has been summoned to an urgent case and wishes you to ready yourself and accompany him forthwith.'

'Do you know where we are bound?' he asked, reckoning a carriage journey would give him time to fully wake up and gather his wits.

'Nearby, I gather. Albyn Place.'

'Not two hundred yards away,' Raven observed. 'At least for once the patient should be able to properly compensate Dr Simpson for coming forth at such an hour.'

Jarvis audibly scoffed. It was hard to see his expression in the half-light but Raven could vividly imagine it.

'What?'

'You have been studying under the professor but you have observed so little about him.'

'I have observed him refusing payment from the poor, but surely he would not need to extend such exceptions to the rich.'

'Mr Raven, there is not the time to discuss this at length, but may it suffice for me to tell you that I have on occasion found Dr Simpson to be using rolled-up five-pound banknotes in order to stop the rattling of a window.'

Raven and Jarvis made it to the foot of the stairs as Simpson emerged from his office on the floor above, grasping his bag. Jarvis held out his hat and coat in readiness, sweeping the latter about the professor and placing the former upon him in a practised motion before opening the door.

The cold hit Raven like the cup of water Jarvis had threatened and he eyed the professor's sealskin overcoat enviously as they swept westward along Queen Street.

'An early start to a Monday morning, but an exciting one, no doubt,' Simpson said, a croak in his voice betraying how he had been recently hauled from sleep.

'You were late to bed, were you not?' Raven asked, knowing Simpson had still been out when he turned in for the night.

'I had dinner at Professor Gregory's house. We talked a very long time.'

'Have you bumped into McLevy again on your travels? I was wondering what emerged from the post-mortem on Rose Campbell.'

'I have not heard anything, no. What specifically is your interest?'

'I remain curious as to what might have caused the body to be so contorted. Is it possible that this was evidence of poison?'

'I wouldn't know,' Simpson replied. 'If it's poisons you're interested in, then Christison is your man.'

Raven felt his pulse race. This could make being dragged out of bed into the darkness worthwhile.

'Professor Christison? You would make an introduction?'

'Introduce you to his work, for sure. I have his treatise in my office. You would have much to learn from studying it.'

'Thank you,' Raven said, though gratitude was not what he felt.

Simpson had no curiosity over the fate of Rose Campbell, beyond perhaps a physiological explanation for what had happened to her corpse. The greater drama around her did not seem visible to the man. Perhaps he only saw such things in abstract, and that was why he was able to distance himself from the horrors and tragedies that he dealt with in his job.

He thought about Jarvis's story of Simpson fixing a rattling window with a banknote. Money meant nothing to him. He inhabited a realm of books and theory.

If Mrs Gallagher had come to Simpson instead of Raven, he would have treated her injuries, but it would not have occurred to the professor how he might address the cause. When he went to dangerous parts of town, the crowds parted for him. They all knew his name, looked up to him, wished him well. He was like a god who did not inhabit the same plane as mere mortals, and though he would help them, he was not affected by their plights.

'Now, let us test how your faculties serve you at this ungodly hour,' Simpson said as they approached Albyn Place. 'The patient we are about to treat is a young woman in her eighth month of pregnancy, who suddenly started bleeding, painlessly but heavily. Diagnosis?'

Raven searched his tired brain for the answer. A number of possibilities presented themselves, but he dismissed those that would not justify their hurrying to her aid at this hour.

'*Placenta praevia*,' he said.

Simpson nodded sagely as a door opened ahead of them.

A maid stepped forth to greet them, anguished and on the verge of hysteria. She babbled indecipherably, tripping over her own incoherent words as she pointed to the stairs inside. All Raven caught was the name: Mrs Considine. The maid's hand, he noticed, was smeared with red, and a livid crimson streak extended from the waist of her skirt to its hem.

Simpson took the stairs two at a time. Raven was a little slower, his climb burdened by memories of what had happened by his hand at another New Town address not two weeks ago. It was ever-present in his mind that someone had died as a result of his actions, yet he was equally consumed by the question of how this had happened. Had he been incompetent? Was ether itself dangerous?

He had attempted to discuss the issue in a general way with Dr Simpson, in the hope of salving his conscience.

'Do you have any concerns about the safety of ether, given that a small number of deaths have been attributed to its administration?' he had asked one morning after breakfast.

'The deaths that you refer to occurred two or three days after severe operations, and should not be attributed to the inhalation of ether itself. Many of the alleged failures and misadventures ascribed to it are to my mind the result of errors in its administration,' Simpson said, a reply that did not allow Raven much comfort. 'Successful etherisation requires a full and narcotising dose be administered by impregnating the respired air as fully with the vapour as the patient can bear, and the surgeon's knife should never be applied until the patient is thoroughly and indubitably soporised.'

Raven thought of Mrs Graseby's initial reluctance to inhale the ether and her sudden movement in response to Beattie's manipulation.

'Have you ever experienced any difficulties?' he asked.

'For the past nine months I have employed it in almost every case of labour that I have attended, without any adverse consequences. I have no doubt that in some years hence the practice will be general whatever the small theologians of the kirk might say.'

Simpson had laughed then, incognisant of Raven's growing unease.

But what was a soporising dose? How could such a thing be measured? What was the difference between Simpson using ether for the first time and Raven using it unsupervised on Mrs Graseby? It occurred to Raven that it was as much an art as it was a science, and that his own efforts had surely not deviated so far from what was required as to have caused a death. Yet he had no other explanation for what had occurred. Without that he was still inclined to blame himself.

They found the patient in a bedroom on the second floor, the door thrown wide to the wall. Lamps and candles had been placed upon every available surface, the flickering play of light picking out a dark glistening seemingly everywhere, a gory spectacle that made Raven grateful he had not breakfasted. Mrs Considine was supine upon the canopied bed, her nightclothes a red-soaked mass of material hauled up around her knees. There was blood over the bed, upon the carpet and on every item of furniture that had been touched by the patient or her maid.

Mrs Considine appeared to have lapsed into unconsciousness, which was a source of some mercy to Raven, in that there would be no need for him to administer ether.

Simpson had his coat off and his sleeves rolled up by the time Raven had closed the bedroom door. He performed a rapid examination in order to ascertain the cause of the haemorrhage.

'Prepare a dose of ergot, Will,' he stated without looking up. 'Hurry, man. I must deliver the child without delay. It is the only way to arrest the bleeding.'

The doctor all but shouted his instructions. Raven had never heard him raise his voice before, which was almost as disturbing as the blood. His anticipated diagnosis had been correct: a low-lying placenta, the afterbirth, situated at the opening of the womb so that it had presented before the child. Raven remembered the description word for word from the textbook, principally because of the lines that followed: *In such circumstances, catastrophic haemorrhage is inevitable, with one in three mothers dying as a result.*

With fumbling hands, Raven did as he was instructed. He was still measuring out the required dose as Simpson brought down the breech and delivered the infant, who remarkably was found to be alive. The troublesome placenta was then removed, the ergot given and pressure applied to the flaccid but now empty uterus.

The bleeding slowed to a trickle and the patient roused a little, but Raven was reluctant to feel any relief while Caroline Graseby remained fresh in his memory. She had shown signs of recovery too, only to succumb hours later while he waited anxiously for news.

A small army of housemaids appeared, armed with hot water and towels. The infant was wrapped up and placed in a corner while the worst of the mess was cleaned.

Mrs Considine attempted to sit, but found this more than she could manage and sank back onto her pillows, exhausted. She cast a tired but fond eye towards the newborn, and only then did Raven feel he could breathe free.

Then Mrs Considine began clutching at the front of her nightgown, a look of fear upon her face. Raven tried to assist by loosening the fastenings at her throat. She was breathing rapidly, gasping, her eyes wide with panic. It was as though she was struggling to find enough air in the room to sustain her.

Raven looked to the professor, who stood at the other side of the bed, wearing an unusually stricken expression.

'Dr Simpson, what should we do?' he asked.

Simpson swallowed, and when he replied, it was in a quiet, hollow voice.

'Speak to her.'

Three words that told him it was hopeless.

Raven held her hands and tried to say reassuring things, his own voice distant as though he was witnessing himself from without. Mrs Considine continued to stare at him, her gaping eyes and terrified expression reminding him of the look on Evie's face when he had found her. He willed her to keep breathing, hoping that she had retained just enough blood to remain alive.

Her breathing slowed and then ceased.

Raven looked to Simpson, hoping for some words of wisdom, some consoling thought to help make sense of what had just happened. Instead Simpson turned and made his way to a chair in the corner of the room, heedlessly spreading gore over an ever-increasing area. The professor sat down heavily and placed his head in his hands.

An eerie silence settled upon the room, broken only by the disconcerting sound of dripping. Then the baby began to cry.

TWENTY-EIGHT

o. 52 Queen Street was in a strange state of suspension. Raven sat by a window in the drawing room, Professor Christison's *Treatise on Poisons* weighing heavily upon his lap, while George Keith and James Duncan were perched either side of the fireplace, also poring over papers and books. The house was unsettlingly quiet and still for this time of the morning, nothing functioning according to normal manner. For the second day, the morning clinic had been cancelled, and everyone was quite at a loss as to how they ought to occupy themselves.

Breakfast had been served without Dr Simpson arriving to say grace, which indicated that the staff knew not to expect him. Upon returning from Albyn Place the previous morning, he had taken to his bed and had not emerged since. Mrs Simpson had joined them but briefly today in the dining room, eating a few mouthfuls of toast before withdrawing again without speaking a word.

All was silent but for the crackling of the fire and the occasional shriek from the parrot. Nonetheless, despite the absence of distraction, Raven was not making any headway in finding a possible cause of Evie and Rose's apparent agonies.

Raven became aware that Duncan had closed the volume before

him and was gazing thoughtfully in his direction. This was seldom the overture to anything good.

'Tackling Christison, eh?' he said. 'An excellent resource, incontestably, but as physicians we must all take care not to be throwing the baby out with the bathwater.'

Ordinarily Raven would not have encouraged him to expand, but right then he was content to be drawn away from the labour of his fruitless search.

'What do you mean?'

'One could argue that all poison is essentially an overdose. For surely there are properties in everything mentioned in Christison that may be beneficial in the right measure, or that may induce an effect we can harness in the patient's interest.'

'Yes, but establishing the relationship between dose and effect is fraught with difficulty. Speaking as one who has been exposed to all manner of foul vapours after dinner most evenings.'

'Yes, but through such endeavours, posterity might at least find a footnote for you in medical history,' Duncan replied.

Keith smirked at this, which provoked a smile from Duncan. Raven strongly suspected the latter did not appreciate which of the pair the former had been amused by.

Raven was less inclined towards levity; he regarded the on-going testing model as a catastrophe in the making. Simpson had every professor and chemist of his acquaintance on the lookout for prospective compounds that might exhibit anaesthetic properties. Any time one of them identified a new one, they would bring a sample to the house and it would be tested after dinner by all of the medical men present. Professor Miller, the surgeon who lived next door at No. 51, had taken to dropping in most mornings on his way to the Infirmary just to make sure everyone had survived the night. So far, nothing they tested had provoked anything more dramatic than dizziness, nausea and blinding head-aches, but Raven couldn't help thinking this was down to good fortune rather than sound judgment. It was not difficult to imagine

Professor Miller arriving too late and discovering the entire gathering fatally poisoned.

'I would rather my honour not be posthumous before I even qualify to practise,' Raven said.

'Oh, don't be melodramatic. Though you are right in that testing remains the great challenge, not helped by the vocal opposition abroad these days to using animals as subjects. How else are we to establish lethal doses, and how else to determine effects if we cannot dissect the creatures afterwards?'

'I am of the mind that anyone opposed to a dog testing poison should volunteer himself in its stead,' Raven suggested. He was not serious but it amused him that Duncan would not realise this.

'Indeed. The problem is that canine physiology is insufficiently similar to our own for us to draw accurate conclusions. I only wish we had such a supply of disposable human subjects.'

'How about prisoners?' Keith suggested.

Raven glanced across and caught the gleam in his eye. For pity's sake, don't give him ideas, he thought.

Too late.

'Indeed,' Duncan mused. 'It would be a means by which murderers and thieves could contribute something to the overall good of humanity.'

'Why not whores?' Raven asked, his tone more aggressive and forceful than he intended.

Duncan responded with a strange look, as though weighing up what might be behind this interjection. The ensuing tension was accentuated by the house's unaccustomed silence, until it was dispelled by Keith diverting the subject.

'At any dose, there are some poisons that have no effect but harm, and yet they continue to be prescribed. Mercury, for goodness' sake. Apart from causing ulceration of the mouth, the loss of both teeth and hair, its only effect is to precipitate salivation, which flimsy wisdom interprets as the body purging itself in order to balance the humours. Such thinking is positively medieval.'

'This is why homeopaths continue to prosper,' Raven offered. 'So much allopathic medicine is toxic, so the benefit of homeopathy is that you don't get sicker other than from the natural progression of your disease.'

'And as you will learn, Will, patients demand pills, and doctors are only too willing to supply them while there is money in it. Polypharmacy is as much the resort of greedy charlatans as homeopathy: doctors selling complex combinations of remedies, then still more to offset the side effects of those. I feel I am shouting into the wind telling patients that the surest route to health is good diet and regular exercise. They feel they have not had their money's worth if they do not leave with a prescription, and in their minds, the more complex the physic, the more impressive the physician.'

'Nonetheless,' Duncan argued, 'we have established the efficacy of some truly remarkable medicines, so there are surely more to be discovered. And I don't mean some nebulous tonic such as Gregory's powder. Who knows what conditions might be improved or actually cured by some natural derivative or by simply the right compound? I have made it my purpose to find out.'

'Though until you can solve the aforementioned problems of testing them,' Raven said, 'it will be your destiny to fail.'

Duncan got to his feet and regarded Raven for a moment, much as an owl might regard a field mouse.

'We shall see,' he said quietly, then walked from the room.

Raven returned to the Christison, though his commitment was hardly redoubled by having had a break. He pored over another few pages and issued the deepest of sighs. It would have been simple enough if he knew the name of a poison and wished to learn more about its catalogued effects, but he was attempting the very opposite.

Keith put down the journal he was reading and glanced across.

'Is everything all right with you, Will? You seem profoundly restive.'

'I think the mood of the house is infecting me.'

Keith nodded, sitting back and contemplating for a moment. 'The majority of cases that you will see with the professor will be difficult ones. You must prepare yourself for that.'

Raven offered a weak smile in response, thinking that the true reason for his having witnessed so few normal deliveries since he began his apprenticeship was that he was not permitted to accompany the professor to see his more aristocratic clients. The obstructed labours of the poor – that's what he was left with.

'You would benefit from a diversion,' Keith continued. 'A non-medical pursuit that would provide you some fresh air and a new perspective.'

Keith was trying to sound like he was mulling over the possibilities, but Raven could tell he already had something specific in mind. Raven also suspected he had an agenda.

'If it will deliver me from Christison, I am open to any suggestion.'

'Have you heard of photography?'

Raven perked up. This was the remarkable means of capturing reflected light upon treated paper, creating images far more accurate than the hand of the finest painter.

'I have heard of it, but I confess I have never seen an example. Do you know someone who has a camera?'

'I know two people who are among the most renowned exponents of the art. You may remember my friend David Hill: he visited the house a few days ago.'

Raven nodded. He vaguely recalled Keith introducing an acquaintance to Simpson, but he had not heard the details as he was on his way out, having been dispatched to pick up some chemicals for Dr Duncan.

'He and his partner Robert Adamson have their studio on Calton Hill, where they are utilising a new process, the calotype. They have requested Dr Simpson sit for a photographic portrait, but I doubt he could be imposed upon to remain still for the length of time required. The man is never at peace.'

Raven smiled at the thought of the professor attempting to hold a pose for more than thirty seconds.

'You on the other hand would be ideal. They are looking for subjects with interesting faces. Would you sit for them?'

Raven didn't like to think of his face as 'interesting'. Among the medical fraternity this was seldom a complimentary adjective. He wondered if Keith was referring to his features in general or to his scar, which although healing still tended to draw unwanted attention.

'As a subject?'

Keith nodded. 'I am seeing Mr Hill later today. I will suggest we visit tomorrow, first thing. It has to be when the light is brightest.'

'I should be honoured,' Raven said.

Keith gave him an odd smile; approving and yet calculating.

'You were out on Sunday with the maid, Sarah, were you not?'

Raven felt rather exposed. He had not thought of the repercussions of their excursion, beyond reporting back to Simpson about Grissom's oratorical expertise in turning humility into self-aggrandisement.

'What of it?'

'If you have a certain rapport with her, then you might ask her to join us too. They are particularly interested in working women. I think she would make a splendid subject.'

Raven realised this was the agenda he had suspected. Hill must have caught a glimpse of Sarah during his visit, and it was she he was truly interested in. Keith was engineering a pretext to deliver her there, with Raven as his instrument.

He didn't mind. He would rather be Keith and Hill's instrument than be Duncan's, and if it got him out from beneath the shroud of despond blanketing the house, he would welcome the chance.

TWENTY-NINE

arah was walking into the teeth of a chill and blustery wind, but she was relieved to be outside. Even opening the front door to commence her journey had felt like lifting the lid on a boiling pot, venting the pressure that was building up within. An atmosphere of gloom had descended upon No. 52, and from experience Sarah knew it was destined to continue for at least another day or so.

Dr Simpson had a tendency to retreat to his room from time to time, when his reserves of energy and enthusiasm had been drained to the very dregs by what he was forced to confront on a daily basis. She understood there had been a case that had gone badly and for which he blamed himself. In the year or so she had been working at Queen Street, she had learned that Simpson was generous in spreading the happiness of his successes, but the corollary was that his failures he took very much to heart.

So when this outing was suggested, Sarah had seized the opportunity, despite Mrs Lyndsay's reservations about the propriety of it.

'Whoever heard of such a thing?' she had said, kneading dough with a degree of violence provoked by having had her well-developed sense of decorum thus offended. 'A housemaid accompanying the gentlemen of the house on a walking tour of the city? No good will come of it, you know.'

She would have forbidden it altogether, Sarah had no doubt, but that it was Dr Keith who had requested Sarah's presence and secured Mrs Lyndsay's agreement before telling her why he required her. The cook was already simmering that her suspension of Sarah's clinic duties had been cut short at Dr Keith's insistence, so Sarah knew she would be made to pay for this later in extra chores and Mrs Lyndsay's glowering disapproval. Nonetheless, she was determined to enjoy her excursion in the meantime.

Sarah had thought that the walk might provide an opportunity for sharing any new intelligence on the matter of Evie and Rose. She had been attempting to make her way through Christison's *Treatise on Poisons* (the book having been surrendered by Raven, who had entirely given up on it) but it was an imposingly weighty volume and her time was limited. She was finding the book fascinating, but her reading so far had failed to shed any light on their particular area of interest. She wished she had all day to study it. How blessed was the lot of a student, she thought.

Raven was unusually quiet, as if the pervading melancholy of the house was proving contagious. He was often sullen, but he usually had something to say for himself, even when it seemed inappropriate; in fact, especially when it seemed inappropriate. He walked beside her in silence, hands in his pockets, kicking at loose stones on the cobbles.

'How did he talk you into this?' Sarah asked. She nodded towards George Keith, who was striding on ahead, muttering excitedly about the clear conditions and the implications this had for the morning's events.

'He thought I was in need of distraction.'

'Are you?'

'I suppose I am. I'm beginning to feel that I am in over my head, entering into a profession that is doomed to be forever fighting a losing battle.'

Sarah felt her hackles rise at this pompous perspective, putting himself at the centre of an almighty drama. He was exhibiting the male trait of believing the world revolved around them, usually because it did.

'That seems a rather self-indulgent interpretation,' she told him, attempting to keep the annoyance out of her voice, though it was evident enough in her words.

'What would you know about it?'

'You forget that some would be happy to have your problems. To be learning a profession,' she added pointedly.

Raven took on an unusually sheepish demeanour. Unlike some men, at least this indicated he had understood her point.

'Nonetheless, that doesn't make it any easier to be every day confronted with suffering and death.'

Sarah looked at his face, the dark circles around his eyes, the scar still livid on his cheek, and felt her anger subside.

'My grandmother once told me about a king who sought a single thought that would raise his spirits when they were low, but keep him vigilant when he was happy.'

Raven lifted his head, curious if not optimistic about what she might be able to offer.

'A wise man told the king but four words: "This too will pass." Dr Simpson won't remain cloistered in his room for long, and things have been worse than this before now.'

'In what way?'

'You'll have noticed Mrs Simpson is in mourning?'

'I had not thought black to be the new fashion.'

'They lost their daughter in February. Mary Catherine. Just before her second birthday. They had already lost their first daughter, Maggie, at the age of four.'

'What did they die of?'

In other company Sarah would have considered this to be a heartless and insensitive enquiry, but she was sufficiently used to medical men by now that it came as no surprise. It would have been unusual if he had not sought clarification upon this point.

'Maggie was before my time,' she replied. 'Mary Catherine died of scarlet fever. It was awful. She kept crying out for water but couldn't drink it.'

'I'm sorry,' he said. 'It's difficult watching a child die.'

'It's difficult watching anyone die, is it not?'

Raven looked pensive. 'Some deaths are easier than others.'

'I suppose you're in a better position to judge, though I have seen my fair share.'

'Have you, now,' he said. His tone was distinctly sceptical.

Sarah stopped walking.

'My mother died in childbirth and my father followed shortly after. Of a broken heart, the doctor said. That is how I came to be working here. I had no one, and our minister knew Dr Simpson.'

Raven had the decency to look contrite.

'I'm sorry if I seemed insensitive. Hazard of the job.'

They walked on again in silence for a few yards, George Keith pressing on ahead of them up the slope. Despite the cold it was a fine day to be out, as the wind had blown away the fog and the sun was shining from a clear sky. As they ascended Calton Hill, Edinburgh fell away beneath them in all directions. To the north Sarah could see all the way to the Forth and beyond, sails dotted along the water in a procession in and out of Leith. The geometry of the New Town was strikingly vivid from up here too, its layout so precise and uniform in contrast to all the districts that surrounded it. It spoke of order and elegance, but also of rigidity and unbending rules.

When Raven spoke again, his tone was pitched a little brighter.

'Miss Grindlay seems remarkably unaffected by the prevailing gloom, don't you think?'

It was true that Mina had been in unusually high spirits for the best part of a week.

'Why do you think that is?' he continued.

'I imagine we have your acquaintance Dr Beattie to thank.'

'Beattie?'

She could be wrong, but Raven seemed oddly uncomfortable at the mention of his name. She had assumed they were friends, but she knew how medical men were in the habit of falling out.

'Yes. They have been seeing a great deal of each other.'

Raven nodded to himself. 'Now that you mention it, I was sure I had smelt his cologne on occasion when I returned from my duties.'

'I would have thought you more surprised,' she confessed.

'Why?'

'I had not thought Mina the type to take Beattie's interest. She is older than him and I cannot think that he would want for younger ladies' affections.'

Raven snorted. 'Jealous, are you?'

'Don't be ridiculous. What interest would I have in such a man?'

'The same interest that a great many women seem to have. As you say, he does not want for younger ladies' affections.'

'Jealous, are you?' Sarah batted back.

Raven ignored this. 'Beattie is older than he appears, and he told me he has come to find such flirtatious attentions trivial and tiresome. I got the impression that he might have found something in Mina that these other women lack.'

'Yes,' she replied, 'her brother-in-law's name and the connections attached to it.'

Raven seemed shocked at her bluntness, enough to make her fear she had overstepped the mark.

'I only say this because I would hate to see Miss Grindlay deceived.'

'It is not an outlandish suggestion,' Raven conceded. 'But equally, though Mina may be in want of a husband, she does not strike me as naive in such matters. What they see in each other may not be what the rest of us assume. She may be aware that the Simpson connection confers certain advantages, but that does not preclude a companionship.'

Sarah frowned. 'You make it seem like a business transaction. It makes sense but it sounds terribly bloodless.'

'In marriage, there are worse things to be than bloodless,' Raven replied.

'How do you mean?'

She could tell from his eyes that he was not going to elaborate.

'Let's just say that while you lost your father too soon, I did not lose mine soon enough.'

As they skirted the Royal Observatory, hurrying to catch up with Dr Keith, Sarah tripped on a loose cobblestone. Raven grabbed her arm to prevent her from falling, keeping hold of it thereafter. His grip was strong and she found she had no objection to it.

'Do you have an interest in photography?' he asked.

'I can't say that I know much about it, but Dr Keith has been kind enough to show me his daguerreotypes. From his travels in Palestine and Syria.'

'Lucky you,' said Raven, smiling for the first time that day.

THIRTY

aven felt himself already in better spirits by the time they arrived at Rock House, the walk having the effect Keith so faithfully promised. He would have to admit that the chance to talk with Sarah had done him good too. Perhaps it was merely relief at the contrast to how badly their early encounters had gone, but he derived a degree of satisfaction from merely conversing with her without rancour.

He had even found himself smiling for the first time in days, and was pleased that he could do so without producing any sense of pain or tightness in the left side of his face.

Rock House was a two-storey building with a courtyard to the front of it boasting a small fountain with a Grecian urn in its centre. It was only a stone's throw from Princes Street and yet seemed to be held in an arboreal cocoon, sheltered from the noise and smog of the city. It was surprising then that Keith had to knock several times before the door was answered.

'They'll be in the garden, I should imagine,' he said as they waited. 'They generally take their photographs outdoors.' He pointed at the sky. 'For the light.'

When the door opened it was a woman who greeted them. She wore an apron but no cap, and had a black stain on the back of one hand, visible when she tucked a stray curl of greying hair behind her ear.

'Good day to you, Miss Mann. We are expected.'

'Of course, Dr Keith. Come in. We are all out at the back.'

She turned and led the way through the house to the garden. Raven followed Keith, leaving Sarah to close the door.

'Miss Mann is the indispensable assistant of Mr Hill and Mr Adamson,' Keith explained as they marched in procession through the narrow hallway.

They emerged into the garden, where it appeared that the house had extruded most of its furniture. There were chairs, a table, wall hangings and a birdcage all arranged as if it were the corner of a well-appointed drawing room. Two men were busy manoeuvring the camera into position. They were so absorbed in their task that they were initially unaware of the arrival of their visitors. Miss Mann loudly cleared her throat and the pair of them looked up in unison.

'Ah, George. You have brought us some willing subjects, I see,' said one, as though this had not all been carefully arranged. The speaker was lively in his features, a great mane of hair spilling about his face. He strode forth and enthusiastically shook their hands, including the surprised-looking Sarah.

'David Octavius Hill at your service. And this,' he said, waving his hand in the direction of the other man, 'is my good friend and colleague Mr Robert Adamson.'

Mr Adamson was the younger of the two, thin and frail-looking. He merely nodded in acknowledgment and resumed his work.

'Mr Adamson is the technical genius within this partnership,' Hill continued. 'He has mastered the method of creating the calotype. I know not the process though it is under my nose continuously, and I believe that I never will. I for my part organise the subject. Together we make art.'

Raven considered this a rather grandiloquent claim to make

until he was shown some of the fruits of their labour. A picture of the Scott Monument before its completion made a particular impression upon him. The clarity of the image and the detail that could be discerned in it were remarkable, a moment frozen in time.

'We had to climb onto the roof of the Royal Institution with the camera to get that one,' Hill said.

The rest of the album of prints consisted principally of sombre men in dark suits. Before he could ask about these uniformly severe-looking sitters, the doorbell rang out and Mr Hill rushed off to answer it.

He returned with another visitor, a tall woman towering a full head above him.

'Here is Miss Rigby,' he explained. 'Writer, patron of the arts and a great supporter of our endeavours here.'

'Not to mention occasional sitter,' said Miss Rigby, removing her hat. 'When you can be forced to drag your attention away from the fat martyrs of the Free Kirk,' she added, indicating the prints Raven was looking at. 'Mr Hill has spent an inordinate amount of time procuring the images of all these ministers for his great Disruption painting. But between you and me, I can't see it ever being finished. He has fortunately begun to cast his artistic net a little wider.'

She regarded Raven with an intensity that he found disconcerting, as though he were being physically assessed. He looked instinctively for Sarah, uncomfortable beneath this woman's forthright scrutiny, though he could not rightly say what succour he thought she might offer. In any case, she had wandered off to the other end of the garden, watching Mr Adamson and Miss Mann as they made various adjustments to the camera.

'I think you will find that the Newhaven photographs are far more interesting,' Miss Rigby said as Raven continued to turn the pages of the book, an on-going catalogue of grim-faced clergymen.

He stopped suddenly, recognising the face that presently glowered at him from the open page.

'Here's one I am familiar with,' he stated. 'The Reverend Malachy Grissom.'

'You're not of his congregation, are you?'

The manner of Miss Rigby's asking indicated that an affirmative answer would be met with disapproval.

'No, though I have heard him preach. He was blaming immodest women for male lust and railing against prostitutes.'

Miss Rigby wore a slyly amused smile. 'Railing against them? That's a term for it I haven't heard before.'

Raven looked up at her. 'I'm sorry, I don't understand.'

Rigby was remarkably tall and thin, her hair clamped in tight coils at the side of her head. She spoke with authority and candour, which was surprising in that she was undeniably a lady and yet seemingly prepared to discuss all manner of subjects with a man to whom she had only just been introduced. Raven suddenly had an image of her picking up the miserable Reverend Grissom bodily and breaking him over her knee.

'From what I am told, the Reverend Grissom knows of what he speaks. Strident denunciations most often hide a secret shame,' she continued, entirely unabashed by the direction she was taking the conversation.

Raven could not envisage her being abashed by much. He preferred this manner of dialogue to the empty pleasantries that one was normally forced to endure in such circumstances.

'Are you saying he has been consorting with prostitutes?'

'Not *consorting* with them, Mr Raven. Using them. Exploiting them.'

The word fell from Miss Rigby's lips so matter-of-factly, and yet as it lit upon his ears it echoed like thunder.

Raven was simultaneously in awe of this woman and terrified of her. She seemed to grow even taller before him, or perhaps it was that he felt like he was shrinking as he considered what she might think of him if she knew that he had thus used Evie.

'But how could a fellow in his position expect to get away with such behaviour?'

'It is the downfall of many a proud man to imagine everyone around him stupid. He frequents places where he thinks he is unknown, although perhaps the good Reverend should have travelled a little beyond Leith and Newhaven. He forgets that even prostitutes will sometimes attend church.'

Further conversation was interrupted by Mr Hill deciding that Raven should now be positioned for his portrait.

He was placed in an upholstered chair beside the birdcage, his face examined from every angle. The position of his arms was arranged and rearranged several times before Hill was satisfied.

Miss Mann handed Mr Adamson a wooden box that was slid into position at the back of the camera. Adamson buried his head under a piece of cloth and removed a cap from the front of the machine while Miss Mann counted off the seconds with a pocket watch.

Raven thought he had remained still, but he noticed Adamson shake his head.

'You moved your arm,' Hill stated wearily.

'A full minute is required for the exposure,' Miss Mann reproached him with a sigh. 'I'll get some more paper.'

Raven was posed a second time, on this occasion with the aid of a box to rest his arm upon, assured its black colour would render it invisible in the finished picture. He felt he was entirely still throughout the ensuing minute, but neither Hill nor Adamson looked particularly pleased.

'We usually pose children as though asleep,' Miss Mann muttered. 'Perhaps we could try that.'

This suggestion turned out not to be in earnest but by way of reproach, and Raven was relieved of his role as sitter. A short time later, he was warming himself with a cup of tea while watching Hill position Sarah. She was seated in a chair, her head turned to the side and resting gracefully on one hand. She had a purple shawl wrapped around her shoulders and her hair was loosely tied at the nape. Hill stepped back and examined her from several angles before announcing that he was content. He implored her to remain as still as possible, looking pointedly at Raven.

Sarah exhibited no similar difficulty, remaining entirely immobile as though she had fallen into an open-eyed trance.

She was not the only one. Raven found himself gazing rapt at her face, the paleness of her skin, the golden highlights in her hair. A sense of tranquillity settled upon him, as though the serenity of her stillness had somehow been transferred to him.

'You seem transfixed,' observed Hill quietly, walking past. 'A pity you could not have held such a pose earlier.'

THIRTY-ONE

arah watched Miss Mann carefully remove the plate from the camera, handling it like a newborn. Her gaze was trained intently upon what she was about, but she still noticed Sarah's attention.

'You made an excellent subject, Miss Fisher. You could sit for a painter with such poise.'

It was a pleasant thought, but Sarah could not imagine ever having such a luxury of time.

'I would be most interested to know what happens next,' she observed. 'The calotype process is a matter of chemistry, is it not?'

Miss Mann looked at her with a degree of consternation that made Sarah fear she had misspoken.

'Or am I mistaken?'

'No, you are quite correct. I was simply taken aback. Most of our subjects are more apt to believe it the work of fairies and angels. And that's just the clergymen. Do you have an interest in chemistry?'

'I have read Professor Gregory's work, but I have not had the opportunity to practise experiments.'

Miss Mann seemed pleased with her answer, which in turn pleased Sarah.

'Would you care to accompany me? I can show you how it's done.'

'I'd like that,' she replied.

They strode towards the house together, the plate still clutched possessively in Miss Mann's hands.

'You took Mr Hill's instruction very well,' she said.

'I am a housemaid. I am used to doing as I am told.'

'You would be surprised. The most subservient of people can nonetheless struggle to follow instructions, while the mighty are prepared to humble themselves when a portrait is at stake. I once photographed the King of Saxony, and had you been there that day, you might have believed I was the monarch and he my subject.'

'You photographed a king?'

'Yes. He turned up at Rock House unannounced, Mr Hill and Mr Adamson's reputation having reached him abroad. Unfortunately, neither of the gentlemen were at home. I told him I could carry out the procedure and he gladly acquiesced.'

Sarah was agog. She thought of the leering squirt rolling pills behind the druggist's counter not a mile from here. Clearly there were some customers who did not always believe that 'only a man will do'.

'And was he pleased with the result?'

'Enchanted. He said it would have pride of place in his palace. Though as the name Jessie Mann is of less renown than Hill and Adamson, I suspect it will be theirs and not mine attached to it.'

'That is unjust,' Sarah stated.

Miss Mann did not reply, for what else could be said?

She led them into a room in which newspaper had been affixed to the window to block out the light.

'We need relative darkness for the preparation of the calotype paper,' she explained.

Sarah went to close the door, out of habit.

'Leave it for now, otherwise I won't be able to show you anything.'

'Of course.'

Miss Mann indicated a table laden with bottles and shallow trays. 'A piece of good-quality paper is first washed in a solution of silver nitrate then a solution of iodine. Once dry, this iodised paper is dipped in a mixture of gallic acid and silver nitrate, and it is this which is placed in the frame that is slid into the back of the camera.'

Miss Mann held up her right hand, which was streaked with black. 'It is a dark art,' she said. 'The silver nitrate stains the skin.'

'How did you come to be involved with Mr Hill and Mr Adamson?' Sarah asked, watching as Miss Mann pinned a piece of prepared calotype paper to a wooden frame.

'My brother Alexander and Mr Hill are friends,' she replied. 'I am a supporter of the Free Church, and have been helping him with the photographs for his Disruption painting. His interests have extended beyond that now, of course, which makes me wonder sometimes if the painting will ever be done.'

'What exactly will the painting depict?'

'It will be a representation of the meeting at Tanfield Hall that followed the mass walkout from the General Assembly by two hundred ministers and elders. As Mr Hill wishes to depict all who were present, he is using calotype to record their faces, that he may work from the photographs.'

Sarah thought of her grandmother, who dispensed wise words as well as herbal remedies. *Where there are men, there will be dispute*, she once said. *Put ten of them in a room and soon enough you'll have two groups of five.*

Sarah watched Miss Mann carefully prepare the next plate.

'You must have a remarkable knowledge of chemistry to be able to do all of this.'

'Only as it pertains to the photographic process. Mr Adamson is a patient teacher. Why do you ask?'

Sarah paused for a second. She felt oddly dishonest to be speaking about this, though she was bearing no false witness.

'An acquaintance of mine died recently, and when she was found, her body was contorted as though she had suffered a fit of some kind. There seems a possibility that she took a poison, though unless I can discern what, I will never know whether she died accidentally or . . .'

Sarah let the other possibility remain unspoken.

Miss Mann put down the framed sheet she was holding. 'I am most sorry to hear that.' She placed the stained hand on Sarah's arm and spoke softly. 'Was it likely that your friend meant herself harm? I mean, did she have reason?'

'I believe she was most troubled. But it makes no sense that she should choose a means whose effects would be so unpleasant.'

'Your description does remind me of something,' Miss Mann said. 'A relative of mine was suffering from a neurological palsy. She was given a tonic medicine which helped for a while, but she kept increasing the dose. It brought on increasingly severe convulsions and eventually killed her. Her body remained in a contorted pose for a long time after. It made it impossible to lay her out properly, which caused a deal of additional distress for the mourners. There was some concern that they wouldn't be able to chest her. You know, fit her into a casket.'

'Do you know what was in the tonic?' Sarah asked.

'Yes. It contained strychnine.'

THIRTY-TWO

he pavements seemed busier as they made their way back down Calton Hill towards Princes Street. Sarah heard a whistle carried on the wind, and in the middle distance she could see steam rising from the new North Bridge station. The sight of clouds rising from below rather than floating up above was one she might be a long time in getting used to. She had only once travelled on a train and had found the experience noisy and frightening.

Dr Keith was not with them, having remained at Rock House taking lunch with his friends. Sarah had explained that she needed to return to Queen Street and her duties, and expected to be walking back alone, but Raven had announced that he also had matters to attend. Sarah was not sure whether this was true, given Dr Simpson's on-going self-confinement, and allowed herself a moment of pleasure that Raven had chosen accompanying her over the prospect of what would undoubtedly have been a sumptuous meal in the company of Messrs Hill and Adamson, as well as the remarkable Miss Mann and the formidable Miss Rigby.

However, once they began talking, she realised that perhaps his principal motive was his impatience to impart Miss Rigby's revelation.

'The Reverend Grissom using prostitutes?' Sarah asked. She

kept her voice low, wary as much of passing pedestrians as of being overheard by someone at an open window. 'Surely she must have been mistaken?'

'She was adamant that he is well known to the pinch-cocks of Newhaven and Leith. Is it so hard to believe?'

Sarah was conscious of an innate sense of duty driving her to question it, and she wondered why this should be so. What made a minister's word or reputation seem beyond question? It was possible that Miss Rigby might be mistaken or even motivated by malice (she certainly had not spoken with much reverence for the 'fat martyrs', as she described them), but Sarah could not envisage the woman making such a serious accusation without having a profound conviction that it was true.

'I suppose such a thing is easier for you to believe,' she replied, which made Raven's cheeks burn a little.

'I sorely doubt I was the only student to do so, as much as I doubt Grissom to be the only minister. And as he is connected to the Sheldrake household, I have to ask myself where else he might have spilled his seed.'

Sarah's voice dropped to barely more than a whisper. 'Are you suggesting . . .?'

She stopped there, unprepared to even voice the words.

'When we heard him preach, he seemed intent on blaming women for the temptations to which men succumb. Miss Rigby suggests he has often fallen to such temptations. Grissom is the Sheldrakes' minister. Rose would have attended his services and I am sure he must have visited the Sheldrakes' house, as I believe Mr Sheldrake is a benefactor of his new ministry.'

Sarah recalled her impression of an awkward and self-regarding little imp. She would admit that she could imagine him using prostitutes to slake his lust, but housemaids were another matter.

'What would make Rose want anything to do with him?' she asked.

'He is an important man. Status, influence and respect might exert an intoxicating influence on a young woman who has none of those things. And if she found herself pregnant by him, he might find himself in a difficult spot.'

Sarah felt a shudder run through her, as though she might face a terrible reckoning for even entertaining these notions. It was one thing to claim that the Reverend Grissom was a hypocrite, but quite another to suggest him capable of murder.

'We are looking for a common cause for Rose and Evie's deaths,' she reminded him. 'My conversation with Miss Mann leads me to believe that strychnine might have been responsible for their contorted conditions. She knew someone who died of it and was left similarly twisted. There is nothing that connects Grissom to Evie.'

'Is it unreasonable to speculate that his appetites took him to the Canongate as well as to Newhaven?'

'I can accept that complacency might make him think he would not be recognised further afield, but surely he would not go whoring half a mile from his own church?'

'Such a man might believe himself beyond suspicion. If he was seen entering or leaving a bawdy house, he could claim he was interested in their souls, not their bodies, trying to convince them away from their lives of sin. Nobody would believe the word of a whore over that of a minister.'

Sarah had to concede this point, but in it also lay the reason Grissom would have had nothing to fear from Rose.

'Nor would they believe the word of a housemaid claiming a man of the Church had got her pregnant.'

'Unless Grissom feared Rose's employer might believe her. Why would she lie about something so heinous?'

Sarah failed to suppress a scornful look. 'Speaking as a housemaid, I find that extraordinarily unlikely. The family would not entertain the scandal. A pregnant housemaid would be embarrassing enough, but an accusation against their reverend minister would be intolerable. No, I consider your hypothesis hopelessly flawed, Mr Raven. Nor have you offered any reason why he would wish to harm Evie.'

Sarah turned to him for a response, but his eyes were looking down Leith Street.

'Do you ever recollect seeing him around Evie's lodgings?' she asked.

'I vaguely recognised his face when we went to the church, but no, I don't recall seeing him down at that end of the Canongate. I certainly don't remember seeing him the night I found Evie dead. One of her friends said the only person who visited that night was a woman.'

'Who was this friend?'

Raven did not answer. Instead he put a hand around Sarah's waist and pulled her bodily into the darkness of a narrow close. In the work of a second she found herself plucked from the brightness of the street and thrust against the wall in a cramped and dank passage, just beyond where the light spilled in.

'What on earth do you think you're doing?' she tried to ask but Raven had already clamped a hand across her mouth. She grabbed his arm with one hand, her other pushing his chest, but he was strong and lithe. Physically she was no match for him.

Shock and anger quickly gave in to dread and fear as she wondered what outrage might be inflicted upon her. Was this the real reason he had opted to leave Rock House and accompany her alone? She tried to wriggle free, but Raven's grip only tightened. She looked desperately into his eyes, which stared back manically, pupils ever widening. Loosening his hold of her with one hand, he put his index finger to his lips. He gestured with his eyes towards the mouth of the close.

Sarah heard male voices approach, one of them rumbling and gruff, the other reedy and nasal. She saw two fellows briefly pass: a rodent-like specimen who looked all the smaller next to the freakish creature alongside. She was allowed only the briefest glimpse as he strode past, due to the speed of his lolloping and awkward gait. He was an ugly and overgrown individual, benighted by some hideous condition that had inconsistently enlarged certain parts of him in the most grotesque manner.

She looked back at Raven as the voices receded, saw the tension in his face lest they turn around again.

She realised that these were the people Raven had been so vigilantly looking out for. Also in that moment, it struck her why he was in their debt, and she felt a little ashamed for not having worked it out before.

Evie had asked him for money, in urgent need. Raven had borrowed it from them though he had no swift means of paying it back; had put himself in danger to help her.

She hardly dared breathe now, her eyes drawn to the scar barely hidden by Raven's developing beard. She recalled the mess of his face when he first arrived at Queen Street, the deep slash upon a cheek held together by cat-gut, and the bruising upon his body. The men who had inflicted it were mere yards away, still in earshot. She stood perfectly still, perfectly silent, not daring to make a sound until they were sure the danger was truly past.

Long after the footsteps and voices had receded, she and Raven remained motionless, their faces barely inches apart, hardly breathing. The intent look in Raven's eyes became something else, their gazes locked upon one another. With her hand still pressed upon his chest, Sarah could feel his heartbeat and thought he must be able to hear her own.

She felt unaccustomed stirrings in unaccustomed places. She wanted to feel his lips upon hers, wanted him to pull her closer.

Raven backed away, though. Edging to the mouth of the passage, he risked a look along the street. The moment had passed. With the spell broken, Sarah felt a flush of relief that nothing had happened. Nonetheless, as she stepped back into the light, she was trembling from head to toe, and not from fright.

THIRTY-THREE

here was frost on the ground as Raven accompanied Simpson along Princes Street, the paving stones slippery underfoot, a glowering sky above promising snow. Adding a further element of hazard was Glen the hound, which seemed determined to entangle him in the coils of its lead as it looped and slalomed before its master.

They were late, or in growing jeopardy of being so, and what was particularly annoying was that Raven had no enthusiasm for reaching his destination. He was being excused from assisting at this afternoon's lectures because Professor Syme was carrying out surgical procedures and Simpson felt Raven should take the opportunity to observe. Having once studied under Syme, Raven had not wanted for such opportunities and lacked any desire to seize another, but he knew not to question the professor's will in such matters.

They were proceeding on foot rather than enjoying the speed and comfort of the brougham because, since Simpson's emergence from his great depression, George Keith had been prevailing upon him with typical evangelism regarding the benefits of simple diet, fresh air and exercise. Simpson had listened with much patience and consideration before ultimately deciding that two out of three would have to suffice. 'I agree with much of George's thinking,' he had told Raven, 'but I draw the line at there being any benefit to culinary asceticism sufficient to offset the impact on one's soul. I am of the opinion that we should live to eat, not merely eat to live.'

Spoken like one used to Mrs Lyndsay's cooking rather than Mrs Cherry's, Raven mused.

Simpson walked for the most part at a brisk pace, barrelling along the pavement with a redoubtable energy that Raven was relieved to see fully restored. However, their progress was slower than it ought to have been due to the fact that Simpson knew simply everybody. With most people there was time for merely a nod and a greeting, but with others there were longer courtesies to be observed, particularly as Simpson had been in confinement and there was catching up to do.

As they passed Kennington and Jenner's store, the professor stopped once more, he and a fellow pedestrian having recognised one another with mutual surprise and delight.

'I would not have known you, sir,' Simpson told him. 'You are considerably changed since our student days.'

'I will take that as a compliment,' the man replied.

'Will Raven, this is Mr David Waldie,' Simpson said warmly, and they shook hands, Waldie's encased in fine leather gloves against the cold. He was a slight man about the same age as the professor, mid-thirties, and peering through spectacles as though Raven was under his microscope.

'Are you currently residing in Edinburgh?' Simpson asked. 'I had thought that you moved away some time ago.'

'I am visiting relatives. I live and work in Liverpool these days, as a chemist for the Liverpool Apothecaries Company.'

'I know the city well,' the professor replied. 'My wife hails from there.'

Having heard that Waldie worked as a chemist, Simpson was not long in turning the conversation to his great quest, explaining the work that had been done with ether and his search for an improved alternative.

'In all your chemical endeavours, have you encountered anything that might exhibit comparable properties?'

Simpson was truly indefatigable in the search for his Holy Grail, but Raven feared his efforts were ultimately going to prove as fruitless as every knight before him. He was beginning to think that ether might prove as good as it got, and far from being the first in a series of ever-improving anaesthetic agents, it would turn out to be an anomaly, the mirage promising water in the desert.

'There is something called perchloride of formyle,' Waldie said.

'The name is not familiar. What is it?'

'A component of chloric ether cordial, a popular remedy in Liverpool for the management of asthma and the relief of chronic cough. The vapour of this cordial has been tried as an anaesthetic on several occasions but was unsuccessful. Nonetheless, I think it may have potential.'

Simpson's features were alert, and Glen, sensing his master's interest, was looking up at Waldie with eagerness as though he might throw the dog some meat.

'Why?'

'The lack of success with the cordial is unsurprising as the amount of the perchloride in it is small – the patients would have been in effect breathing only the vapour of alcohol. I have devised a method of manufacture that produces a pure form of the chemical, which is then dissolved in rectified spirit. It is this pure form that I think may be of interest to you. On my return to Liverpool I would be more than happy to send you a sample.'

'I would be much obliged to you, sir.'

One more thing to sniff after a future dinner, Raven thought.

'A serendipitous encounter?' he asked as they resumed their progress.

'Och, you never know,' Simpson replied, sounding less enthusiastic than he had during the conversation. 'I have to investigate every avenue, but if I remember Waldie, he is as apt to blow up his own laboratory as to come up with something ingenious.'

They did not make it as far as West Register Street before Simpson encountered another acquaintance, this time Professor Alison. At this point, Raven was compelled to make his apologies. 'I will need to take my leave and walk on, sir. Professor Syme deplores late-comers.'

As he deplores most things, Raven thought, hurrying towards the North Bridge.

Raven broke into a run to make up time, though he was conscious this might make him conspicuous. It spoke of his enduring terror of Syme that he was more afraid of incurring his wrath than of increasing the risk of being spotted by Flint's men.

His thoughts turned to his most recent sighting of them, on his way back from Rock House. In truth, his thoughts had turned to it frequently in the days since, but only because of what his evasive action had precipitated. That briefest frisson between him and Sarah, a glimpse of tantalising possibilities. Raven's instincts warned him that less trouble awaited down the path leading to the Weasel and Gargantua. Nonetheless, his mind kept returning to the moment, and wondering whether hers did too.

As he walked past the courtyard at the university, Raven became aware of an unmistakable smell of oranges – or bergamot, as Beattie had corrected him – and a moment later the man himself fell into step alongside. A cold breeze was blowing in from the east, from which Raven's care-worn jacket was offering scant protection. His companion, by contrast, was swathed in a flowing greatcoat that made him appear to glide along the cobbles. It made him appear taller too, while Raven's lack of a similar garment caused him to shrink into himself.

Though Beattie had visited Queen Street a number of times since the death of Mrs Graseby, Raven had not found himself alone with him and had therefore enjoyed no opportunity to discuss it – or indeed anything else. The estrangement saddened him. He had felt they were on the verge of a valuable friendship, but knew now that this dreadful thing would always be between them – unless this was another lesson he needed to learn: that such professional tragedies were part of the job. He therefore wasted no time in broaching the subject.

'I have been meaning to enquire, was there any manner of investigation following what happened at Danube Street?'

Beattie wore a burdened expression as he replied: 'She died under her doctor, so I was able to handle the formalities. However, the smell of ether hung about the place for a long time afterwards, raising curiosity among the staff. They were too ignorant to ask the right questions, but one's concern is always who they might have mentioned it to.'

This was not the stuff of Raven's dread fears, but nor was it entirely reassuring.

'I am sure I didn't overdose her. She must have had an unforeseen reaction.'

'Possibly. What is without doubt is that my patient died as a result of your anaesthetic, though why that was, we may never know. Which is why I have endeavoured to ensure that you do not find yourself accused.'

'And thus I am indebted to you, John. Whatever I can do to repay you, please let me know.'

Beattie gave him a sincere nod. 'I will hold you to that. In the meantime, I am sure you must be aware of my interest in Miss Grindlay, so if Dr Simpson or anyone else in the household should ask about my character, I assume I can rely upon you to speak generously?'

Raven stopped his tongue before offering the assurance Beattie sought, recalling his discussion with Sarah. He owed Beattie a debt, but felt compelled by an instinctive loyalty towards the household that had taken him in.

'If you can guarantee that your affections are genuine and that Miss Grindlay is the sole object of them.'

Beattie stopped and shot him a piercing look, a volatile mixture of shock, dismay, insult and outrage. Raven had never seen such fury in his face before, which was usually a picture of concentration or composure.

'I do not mean to offend,' he attempted to explain. 'It is merely that—'

'You have such a low opinion of Miss Grindlay that you cannot believe I would be drawn to her?'

'Quite the opposite. We are all of us at Queen Street protective of Mina, so the household would not forgive it if I were party to an advance that proved –' he sought for the word '– insincere.'

Beattie opened his mouth to retort, then appeared to think better of what he was going to say. That familiar composure fell over his face like a mask covering his anger.

'Do you recall how I told you that true sorrow would grant you perspective?'

'Indeed,' Raven answered humbly.

'It does not merely apply to medicine. I was once betrothed, to a young woman who lit up the world like the morning sun. You would have no difficulty in imagining my intentions towards her sincere. She was the love of my life, as she would have been the love of anyone's. But she died the day before we were to be married. She was thrown from her horse.'

Raven felt half Beattie's height. The man's life had been ripped apart, not once, with the deaths of his parents, but twice, and here he was, questioning his motives.

'I am so terribly sorry. What was her name?'

Beattie took a while to answer, as though he had to think about it. Clearly he was bracing himself for the pain of saying the word.

'Julia. Her name was Julia. After her death, I could not imagine a future with anyone else. I saw small aspects of her in every woman who ever showed an interest in me, and that brought me only pain. That was until Mina. Mina is the first woman I have truly seen for herself, because when I look at her I am not searching for Julia.'

Raven and Beattie resumed their march past the main Infirmary building towards the new surgical hospital in High School Yards, where they followed a large group of gentlemen making their way towards the operating theatre. It seemed half the doctors in the city would be present to observe. Syme would love that.

'I imagine it will be full today,' said a familiar and unwelcome voice. 'Novel operations always draw a crowd.'

Raven turned to see James Duncan inviting himself into their company. Perfect.

'Have you seen Syme operate before?' Duncan asked.

'Indeed,' Beattie replied.

Raven said nothing. He had seen Syme operate many times, but had no desire to share this information with either of this pair, for fear of where the conversation might lead.

'One could argue that he is the best surgeon in the country,' Duncan ventured.

Raven certainly had little doubt that Syme himself would agree.

'Did you know that he was the first in Scotland to perform an amputation through the hip joint?'

'I did,' Raven replied, suppressing a note of irritation. He disliked the way Duncan presumed upon his ignorance. As though one could be a medical student in Edinburgh and be unaware of such a thing. 'The patient died, though,' he added.

'Not for several weeks after the operation, which matters little enough.'

'I'd wager it mattered to the patient. Anyway, I don't think Dr Simpson would agree with you regarding Syme's pre-eminence.'

'Probably not,' Duncan admitted. 'I gather there is a considerable degree of animosity between them. I am told they nearly came to blows on the stairs outside a patient's bedroom.'

'Why?' asked Beattie, his face lit up with delighted curiosity.

'I believe Syme wrote an article in a professional journal in which he criticised Dr Simpson's management of a case.'

'I see,' said Raven, though he truly didn't. The senior men of medicine all seemed to indulge in this sort of behaviour. Criticising one's colleagues in the pages of a publication was not generally regarded as grounds for fisticuffs, so there had to be more to it.

The operating theatre was indeed already packed by the time they made their way inside. They found some seats at the back, where the view of the operating table was obscured by an undulating sea of headwear, a situation Raven was not inclined to complain about. Then above the low murmur of the crowd, someone shouted 'Hats! Hats!' and in a seemingly synchronous movement, all obstructing millinery was removed. Duncan leaned forward eagerly, while Beattie settled back into his seat and folded his arms in a relaxed attitude, as though it were a playhouse they were attending. Alongside them Raven felt stiff with a growing unease about what was to come.

A few minutes later the door at the back of the theatre opened and all conversation ceased. The first to enter was the instrument clerk, a small man in a large apron, who made a final check of the well-stocked table under the window. The door then opened again and Professor Syme entered, followed by Henry, who was his house surgeon.

Raven was always a little surprised by the professor's meek appearance. This leviathan of surgical practice was a small, thin man with a severe, unsmiling face. He was rather grey – eyes, hair and clothing – and his voice was muffled and lacking in power. He had neither the energy and flamboyance attributed to Liston nor the reputed oratory talents of Knox. In fact, there was something altogether miserable about Professor Syme, and Raven would have doubted the many stories of his voluble ill temper had he not experienced such displays first-hand. Despite this, he was reputed to induce a profound loyalty in those who worked closely with him. Perhaps beneath his sullen exterior lurked a magnanimous and caring individual, but Raven had encountered no evidence to support this notion and plenty to refute it.

Syme had demonstrated an open disdain towards Raven during the brief period he studied surgery under him, the roots of which he attributed to one unfortunate incident in this very theatre. It happened during a warm afternoon in August, shortly after Raven began attending the university. The room had been as crowded as it was today, but also stiflingly hot, and Raven was feeling light-headed even before the operation began. He recalled how the smell of putrefaction from the patient's diseased limb filled his nose and his throat, as though he might choke on it, then the grinding of the knife cutting through bone, combined with the horrifying screams of the patient, caused him to feel sick. He had tried to rush from the room, but his way was barred by spectators, too intent upon the spectacle to notice his urgent need to get past. Thus delayed, he had vomited as he neared the door, in full view of Syme, thereby marking him in the Professor of Surgery's sharp and unforgiving eyes. Syme had thereafter treated him like a cur, singling him out for ridicule any time he needed to make a point to Raven's peers.

He particularly recalled the laughter and mockery of Syme's surgical dressers. Raven recognised some of the same men standing in the theatre now, lengths of cat-gut spilling from their pockets in readiness to be handed to the surgeon. Before that, they would be required for more brutal purpose.

Syme took a seat on a plain chair to the left of the operating table, bobbed his head to the assembled dignitaries in the front row and then signalled for the first case to be brought in.

'It has been said that he wastes not a word, nor a drop of blood,' Duncan whispered in admiration.

The four dressers carried in the patient upon a wicker basket, a rough red blanket pulled about him and his face buried in its folds. When he raised his head, Raven was appalled to recognise the man he had confronted over beating his wife.

Gallagher looked about himself apprehensively, taking in the large congregation of strangers who had gathered to witness his operation. He was initially reluctant to let go of the blanket, gripping it in his good hand and causing a ripple of laughter amongst the audience. This was quickly silenced by a reproving look from the still-seated professor.

Raven too could find no levity in the situation. The mirth from the gallery called to mind the words of Simpson regarding this tendency among medical men to make light of suffering: *They jest of scars only because they never felt a wound.*

Raven's hand went automatically to his cheek. He had felt that wound all right, but he was feeling something deeper now: guilt and shame.

Syme rose, and with his back to the patient addressed the room.

'This man has a putrid inflammation of the right hand,' he said, pulling back the blanket to reveal the offending appendage, which was grossly swollen and horribly discoloured. The smell of rotting flesh, synonymous with the surgical wards of the hospital, wafted all the way to the back row. Those in the audience less inured to the odour quickly sought out handkerchiefs in an attempt to blot out the olfactory assault. To Raven's nostrils it smelled all the worse for his part in it.

'It is obvious,' continued the professor, 'that amputation is required.'

Gallagher gestured at Syme with his good hand. 'I beg you, sir, is there no other way? For I am a joiner, and without my hand, my wife and I shall be for the poorhouse.'

'If I do not amputate, you will be for the grave, and what of your poor wife then?'

Gallagher offered no response other than a look of fear and confusion. The man was right, though. He would lose his livelihood:

had done the moment Raven goaded him into punching that wall. Through his vainglorious actions, Raven had condemned Mrs Gallagher to penury, driven more by his need to punish her husband than to offer her genuine help.

Syme continued to describe the procedure to the audience, oblivious to the anxiety of the patient who was being roughly coaxed from his basket. Raven had more than once witnessed those in Gallagher's position yelling and sobbing in a panic of fear, trying to escape the hefty assistants as they were hauled to the operating theatre like it was the gallows. Gallagher said nothing as one of the dressers held up the diseased limb.

'The forearm ought to be amputated by making two equal flaps from before and behind,' said Syme, pointing out to the audience where he intended to make his incisions. 'The arm should be held in the middle state of pronation and supination in order to relax the muscles equally and facilitate the operation. The hand may be removed at the wrist joint but the larger stump thus obtained is not found to facilitate the adaptation or increase the utility of an artificial hand, and the large articular surface which remains, though it may not materially delay a cure, must always cause a deformity.'

Raven wondered at the professor's insensitivity. Without doubt the patient was fortunate such an eminent surgeon was to perform his operation and thereby save his life, but surely it was a form of torture to describe within his hearing the mutilation that was about to occur. His mind was taken back to George Heriot's school, where a singularly vicious mathematics master administered the strap if one's marks did not meet his standards. Raven was a dedicated and eager pupil, but he unavoidably fell short on occasion and condemned himself to be beaten. What he recalled more than the pain was the ritual with which it was delivered. The master produced the dreaded tawse and laid it on Raven's desk, forcing him to contemplate it for the duration of the lesson, before finally delivering his thrashing at the end. To this day, Raven still harboured murderous thoughts towards the man.

While the professor was speaking, the patient had been strapped down to the table and the four surgical dressers had positioned themselves around him to provide additional physical restraint if required. It was at this point that Raven remembered Henry saying that Syme had given up on ether, finding it unreliable, not fit for purpose. This operation would be performed without it.

Raven felt suddenly sick, his guilt compounded further by his knowledge of the horror that was about to unfold. It was impossible to predict which patients would submit to their fate meekly and which would struggle; sometimes the frailest-looking specimen would find remarkable strength and attempt to withdraw the limb just as the surgeon's blade descended for the first cut. Gallagher seemed of the more submissive sort, weeping quietly and then whimpering when the professor was handed his knife.

An assistant grabbed the patient's arm just above the elbow, holding it steady. Syme began immediately, cutting through flesh with absolute certainty and precision, undistracted by Gallagher's screams. Raven was both awed and horrified by this, for he felt the anguish of every cry, and had he been holding the knife, such screams would surely have stayed his hand. He failed to understand how surgeons could work as they did, insensitive to the pain that they inflicted, speed their only clemency. It was this more than anything that had told Raven he had no future in it, and which led him to seek another field.

The professor himself was silent in his task, gesturing to the instrument clerk for what he required. Raven felt sweat run down between his shoulder blades and realised he was holding his breath. Alongside him, Beattie and Duncan watched with detached fascination, evidently troubled by no such emotional responses. They might as well have been watching Mrs Lyndsay carve a joint of ham.

Within minutes the gangrenous hand was slung into a sawdust-filled box at the end of the table, spurting vessels were quickly tied, the edges of the wound stitched together and a dressing applied to the stump.

An animalistic keening emanated from Gallagher, his eyes shuttling incredulously between the box of sawdust and the stump where his hand used to be.

One of the surgical assistants quickly wiped the blood that had collected on the operating table. Another threw fresh sawdust onto the floor, covering the majority of the blood spatter and lumps of tissue as though hiding the evidence of what had just occurred.

Raven understood now why Simpson had all but insisted he attend, why his mentor was relentless in his quest for that Holy Grail, and why he would never again complain about sniffing strange potions.

There had to be a better way than this.

THIRTY-FOUR

ain was bouncing off the pavements as the brougham drew to a halt close to the Royal Exchange. As George Keith had explained, Simpson did not keep anything so conventional as an appointment book, claiming all such relevant information to be locked safe in his head. Consequently Raven seldom knew their destination much in advance, or what the next case might involve.

He did know there had been a messenger to the house this morning during clinic, resulting in their first stop being an address in Canonmills, where Simpson had delivered a baby using his forceps. It had been an unnecessarily traumatic affair, the household being another contaminated by the Reverend Grissom's leaflets and therefore ether had not been permitted. Raven's lingering anger had occupied his mind on the subsequent journey, and he had not thought to enquire as to what was next on Simpson's mental list.

He looked up at the grimy windows looming above the pavement, wondering what sights and smells awaited inside the ramshackle tenement before him. There was a lodging inn on the ground floor, an establishment he had passed many times, but the unfamiliarity of the building itself made him realise how seldom his gaze was drawn above street level. Gazing up for too long in the Old Town was merely an invitation to pickpockets.

Simpson looked out into the driving rain and waved acknowledgement to a fellow hailing them from a doorway. Raven quickly recognised him as McLevy, the police detective, accompanied by one of his burly assistants.

Simpson turned briefly to Raven, an odd look upon his face. 'We are here to assist with a police inquiry,' he said. He seemed rather bemused by this notion, but offered no further detail as to why. 'It is always advantageous to have the constabulary owing one favours,' he added.

Raven wondered whether Simpson was waiting for a break in the rain, then observed that McLevy was coming to join them inside the carriage. He clambered in, water running around the brim of his hat even from the journey of a short few yards.

Simpson made introductions. At such moments, most men of station inferred that they could now safely ignore the apprentice, but McLevy looked Raven up and down carefully, as though taking the measure of him.

'May I pick your brains before we proceed?' McLevy asked. Though he was looking directly at him, it still took Raven a moment to realise that McLevy meant him and not the professor.

'By all means,' Raven replied.

'You may have heard tell of a scavenger discovering a bairn's leg in a gutter pipe, not far from here?'

Of course. It had been near the Royal Exchange.

'I have indeed. And I have heard all manner of gruesome explanations for it. From devil-worshipping child sacrifice to cannibalistic Irish immigrants.'

'And what do you think to it yourself, Mr Raven?'

'I would expect the cause to be more prosaic. An unwanted baby, disposed of in a hurried manner suggesting desperation and panic. The act of a person not thinking clearly.'

'Aye,' McLevy said with a nod, causing more rain to run from his hat. 'The leg was found inside a main pipe, into which pipes from all the nearby dwellings feed as well as Mr White's inn, wherein several females dwell. There are many females of a higher grade resident hereby, thus I have had to be most delicate in my investigations; perhaps too delicate, hence my lack of success up until now. This inquiry contains an imputation wont to stain a woman's name forever after.'

Raven noted that such delicacy was only to be extended when the subjects laid claim to a certain level of respectability. He could not imagine the policeman treading so lightly around Evie's lodgings. Nor did he care for how McLevy used the term 'females'. He made it sound as though he were talking about some other manner of species; exotic and of interest, no doubt, but somehow beyond the human. Or beneath it.

He wondered how McLevy would get on against Miss Rigby. She was a species apart, for sure, but one beneath nobody.

'My enquiries have so far borne little fruit, but I recently heard it said that Mr White, the landlord, has been known to impose himself upon some of the young ladies in his employ. There are staff who have bed and board in part lieu of a wage, and that can bring its complications.'

Impose.

Complications.

Raven thought there an obscenity about this politesse.

McLevy led them from the carriage and into the inn. They gathered at the foot of a staircase leading up to the lodging rooms; to their right, next to the kitchen, was a common area in which several young women were about their duties.

White was ill-named for such a red-faced individual. He did not look pleased to see McLevy, but quickly concealed this behind an oily display of obsequiousness.

'How may I help you on this occasion, Mr McLevy? Did you ever get to the bottom of that unpleasant matter that brought you here before?'

'That is indeed what brings me back, sir. I need to speak to the female domestics once again.'

White's eyes narrowed. 'As I assured you before, it would not have escaped me had one of them been in such a condition. And I would have surely acted upon it, as my house has its pride and reputation to uphold.'

As he spoke, McLevy turned his gaze to the young women, picking out one in particular for his piercing stare. She was sweeping the floor near the back door, keeping her head down just a little too keenly.

'That one there,' McLevy announced. 'I don't recall seeing her the last time.'

Raven was beginning to suspect he knew why, though he remained unsure what Simpson's role in all this might be.

'What is her name?'

'Mary Brennan,' White replied.

The girl started at the mere mention. She looked to her landlord in pale fright, though Raven was not sure whether it was him or McLevy she was more afraid of.

'We would speak with her alone.'

White issued a sigh, then told the other girls to leave the common area.

'I said we would speak with Mary alone,' McLevy reiterated with a firm tone, his eyes fixed on White.

The landlord retreated with hesitancy, sending one last look to Mary before the door closed. Raven did not imagine it escaped McLevy's notice.

Mary Brennan stood before the four of them, clutching a broom as though she might fall down without it. She was trembling.

'We are investigating the discovery of a bairn's leg, wrapped in cloth and flushed down a pipe. Do you know anything about this?'

Her eyes searched back and forth along the line, as though seeking an ally.

'No, sir,' she replied, her voice feeble. There was a determination there, however: an awareness of the stakes should she crumble.

'Do you know who this gentleman is?' McLevy asked.

'No, sir.'

'His name is Professor James Young Simpson. Does that name mean anything to you, Mary?'

Her expression was blank, but all the more worried for not knowing the potential significance of this esteemed gentleman's presence.

'He is one of the foremost medical men in the city, specialising in the care of pregnant women, and assisting them in their time of labour.'

McLevy then turned to address the professor.

'Dr Simpson, if you were to examine a young woman such as Mary here, would you be able to ascertain whether she had recently given birth?'

'Most certainly and unmistakably,' Simpson replied.

That was all it took. The girl dropped to her knees and broke down in tears, spilling forth a confession there on the floor as though relieved to be finally shedding her burden.

'God forgive me, I confess that I bore that child, but it was dead when it came into the world. Wild with sorrow and pain, I cut it into pieces and put it into the soil pipe so that nobody would know my shame.'

'Did anybody know of your condition?'

'No, sir. I kept it secret for fear I would be cast out onto the street. Mr White insists he keeps a respectable house.'

She looked to the door as she said this. A greater threat lay beyond it than anything she faced inside this room.

'Whose child was it?' McLevy asked, though the question struck Raven as redundant.

She hung her head, her hair all but sweeping the floorboards.

'A wicked man seduced me,' she answered, not looking one of them in the eye.

McLevy pressed her, but she would not name him.

She did not have to.

McLevy's assistant helped her to her feet and led her away. She looked hollow-eyed, as though entranced, then a panic enlivened her face. 'Am I to hang?' she asked McLevy, terrified.

'Not if what you told us was true, about the child being stillborn. You will only be confined a short while.'

Simpson shook his head sadly as she was led away.

'It is a tragedy that this young woman should be facing any greater punishment than that which she has already endured,' he stated.

'And it sorely compounds the injustice that there should be no consequence for the landlord,' ventured Raven, struggling to keep bitterness from his voice.

'I'll have a stern word,' McLevy assured him. 'He'll understand I have my eye on him, but what more can I do?'

Raven thought of what more he would like to do, then remembered the fate of Mrs Gallagher, in danger of the poorhouse as a consequence of his previous thirst for justice.

McLevy thanked Simpson for his assistance, which had amounted to little more than his august presence, but Raven had to commend the policeman's cunning in knowing this alone would do the trick.

'You are most welcome, as always,' Simpson replied.

'If I may ever be of assistance, just say the word.'

'Certainly. But in the meantime, I believe Mr Raven was curious about another case you were looking into.'

Raven looked at him in some surprise, and wondered how conspicuous his interest might have been.

'Which case would that be?'

'Rose Campbell,' Raven replied. 'She was a housemaid of Mr Sheldrake, the dentist. Her body was pulled from the water at Leith.'

'Oh, yes. Dr Renfrew, our police surgeon, carried out a full examination of her remains. He concluded that she had drowned.'

'So he found no trace of poison?'

'Why would he?'

'The agonised posture of her body. It is my understanding that it can be a symptom of strychnine.'

Raven was aware of Simpson regarding him with some scrutiny, but had to press on while he had McLevy here before him.

'As I say,' continued McLevy, 'no evidence of poison was found. When the bodies of the drowned are removed from the water their limbs may be contorted, indicating their final struggles, contortions which persist because of the rigidity that follows on after death.'

That may well be true, thought Raven. But Evie did not drown.

'This was a case of accidental death,' said McLevy, with a finality that suggested further questions were superfluous. Raven ignored this.

'Didn't you previously entertain the notion that she had done away with herself?'

McLevy looked at him with wariness and some surprise.

'I did indeed, as I was informed she was pregnant, as much as five or six months. But here's the strangest thing: when the post-mortem was carried out, she did not appear to be with child after all.'

Raven reeled from this, as though the walls around him had moved. 'Are you sure?'

McLevy allowed himself a grin. 'Speaking candidly, Dr Renfrew is not the greatest medical mind I have ever encountered, even on the rare occasions he is sober, but I am confident that even he would not have made a mistake about something like that.'

Raven felt numb in his confusion, the world swirling around him as the brougham pulled away, rain hammering upon its roof.

'You did not hear the answers you were hoping for,' Simpson observed.

This was to say the least. His belief in a connection between

Rose and Evie, about which he had been so certain, now appeared to be groundless. He had no real evidence that either of them had been poisoned, McLevy having provided an adequate explanation for the condition of Rose's body when he suggested rigor had set in while she was still in the water. Now it transpired that Rose had not been pregnant, and he was forced to own that it had been mere speculation on his part that Evie was with child.

'I will not intrude to ask why you were so exercised by Miss Campbell's death, but I will impart a lesson that will serve you well in all your dealings as a doctor.'

Raven looked up, eager for the comfort wisdom might bring.

'Always remember that the patient is the one with the disease.'

Raven's expression betrayed that he did not understand.

'It is easy to become burdened by responsibilities, to become so obsessed with a problem that you lose perspective. Evidence can be confounding, unlikely coincidences do happen, and an over-wrought mind can leap to wrong conclusions. Remember your own good judgment when McLevy asked how you would explain the dead baby's leg. In that instance, your detachment served you well. People often hypothesise the sensational, and become inexplicably blind to the obvious that is before their very eyes.'

THIRTY-FIVE

he rain let up as the carriage took them down the Mound and north again into the New Town. Simpson occupied himself with a book, while Raven was left to mull over what the professor had told him. He began asking himself whether he had concocted some greater malfeasance on the part of an imaginary villain as a means of dealing with his own guilt over Evie. In his need to do something for her after her death, he feared he had constructed a fantasy, pulling elements in from around him to support it, tilting at windmills like Don Quixote. Worse still, he had drawn Sarah into it too.

The brougham began to slow after turning a corner into a street that was familiar to Raven in the most uncomfortable way. With a horrible inevitability, the coachman drew his horses to a stop outside a handsome enough building, but one that he could no longer lay eyes upon without a stomach-churning guilt.

The Graseby residence.

Raven endeavoured to keep the alarm from his expression, already worried enough about how transparent Simpson found the inner workings of his mind. The professor looked up from his book as the carriage halted. His expression was briefly curious, as was often the case as he sought the item on his mental list that had brought him here. Then his visage darkened.

'Here, Mr Raven, I'm afraid I must insist we part ways. I have been called to this address on a very sensitive matter, under condition of such strict confidentiality that I am not permitted to discuss with anyone the reason for my visit.'

Raven experienced a sickening dread. It was as Beattie had feared. Someone had mentioned the lingering smell of ether in the aftermath of Mrs Graseby's death, and this had led to the summoning of the man regarded as the city's primary expert on the stuff. If there was one stroke of fortune, it was that this need for confidentiality spared Raven having to walk in there right now, to be recognised.

It would only be a matter of time, however.

'I should stay here in the meantime?' he asked.

'No, I need you to busy yourself with an errand. You recall my encounter with Mr Waldie, who told us of a cordial containing perchloride of formyle and promised to send me some?'

'I recall you said he was as likely to blow up his own laboratory as to come up with something ingenious.'

'Proving that many a prescient word is spoken in jest, his sample was never dispatched on account of a fire at the Liverpool Apothecaries Hall. It remains unclear whether Waldie was personally responsible for it, but I was intrigued by his suggestion, and as he is unlikely to make good on his promise any time soon, I asked Duncan and Flockhart to prepare a batch for trial. I need it collected.'

'Very good, sir.'

Raven hastened from the carriage, keeping his head down though the rain had stopped. He did not want to risk being seen by one of the staff at a time when they were casting their minds back to the night the mistress of their house died.

He was grateful for the walk in the fresh air, the carriage having begun to close in on him like a cell as soon as Simpson announced his reason for being there. His legs felt heavy, though. Simpson's enquiries would now surely lead to Beattie, and there would be no reason for Beattie to protect him. As he strode east along George Street, he was conscious that at that very moment, the mechanism was being set in motion whereby his medical career might soon be ended.

As he approached the druggist's, his nose was assailed by a variety of medicinal scents. Through the glass of the door, he could see a young assistant rolling pills on the marble counter and the well-dressed, bespectacled Mr Flockhart pouring a clear liquid into a number of small glass bottles. All his senses seemed enhanced right then, as though drinking in all they could because this might be the last time.

These premises had always held a fascination for him, more so than any baker's or confectioner's in his youth. The cabinets accommodated neatly ordered rows of soaps, tooth powders, lotions and liniments, while upon the shelves a hundred bottles and jars glinted in a play of colours. The floor was always swept and polished, a place where neither dirt nor disorder would be tolerated. Its greatest pull upon Raven, though, was the knowledge that within these premises they made medicines. Here they powdered, mixed, brewed and diluted, creating tinctures, pills and potions from roots, herbs, minerals and sundry other substances. Here, they experimented, developing remedies for all manner of ailments. Here, progress was made.

He had always wanted a part of this, and had relished each visit, even upon errands for Dr Duncan. He had begun to believe it a part of his world, a part of his future, but now he feared it was all about to be taken away.

Flockhart looked up from what he was doing.

'Mr Raven. You'll be here for *this*,' he said with pointed emphasis, and picked up a bottle that was sitting to his left upon the counter. It contained a fluid so viscous you could have stood up a spoon in it.

'Yes, sir. For Dr Simpson. I believe he asked you to reproduce a formula suggested by a Mr Waldie of Liverpool.'

Flockhart issued a stern sigh. 'That we did. Resulting in a small explosion which scorched our walls and ceiling and could have resulted in irreparable ocular damage had we not been wearing our spectacles at the time. I trust we can add the repainting cost to Dr Simpson's account?'

Raven did not reply, unsure whether he had the authority to approve this or even whether Flockhart was joking. He took the bottle and departed.

When he reached Queen Street, he made straight for the dining room, where he intended to leave the bottle, ready for trial after that night's dinner. He found James Duncan knelt by the open doors of the sideboard, all the previous samples and a dozen other vials laid out on the top.

'I'm attempting to rationalise this mess and dispose of a few things,' he said, his tone indicating irritation at Raven's interruption, or maybe his mere presence. 'What do you have there?'

'Something Dr Simpson requested from Duncan and Flockhart. I imagine he wants to test it after dinner.'

'Let me have a look.'

Duncan took the bottle, tilting it on its side, and frowned in disapproval at the dense liquid. He unstopped it and held the open neck to his nose, which he wrinkled, though not in reflexive response. He sniffed deeper, then shook his head, handing it back.

'Most unlikely to serve,' he predicted.

Raven had a sniff too. He thought he felt a hint of light-headedness, but this might have been resultant of having just hurried to get there.

'Perhaps if it was warmed to make it more volatile,' Raven suggested, conscious that the bottle was chilled from being outside. 'The heat of the room will render it so by the time dinner is concluded.'

'*Peut-être*,' Duncan replied, in a tone that did not sound hopeful. He had an irritating habit of slipping into French, an affectation no doubt intended to remind everyone of his having recently arrived here from his prodigious studies in Paris.

Raven felt reluctant to dismiss the bottle so quickly, then remembered Dr Simpson's entreaty not to make it about oneself when dealing with matters of evidence. He was attributing the stuff significance due to the fire it might have caused in Liverpool and the subsequent explosion in the druggist's lab, not to mention the distance he had walked in retrieving it.

'I have higher hopes for this, though,' Duncan said, holding up another bottle. He took out the stopper and held it beneath Raven's nose. There was something sharp and acrid about it, causing him to recoil. He felt an immediate sense of dizziness too. Raven could understand Duncan's optimism, but equally could already anticipate tomorrow's resultant headache.

Duncan observed him with a wolfish grin.

'What is this stuff?'

'I suggested a formula to Professor Gregory.'

'So this is of your own devising?' Raven asked. That would certainly account for Duncan's enthusiasm.

'Indeed, though this is merely a preliminary distillation. He assured me a refined batch will be ready tonight. Now that you are here, you can go and retrieve it.'

'I have to get back to Dr Simpson,' Raven protested. 'His visits are not complete.'

'Don't you have duties at the Maternity Hospital later?'

'Yes.'

'Then you can go once those are concluded. Professor Gregory works late at his laboratory. In fact, I suspect he sleeps there.'

It was not strictly true that Raven had to return to Dr Simpson, as the professor had made no direct instruction regarding the matter. It was more the case that Raven felt an urgent compulsion to report back to him, due to a combination of guilt and anxiety and his resultant impatience for this uncertainty to be at an end.

If there was a reckoning, he wanted to face it sooner rather than later, though not so much that he was prepared to expedite this himself by coming clean. While there was still hope that his role in Mrs Graseby's death might never emerge, he would cling on, though it become ever more agonising.

He set off towards Danube Street, striding briskly north along Gloucester Lane. He had no guarantee Simpson would still be at the Graseby house, but little over an hour had passed since they parted. It was as he crossed the junction at Doune Terrace that he spied a brougham and its pair, halted not fifty yards away. He saw Simpson emerge and quickly cross the pavement towards the door of a terraced townhouse.

Raven hastened to catch up with him, but as he did, Angus the coachman stepped into his path to arrest his progress.

'The professor is not to be disturbed,' he said.

'What, here too?' Raven asked.

'Here too,' the coachman confirmed with a solemn nod.

Raven glanced towards the house, where the door was closing behind Simpson. Perhaps it was his imagination, but he thought he detected an anxiety about Angus, a degree of alarm at Raven having come so unexpectedly upon them.

Raven was about to turn towards the carriage when he saw movement through the window of the large front room. He watched an elegantly dressed young woman rise to her feet and greet Simpson as he strode into the room. They embraced warmly, exchanging words Raven could not hear.

The professor bent briefly out of sight, and when he stood up again, he was holding an infant: a baby of perhaps eighteen months, swaddled in a pink dress. Simpson hugged the child to him while the woman looked on, smiling with the most tender affection.

There did not appear to be any medical matters to attend, far less an emergency.

'What is Dr Simpson's business here?' Raven asked. He did

not expect a straight answer, but sought to measure subtleties in how Angus evaded it.

'I know only that it is a private matter, and I know not to ask further detail. You would be wise to follow suit, unless you would rather Dr Simpson was made aware of your curiosity.'

'May I wait in the carriage?'

Angus gestured him welcome. Raven wondered at his loyalty: what secrets he might know; what further secrets he did not *know* he knew.

His thoughts were called back to the fraught conversation he had overheard between Mina and Jessie: '*He is paying out twelve pounds a year to another woman. Isn't the obvious question: why?*'

'*It is an act of charity. Surely no one can cast aspersions over something so noble.*'

'*In my experience people are happy to cast aspersions over anything when the morality of an action can be called into question.*'

Raven recalled Simpson's own advice to him this morning regarding sensational hypotheses. Nonetheless, this woman was in no need of charity, and here was Simpson visiting her alone, knowing Raven had been sent elsewhere, his coachman acting to protect his privacy. Had Mina been trying to make Jessie see what should be obvious before her eyes?

Simpson was not there long, perhaps half an hour. He strode back out to his carriage, a look of surprise lighting upon him at the sight of Raven waiting there. If it was accompanied by alarm, he concealed it swiftly. Nonetheless, there ensued a moment of silence once they were both seated, an uncomfortable intermission during which it was evident that Raven's presence was as unwelcome as it was unexpected.

'I was making my way back to Danube Street when I saw your carriage,' Raven ventured by way of explanation. He swallowed, the better to keep his voice steady and bright during his next words. 'What of your visit there? I appreciate it was confidential, but went everything well?'

Simpson's countenance became regretful, like clouds gathering. He let out a deep sigh. 'A bad business,' he said, gazing through the window. Then he turned to look at Raven. 'And one not yet concluded to my satisfaction.'

THIRTY-SIX

arah elbowed her way into the room, balancing the tea tray on one arm. She manoeuvred carefully around the mess on the floor, trying not to stand on any remnants of material or any part of the seamstress who was lying prostrate at Mina's feet, making adjustments to the hem of her new dress. The tray contained but one cup, Miss Tweedie the seamstress considered too lowly a person to merit refreshment.

Sarah placed the tray on a small table in the corner.

'Shall I pour, ma'am?'

'In a minute, Sarah. I think we're almost finished here.'

Mina swung around to face Sarah, ignoring the fact that Miss Tweedie was still in the process of pinning the hem.

'What do you think?'

Sarah stood with her arms folded, making a convincing pretence of considered study. She knew from experience that it did not do to answer too quickly. The dress was a damson silk satin, wide at the neckline, narrow at the waist, with a full skirt.

'It's beautiful, Miss Grindlay.'

As indeed it was, but Mina was looking good in whatever she wore these days simply because of the glow of contentment she was giving off.

'As you know, Sarah, I was in desperate need of a new evening gown.'

A slight emphasis was added to the penultimate word to remind Sarah, lest she had forgotten, that Mina was now being escorted with some regularity to evening functions.

'Plain is the fashion now,' piped up Miss Tweedie, kneeling on the floor and speaking through two pins gripped between her lips. 'No applied decoration.' She groaned a little as she stood up. 'Now, we'll get that off you and I shall make the adjustments we discussed.'

Sarah helped the seamstress wrestle Mina out of the dress and into her old one.

'When will it be ready?' Mina asked. 'I have a number of important engagements in the near future.'

The word *engagement* was also given extra stress, Sarah noticed, though not so much that Miss Tweedie would surely infer its significance.

'End of the week, I should imagine,' Miss Tweedie said, collecting up her pins.

'I think Dr Beattie will like it,' Sarah said, offering Mina the opportunity to talk about him, though she seldom needed prompting.

'Yes, I do believe that he will.'

'Is he your intended?' asked Miss Tweedie, gathering up the garment under discussion.

'Nothing has been made formal,' replied Mina, although the implication was that it would be soon.

This gave Sarah pause, prompting an involuntary tightness in her chest. Happy as she was for Mina, Sarah retained an instinctive suspicion about Beattie's intentions. Perhaps it was a natural caution born of concern that Mina should not get hurt. Mina was a sensible and strong-minded woman, but if there was one area where she might be vulnerable to deception – and most danger-ously self-deception – it was in the matter of finding a husband.

When she had first mentioned her reservations to Raven, he had told her how Beattie insisted that he was not interested in trivial flirtations. This sounded well and good, but did not entirely tally with how she often felt Beattie's eyes lingering upon her as she went about her business. Men deluded themselves that you didn't know they were staring – or *where* they were staring.

Looking and desiring were different things, however, and she would admit to being moved when she learned from Raven how Beattie had lost his bride-to-be on the day before their planned wedding. It was truly tragic, like something from a novel. Nonetheless, she was not convinced that his previous loss meant his feelings for Mina were everything Mina would like to believe. Simply not reminding him of the woman he lost did not strike Sarah as a strong foundation upon which to build true feelings. In fact, it seemed the opposite of true feelings: a bulwark against genuine emotion.

'Do you believe an announcement is imminent?' Sarah asked.

She realised her question might be considered impertinent, but she was confident that this would be overlooked in Mina's desire to share her news.

'I believe so.'

Mina had a flush of colour rising from her neck to her face.

'How wonderful,' said Miss Tweedie, sounding like she meant it.

'Yes,' agreed Mina. 'I was beginning to think that it might never happen.'

Sarah noticed that she spoke this more quietly, as though to herself.

'Is remaining unmarried such a disaster?' Sarah asked. She knew that Mina was in love with Beattie; she was less sure that these feelings were being genuinely reciprocated. Sarah thought about Rose Campbell, perhaps similarly afflicted by an all-consuming passion that left no space for doubt. Look where that had led.

Mina looked at her as though she might have lost her mind. 'To be a spinster aunt reliant on the generosity of family? What kind of life would that be?'

'Can't a woman have aspirations for herself beyond marriage?' Sarah responded.

'"Aspirations"? What on earth can you mean?'

Sarah thought of Miss Mann and Miss Rigby, and of Mina's love for the written word. Nobody she had met knew more about novels and poetry. It seemed a shame that there was no means of harnessing this.

'A profession of some kind. I mean, do you not wish there was a worthwhile way to use your intellect and knowledge?'

'Sarah, a woman's God-given role is to be a wife and mother. Any profession is a poor substitute for that. And what sort of profession would be suitable for a lady? Governess? I shudder at the very thought.'

Mina turned back to the mirror and adjusted her hair, pinning a loose strand back into position.

Sarah poured the tea, thinking how narrow Mina's assessment of a woman's role was, how restrictive. Why couldn't a woman aspire to more? Why shouldn't she? Why did Raven get to do whatever he wanted? She was convinced that they were of similar backgrounds and she was damn sure they were of similar intellect, yet he had opportunities that were denied to her, and seemed not always to appreciate his privilege.

Sarah bent down to retrieve a stray pin from the carpet. As she did so her hand brushed against the new dress. She wondered if she would ever wear a garment made from such fine material. She was surely not destined to remain as she was, the hired help, condemned to domestic servitude for the rest of her life. Yet how was she to escape? If a man of means offered to take her away from all of this, would she not leap at the chance? Or would that merely represent the exchange of one form of servitude for another, albeit one with greater comfort and fewer chilblains?

Would it be possible to meet a man who would accept her ambitions to educate herself and be of use? Did such a man exist? If he did, she was sure she hadn't met him yet.

She also thought of Mrs Lyndsay's admonitions about seeking to better herself. Should she just be grateful for what she had, accept her position in society that God had seen fit to give her and avoid the trouble that would inevitably come her way should she try to change things?

She handed the stray pins to Miss Tweedie, who, having wrapped the new dress in a protective layer of brown paper, made her farewells and left the room.

Sarah decided to turn the conversation back to Beattie, a sure way to restore Mina's good humour.

'It is a blessing that you should both have found each other, is it not?'

'Truly. I shudder to think how capricious fate can be.'

'You both deserve such happiness. It warms the heart to know that Dr Beattie should be able to put such painful tragedy behind him.'

Mina gave her a quizzical look. 'What tragedy?'

Sarah froze for a moment as it dawned that Beattie had not told Mina about his previous engagement. She cursed her own foolishness: she could suddenly see all of the reasons he might choose to keep it from her. Why he had chosen to confide in Raven was a more curious question, but no matter.

'That he lost his parents so young,' she said, by way of covering her misstep.

'Yes. His life has not been easy. But I am sure that it is about to improve.'

As she left the room and made her way downstairs, Sarah thought about how Mina had looked in her new dress. She radiated the joy of being admired, esteemed, raised above her peers. If love was a potion that could be bottled and sold, it really would be the cure for many a drawing-room malady.

She tried to assuage her doubts about Beattie. It was a good match in many ways, after all, and perhaps he did love Mina in a way he could love no other after losing his first intended wife.

Unlike Raven, Sarah was prepared to accept that her instincts were not infallible. But they were seldom completely wrong.

THIRTY-SEVEN

he girl on the table in front of Raven looked fourteen at the most, and plainly terrified.

'Lynsey Clegg. Been living on the streets for months,' Mrs Stevenson had told him earlier. 'Thrown out by her father when it was discovered she was pregnant, and I wouldn't be surprised if he was responsible for her condition too.'

Mrs Stevenson did not say what her grounds were for believing this. She didn't make such accusations lightly, however, and Raven had come to learn that she made it her business to find out as much as possible about the women who passed under her roof.

Lynsey was slight, about four and a half feet tall with a skinny frame that spoke of years of malnourishment. It would have been impossible for her to disguise her condition long past the quickening.

'The child is breech,' Ziegler observed quietly. 'I anticipate problems delivering the head.'

He kept his words out of the girl's hearing, but Raven did not imagine she would have picked up much anyway. She was nearly hysterical from the pain and her growing panic.

'She is not built for this. She has such a narrow pelvis. She is but a child.'

'Ether?' Raven suggested, the word emerging before he could question himself.

Ziegler merely nodded.

The contrast was, as always, astonishing. The girl went from torment to easeful sleep in a matter of minutes, and remained oblivious of the violent manoeuvres Ziegler was necessarily inflicting upon her. Despite all of this Raven could not help but think about Mrs Graseby. He remained ignorant as to what had gone wrong, what had caused her adverse reaction and why it had proven fatal after she appeared to rally. But then, such ignorance was the very reason he should not have been administering ether unsupervised.

Ziegler brought forth a baby girl and handed her to a nurse while he delivered the placenta. Raven hoped the infant would see more than fourteen years before she was giving birth too. The mother started to come around, her oblivion one last sleep before waking up in a new world.

Having swaddled the child, the nurse held her out towards her mother. The girl simply looked afraid of it.

At that point, they were interrupted by Mrs Stevenson, hastening towards them down a corridor and calling out as she ran: 'Dr Ziegler! You are needed urgently. You too, Mr Raven.'

In the lobby of Milton House, just inside the door, a young woman lay writhing upon a cot, while alongside her stood a burly fellow, clutching his hat nervously.

'He carried her here,' Mrs Stevenson informed them.

'They wanted to call for a doctor,' the man said, 'but I suggested I fetch her here, as that would be quicker. We came from just along the street.'

'Who is she?' Ziegler asked.

'Her name is Kitty. That's all I know.'

There was a smell of brick dust about the man, and he had the rough hands of a labourer.

'And who are you?'

The man paused, mulling it over before venturing his name. 'Mitchell, sir. Donald Mitchell.'

Ziegler examined the woman, as much as she would allow. She was squirming in pain, sweating and incoherent. He asked her some questions, but it was as though she was not in control of her faculties. Ziegler looked again at the man who brought her in.

'What can you tell us? What did you see? What do you know of her?'

Again, he seemed reluctant to answer. Raven reckoned he knew why.

'Were you *with* her, sir?' he asked pointedly, so that the man could make no mistake as to his meaning.

He eyed Raven with surprise, but the surprise of one who has been caught out.

'I was with another,' he admitted. 'Across the landing. We heard her cry out like the very devil was about her. I kicked in the door because I feared she was being attacked, then when we discovered her ill, as I say, I opted to bring her here directly.'

Raven contrasted this with his own conduct, sneaking away so that he was not seen. He liked to think it would have been different had Evie not already been dead, but had no doubt that Mitchell was a stronger man than he, in many ways.

They wheeled Kitty to a room where they had better light, though at this hour that was not saying much. She seemed to pass out momentarily, which allowed Ziegler an opportunity to put his hands about her.

'She's pregnant. Past the quickening.'

The calm did not last. As soon as her eyes opened again, her body buckled and twisted on the bed as though indeed the devil was not merely about her, but inside her. Raven watched her contort herself and felt sure he was witnessing what had happened to Evie before he got there that night.

'Did you take a draught or a pill?' he asked her. 'Did you seek to rid yourself of what grows in your womb?'

Her eyes fixed on his long enough for him to believe she had heard the question, but she offered no word of answer.

'She wouldn't tell you if she had,' said Mrs Stevenson. 'For fear.'

'We are here only to help you, Kitty,' he insisted. 'Please, if you took something, let us know.'

At that point, the convulsions worsened as though Raven's words had angered the demon that possessed her. Her limbs became rigid, her head thrown back.

Ziegler tried to dose her with some laudanum but her jaw was clamped shut. Her convulsions continued unabated and it was clear they were powerless to intervene.

'There is nothing we can do,' he said quietly. 'You should leave now, Raven. Go home and rest, for this all begins again tomorrow.'

'I would stay,' Raven replied. 'If there is nothing else anyone can do, then this much I can offer.'

Ziegler looked upon him curiously for a moment, then nodded by way of acquiescence.

Raven sat with her for the next few hours, watching her tormented mercilessly, her body pulled around as if she was trying to escape her very being. Though she barely seemed aware he was there, he would not let her endure these throes alone as Evie had.

Even the end was not a gentle fading, but a final, brutal jolt.

Raven remained still alongside her, his heart anxious that she might resume her agonies. After a short time, he tested for a pulse and found none.

'She has passed?' Ziegler said, appearing in the doorway. He had absented himself upon Raven's insistence, but Raven wondered whether he had ever been far.

'Indeed. I will tell Mitchell.'

Ziegler looked apologetic. 'He left some time ago. It was mercy enough for him to bring her here.'

'Did he tell you anything else? From where he brought her, at least?'

'No. He did not wait long. I don't think he knew her.'

'Then have we any means of knowing who she was?'

'Not unless someone comes to claim her remains.'

Raven thought of Evie, hauled down the stairs wrapped in a soiled shroud and slung onto a cart.

No funeral, no mourners, no headstone.

'I never knew her surname,' he said.

'Mitchell didn't give us it.'

But Raven wasn't talking about Kitty.

THIRTY-EIGHT

he hour was getting late by the time Raven left the Maternity Hospital, sharp pangs of hunger bringing him back to more immediate concerns. Dinner would be over by the time he returned to Queen Street, but Mrs Lyndsay should be able to offer him something, he was sure. Perhaps Sarah might even keep some leftovers aside for him, though he knew not what he would tell her about today's contradictory discoveries.

What made it worse was that though he would be too late for the meal, he would most likely return in time for the testing afterwards. His brief exposure to the nasty stuff Duncan had concocted was sufficient to suggest that all his previous headaches would prove joyous memories compared to the after-effects of that.

With this thought, he realised he had a means of avoiding it. Duncan had exposed him to a preliminary distillation, and Raven had been instructed to pick up a more refined sample. Professor Gregory might well have gone home by this hour, but he would take a walk up past the college building anyway. Either way, it would provide a plausible reason to delay his return until the testing was over and everyone had removed to the drawing room to smoke pipes and sip whisky.

Professor Gregory's laboratory was housed in a far corner of the university buildings, Raven attributing its remote location to the potentially explosive nature of his work. It was not easily found, Raven traversing a labyrinth of passages and stairs, though it was possible to discern that he was drawing nearer because the smells became stronger.

The laboratory was the very antithesis of Duncan and Flockhart's pristine premises: a claustrophobic and permanently cluttered chamber lined from floor to ceiling with bookcases and shelves, its floor an evolving hazard of boxes, crates and discarded equipment. The bookcases housed an extensive collection of ancient and in some instances dusty tomes, some of which Raven suspected had not been disturbed since being placed there, not by the incumbent, but by his predecessor.

In the centre of the room was a large wooden table etched with stains and scorch marks. A stooped figure was holding a flask above a spirit lamp, the purplish flame licking the underside of the glass, which caused the liquid inside to bubble furiously as though incensed by the application of such heat. Raven waited in the doorway so as not to interrupt, but without looking up the professor beckoned him with a wave of his hand before brushing a long strand of black hair from his forehead.

William Gregory was a thin man who appeared older than he was. He hobbled when he walked, the result of a childhood illness from which he had never entirely recovered, but he had a lively energy about him when his enthusiasm was piqued – usually by his work. His father James Gregory had been the renowned formulator of Gregory's powder, the most prescribed medicine in the *Edinburgh Pharmacopoeia* and thus the standard by which James Duncan intended to measure his own success.

According to Simpson, Gregory Sr had been by nature a belligerent man, prone to feuding with individuals and institutions alike. He had carried a cane and on one notorious occasion used it to attack the then Professor of Midwifery, James Hamilton, following a dispute. This resulted in a court hearing at which Gregory was ordered to pay Hamilton £100 in damages, which he said he 'would pay all over again for another opportunity of thrashing the little obstetrician'.

By contrast, William Gregory was known for his calmness and self-possession, having inherited only his father's academic brilliance. Simpson told Raven that early in his career, he had developed a process to produce morphine in a high state of purity. However, Dr Simpson could not help but also impart that Gregory was an enthusiast for phrenology and hypnotism, and it was said that his choice of wife had been made only after phrenological examination.

Raven approached, stepping around a three-legged stool upon which sat a beaker with a long retort just asking to be knocked over and smashed. Next to that was a pile of leather-bound volumes and what appeared to be two dead rabbits in a wooden crate. Raven wondered if they had been delivered thus on order, though he did not wish to dwell upon what purpose they were about to serve.

Gregory removed the flask from the flame and held it up, swirling the contents under the dim light of a gas lamp, a look of dissatisfaction upon his face at the results.

Raven took in the ramshackle chaos of bottles, jars and vials arrayed close to the professor. His eye was also drawn to several jars of a bright red powder, one he did not recognise.

'Mr Raven,' Gregory said. 'Here at Dr Duncan's request, I assume?'

'Indeed.'

'He's fairly got you people fetching and carrying for him. The initial distillation of this stuff was collected by some young girl. Gave me quite the interrogation, too. Would you know who that might be?'

Raven could not help but smile. 'She is Dr Simpson's house-maid.'

'Really?' Gregory replied, given pause. 'His housemaid. I wish my students were half so inquisitive. Or as informed. Now, where did I . . .'

Gregory turned to the array of glass containers before him, reaching towards the vial Duncan was waiting for, but then his attention suddenly diverted to the red powder.

'I forgot to say to the young girl when she was here. You must take this to Dr Simpson as a gift. I was sent a batch of the stuff by Professor Joao Parreira of the University of Coimbra in Portugal. We met in Paris over the summer.'

'Is he a chemist?'

'Yes, and an esteemed one, but this is not a chemical compound. It is a powder ground from dried capsicums: a powerful strain originally deriving from Africa, I believe. They call it *peri-peri*.'

'What does it do?'

Gregory became animated, his face charged with enthusiasm.

'It adds the most enlivening flavour to food. It is the stuff of miracles, believe me. It can transform the most miserable and mundane of stews into something that will delight your palate.'

Having had his scale of miserable cuisine calibrated by life at Ma Cherry's, Raven looked sceptically upon the jar Gregory was proffering.

'Try some,' he said, unscrewing the lid. 'Just take a pinch.'

Raven dipped three fingers into the neck of the jar and scooped out the equivalent of a teaspoon, transferring it swiftly between his lips.

Gregory's admonition – 'I said just a pinch!' – hit his ears at the same moment the powder had its seemingly incendiary effect inside his mouth. His tongue felt aflame and his eyes began to stream. He spat it out, but the burning continued.

'Water,' he coughed, to which an amused Gregory held out a cup. Raven poured it into his maw, but this only seemed to exacerbate the intensity, like pouring water upon burning oil.

He would have to admit that there was an intriguingly smoky

flavour about it, but worried that he was tasting his own burnt flesh.

Gregory's eyes were moist too, but merely from mirth at Raven's affliction.

'I won't have to warn you to tell Dr Simpson's cook she should use it sparingly.'

Raven was sceptical as to whether Mrs Lyndsay could be prevailed upon to use it at all. She was a fine cook, but according to Sarah, extremely set in her ways. Nonetheless, Raven looked forward to offering a taste to Jarvis, and to Duncan. He would recommend a generously heaped spoonful to each of them.

He replaced the lid and placed the jar in the pocket of his jacket so that his hands were free to carry the vial for which Gregory was now reaching.

'I thought I could improve the distillation process, but in truth it is all but identical to the first attempt. I wasn't so sure about some of the ingredients Duncan suggested. The combination struck me as potentially lethal, a danger he seemed to be blithely ambivalent towards.'

Yes, that sounded like Duncan, Raven thought. He couldn't imagine the man shedding many tears if his experimentation happened to kill somebody. He'd probably view it as a necessary sacrifice on the altar of progress. With that thought, he resolved to walk home slowly despite his rumbling stomach.

'That said, I think he may be onto something,' Gregory added. 'I was reluctant to test the formula on myself, so I experimented on some animal subjects a short while ago. They became quickly unresponsive, proving impervious to painful stimuli. I was intending to check on them again, but your arrival distracted me.'

'What manner of animals?' Raven asked.

'A couple of conies.'

'Do you have a lot of rabbits that you experiment on?'

'No, just the two over there.'

Raven felt something solidify within him, like mercury in the chill. He reached into the crate, placing a hand on each of the rabbits in case he had misapprehended their condition.

He had not.

'These rabbits are quite dead. How much did you give them?'

'It was but the slightest dose of vapour. A single drop upon the muslin.'

A single drop.

Raven bolted from the lab, clattering his way down the stair-cases and halls. In keeping with the normal testing practice, Simpson and the others would be gathered around the dining table, dispensing ever more liberal quantities, sniffing it deeper and deeper until it had an effect or was declared useless. He had to get back to Queen Street, though it may already be too late.

Raven barrelled out of the college and onto rain-swept Nicholson Street, where he looked about for a hansom cab. He didn't have the funds for such a journey but he would borrow the fare from the professor, and if he got there too late, payment would be the least of his worries.

The streets were all but empty: a few damp souls wending their way home upon the pavements, and not a carriage to be seen. Ruefully he recalled guests to Queen Street complaining that there was never a cab to be had in Edinburgh, particularly when it rained. The hour was late too: most respectable people would be digesting their dinner or preparing for their beds. The only people on the street were drunks. One of them swayed into his path, suddenly enraged and irrationally regarding Raven as his enemy. He screamed out an oath and challenged him to fight. Raven checked his stride and harmlessly passed around him.

Then up ahead he saw a carriage approach the junction with Infirmary Street. The gentleman inside was bound to have heard of the professor. Surely he would assist when he heard how he was imperilled.

Raven ran towards it, waving his arms and beseeching the

coachman to stop. He heard an urgent voice from within as the coachman urged his steeds to hurry, cracking his whip at the approaching Raven to warn him off. He was not surprised. He must have looked like a madman trying to attack them.

He had no option but to run. And though it burn his muscles and crush his lungs, he would drive himself without rest until he reached Queen Street.

He calculated the most direct route as he ran, his splashing footsteps echoing off the buildings. The rhythm of his lengthening stride was soon accompanied by another beat in his chest, though he felt a welcome easing as his route took him steeply downhill on Cockburn Street, where he was able to run faster with less cost to legs and lungs. As he picked up momentum, he skidded on something – he didn't stop to consider what – and almost tumbled. It was a near thing: a twisted ankle would have ended his mercy dash right then and there.

Righting himself, he stepped up the pace again, his eyes trained upon the flagstone and cobbles, straining to pick out potential hazards in the gloom. Then he felt an impact that shuddered every bone, and almost bit through his tongue as his teeth clattered together. It felt as though he had run into a wall, except walls weren't usually warm and clad in cloth. He rebounded and tumbled to the ground, feeling a blow against his thigh and a crack as the jar in his pocket smashed between his falling weight and the hard stone beneath. As he tried to focus in his daze, two horribly familiar faces loomed over him beneath the glow of a street lamp.

He had run straight into the Weasel and Gargantua.

THIRTY-NINE

aven felt Gargantua's huge hands about his shoulders, gripping him and hauling him upright like he was a carcass in a slaughterhouse.

'Mr Raven,' the Weasel said, a vicious delight dripping from his voice. 'What a lovely surprise to run into you. Now, do you know what time it is?'

He theatrically produced Raven's father's pocket watch and dangled it from its chain.

'Well past time you paid up – either in coin or in kind. I think I said an eye, didn't I?'

The Weasel put the watch back in his pocket and took out the same blade that had ripped Raven's face the last time they met.

Raven started at the sight of it, but Gargantua's hands held him firm.

He felt sick with fear. He was barely able to think of anything other than the pain he would endure, but some part of him was thinking of the consequences beyond. Could he still have a career with one eye? It was a moot question, he realised. Being held here and mutilated meant his mission tonight was at an end. With Simpson dead, he would have no apprenticeship anyway. It was all about to be lost, for the price of trying to help Evie.

To add insult to imminent injury, he hadn't even helped her. In fact, it was quite possible he had merely borrowed the means by which she purchased her own death.

Fear caused his mind to race, revisiting the events of the evening like he was experiencing them all simultaneously. Every sight, every smell, every sensation and emotion flashed before him, and amidst it all, something stuck.

Raven's shoulders remained gripped, but his hands were free and he could bend his elbow.

'No, I have it,' he implored. 'I have Mr Flint's money upon me. Please, I beg you. I have just sold a treasured heirloom and I have it here in my pocket.'

Mindful of the broken glass, he dipped his fingers carefully and scooped up a quantity of the red powder. Then he closed his eyes and tossed it backwards into his captor's face.

Gargantua let go immediately and spun away, bending over and howling as he put his hands to his eyes. Even as he did so, Raven was scooping another handful, which he cupped in his outraised palm and blew, sending a red cloud to engulf the Weasel's eyes, nose and mouth.

The Weasel fell, his screams echoing about the walls, while behind him Gargantua remained bent, emitting a low moan and muttering about being blinded by hot coals.

Raven crouched over the Weasel and swiftly retrieved his stolen pocket watch. Would that time itself could be recovered so easily.

Raven resumed his running, powering down the grass of the Mound in darkness, his eyes fixed on the lights of Princes Street ahead. His heart was fluttering both from his fear and from his exertion, but he felt as though some analgesic draught was surging through him, dulling the pains in his legs and in his chest.

The draught had worn off by the time he was careering down Frederick Street, but by that time gravity was assisting his flight. He almost flattened a gentleman alighting from a carriage as he turned the last corner, the front door of No. 52 in sight ahead of him. He barely dared to consider what awaited him behind it.

Raven burst into the hall past a startled Jarvis, his thighs screaming from his efforts. His breath was so short he feared he would not have enough left to speak, but as he bowled through the door into the dining room, he discovered that it didn't matter.

He was too late.

The room was in disarray. The lace tablecloth was hanging askew, a number of glass tumblers lay smashed upon the wooden floor and several of the dining-room chairs were on their sides. Amongst the detritus on the floor, beneath the mahogany table, were the lifeless bodies of three men: Simpson, Keith, and one he did not recognise. A fourth, James Duncan, was slumped face-down on the table, a single bottle open in front of him next to a folded cloth.

Raven cursed the man. In his blasted quest for a place in history, he had killed them all.

FORTY

arah carried a tray into the drawing room bearing a pot of tea, three cups and a tray of fancies. She did not think that anyone could still be hungry after the bounteous meal she had watched them consume, but she was aware of Agnes Petrie's eyes tracing the progress of the little cakes from door to table. Mina often claimed to have 'a second compartment for sweet things' to excuse how she fell upon such treats after a generous dinner, though Sarah had noticed that her habits had been more abstemious in recent times: specifically since Dr Beattie started showing an interest in her.

The ladies had retired upstairs to the drawing room while the gentlemen remained around the dining table to commence the professor's preferred after-dinner pursuit: that of testing new candidates to improve upon ether as a drowsy syrup. Drs Simpson, Keith and Duncan were joined by a layperson, Captain James Petrie, but as he described himself as 'a man of intrepid spirit', he had had no qualms about throwing his weight behind the medical men's pioneering quest.

Captain Petrie was Mrs Simpson and Mina's brother-in-law, the widower of their late sister. He was a voluble personality, a man who looked like he did not quite belong amidst domestic gentility. He had been friendly and polite to the staff, however.

Indeed, while Sarah waited at the table, he had asked her to pass on his compliments to Mrs Lyndsey for a remarkable meal, though it became retrospectively clear that this was merely a pretext for him to hold forth on the subject of 'the only meal I might be permitted to consider more remarkable'.

He proceeded to talk at length of his exploits defending Britain's interests in the American War, telling of how in 1814, following victory in the Battle of Bladensburg, his company had marched on Washington. 'We took the city with such swiftness and audacity that James Madison's dinner was still warm upon the table when we stormed his house and set it ablaze. I fetched a leather-bound book of poetry from the library shelves and briefly sat down to finish the abandoned meal before the flames took over, for it is a sin to waste good food.'

Sarah was most impressed with this tale, thinking Captain Petrie sounded gallant and colourful; certainly a good deal less dusty than most of the grey-faced medical men who had dined there. It was only as they ascended the staircase that she overheard Mrs Simpson say to Mina: 'I wonder how many times we have sat through him telling that story.'

'Almost as many as the number of soldiers who claim to have eaten of that meal,' Mina replied. 'Truly, it must have been quite a plateful.'

This exchange had, of course, taken place out of earshot of Agnes Petrie, the captain's daughter and Mrs Simpson's niece. Agnes was a plump and rather giddy creature who did not strike Sarah as blessed with the highest level of intelligence, though at least this did not mean another fine female mind condemned to atrophy through disuse. Neither had she inherited her father's easy grace in dealing with the staff, and came across as a rather spoiled and self-regarding young woman.

Sarah was pouring the tea when the entire house was shaken by the crash of the front door being thrown open against the wall. It was followed by a sound like rumbling thunder, the shuddering thump of someone rushing down the hall with such haste and force of weight that she could feel it vibrate through the boards beneath her feet.

'What on earth is that?' asked Mrs Simpson.

Sarah hastened to investigate, the ladies rising to their feet at her back. She looked over the banister and observed Jarvis standing against the wall with an affronted expression upon his face.

'What occurs?'

'Mr Raven just came charging through here like he had the devil at his heels,' he said.

Sarah hastened downstairs into the dining room. She found Raven crouched over Dr Simpson, who lay face-down upon the floor, the bodies of Dr Keith and Captain Petrie motionless alongside. Raven rolled Dr Simpson over and placed his ear to his chest.

'He breathes,' he announced, panting heavily, a near-tearful anxiety in his voice. He was soaking wet, his hair plastered to his face, which was red with exertion.

'You've been running.'

'I rushed here from Gregory's lab,' Raven said, still struggling to catch his breath. 'The formula Duncan ordered is poisonous. It rendered two rabbits unconscious before killing them shortly after. I fear it may yet do the same here.'

Sarah noticed a bottle sitting on the table where Dr Duncan sat slumped, his arms sprawled before him as though reaching for it. She recognised the handwriting on the label.

'But this bottle isn't from Professor Gregory. It came from Duncan and Flockhart. "Perchloride of formyle",' she read.

She handed it to him, Raven's hand outstretched impatiently. He read the label, a look of confusion upon his face, and as he did so, Dr Simpson's eyes opened.

Sarah thought back to earlier in the day, when she had come here to prepare the dining room and lay the table for dinner. She had found easily a dozen bottles untidily ranged on top of the sideboard, still others seemingly abandoned on the floor. As she endeavoured to tidy the former away, she had knocked one onto its side, causing it to roll to the back where it dropped into the gap between the wall and the cabinet.

She didn't have the strength to move the sideboard on her own, and besides, at that moment, Dr Duncan had come in and begun chastising her for interfering. She therefore decided it best not to mention how she had just mislaid one of his bottles.

Dr Simpson tried to sit up then lay back again, blinking several times and looking at his surroundings as though they did not make sense. Sarah fetched a cushion to help support his head as Mrs Simpson and Mina appeared in the doorway.

'Oh, dear heavens, what has happened?' Mina asked.

Mrs Simpson rolled her eyes. Clearly it was not the first time she had witnessed such a sight.

The professor focused upon his wife and propped himself up with his elbow. He looked at the concerned faces crowded above him and smiled.

'This is far stronger and better than ether,' he said.

Dr Keith was next to stir, but there was no gentle waking for him. Instead he began to thrash about, kicking at the table as though trying to overturn the few items that had thus far managed to remain upright upon it. This was accompanied by loud snoring on the part of Dr Duncan.

After several minutes of this, Dr Duncan began to rouse and George Keith, having ceased his semi-conscious violence, raised himself to his knees. He gripped the table, only his eyes visible above the edge, and stared in an unfocused way, with a hauntingly vacant expression on his face, as though his human spirit had abandoned him. For some reason he directed this ghastly gaze at Mina, who looked reciprocally transfixed, horrified by what she was seeing. Thus, just as everyone else was regaining either consciousness or composure, Mina threatened to faint. An upturned chair was righted for her, and Sarah was dispatched to find her fan and fetch her a glass of water.

Dr Simpson climbed to his feet, assisted by his wife.

'Waldie was right,' he declared, delight in his voice. 'This is by far the most promising of all our experiments.' He looked about himself eagerly. 'Where has it gone? Is there any left?'

The sopping Raven held out the bottle to him, but Mrs Simpson gestured him away.

'I think perhaps we have all had enough excitement for one evening.'

The professor would not be denied. 'But this is just the beginning. We may well have found what we have been searching for. Who else would like to try?'

Mina was first to find her voice. But not in the affirmative. 'I for one will not be making such an exhibition of myself. The look on Dr Keith's face just now will haunt me for the rest of my days.'

'Oh, come away now, Mina. It may be your chance to form part of history.'

Dr Simpson grabbed the bottle from Raven, removed the stopper and waved it in Mina's direction. Looking suddenly alarmed, Mina got out of her chair and backed away from him. The professor then began to chase her round the table as she shrieked her objection.

The pursuit was short-lived as Dr Simpson subsided into laughter and had to give up. Raven rescued the bottle before its contents were inadvertently poured onto the carpet.

'I'll try it,' said a voice, which turned out to belong to Agnes Petrie. She had been standing in the doorway and now pushed forward into the room. 'Oh, do let me have some.'

Dr Simpson looked to her father, who nodded assent. Sarah suspected he had said no to few requests where his daughter was appellant.

Agnes squeezed herself into a dining-room chair and began to inhale the saucer of liquid that had been poured for her. Within a matter of moments, her eyelids fluttered and she declared herself to be lighter than air, which seemed all the more remarkable given her size. She then began shouting 'I'm an angel, I'm an angel,' before sliding to the floor in a manner far removed from the seraphic. She remained there, peacefully unconscious, for a full five minutes.

Dr Simpson decided he would try it upon himself again, ignoring the concerned looks of his wife. Dr Duncan joined him and Dr Keith took out his pocket watch to time the duration of the drug's effect.

'Perchloride of formyle,' Keith stated, taking a note. 'Somewhat more of a mouthful than "ether". Can we give it a shortened name?'

As Dr Simpson raised the glass to his nose, he paused momentarily. 'I believe Waldie said it was also known as "chloroform".'

FORTY-ONE

arah watched Raven quietly withdraw from the dining room, suspecting she was the only one who noticed. Everyone else remained fixated upon the experiments, though in Mrs Simpson and Mina's cases this seemed more an act of vigilance than enthusiasm.

Raven had observed the recent activities wordlessly, and declined the offer of partaking in subsequent experiments. The man looked drained. He had turned up looking like he'd been pulled from the river, and if anything for a while he had become wetter. The warmth of the room made him sweat all the more following what appeared to have been considerable exertions. It had been half an hour before his face returned to a normal colour.

None of the people he had exhausted himself to protect were even aware of his efforts. That they had never truly been in danger because of Sarah's earlier mishap was something she decided she should not immediately share with him, though he would have to be told.

With the hour drawing on and her own services seeming superfluous in the face of this new distraction, she followed him out a few moments later, ascending the stairs at his back. He heard her and stopped just before reaching his room, turning to see who was there.

'Would you like some supper, Mr Raven?' she asked. 'You didn't eat yet.'

He managed a weak smile. 'That would be most welcome.'

His voice had a tremor to it. She realised he must be cold now, and would get colder.

'You need to get out of those clothes at once. You'll catch a fever. Come on,' she said, following him into his room, where she lit a gas lamp. She turned to help him remove his jacket, which felt twice its normal weight.

'I'm perfectly capable . . .' he began, then seemed to surrender to her assistance, lacking the strength or the will to resist.

'You really need to get yourself a proper coat, Mr Raven. Before winter truly bites.'

'I know.'

She lifted the damp garment from his shoulders, her gaze drawn by how his hair was stuck flat about his face.

'You ran all the way from the college?'

'Yes, but that was not even the worst part of my evening. I watched a young woman die in agony before me at the Maternity Hospital. And I am certain she died the same way as Evie: racked with spasms, and pregnant too.'

'"Racked with spasms": the way Miss Mann described one who had taken strychnine?'

'Precisely. But what is confounding is that earlier today, I met McLevy, and he said that there was no trace of poison in Rose Campbell's remains. More confounding still, that neither was she found to be pregnant.'

Sarah could well understand Raven's consternation. One part of this made sense to her, however.

'I have been reading about strychnine in Christison's *Treatise*. An added boon to any malefactor is that there *is* no test for it. It would not be traceable in any post-mortem examination. So it remains entirely possible that strychnine was responsible for Rose's death.'

'Yes, but there is an irrefutable post-mortem test for pregnancy, and McLevy insisted no baby was found.'

This part, Sarah had to concede, truly was confounding.

'Milly was not mistaken about this,' she argued. 'It is the very reason Rose feared she would be dismissed.'

'McLevy insists otherwise, and they cannot both be right.'

But as Raven spoke, Sarah realised there existed a reason that they could.

'Perhaps she was not pregnant by the time she went into the water. What if she successfully rid herself of her unwanted burden? Strychnine brings on spasms. Could it have been used in a medicine to bring on the contractions of premature labour, which in Rose's case it succeeded, only for her to die later?'

Raven's eyes widened. 'It is my suspicion that the girl who died tonight took something to get rid of her child. Perhaps Evie did too, but in each of their cases, it killed them before it could have any other effect.'

'Who was this girl? Could she have any connection to the Reverend Grissom?'

Raven wore a look of regret. 'I know nothing about her. Not even her full name, only that she was known as Kitty. I know not where she lived, other than that it was near enough for a man to have carried her there. But in the Old Town, that radius might include a thousand dwellings.'

His voice wavered again, shivers taking him. Even his shirt was wet through. Without asking, she began to unbutton it for him.

Sarah had seen Raven fully naked when he first arrived and was in need of a bath. This felt different, now that she knew something of him. She recalled her words – *whatever you've got, I've seen it before* – and though she had now indeed seen him before, this time her eyes wished to dwell.

Her hand brushed his chest as she tugged at his wet shirt, the cloth sticking to skin. She felt something surge inside herself, and the insistence of it unnerved her.

As she undid the final button, she sensed a stirring close to where she touched him, and belatedly understood what was meant by the expression 'proud below the navel'.

Raven flinched away from her in response, presumably because he could not flinch away from himself.

Sarah stepped back from him, looking to the floor.

'You must be starving,' she said quietly. 'I'd best get down to the kitchen and fetch you something to eat.'

He said nothing as she departed. She waited a moment outside his door, as she felt so light-headed as to fear she might trip on her descent.

Upon reaching the kitchen, Sarah took a plate and gathered some leftover pie, a slice of ham and a hunk of bread. She held it in her left hand, grabbed a bottle of ale with her right, then made for the stairs once again.

When she reached the top landing, she found Raven deeply unconscious, and no chemical agent had been necessary to produce the effect.

FORTY-TWO

arah entered Kennington and Jenner's on Princes Street and was immediately grateful to be out of the cold. Her callused hands were cracked and sore, the result of washing household linens the day before. Her hands were always bad in the winter. The cold made everything worse.

The shop was warm and inviting, a place she had always enjoyed spending time, fancying what she might buy if she only had the money. It was always brightly lit either by daylight streaming in through the windows that lined the front of the shop or from the large gas chandeliers that hung from the ceiling. Bolts of cloth in every conceivable colour were stacked on shelves, smaller samples of fabric arrayed across the counters.

The shop had been established by two draper's assistants who had found themselves out of work following an unauthorised leave of absence to attend the races at Musselburgh. In opening their own store they had been determined to provide the ladies of Edinburgh with the finest silks and linens, previously only available in London. They had thus far been successful in their endeavours, having recently acquired the neighbouring premises to expand their textile emporium.

Sarah liked this story; ordinary people making their own way in the world. It gave her hope. Or at least it used to. Now

Kennington and Jenner's would always remind her of the last time she saw Rose Campbell, a young woman cut down in her prime, all her potential lost. It would make her think of the husk Rose had become even before she died: ground down by a life of servitude, a dead-eyed and depleted version of the girl whose confidence and energy Sarah once found intimidating.

She gazed at the fabrics that were, as always, elaborately displayed. Today yards of expensive material in a variety of vibrant hues had been pinned to a high point on one wall and allowed to cascade down onto one of the counters as though a flood had occurred. She used to daydream about the goods on offer in this place. Now they seemed an affront, and not merely because the limitations placed upon her meant she would never own such luxuries. They served to remind her that it wasn't only those women below stairs who would never be permitted to realise their potential. Those above could aspire to no more than marriage and motherhood, and thus were encouraged to fuss over fripperies as they concerned themselves with how they might adorn themselves the better to please men.

Sarah would have turned and departed from the place if she could, its previous pleasant associations tarnished, but her time was not her own to command and she was obliged to go wherever she was sent. She had been dispatched by Mina to collect a length of black velvet, ordered the week before, which was to be made into a cape to go with her new evening gown.

She proceeded towards the main counter, but as she approached it she became aware of a familiar smell, of citrus and sandalwood, though it was a fragrance that seemed incongruous here among women's finery. This, she realised, was because she associated it with a man, and there indeed he stood at a sales counter, in conversation with the assistant.

Sarah loitered behind a pillar, reluctant to be seen and perhaps recognised. Beattie never struck her as the type to notice much about servants beyond the pair of hands that was handing him something, but having accompanied Mina so often, if he was going to remember any housemaid, it would be her. His attention was upon the counter, however, so she felt emboldened to peer around the pillar, which was close enough for her to overhear the exchange taking place.

Beattie was turning a pair of gloves over in his hands upon the counter top.

'These are the very best that we have, sir. Kid, although we have silk and cotton too if you would prefer to see those.'

'It has to be kid. Silk and cotton are a little vulgar, don't you think?'

Sarah watched the assistant nodding in agreement, beaming pleasantly, flattered by Beattie's easy charm.

She looked again at her own hands, turning from white to red in the warmth of the shop. She knew that she ought to be reassured by what she was witnessing. Buying expensive gifts was, after all, the way a man was expected to show his affection, and Mina would be delighted with such a token. Yet Sarah felt a persistent unease. On paper, when all was totted up, he seemed eminently suitable, but she couldn't help thinking there was something beneath the veneer that was not as it appeared.

Whenever she raised her concerns about how sketchy their knowledge of him was, Mina was ready with excuses. Little could be known as to his background, as both his parents were dead. Beattie's father had been a merchant, his unfortunate early demise much lamented. His mother hailed from just outside Edinburgh, on the Morningside. She was survived by her brother, one Charles Latimer, who still lived in the family home he had inherited in Canaan Lands. He was a frail man, more or less confined to his house these days, but it was furnished with large gardens and had views to the surrounding countryside, which made it an agreeable confinement. 'The uncle has a large hothouse,' Mina had said, 'wherein he grows exotic fruit and flowers. I have been promised orchids and pineapples.'

Such treasures, Sarah noted, had so far not been forthcoming.

Mr Latimer's home sounded very much like Millbank, where Professor Syme lived, half an hour's walk from Princes Street but far removed from the smoke and bustle of the city (and more significantly from his patients). It had extensive gardens and beautiful views towards Blackford Hill. Sarah knew this because Mrs Lyndsay had a relative who worked there.

Mrs Lyndsay often made comparisons between the regime at Millbank and that of Queen Street, trying to inculcate a sense of gratitude in Sarah about her place of work. She was conscious of Sarah's restlessness and talk of wanting more than she had. To Mrs Lyndsay's mind, this lack of appreciation was likely to provoke some form of divine intervention that would see Sarah much reduced in circumstances by way of punishment.

Sarah remained unconcerned about providential retribution, being more troubled by Mina's mention of the debt currently being accrued by Beattie as he struggled to establish himself in medical practice in Edinburgh.

'Don't look so alarmed,' Mina had said. 'It is often how things are in the beginning. Dr Simpson himself owed a considerable sum of money at the time he married my sister.'

Perhaps, Sarah had thought, but Beattie is no Simpson.

Sarah watched him as the assistant wrapped his purchase. Oblivious of any onlooker, his gaze lingered upon the girl's behind as she bent to retrieve paper and string from a drawer beneath the counter. Sarah had never seen him look at Mina that way, but it was Mina he was buying gloves for, so perhaps she should be assured that it was this way round.

When the assistant presented the bill, Beattie told her to add it to his account. He then picked up his package and made for the door with an unhurried gait, the smell of his cologne lingering long after his departure.

FORTY-THREE

aven doubted there had been a more crowded meeting of the Medico-Chirurgical Society. News of chloroform had already begun to spread throughout the city's medical men, though the knowledge that Simpson and Syme were both to be present no doubt played a part too. The prospect of an argument between these two known adversaries would often draw a crowd.

Though this was to be the first formal announcement of his discovery, Simpson was making no secret of his new anaesthetic agent, and had used it in an obstetric case a mere four days after the experiments at Queen Street. He was called to see a Mrs Jane Carstairs in Albany Street, the wife of a physician recently retired from the Indian Medical Service. A difficult labour was anticipated due to a previous confinement having lasted three days and ending with the baby's head having to be broken up to permit extraction. (Raven frequently had to remind himself that many infants did in fact make it into the world alive and fully intact.)

Mrs Carstairs was persuaded to try the chloroform when her pains became severe.

'I've taken it myself,' Simpson assured her. 'It is really quite pleasant.'

Half a teaspoon of liquid was poured onto a pocket handkerchief, which he rolled into a funnel shape and held over her nose and mouth. She quickly drifted off into what appeared to be a comfortable sleep, and the child was born without difficulty some twenty-five minutes later.

The crying of the newborn had failed to rouse the sleeping mother, which caused Raven to feel a pang of anxiety at the memory of Caroline Graseby. His hands became sweaty, his mouth dry and he found himself offering a silent prayer to a God he was convinced had no interest in helping him. Punishing him, yes. Helping him, no.

The placenta was expelled and the child removed by the nurse to another room before the mother began to waken. But waken she did, to Raven's profound relief. When she had returned to full consciousness she expressed her gratitude at having been provided with such a restful sleep. 'I now feel quite restored and better able to deal with the trial ahead of me,' she said, which to Raven did not sound like the most optimistic view of motherhood. Then he noticed the look of concern spreading upon her face.

'I fear that my sleeping has somehow stopped the pains.'

Simpson smiled and patted her hand. 'Your trial is at an end,' he said.

He called to the nurse in the next room, who appeared with the newly bathed and swaddled child, to the mother's astonishment.

'I cannot believe it,' she said. 'It is a miracle. She is here and I have suffered hardly at all.'

'Perhaps you should name her Anaesthesia,' Simpson suggested.

At that juncture, she had discovered a limit to her gratitude.

The meeting was called to order by the society's president, Professor William Pulteney Alison, and the audience began to settle themselves into their seats. Raven noticed Henry in the crowd and quickly beckoned his friend sit with him. He had spotted Beattie also but failed to catch his eye in the throng.

'Is this new discovery truly better than ether?' Henry asked as he sat down.

'So much so that even Syme might be convinced to use it.'

Henry looked sceptical, as Raven knew he might. This was a long-standing source of frustration. 'Then may he set the rest of the dominoes to fall,' he replied. 'There are still surgeons who believe that the patient's pain serves as a useful guide to their endeavours. In my opinion, this merely demonstrates that they lack a sound knowledge of anatomy and the appropriate skill.'

'Simpson receives letters from the outraged on a regular basis.'

'Yes, you told me about the Reverend Grissom and his leaflets. The primeval curse and all that.'

'In fact, the religious types tend not to write. The most vociferous correspondents are other obstetricians. Barnes, Lee and Gream in London; Meigs in Philadelphia.'

'And what is their objection?'

'God, nature and bad language.'

Henry looked at him askance. 'Please explain.'

'Pain in labour is natural, a manifestation of the life force, an ordinance from the Almighty and therefore painless childbirth is unnatural and improper. Under the influence of anaesthesia, some women have been heard to use obscene and disgusting language – words that they should never have had the opportunity to hear – which of course means that it is wrong ever to employ it.'

Henry began to laugh. 'I can't imagine any of the women of my acquaintance sharing such concerns. What does Simpson say about it?'

'That the same logic would suggest it is unnatural to wear clothes, to use condiments in aid of digestion, and the stagecoach to relieve ourselves of the fatigue induced by walking.'

Dr Simpson stood and walked to the podium. Silence descended upon the crowded hall.

'I wish to direct the attention of the members of the society to a new respirable anaesthetic agent which I have discovered,' he began.

Simpson proceeded to outline the events which had led to the successful trial of chloroform and stressed the many advantages it had over ether: the relatively small dose required; a more rapid and persistent action; a more agreeable smell; and that no special equipment was necessary for its administration.

When he concluded his presentation, there was much discussion amongst the assembled throng, many of those present asking if they could try it for themselves. A bottle of the stuff appeared and chloroform was liberally applied to several handkerchiefs, which were then passed round. One arrived in Henry's hand and he put it to his nose.

'Don't let it touch your skin,' Raven warned him, indicating a tender spot beneath the bridge of his own nose. 'Direct contact results in irritation, like a burn. I learned that the hard way.'

Henry inhaled but there was an insufficient dose on the handkerchief to produce anything more than a pleasant feeling of intoxication. The effect was nonetheless enough that Henry took a seat, which cleared a line of sight between Raven and Beattie. He began striding across the room, intent upon sampling the stuff himself. James Duncan made his way over also, no doubt keen to claim his role in the new agent's discovery.

'May I?' Beattie asked, though his hand was already gripping the bottle.

'By all means,' Raven replied, watching him pour an injudicious dose onto the cloth.

He considered warning them about direct contact, but held his tongue, some bitter instinct eager to inflict damage upon Duncan for a change. More surprising was an ambivalence about Beattie inflicting a mark upon his otherwise unblemished face. Raven was not sure where this unpleasant sentiment came from; perhaps a lingering anger over his scar, or a latent resentment at Beattie having dragged him into the Graseby incident. (That was how he thought of it – the Graseby incident. He was unable even within the confines of his own head to label it for what it was: a death for which he was responsible.)

Beattie having over-soaked the handkerchief, the vapours hit him before he might press it to his face. He lay himself down on a bench as around him others staggered and fell over. Beattie slept peacefully for several minutes, during which time Raven found himself making a careful study of his deceptively youthful features, contemplating how old he truly was, and what events had shaped him. Raven wondered also at his greater ability to deal with their shared disaster. Granted, the larger part of the blame lay upon Raven for attempting something beyond his experience, but Beattie seemed untroubled by remorse while Raven was incessantly tortured by what had occurred that day. Was he really as unperturbed as he appeared? Was such detachment a good thing in a doctor? A necessity for self-preservation? Perhaps it was.

He knew it was unworthy, given all Beattie had done for him, but again he felt a sting of envy towards the man: of what he had and of all he was going to have. No doubt he would soon marry Mina, which as Sarah noted, would instantly confer a considerable advantage in his field. That was how it went: a doctor from a wealthy background would swoop in, trade on his association with the great Dr Simpson and accumulate a wealthy client list on the back of it. Raven, by comparison, would merely pass through the house and be gone, replaced by another apprentice once he had served his time, then promptly forgotten.

Henry got to his feet, regarding the host of sleeping doctors around him with some amusement. 'I do hope I can come to Queen Street some evening and participate in the experiments there,' he said.

'Be careful what you wish for,' Raven replied, thinking about the prostrate forms lying under the dining-room table.

'Why?'

'There is a want of caution which at times disturbs me. I have no wish to sacrifice myself at the altar of scientific progress.'

Duncan scoffed. 'Boldness and a certain want of caution are necessary for scientific progress to be made,' he said.

'I'm not convinced lives should be put at risk,' Raven replied.

'We should certainly be endeavouring to make our methods more scientific,' Henry suggested. 'With the use of statistics and experimentation, we would soon get rid of the quacks, charlatans and snake-oil salesmen once and for all.'

'But there must always be room for a certain degree of resourcefulness, inventiveness, ingenuity,' Duncan argued. 'And the march of progress should not be restrained by faint hearts.'

Raven looked at him, wondering if this statement was general or making reference to particular circumstances.

'Simpson likes to think of medicine as more than pure science,' he countered. 'There must also be empathy, concern, a human connection.'

'I suggest that both elements are required,' offered Henry. 'Scientific principles married to creativity. Science and art.'

If it is an art, it is at times a dark one, Raven thought, though he chose to keep this observation to himself.

FORTY-FOUR

ohn Beattie was in Dr Simpson's study, an unusually sincere expression upon his face as he sat opposite the professor. Sarah had brought in a pot of tea and was prolonging the pouring of it in order to ascertain what was being discussed, as the mood suggested something of great import.

She often thought that the household's preoccupation with tea-drinking provided her with untrammelled access to important conversations: hers was such a familiar presence that it was sometimes as though they all ceased to see her. However, there was only so much time to be taken in the pouring of tea without breaking this spell, and Sarah was forced to leave just as Dr Simpson tantalisingly stated: 'You will of course have to write to her father in Liverpool, but in truth I can foresee no objection.'

Sarah had to stifle a gasp as she left the room. This could mean only one thing. She hovered just outside the door in her determination to hear what else was being said.

'What of Mr Latimer?' Dr Simpson continued. 'Is he happy with the arrangement?'

'My uncle is terribly frail at the moment and his physician has proscribed excitement of any kind. A visit is therefore out of the question, but a carefully worded letter has been written and sent. I expect a reply imminently. I have no doubt he will be entirely in agreement with the match. It will do much for his morale, in fact.'

Sarah's joy on Mina's behalf was short-lived, giving way instantly to suspicion. How convenient that the old man could receive no visitors. She was also annoyed at these discussions taking place in the absence of Mina herself. It was as though she was the inanimate part of a business transaction, a consignment of whale oil or shares in a coal mine – profits could not be guaranteed but the prospects were good.

Sarah was so intent upon hearing what was being said on the other side of the door that she did not hear an approach from behind her, and consequently jumped at the sound of someone clearing his throat.

'What are you doing, Miss Fisher?' Raven said with open amusement, though from the merciful quietness of his tone it was clear he knew precisely what she was doing.

Sarah scowled at him and put her finger to her lips. She turned back to the door to listen again but the sound of footsteps on the stairs put a definitive end to her eavesdropping.

She pulled Raven into an adjoining room to avoid them being seen. They stood in silence, waiting for whoever ascended the staircase to pass, her hands on his lapels. She was sharply aware of his proximity. His breathing seemed loud in her ears and she sensed the heat coming from him. He smelled clean, of soap, and his clothes had benefited from being properly laundered and mended. His overall appearance had improved considerably in his time at Queen Street, in fact. His face had lost its gauntness, having filled out from regular food. An image of him naked in his bath on that first day came to mind, and Sarah felt her cheeks flush at the memory. She was glad that he was unlikely to notice: as the room was unoccupied, the lamps had not been lit.

She realised she was clinging on to him and let go, embarrassed.

'Care to tell me what is so compelling?' Raven asked.

'It's Beattie. He has asked for Mina's hand.'

'Well, we all knew that was coming.'

He seemed oddly regretful about this, and yet resigned to it.

'I don't like it,' she stated.

'It is hardly a matter for you or me whether we like it or not.'

'I have my concerns. There is a whiff of deceit about that man. I can sense it.'

'Are you still suspicious that he did not tell Mina about this Julia? Because it is hardly a damning omission. What woman would wish the ghost of another haunting her marriage?'

Sarah felt a surge of irritation. 'He hasn't given her the gloves,' she said.

'What gloves? What are you talking about?'

Sarah tutted at her own impatience. She had sought to clarify things for him, but only succeeded in confusing him further.

'I saw him buying ladies' gloves and assumed they were a gift for Mina, but he has not given them to her.'

'Perhaps he intends to give them to her at a later date.'

'Perhaps he intends to give them to someone else. And there have been no orchids. Or pineapples for that matter.'

'Sarah, you are making little sense.'

'He promised gifts from his uncle's hothouse and they too have failed to arrive.'

'What is it exactly that you suspect?'

Sarah had no ready answer for him. There was something about Beattie that troubled her, but she could not put it into words.

'And anyway, what can you do about it?' he asked.

Looking back, Sarah might have left it at that, but the assumption that she was powerless lit a fire under her.

Why it burned the hotter for coming from Raven was a question she did not wish to dwell upon.

FORTY-FIVE

he final outcome of any sequence of events can turn on many pivots: there is always a multiplicity of nodes, intersections in a fragile system of happenstance whereby the slightest divergence at one would have altered all. The fate of chloroform and the mystery of Evie's death were intertwined in just such a system, and either could have easily been diverted down a path to a dead end by the slightest whim of chance.

For instance, Professor Miller was equally enthusiastic about his Queen Street neighbour's discovery and was keen to be among the first to use it in a surgical case. A messenger had arrived at No. 52 the day after the Carstairs case, looking for Simpson to administer chloroform to a patient suffering from a strangulated hernia at the Infirmary. Unfortunately, the doctor was not at home and his whereabouts unknown, prompting Raven to once more lament the lack of an appointment book, as well as to wonder if the refusal to keep one was a deliberate tactic to hide the doctor's more clandestine calls. Several students, including Raven, were dispatched to find him, but to no avail. Sarah even suggested Raven stand in for the professor. He scoffed at this proposal but was secretly pleased that she thought him capable of such a thing.

Professor Miller was forced to proceed without any anaesthesia, as the surgery could not wait. Upon the first incision, the patient fainted and could not be revived. He died with the operation unfinished. If chloroform had been administered, it would have been blamed. If Raven had administered it, so would he.

Dr Simpson posited that it was fortunate he could not be found on this particular occasion. The damage to chloroform's reputation at this early juncture could have been irreparable. Raven felt obliged to comment that this was surely no justification for not keeping an appointment book.

Though it was not ultimately crucial in terms of the information it imparted, Raven would have reason of his own to thank serendipity, given how easily a particular encounter that occurred shortly after this might never have taken place.

It was amidst the chaos of the morning clinic, such sessions becoming steadily more crowded as the weather grew colder. Raven emerged from his consulting room to summon his next patient and found himself confronted by Mitchell, the burly individual who had conveyed poor Kitty in his arms but left without conveying much else. Had Raven been delayed a little longer by the previous patient, or had George Keith finished with his but ten seconds sooner, Mitchell might have passed through and been gone again without Raven seeing him.

It had been a hectic – if exciting – time since the night their paths last crossed, given it had been the same night Simpson discovered the effects of chloroform. The matter of Kitty's death was seldom far from Raven's mind, but opportunities to investigate further had been limited. Not only was he hard-pressed to find time away from his duties, but a greater factor was his reluctance to traverse the Old Town other than via the safety of Simpson's carriage. He knew that Flint's men would be looking for him with redoubled interest now, and in certain cases with vengeance on their minds. It seemed reasonable to fear that Flint might even wish to make an example of him.

Raven had briefly happened upon Peggy, who had shared lodgings with Evie at Mrs Peake's house. He asked if she had heard of a girl named Kitty, but was sent away with a flea in his ear when he further explained that they shared a profession. 'We don't all know each other,' she scolded him. 'We're not all friends, or some sisterhood of hoors.'

Mitchell stood clutching his cap in much the same posture he had done before. When he looked up, his expression betrayed that he recognised Raven, though a degree of puzzlement indicated further that he did not remember from where.

Raven showed him into the seclusion of his consulting room and let him outline his complaint, his uncomfortable hobbling gait providing an overture.

He rolled up his trouser leg and showed Raven a long cut, slightly swollen and weeping pus. 'I cut it upon a splintered board about a week ago. I thought it just needed time to heal, but what started as a scab has turned into this.'

Raven immediately thought of the preparation Sarah had given him for his face when first he arrived at Queen Street. He said nothing of that quite yet, however.

'Mr Mitchell, I work also at the Maternity Hospital. You were the gentleman who so kindly carried a stricken woman to us recently, weren't you? Kitty, you said her name was.'

He looked on his guard. 'Yes. I gather it did not go well.'

'No, sadly we were unable to do anything for her. I need to know who she was, where she lived. Can you tell me from where you carried her? Or the name of the girl you were with, that I might find her?'

Mitchell sat back in his seat, folding his arms. Raven had anticipated this. It was one thing to act upon the spur of the moment, quite another to speak of one's dealings with whores.

'I am not sure I recall the details of that night,' Mitchell said, 'and nor do I particularly wish to.'

Raven nodded, as though understanding. 'A pity. Just as I am not sure I recall the formula for the ointment that would surely cure your wound.'

A few hours later, Raven was standing inside a ramshackle building on Calton Road being confronted by a woman about whom he had been warned by Mitchell. He had come here on his way to the Maternity Hospital, reasoning that not only would it be easier to spot the Weasel and Gargantua in daylight, but also less likely they would attempt to assail him in full view of a busy thorough-fare.

The madam of the bawdy house to which he had been directed was a corpulent and intimidatingly ugly woman by the name of Miss Nadia. Raven could not imagine her ever having worked on her back, but reckoned she was particularly suited to her role in that by the time the customers got past her, any girl they were presented with would look like Venus by comparison.

'I wish to see a woman by the name of Mairi,' he stated. 'I am informed she works here.'

Miss Nadia gave him a cold smile. 'She does indeed. I can enquire if she is available, but I'll be wanting to see the colour of your money first.'

If Raven's finances had a colour, it would be deathly pale. His mother had sent the regular allowance permitted by his miserable uncle, but that had been almost three weeks ago. How he envied the likes of Beattie, typical of those he had studied with whose family riches comfortably financed their living while they learned their profession. His uncle had plenty more to give, and his mother would go to any lengths to secure it if he asked, but Raven would not have her further humbled before him. Once he began to make money in earnest, he would free her from ever having to ask Malcolm for another penny. For now, however, he had to find another currency.

'I am a doctor at Milton House. I recently treated a girl named Kitty, late of this establishment.'

'Didn't treat her very well, did you? She never came back from Milton House. Are you after payment in kind for services rendered? Because it doesn't work like that.'

Raven fixed her with the same look he had given Mr Gallagher. His dealings with Effie Peake had let him know it was best not to show any weakness. Such women dealt in counterfeit emotions, and in this place there was no reward for honesty.

'There is growing police interest in what might have brought on Kitty's condition. So unless you would prefer James McLevy and his men knocking on your door instead of me, I would suggest you do me a courtesy.'

Miss Nadia considered this for a moment, then bid him follow, leading him to a room on the second floor. Mairi was tall, appearing all the more so for being undernourished. Her olive skin suggested a more exotic provenance than was usual in these parts, though sadly it most likely derived from a father who briefly put to shore some twenty years previous on a ship from Spain or Italy.

'Give him what he wants,' Nadia instructed her. 'And by that I mean answer his questions. Anything else comes at the usual rates.'

Raven closed the door. Mairi was sitting on the bed with an anxious look, detecting that the circumstances were out of the ordinary.

'I treated Kitty at Milton House,' he explained. 'Your client brought her to us. There was nothing we could do to save her, so I sat by her until the end.'

Mairi bit her lip, sadness immediate upon her face. 'Thank you for that,' she said.

'I would know what caused her agonies. She was with child, wasn't she?'

Her expression betrayed that Mairi knew this and more.

'I believe she took measures to get rid of it, and I believe you know that too.'

'I know nothing about that,' she answered, a little too fast.

'Then let's talk about what I think you do know. If you were to find yourself with child, you would have a notion who to speak to about dealing with it, would you not? Who did Kitty speak to?'

Mairi said nothing, but from the widening of her eyes, it was clear that there was a specific something she was not saying.

'Have no fear. I am not looking to get anyone into trouble. But I am a man of medicine and I need to know how this happened. Kitty was not the first to die in this manner and I would ensure a similar fate does not befall any other women.'

She swallowed, looking about herself as though afraid someone might overhear.

'There is a French midwife,' she answered quietly. 'Worked in the service of queens and contessas, Kitty reckoned. She had special training. Knows how to do things that doctors won't, if you know what I mean.'

'Well enough. Do you know her name?'

Mairi answered in a whisper, 'Kitty called her Madame Anchou. Said she wore a hooded cape of the finest cloth and spoke with a strong accent.'

'How did Kitty get in touch with this woman?'

'She has rooms at a tavern. You have to speak to the landlord, though. He makes the arrangements.'

'For a slice, no doubt.'

Mairi nodded. 'It cost a lot of money, I know that. Kitty had this locket her mother gave her that she had to pawn. Broke her heart to part with it, but she had no option.'

'What exactly did her money buy her?'

'That's the thing: only pills. I told Kitty she was robbed if she handed over all her money just for that, but she said there was an agreement. Madame Anchou assured her the pills would deal with the problem: you know, make the baby come right soon. But as a guarantee, if that didn't happen, Kitty should come back and she would perform her service in respect of the fee. Kitty reasoned she would rather take the pills and see how that worked out if it spared her knives and knitting needles.'

Raven recalled his discussion with Ziegler and Mrs Stevenson. Desperate women would pay handsomely for a 'secret remedy', especially if it was dispensed by a midwife from Paris, trained at the famous Hôtel Dieu, and formerly in the service of French aristocracy. But as Mrs Stevenson warned, it was not always harmless pills their money bought them.

'And where is this tavern she works out of?' Raven asked.

'It's down in Leith. It's called the King's Wark.'

FORTY-SIX

arah sat at a table by the window, chosen for the view it afforded of Leith Shore stretching southwards towards Tolbooth Wynd. On Sunday morning, she could have accurately stated that she had never been inside a tavern in her life, and now she found herself patronising such an establishment for the second time in three days.

She was nursing a glass of gin, purchased primarily for appearance's sake. It was her first taste of the stuff, and she had resolved that it would also be the last, until she discovered the ameliorating effect it had upon her anxiety. She could not imagine why anyone would choose to drink it for pleasure, but under needful circumstances, the flavour was to be tolerated like that of any other medicine.

'It is the only way to draw out this Madame Anchou,' Raven had insisted. 'I can't go myself, for what reason would a man have to be seeking her services?'

'You could be seeking them on behalf of your lover.'

'Yes, but this landlord would recognise me. He followed me after I went to the King's Wark asking questions about Rose's body.'

The landlord's name was Spiers, according to a plate above the door. He was exactly as Raven described: bald-headed, tall and burly, an intimidating presence fit for rousting drunks. He had come over to her table unbidden, seeing her sitting there alone. Sarah guessed he already knew what she was there for.

Sarah had never considered herself to have any kind of gift for the dramatic. Her sole experience had been staging scenes from Shakespeare at school, where she had distinguished herself only by her recall for the lines, an ability entirely down to hours of rote learning. However, as Spiers approached her, she had realised she would need no talent for acting in order to deceive him. She was there to play the part of a frightened housemaid, and that required no pretence.

'Are you quite sure you are in the right place, miss?' he had asked.

'I am not sure. I have been told you have a tenant, a French-woman by the name of Madame Anchou. Is she present? I would speak with her, if you please.'

'And what would you speak with her about?'

'That is a personal matter, between ladies.'

'Madame Anchou is not present. She does not reside here, but keeps a room for consultations. However, I can arrange an introduction.'

'I would be most grateful.'

'Your gratitude will suffice for that, but should you require her services –' Spiers paused, casting an eye towards her middle '– and if you've come here, I wager you do – then the fee is two guineas.'

Though Raven had warned her about the likely cost, Sarah's eyes still bulged. This was more than two months' wages. It was the cruellest extortion of the desperate.

Spiers had noted her reaction. 'If you cannot meet the price, you and Madame Anchou should not waste each other's time.'

'I can . . . obtain it.'

'Good. For though her services are expensive, they are worth it. She was trained in Paris and retained by French aristocracy.'

Sarah had already heard about her reputation. 'Such are her reputed abilities,' Raven had said, 'it is a pity she was not around during the Revolution, for she surely would have had a balm fit to reattach Marie Antoinette's head. All of which begs the question of what happened to her that she's plying her trade here.'

Spiers had offered to arrange an introduction the very next day, but Sarah knew that Monday's duties allowed no opportunity to absent herself. She had therefore agreed to return on Tuesday, when she always had errands to run during the afternoon, giving her dispensation to be out of the house. Procuring two guineas in such a time frame was mercifully not a task upon which the success of their plan was predicated.

Even within the bounds of such dispensation, she knew she was still risking her position by partaking in these activities. It had preyed upon her mind from the moment Raven asked her to come to Leith, and yet it had not occurred to her to say no. Though it set her trembling from her gut to her fingertips, pursuing these investigations gave her a sense of freedom and usefulness far greater than anything she felt assisting at clinic.

Sarah glanced out of the window, checking that she could still see Raven on the dockside. He had chosen a discreet vantage point where he was unlikely to be noticed by the landlord, but close enough to move in and join them once Madame Anchou was settled at Sarah's table.

A twelfth glance at the clock told her the appointed time had come and gone. Spiers had warned her not to expect sharp punctuality, but Sarah was more concerned about completing the errands she still had to run before returning in time for her pre-dinner duties.

Then, as she gazed into the ever-shifting traffic upon the quayside, she noticed a distinctive figure approaching from the south. She wore a flowing black cloak with a capacious hood, and though her head was slightly bowed, there was an upright confidence about her as she walked. Sarah had no question but that this was her, as described in the albeit second-hand accounts Raven had relayed. She was tall and graceful, gliding through the crowd as though she was not of them.

Sarah downed the rest of the gin, wincing against the taste. She needed something to steady her, already feeling intimidated by this woman before she had even reached the tavern. She felt the liquid burn all the way to her stomach.

Sarah looked along Leith Shore once again, hoping to glimpse the face beneath that hood, but Madame Anchou was no longer in sight. She surveyed the crowds upon the dock, expecting the hooded figure to re-emerge, but the woman was not to be seen.

What she did see was Raven charging past the window, taking off in urgent pursuit.

FORTY-SEVEN

s always in Leith, Raven felt surrounded by bustling movement in every direction; even above, where seagulls wheeled amidst rising clouds sent up by a departing packet steamer. He could barely see the water for sails, and upon the shore there was the liveliest throng and babble, everywhere teeming with activity and busy purpose. Raven heard half a dozen languages spoken in the space of a few minutes, noticed a boundless variety of features, skin colours and clothing upon men toting crates, bales and trunks.

Smells of coffee and spices hung upon the air. Raven breathed them in gratefully, aware the shore was not always so blessed. Simpson had told him about an altogether less fragrant cargo that landed here once, both of them taking pleasure in a tale that reflected poorly upon Professor Syme. In the days before the Anatomy Act, when bodies for dissection were in short supply, Syme had acquired cadavers from Dublin and London, transporting them to Edinburgh via the docks at Leith. During the summer of 1826, the stench coming from a shipment resulted in Syme's crates being opened and their unauthorised contents discovered, generating much outrage and scandal. 'Syme's cargo was marked "perishable goods",' Simpson told him, wheezing with laughter.

Raven thought he had chosen his position well. It was a spot where he would remain largely invisible should the landlord happen to look out of the window, but affording a clear view north and south along the shore, for he didn't know from which direction Madame Anchou would approach. As he had explained to Sarah, his concern was that, should Spiers see him, he might suspect something was afoot and take steps to warn off the midwife. The unspoken further implication was that the landlord might simply move against Raven directly, or God forbid even Sarah.

In order to reduce her exposure to danger, Sarah was under instruction to conduct her conversation only in the tavern and not to agree to a consultation upstairs in the midwife's rooms. She was to discuss the services the Frenchwoman might offer, but then admit she did not have the money yet. This would give Raven the opportunity to follow Madame Anchou and confront her on neutral ground, or even to find out where she lived so that he could choose his moment judiciously.

What he hadn't anticipated was that she would see him first.

He was hopping from foot to foot as he waited, in an effort to fend off shivers. It was a cold day, an unforgiving wind blowing in off the water. Sarah was right: he urgently needed to get a heavier coat.

He ceased his hopping and stood rigid when he saw his quarry moving through the crowd, striding down the incline from Tolbooth Wynd. The moment he saw that hood, he had no question that this was the woman he had heard described. The black cloth was swaying back and forth with each step so that he could only glimpse fragments of her face, never the entirety. The view was further obscured by people moving in and out of her path, sometimes causing her to disappear from view altogether. He thought she might have looked at him, but with her eyes in shadow beneath the hood, it was impossible to be sure. She was getting steadily nearer, though, so he would get a close-up view soon enough.

Again she vanished from view behind a shore porter pushing

a cart, and when next he spied her, she had turned and was running. Raven watched her part the crowd, hurrying back in the direction from which she had just come.

She knew something was wrong.

He took off, signalling through the window for Sarah to follow. There was going to be no meeting. They had to catch her now, or they might never track her down.

Weaving between the people milling along the dockside, Raven quickly began to gain ground. He had always been swift on his feet, and it was easier to run in gentleman's clothing. For that reason, he knew that he would be leaving Sarah far behind, but the important thing was that the midwife did not get away.

She was easier to keep in sight now that she was moving faster, as he could see the movement ahead of her as people stepped out of her way. However, when she reached the first side street, she took a hard turn and was gone from view. Raven stepped up his pace, and to his relief she was back in his sight when he reached the corner, both of them now hurrying along a narrower but altogether quieter thoroughfare.

Anchou glanced back upon hearing his footfalls, then diverted to speak briefly to three stevedores who had just emerged from a doorway. Raven was out of earshot, but as he watched her point towards him, it was not difficult to deduce the crux of their conversation.

She resumed her flight as the three stevedores began marching on Raven, one hefting a heavy stick. He reckoned he could possibly take one of these men on his own, or at least be swift enough to evade him, but not all three at once. He had to back away for his own safety, and in his retreat he did not see where the midwife went. In order to resume his pursuit, he would have to double back and loop around, by which time she would be long away, or at least have plenty of time to hide.

As he turned the corner back onto the dockside, he saw Sarah hurrying towards him.

'She got away,' he confessed. 'She set some dockers to block my path. Must have told them I meant her harm.'

'Why did she run, though?' Sarah asked.

'It is my assumption that she recognised me, enough to know what I was about.'

'And therefore she feared you would recognise her also. But from where?'

'I can't imagine. I don't know any Frenchwomen.'

'Then perhaps she is not French,' Sarah suggested, 'but rather a woman pretending to be something she is not.'

Raven suddenly saw how Madame Anchou's exoticness was part of her attraction to prospective patients. It might be as false as the medicines she was hawking.

Raven waited until he saw the three stevedores pass, then slipped along the side street again. He and Sarah reached a thoroughfare that ran parallel to the dockside, but there was no sign of her. He knew it was hopeless.

'She could have gone anywhere,' he admitted.

'At some point she will have to go back to the King's Wark, surely,' Sarah reminded him.

They had no notion when that might be, nor the option to keep vigil for its happening. However, there was reason enough for them to visit the place.

'We have some questions we ought to ask Mr Spiers,' he said.

'And what if he has a strong will not to answer them? A violent will, even?'

Raven had considered this, but he had his leverage now. 'He has seen you too. I will tell him that you wait for me, and should I fail to return or come to any harm, you will be going straight to McLevy to tell him everything we know.'

'We don't know much.'

'Nonetheless, it is what he fears we know that will restrain him.'

They made their way back towards the King's Wark, approaching from the rear having come around in a circle.

Raven's plan to keep Sarah out of the landlord's sight was immediately dashed as they saw Spiers emerge into a courtyard at the back of the tavern. He pitched forward as though about to sprint towards them, but as Raven altered his stance and put out an arm to warn off Sarah, it became clear that the landlord was in fact staggering. He fell against a stack of beer barrels, gripping one to prop himself upright. As he turned, Raven was able to see a patch of dark red staining his grubby shirt around his middle.

Spiers noticed them and reached out an imploring hand before dropping to his knees.

They hurried into the courtyard.

'She stuck me,' he said, clutching his hand to his side. 'The French bitch. So quick. I didn't even see a blade.'

'Why?'

'I don't know. She didn't stop to explain.'

Raven helped Spiers take his rest against a barrel. The patch of red was widening by the second. He and Sarah shared a look. Spiers was bleeding badly and they both knew he had little time left.

'What was your arrangement with this woman?'

'I will not condemn myself with my own testimony,' he replied, grimacing against the pain.

'Your wound is grave, sir. Without help you will die within the hour. I am a doctor. I can keep you alive long enough for us to get you to Professor Syme, the best surgeon in the city. But only if you answer our questions.'

'Do not take me for a fool, son. There's not a surgeon in the world who can mend this. She has done for me.'

'Then you owe her no loyalty. Speak, man.'

'She is a French midwife who rents rooms. That is all I know.'

'You must know more than that. She carries out abortions on your premises and she pays you a percentage. Who is she really? What more do you know about her?'

'Nothing. She told me if I didn't ask questions, it would protect us both.'

'Well, your silence has not served you well today, has it? What more do you know?'

Spiers considered it, a bitter look on his face, from which colour was visibly draining.

'She has a partner,' he said, swallowing.

'Who?'

'I never knew his name and I saw him but once. I tried to enter her room when I thought her not home and found him there.'

'What did he look like?'

'I saw him but for a few seconds, and even then only from the back. I had barely opened the door when he pushed me out and slammed it shut. He was standing by a table with instruments and potions ranged upon it. A medical man, like yourself. Older, though.'

'And what of Rose Campbell?' Sarah asked.

'Who?'

'She was a housemaid. The one who was pulled from the water.'

'I know nothing about that.'

'You followed me after I asked about her,' Raven reminded him. 'Come on, would you not make your confession that you may face death without fear?'

Spiers winced, the blood oozing between his fingers where he clutched them to the soaking cloth. He looked afraid now.

'She came here, paid the money. The procedure was successful but she was ill afterwards. They often were . . . and we turned them out, though they were barely fit to walk. We let them stay a couple of days, and if it appeared they would not recover, we put them out because we did not want any bodies to dispose of or deaths to explain. God forgive me,' he said, his voice faltering.

Sarah had found a wooden tankard upon a bench and pulled

out the stop from a barrel to fill it. She offered it to Spiers, who sipped it gratefully.

'Your one, Rose . . . she was recovering. She was here a few days, but she was on the mend. I brought her water, meals. Then I was woken by her screaming in the night. When I went to her room, she was in her final throes. She died all twisted and agonised.'

Sarah offered another sip, though he barely had the strength to take it in. Most of it dribbled down his chin, and when he spoke again, his voice was dry and faint.

'I was sore afraid. I feared it would bring all hell crashing down upon me if it was found out what was being done here. I had to get rid of her, so I took her to the water and dropped her in. But I didn't kill her. God as my witness, I didn't . . . kill her . . .'

With these words, his voice became a pitiable whisper and his head rolled forward onto his chest.

'He is gone,' Raven said.

Sarah looked ashen, but it was not merely the sight of a dead man that was troubling her.

'What do we do now?'

'Leave. Quickly.'

'Just abandon him here? Shouldn't we alert the police?'

'Only if you feel confident about explaining your role in all of this to McLevy.'

This silenced any moral qualms Sarah might have about his suggested course of action. They looked left and right out of the back court to ensure nobody had seen them, then slipped quietly down the same narrow lane by which they had approached.

'Why would Anchou kill him?' Sarah asked as they walked briskly but not in a conspicuous hurry back towards the anonymity of the busy dockside.

'I know not, but I fear it was our actions that brought her knife down upon him. She knew we were investigating her, and there was something she feared Spiers might tell us.'

'Then why didn't he? He gave us nothing of any great import.'

'Perhaps there was something she merely feared he knew, and could not take the risk.'

Sarah suddenly pushed Raven against a wall, her hands upon his chest. He could feel his heart thump against her fingers, his whole body still trembling from what he had just witnessed.

'What is—?' he began.

'I cannot be seen,' she said urgently. 'I am supposed to be in the town on errands. I could be dismissed.'

'Seen by whom?'

'Do not look,' she insisted. 'Keep your head down.'

But by that time he had already spotted the problem. Walking south along Leith Shore was the man who was these days affecting to call himself James Matthews Duncan.

'What is he doing down here?' Raven wondered aloud.

'I don't know. Just take care he doesn't see you.'

As though to ensure this, she pulled his head down nearer to hers. She was close enough that he could smell that familiar aroma, like fresh linen. His thoughts returned to their encounter the night he had run home in the rain. Many times since, he had revisited the memory of her hands against him as she helped take off his shirt.

They stayed like that a while. Raven saw Duncan pass from view, but was long in saying so, for he did not wish the moment to end so soon. In time, it had to though.

They broke apart, an awkwardness between them as though they did not know how to acknowledge what had just happened. Fortunately, there was plenty to talk about.

'You were vindicated in your thinking about Rose,' he said. 'What Spiers told us would explain why the police surgeon found her not to be pregnant.'

'Yet clearly, she died in the same way as Kitty and your Evie. If she had successfully rid herself of the baby, why would she take the same pills?'

Raven had been asking himself this question too.

'Perhaps she did not take them voluntarily,' he suggested. 'It might be that she had discovered something about Madame Anchou that the midwife wished to keep hidden.'

'Or about her partner. Could it be that he is the one who actually carries out the procedures, while she brings in the business with the allure of having trained in Paris and worked for the French aristocracy?'

This was an astute supposition, in keeping with the mystique that allowed her to charge exorbitantly.

'Not to mention of being a woman and therefore earning their trust,' Raven added. 'Such an arrangement would allow a doctor to practise this dark art without the risk that would attend advertising such services.'

They strode south in the direction of the city, the crowd thinning as they moved further from the water. Raven could not help but search ahead in case he spied that black hood, while he suspected Sarah's eyes were still concerned with the whereabouts of Dr Duncan.

'In recent months there have been several cases of young women dying following abortions,' Raven said.

'So they might all have been the work of Madame Anchou and her partner?'

'Spiers admitted they turned out the sick ones so that they did not die at the tavern. And if Rose was deliberately poisoned, it could have been either of them who killed her. We came here seeking one anonymous malefactor and depart in search of two: Madam Anchou, who may or may not be the Frenchwoman she pretends, and a doctor of little conscience or humanity.'

FORTY-EIGHT

arah maintained a respectful distance while the parish clerk dealt with the fellow who had arrived at St Cuthbert's just ahead of her. He was a young man but looked as though he carried the weight of the world upon his sloping shoulders. He was attempting to hire the parish mortcloth for the burial of his mother, but there appeared to be some issue over the fee.

The clerk examined the pile of pennies that the man had deposited upon his ledger. He separated them with the end of his pen as though reluctant to sully his fingers with the contents of the young man's pockets. He sighed and then frowned.

'This is insufficient. I suggest that you return with the fee already stipulated or your mother must be buried without the parish cloth.'

Then he smiled at the bereaved man with a chilly politeness and dismissed him as though they had been discussing a frippery of no earthly significance. The man said nothing, rendered mute by the clerk's unbending adherence to his ecclesiastical price-list. Christian charity evidently did not extend to the parish's funeral shroud. He turned and shuffled out of the clerk's office, back into the body of the church.

The clerk watched him leave with a tiny shake of the head,

as though other people's poverty was an affront, then turned his attention to Sarah, peering over the top of his spectacles.

And anyway, what can you do about it? Raven had asked when she told him about her suspicions regarding Beattie. It had been a rhetorical question, to his mind. She would show him otherwise by answering it.

'How may I help you?' the clerk asked, in a tone that suggested he had little intention of doing so.

'I come at the behest of Dr James Young Simpson,' Sarah replied, hoping that the mention of the professor's name would oil the wheels of cooperation.

It seemed to have some effect, as the clerk stood a little more upright and pushed his glasses back up to the bridge of his nose. His tone became oleaginous and a ghost of a smile appeared upon his thin lips.

'How may I be of assistance to the professor?'

'A woman has died at the Maternity Hospital,' Sarah said. 'Her child lives. The woman's name is known but not that of her nearest relative. There is a need to find someone to care for the baby, to see it baptised and properly raised. The professor requested that I consult the local parish registers to see if she was married, and who her parents are, if they are still alive.'

The clerk briefly brightened at the mention of baptism but snorted at the suggestion of a marriage. It was well known that many of the women treated at the Maternity Hospital were not in possession of a spouse. He wrinkled his nose as though assailed by an unwelcome smell.

'I am surprised such an important task has fallen to you. Has the professor not an apprentice or some other suitable person to do it?'

'Indeed he has,' she replied. 'But they are all so busy, what with the recent outbreak of typhus.'

The man immediately sought out his handkerchief and held it to his nose as though the mere mention of the disease would cause it to arrive. He looked at her for a while, weighing up her request. She perhaps should not have mentioned the Maternity Hospital. Or typhus.

'The information you request will take some time to find,' he said at last. 'And I should point out to you that our records are far from comprehensive: those who are not prepared to part with the necessary fee often do not bother with registration at all.'

'I understand,' said Sarah. 'I can see you are a very busy man and I have no wish to impose upon you. Perhaps you would permit me to look through the book myself.'

He looked at his pristine ledger and then down at her hands.

'My hands are clean, sir,' she replied. 'Dr Simpson insists upon it.'

The mention of the professor's name again seemed to tip the balance in her favour.

'You'll have to look through several of the registers. The current one only goes back to 1840.'

Her search did indeed take some time, and bore no fruit. As the vestry began to darken, she tried not to think of what Mrs Lyndsay would say upon her return, what punishment she would have to endure as a result of her tardiness. A suitable excuse would have to be found or her clinic duties would be severely curtailed.

Sarah had always considered herself an honest person, and was feeling increasingly uncomfortable about the lies she now found herself having to tell on a regular basis. She felt that her concern for Mina justified her current endeavours, but she would have to make sure that this propensity for subterfuge came to an end once everything was resolved.

Yet even as she thought this, she considered what she was about and contrasted it with the person she used to be, only a few weeks ago. That meek housemaid would not have dared to deceive anyone, far less embark upon clandestine investigations in the realms of abortionists and murderers. There was a comfort and security in knowing one's place and asking no questions. But she had never felt that a role of meekness and acceptance *was* her place.

Sarah was fastidious in her search, but she could find no record of Charles Latimer or of Beattie's mother. The name 'John Beattie' was cited, but the dates did not tally up unless the apparently sprightly young doctor was in fact approaching his eightieth birthday.

Sarah slumped in her chair, unsure as to what this lack of information represented. She had to admit that it was hardly conclusive evidence that Beattie was a fraud of some kind. Could she be entirely on the wrong track? Were her emotions clouding her judgment, her disapproval of Mina's choices colouring her view?

She regarded the stack of dusty registers piled in front of her and wondered if she was wasting her time. Perhaps in a desire to gain something from her afternoon's efforts, it occurred to her that Raven's family might be listed among them. He was someone else whose account of his own background rang false.

Sarah checked for the clerk but he had disappeared. It seemed he was content to leave her to her own devices as soon as he was sure she had no intention of amending entries, ripping out pages or drooling on the paper.

She estimated Raven's age to be twenty and so looked at the records for the years 1825 to 1830. She found no entry for the birth of Wilberforce Raven, but she did find a record of the marriage of a Margaret Raven to an Andrew Cunningham in 1826. The surname was familiar but for a moment she couldn't think why. Then she remembered: it was the name inscribed inside some of Raven's books.

Sarah looked at the births registered in the following year and found him: Thomas Wilberforce Cunningham.

Raven had changed his name. But for what purpose? She tried to think what else she knew about him, what she had been told regarding his background. His mother lived in St Andrews with her brother, Raven receiving letters from there on a regular basis. She knew his father was dead, hence the removal of his mother to Fife.

Sarah wondered when this tragedy had occurred, from what age Raven had been raised without a father. She turned to the registers again, searching for burials. She looked from the present day all the way back to the year of Raven's birth. There was no entry for the interment of Andrew Cunningham.

According to the records of St Cuthbert's parish, which covered all of Edinburgh and some way beyond, Raven's father was not dead at all.

FORTY-NINE

itken's tavern was crowded, a thick pall of pipe smoke coiling up to the rafters. It was warm, almost uncomfortably so, the press of bodies elevating the temperature and causing the windows to run with condensation. As Raven returned from the bar, it took him a few seconds to locate Henry, who had managed to find a table in a corner, where he was chatting to a man Raven failed to recognise.

He wondered again why he had been summoned here. Henry had accosted him as he stood by Simpson's carriage, waiting to accompany the professor home. Raven had confided in his friend about the French midwife and her medical accomplice, whereupon Henry told him he had news that might be of interest.

'What news?' he had replied, but Henry wagged a finger by way of denying him.

'This is information I will only share with a tankard in my hand, for it has been too long since we supped together.'

Raven feared he was being sold a bill of goods, as he would have much preferred to know the value of this information before he traded it for a safe means of conveyance home.

The man sitting with Henry looked young but exceedingly weary, sporting dark circles beneath eyes that betrayed a profound want of sleep. Raven was unsurprised when Henry introduced him as a doctor at the Royal Infirmary.

'This is Fleming,' he said. 'Replaced McKellar, Christison's resident clerk who died of fever last month.'

Raven sat down and took a long pull of his beer, involuntarily calculating what fraction of Flint's debt the price of a round would have redeemed. '"The poisoned breath of infection",' he said, wiping froth from his beard.

'"A young and early sacrifice at the shrine of professional duty",' replied Henry archly. It was a well-worn phrase trotted out by the medical professors when such an incident occurred, which was a little too often in Raven's opinion. Not for the first time, he felt relief that his present duties seldom required his attendance at the Infirmary.

'We imperil our own health working in that place,' said Henry's lugubrious companion, staring disconsolately into his beer.

Raven wondered why Henry had seen fit to bring him along.

'So what is the news?' asked Raven, feeling disinclined to tarry. He had grown his beard since last he was in Aitken's, but the very reason he needed it had stemmed from being recognised in this place on the night he was attacked. Flint had eyes in here, he had little doubt.

'There's been another one,' Henry said.

'Another what?'

'Another death. Young woman.' Henry nodded at his drowsy companion, who was still staring into his beer. 'Fleming dealt with the case.' He kicked the young man under the table, which caused him to rouse himself.

'Yes,' Fleming said, rubbing his eyes. 'Moribund when admitted. Didn't wake up.'

'What was the cause of death?' Raven asked.

'Peritonitis. All the signs of puerperal sepsis but no sign of a baby.'

Raven could feel his anxiety grow. He had a fear that if he

was going to be caught by Flint's men, it would be due to an avoidable lack of vigilance in the service of an ironically pointless risk. Diverting here merely to learn about yet another victim of their anonymous abortionist definitely came into that category.

As if sensing his friend's deteriorating mood, Henry nudged Fleming again. 'Tell him what you told me.'

'Oh, yes,' he responded, as though in his fatigue his brain needed a shunt. 'She had an unusual smell about her. It was on her clothes when she first came in: a sweet smell. Like over-ripe fruit. And she had unusual marks around her mouth.'

'Abrasions?'

'No, not abrasions.'

'Bruising, then?' Raven suggested impatiently.

'No, it looked like—'

'Ligature marks, as though she had been gagged?'

'For pity's sake, let him speak, Raven.'

'What, then? Why did you drag me here?'

'These looked more like a burn,' Fleming stated.

Raven understood. 'Chloroform.'

'You see?' said Henry, with a flourish of his hand. 'This individual you seek has been keeping up to date with new developments.'

Beyond proving how quickly the new anaesthetic was being adopted, Raven did not see how this assisted in his quest. He took a glum gulp of his beer by way of consolation.

'You seem less than elated,' Henry observed.

'Why should I be other? This does not bring me any nearer to knowing his identity.'

The young surgeon's familiar wily grin informed him there was something he had missed.

'Not at this moment,' Henry said. 'But I can tell you where you will find it written down.'

FIFTY

arah stood on Princes Street, peering through the window into Duncan and Flockhart's. She was choosing her moment carefully, and as she waited for the opportunity she required, she worked on composing herself, because for the first time in her life, she was about to commit a crime.

She was not going to steal anything, merely borrow without leave, but by the borrowing she intended to facilitate a trespass upon this property. Technically, this would be a burglary, albeit one in which, again, nothing would be taken save information. Nonetheless, though there would be no theft and no damage, she would not wish to find herself explaining it to anyone, least of all McLevy. It might be enough to see her in jail, and would be more than enough to see her dismissed.

Duncan and Flockhart were the primary manufacturers of chloroform throughout Edinburgh. Every doctor using it was buying their supplies from here, where their purchases were recorded in the druggist's ledger. Raven had enquired of Mr Flockhart whether he might see who had been ordering the stuff, feigning a curiosity regarding the uptake of the new anaesthetic agent, but Flockhart had told him the ledger had to remain confidential. When it came to the purchase of drugs, customers needed to be able to rely upon their suppliers' discretion. Yet one of those customers was Madame Anchou's mysterious confederate, and very possibly the man who had murdered Rose Campbell.

'I need to see that list,' Raven told Sarah, almost uncontainable in his frustration. 'But how can I do so if it is locked safe in their keeping?'

'Every lock has a key,' Sarah had replied. 'It is simply a matter of acquiring it.'

'I would not be able to locate it, far less procure such a thing unnoticed.'

'A set of keys hangs from a hook on the wall behind the counter, just to the right of the cash register. They are in the charge of Ingram, the assistant. I have heard him talk of how he opens the shop and prepares the premises before the Misters Duncan and Flockhart arrive.'

'And how do you propose that I lay my hands on them unseen?'

'I do not propose that you lay your hands on them at all. For such a task you require a person to whom nobody pays any notice. Such as a housemaid.'

Watching through the window, she observed what she expected: Mr Flockhart tending to some matter at the counter, assisted by the smug and dim young runt whose suitability for employment here was considered greater than hers by virtue of what dangled between his legs. Mr Duncan was, as usual, not to be seen, busying himself in the laboratory towards the rear of the building. Mr Flockhart was the more garrulous of the pair, and therefore more frequently the public face of the partnership.

In time, she saw Mr Flockhart slip out of sight too, either to the lab or one of the storerooms. She knew from experience that he was happy to let Ingram deal with customers of lesser standing, such as a maid running an errand. If someone important came in, the lad would fetch his boss.

This was her moment.

As she stepped through the door and the bell rang, Sarah felt it trilling right through her. She was jangling with tension. She didn't only feel it in a quickened heartbeat and a tightness in her gut; her fingers tingled, her elbows, her knees. It was manifest in a heightened state of perception affecting all sensations. The colours in the room seemed brighter, the smells more distinct, the sounds sharper.

She wondered if this was down to a pronounced awareness of all that she stood to lose should she be caught. Never would she be allowed in this shop again. She would be thrown out of the household, in fact, and what future would be open to her then? Sarah became privately angry whenever someone suggested she should be grateful for her job as a housemaid, but she knew there were worse fates. Nonetheless, there was someone in this city who saw housemaids and other young women as disposable, and she was resolved to see their wickedness unmasked.

'Can I help you, young lady?' the assistant asked.

She wanted to swat him for that. She estimated she was at least a year older than him, possibly two.

'I require some items for Dr Simpson.'

'Dr Simpson of Queen Street?'

This annoyed her too. He was verifying whose account should be billed, even though he saw her at least twice a week. Either he was acting as though he didn't recognise her or he genuinely didn't recognise her, and she wasn't sure which one was the greater insult.

'Indeed.'

'And what does Dr Simpson require?'

Sarah rhymed off a short list and cast an eye upon the high shelves while Ingram retrieved her requests, all of which were within easy reach.

'Oh, and he also wished a quantity of carbonic acid.'

Ingram frowned and turned to search the nearby cabinets. He did not see what he was looking for. This was because she had asked him to supply a quantity of fixed air, the transparent and colourless gas that, according to Gregory's *Outlines of Chemistry*, he was currently exhaling and he hadn't the knowledge to realise it.

'I'll just go and ask Mr—'

'It's right up there,' Sarah interrupted, stepping behind the counter and pointing to a high shelf.

'I don't see it.'

'Then let me fetch it,' she said, reaching for the ladder.

Ingram blocked her way. 'That is not permitted,' he told her in a scolding tone.

'For only a man will do,' Sarah muttered, stepping away from the ladder but closer to the cash register.

As Ingram climbed, his attention firmly upon each spar, Sarah lifted the keys from their hook and slipped them into her pocket.

'I still don't see it,' he reported.

'My apologies. I just remembered that Dr Simpson merely mentioned it. He didn't mean for me to buy some, otherwise he'd have told me a quantity, wouldn't he?'

Ingram sighed with irritation at this stupid woman.

As he began descending, Sarah was already heading for the door, as though some force was pushing her out of the shop before she could be apprehended. She felt heat in her cheeks and it was all she could do not to break into a run once she was back on Princes Street.

She had travelled only a few yards when she heard the voice.

'Young woman! Stop!'

Sarah felt time suspended as the recklessness of her actions came crashing in upon her. She saw McLevy hauling her away, the stern face of a judge, rats and chains in a jail cell.

When she turned to face this grim future, she saw Ingram striding towards her, holding a brown paper bag.

'You forgot to lift what Dr Simpson *did* order,' he said, his tone patronising and heavy with scorn. 'That would have earned you a dressing down when you got back, wouldn't it?'

'Thank you,' she said, relief lending her tone sincerity. 'Indeed it would.'

Much like one might receive for misplacing one's keys.

FIFTY-ONE

aven tried turning another key without success, huddled in the darkness at the back door to the building. Though few people were likely to be passing at this hour, he had opted to approach from the rear as it was secluded from view. Unfortunately it was also secluded from the illumination of the nearest street lamp. Sarah had tried lighting a candle, but the breeze was too strong even back here, whipping through any gap it could find.

His hands were cold and he was shivering. Neither of these things were helping either.

'Are you sure you lifted the right keys?' he asked.

She did not respond to this, but he could imagine her expression. Sarah had only surrendered the keys on the walk here, once everyone at Queen Street had gone to bed. It had been her way of ensuring that he could not go without her. He did not understand why she would wish to, but he was learning that it was usually futile to argue.

'We are equals in this enterprise,' was all she told him.

Raven tried the first key again, and this time it turned. In his trembling anxiety, his fumbling fingers had not inserted it properly before.

The door opened with rather more of a creak than was

comfortable. With the wind blowing so hard, the sound would not carry more than a few feet, but to Raven's ears it sounded like the wail of a banshee calling attention to their crime.

Sarah lit the candle now that she had some shelter. By its meagre light, they found their way into the laboratory, where Raven located an oil lamp. As he turned up the flame, he saw dozens of leather-bound volumes lining a bookcase, amidst shelves upon shelves of powders and liquids. Bottles, beakers and flasks reflected the light. Raven was wary of the many retorts jutting out, inviting accident, which would preclude their intention to pass here without leaving any record.

He held the lamp to the spines. None of them was what he sought.

'I have often seen Mr Flockhart write in his ledger upon the counter,' Sarah told him. 'I imagine it is kept close by.'

They crept through to the front of the shop on quiet feet, though Raven did wonder why he felt an instinct to tread so softly. The glow of the lamp through the window was more likely to be noticed than any footfall.

He turned down the lamp accordingly and they waited for their eyes to grow more accustomed to the dark, alleviated only sparingly by the street lamps on Princes Street.

Sarah went to the back of the long sales counter and rolled out a shallow drawer from beneath. There indeed was the sales ledger.

'Let us take it where we can turn up the lamp,' Raven said.

They withdrew into the laboratory, where they placed the ledger upon a table. Raven turned the pages carefully as Sarah held the lamp close. It was not difficult to find what they were looking for. Sales of chloroform had only commenced in the past month.

Raven ran a finger down the column on the far right, where it stated what had been purchased, and each time he encountered the word chloroform, he traced his finger left, to the name of the customer.

The first few instances were no surprise.

Simpson.

Simpson.

Simpson.

Then other names started to appear: Professor Miller, Professor Syme, Dr Ziegler, Dr Moir. Surgeons, obstetricians. There was Dr J.M. Duncan, insisting upon the extra letter, Raven observed. Mostly they were names he recognised, and it gave him pause to ask whether he was truly considering them to be his abortionist.

He saw a couple of names unfamiliar to him: a Dr John Mors, a Dr Edgar Klein. He was about to bid Sarah fetch some paper to write these down when the next purchaser stopped him with a jolt. Sarah's eyes were quicker than his finger, and she spoke the name aloud even as he read it.

'Adam Sheldrake. Rose's employer.'

Raven gaped, feeling like a fool. He recalled Simpson's lesson outside the inn near the Royal Exchange: *People often hypothesise the sensational, and become inexplicably blind to the obvious that is before their very eyes.*

It had been in front of him all along. He and Sarah attended the Sheldrakes' church in order to talk to Milly, and that led them to suspect Grissom. It had never occurred to him that Sheldrake himself was the obvious suspect.

'Not a doctor, but a medical man, of sorts,' Raven said. 'A dentist. Perhaps the wealthiest in the city. He might even have been responsible for Rose's condition. She was scared she would be dismissed if he found out.'

'I heard Mina make mention of a man in Glasgow believed to have murdered his housemaid because she was pregnant by him. But why would a wealthy dentist risk his reputation to carry out abortions?'

'Perhaps dentistry is not his most profitable practice. And you forget he has an ingenious means of protecting his reputation. Madame Anchou is the public face of the business, while he remains in shadow. Besides, his clients are young women from the lower orders, unlikely to be familiar with him as a dentist.'

'Until one of them turns out to be his own employee.'

Raven opened his mouth to speculate further, but no word issued from it, for at that moment they heard a key in the front door. He looked down the passage and saw the silhouette of a man in a top hat behind the glass.

Though the hour was past midnight, Mr Flockhart had returned to his shop.

FIFTY-TWO

arah had seldom moved so fast in her life. The state of heightened alertness she had experienced in these same premises several hours previously restored itself in an instant and drove her to action. In a quarter of a second, she recognised Mr Flockhart at the door and understood all possible implications as they applied to her circumstances. She also understood that the doom she envisaged earlier, when she heard a voice call 'Stop!', might merely have been postponed, not avoided.

She turned off the lamp as Raven lifted the ledger from the table, and led him swiftly to the storeroom. If Mr Flockhart was visiting at such an hour, it was either to retrieve something or because some idea had come upon him, and both were likely to bring him to the laboratory. The storeroom was off the passageway between it and the shop. There was no reason Flockhart would not need to visit it also, but it was the best chance they had to avoid detection.

Sarah ushered Raven inside and pulled the door to, but not fully closed. She could hear approaching footsteps and knew the sound of it meeting the frame would be too loud. It was not so much a room as a cupboard, a tiny space within intended for one person to reach the shelves on three sides.

They were pressed tight against each other, lest they nudge the door open. Sarah could feel the warmth of Raven against her chest, his scent in her nostrils, her nose almost touching his chin.

She tried not to breathe as she heard footsteps nearing. Through the crack in the door, she saw a dance of shadows, the aura of a lamp as Mr Flockhart made his way through the building.

She heard a cough, a clank of glass upon wood, a bottle or flask being placed on a table. Laughter, a tipsy giggle. Mr Flockhart was a noted socialite. He had stopped off after a night of revelry, but for what?

A few moments later, footsteps approached again. Did he need something from the store?

Once more the shadows flickered, the dancing aura visible through the crack. Sarah felt her heart thump against Raven as the footsteps grew closer.

Then they grew fainter. She heard the front door open. Flockhart was leaving.

Sarah breathed again, then the feeling of relief gave way to something more powerful, as though the lifting of fear had broken a dam within her. Even as the sound of the bolt reverberated from the front door, she pulled Raven closer, though that felt barely possible. She lifted her head in the darkness and found his lips. It felt as though this cramped little space was the whole world, and that world was filled with light.

FIFTY-THREE

aven extinguished his lamp and lay down, though he knew he would not sleep. The events of the past hour felt like they might take days to absorb. He could not even settle his mind to focus upon a single component of it, tossed amidst a storm of information, revelation and emotion. He did not lie alone in the dark as long as he feared, however.

He had barely settled into the pillow when he heard his door open and the sound of dainty feet upon the floor. Sarah stood before him clutching a candle, by the flickering light of which he could see that she was dressed only in her nightgown.

'What are you doing here?' he asked, his voice a whisper. He could not disguise how pleased he was to receive her, but was mindful of the consequences should they be discovered.

'I would hold you just a little longer,' she replied.

She slipped beneath the blankets alongside him, her arms tangling around him and pulling him close. There were but two thin layers of cloth between them as she pressed herself against him.

Raven recalled his youthful excitement when first he saw Evie unclothed, and of all that followed. This felt more powerful, though they merely lay together in silence, unmoving, the darkness enveloping them as though banishing the world outside. There was a rushing in his ears, soothing for being a sound without meaning. Sleep might come yet, though not with Sarah here. Much as he enjoyed the warmth of her against him, for them both to fall asleep would be to court disaster.

In time Sarah spoke softly, but one word.

'Thomas?'

'Yes?'

Raven's response was instinctive, too fast to avert.

He endured a moment of shock, but no fear and no threat. It felt like an intimacy, almost as much as the one that had preceded it.

'How do you know?'

'From parish records. I went in search of knowledge about Beattie, and in particular his family background. While I was there, I confess I indulged my curiosity. I smelled secrets upon you from the moment you entered this house.'

'And what do you smell upon Beattie, beyond oranges and sandalwood?'

Sarah paused.

'Hidden purpose. A man whose true intentions are always occluded.'

'What did you learn of him?'

'There is no record of Beattie's uncle or his mother ever having lived in Edinburgh. Nor is there record of his uncle living here now. I consulted the Post Office directory too.'

'Have you told Mina this?'

'Certainly not, for fear she shoots the messenger. She has an understandable faith in him, and would see it as inexcusable impertinence were I to reveal what I have found or even that I went looking for it. Nonetheless, I will not let her be deceived and walk blindly into a marriage that is not all she believes. There may yet be an innocent explanation, but I suspect Dr Beattie is not all that he pretends, and it is my intention to have answers from him.'

'He will not answer to a housemaid.'

'He will if she might otherwise reveal what she knows to her employer, Dr Simpson. I am tenacious, Mr Raven. And I would have answers from you also.'

She prodded him in the chest accusingly.

'Do not think I failed to notice that you changed the subject. How did Thomas Cunningham become Will Raven?'

Raven had indeed hoped she would forget. It would not do to deny her satisfaction, or some honesty.

'I changed my name when I enrolled at the university,' he said. 'I took my mother's surname and the middle name she chose for me. I wished to be entirely her son and not my father's.'

'Dr Simpson said you attended Heriot's school for fatherless boys. Yet the parish holds no record of your father's death.'

Raven lay quiet a moment, considering how he might best explain.

'I told Dr Simpson my father was a lawyer in St Andrews. That was not true. My father was a philanderer and a drunk, one prone to violent rage. A vintner whose business faltered because he was too fond of his own goods, and who took out his anger at his failings on us. My mother and I lived in permanent fear, never knowing what demeanour would be upon him when he came home.

'Then one night he beat my mother so viciously I feared he would kill her. After that, he walked out and left us. Perhaps when he saw what he had wrought, he finally felt shame, or perhaps he merely sought to escape the debts of his collapsing business.'

'He left and did not return?'

'Days passed, then weeks, then months, until it became clear he had abandoned us. My mother's brother, a lawyer, had some influence with George Heriot's school, and a special accommodation was made, as I was to all intents and purposes a fatherless boy. He took in my mother, as she was left mired in my father's debts.'

'You must feel a great fondness for an uncle who would be so generous. And yet I have never heard you speak of him.'

'I despise the man. His apparent generosity is in fact a cheap bargain for possessing and controlling my mother. He disapproved of her marrying my father and enjoys every opportunity to demonstrate how his judgment was vindicated while hers was responsible for her shameful plight. It is as though every penny he gives her further elevates him and further diminishes her. Thus it is my ambition to make a success of myself and buy back her dignity.'

'Did you ever hear word of what became of your father? Might he one day return? What would your mother do then?'

These were three questions for which Raven was prepared to offer but one answer.

'We are no longer afraid,' he told her.

FIFTY-FOUR

arvis was lighting lamps as Raven descended the stairs from his room, darkness already falling in the late afternoon. He encountered Sarah almost sprinting along the second-floor landing, laundered sheets piled so high in her arms he wondered how she could see where she was going. Raven halted her course before she could trip over David and Walter, who were huddled in her path as they waged an imaginary war down upon the carpet.

'What is your rush?' he asked.

'I am trying to discharge my duties swiftly so that I have a little extra time on the errands I must run before dinner. I wish to factor in an errand of my own while I am out.'

'You mean Beattie. You may not find him at home,' Raven warned. 'I am unsure of the hours he keeps.'

'Then I will make time to return each day until I have the truth from him.'

'After which you will have another problem – that of what to tell Mina.'

'Let us cross that bridge when we come to it,' she said, brushing past him to resume her work. 'I cannot tarry.'

Raven was full of admiration for Sarah's loyalty and sensitivity. He knew she often found Mina a trial and at times rather demanding, but nonetheless, she was prepared to go to great lengths to prevent any harm coming to the woman. The pity was that if Sarah unmasked Beattie as a fraud and a rogue out to take advantage of her, Mina might never forgive her for it.

Nonetheless, he was relieved that Sarah was busying herself with this quest right now. She had frequently insisted upon being involved first-hand in his investigations, but his mission today was taking him into more hazardous territory, and was best carried out alone.

Since their discovery at Duncan and Flockhart, Raven had asked himself how he might best investigate Adam Sheldrake, and the principal answer he had come up with was this: very carefully. He was a man with a great deal to lose, and that made him dangerous. It was possible he had already murdered Rose because of what she might reveal about him. Even if he had not, then his confederate surely had, and with Spiers's killing Raven had witnessed what she was prepared to do, without hesitation, in order to protect herself.

Since the encounter at the dockside, he had worried over how quickly the midwife had recognised him. He searched every face in his memory but still could not think of where they must have seen each other before. This was inclining him further towards the belief that Madame Anchou was an alias for someone else. Did Sheldrake know her real identity, he wondered? Had Spiers? She had murdered him as soon as she calculated he was a liability. Was her true name the thing she feared he might reveal?

Raven and Sarah had speculated that Rose might have been poisoned because she had discovered this forbidden knowledge too. However, if Sheldrake was secretly working as an abortionist, then the dentist had reason of his own to silence his housemaid after her plight led her to the King's Wark.

Perhaps they were both capable of murder: each as ruthless and deadly as the other.

Raven had enquired as to the location of Sheldrake's dental

surgery. Though he also did home visits, he spent several hours each day offering a clinic wherein patients might attend. Raven's intention was to follow him unseen to discover where else he went once these clinics were over, because at some juncture he would have to resume meeting his partner in these dark arts.

The surgery was on the edge of the New Town, on London Street, not half an hour's walk to the Leith tavern. The clinic was likely to finish within the hour, so like Sarah, Raven had no time to tarry.

Raven opened the front door and promptly felt the ice-cold wind sting his cheeks. He closed it again and looked covetously at Dr Simpson's coat, hanging up just inside the hall. The professor was home for the evening now, busy upstairs in his study. He surely wouldn't miss it for a couple of hours.

Raven looked around for Jarvis, who had disappeared into the drawing room. He slung the coat about his shoulders, its weight pleasingly heavy. He felt transformed, like a knight in armour better equipped to face his foe, even if his foe was merely the weather. He only wished that he could take on the professor's mantle so easily as donning his sealskin.

As he stepped through the front door, the coat swirling about him like a cloak, a number of disparate fragments swirling at the forefront of his thoughts coalesced at once into a visible whole.

He saw the figure in the cape, walking towards him on Leith Shore.

Someone pretending to be what they are not.

Each as ruthless and deadly as the other.

A French midwife who may not be French.

A person transformed by a single garment.

'Such an arrangement would allow a doctor to practise this dark art without the risk that would attend advertising such services.'

Sheldrake was not in league with Madame Anchou. Sheldrake *was* Madame Anchou.

He saw it all now. Sheldrake's already feminine face, disguised beneath powder, peering out from the shadows of a hood. And how much easier to hide your true voice when speaking in another language or accent. It was the perfect way to protect his reputation while carrying out his illegal but lucrative sideline.

Raven's head spun with it as he stepped onto Queen Street, which was why he failed to notice the three men rapidly approaching, their eyes fixed upon him. In this moment of revelation, he was heedless of the danger until it was too late.

Two of them grabbed him from either side and bundled him into Dr Simpson's carriage, the third knocking the protesting coachman to the ground and seizing the reins.

Raven did not recognise them, but it took only one name to tell him all he needed to know.

'A Mr Flint humbly requests your attendance, sir.'

FIFTY-FIVE

arah felt a familiar unease about walking the streets after dark, particularly as her journey had just taken her beyond the bounds of the New Town. In her growing fear, she could not help but ask herself what she hoped might come of this. If there was an innocent explanation for Beattie's apparent dishonesty, then she would surely be dismissed once he reported her impudence and accusations to Mina and to Dr Simpson. However, until she had such an explanation, she could not in good conscience allow her employer to be deceived like this, and for Mina to be so ill-used.

There was only one house on the narrow lane, a good thirty yards along Shrub Hill from Leith Walk and the comparative reassurance of its street lights. Beattie's address was a solitary cottage, a glow from the windows enough to guide her path. She recalled Raven saying he might not be at home, but clearly someone was. Sarah didn't know if Beattie kept a housemaid like herself. Perhaps if he did, and he was indeed from home, she might prove someone from whom Sarah could discreetly solicit some information.

She approached the front door on quiet tread, fearful of the sound of her own footfalls. From what she could make out in the dark, it was a neat little cottage, a dwelling she could imagine being maintained with the same attention Beattie afforded his own appearance.

She rang the bell and heard footsteps in response, which she confidently predicted to be male. It was indeed Beattie who opened the door. He looked most surprised to find her there, and not pleasantly so.

'I am sorry to trouble you at home, Dr Beattie, but I have difficult news concerning your uncle, Mr Latimer.'

Beattie was taken aback, though whether his expression reflected concern for the welfare of his uncle or suspicion over the potential unravelling of his deceit remained to be seen.

'You must come in,' he said.

There was a sternness to his tone, at once commanding and yet eager. He bade her follow him into the house. It was brighter than she anticipated. There appeared to be lamps lit in several rooms, as well as the hall itself.

There was no maid in evidence, and Sarah wondered whether the expense of having one would prove an economy over the wasteful burning of so much oil and gas. Perhaps he was busy with activities that required him to flit from room to room, though such matters would surely be simpler to deal with by day.

He ushered her to the drawing room, where he took the time to light still more lamps. An uncharitable part of her wondered if it was so that he might better stare at her bosom. On her way down the hall, she had noticed another open door and caught a glimpse of Beattie's study, which, from the equipment she spied, appeared to function also as a laboratory.

He gestured her to a chair. Beattie sat down opposite, a low table between them at their knees. Sarah was unused to being seated at such a fixture, more accustomed to serving tea upon it.

'So, what news is it that you have for me?'

Sarah swallowed. She hoped that the anxiety she might be displaying would be read by him as evidence of her apprehension at sharing difficult tidings.

'Your uncle's house is in Canaan Lands, is it not? On the Morningside?'

Beattie paused a moment before responding. It struck her that one should not be so wary of a question to which the answer is a simple yes or no. Did he suspect she was testing him? Probably not. Men such as him did not believe the lower orders to have the audacity or imagination to so deceive.

'It is.'

'Miss Grindlay told me how you described it, with its views and fine gardens and even a large hothouse. She said your mother was born and raised there, which makes this all the more difficult.'

He regarded her with piercing eyes, his expression impatient.

'What of it? Come to the point, Miss . . .?'

'Fisher,' she reminded him, though she was unsure he had ever heard her surname before. 'I met a friend today, in the service of a family in Canaan. She was talking about what sounded like the very same house, which was occupied by an elderly gentleman who lives alone. Canaan Bank, I think she said the house was called. Is that your uncle's? Or did she say Canaan Lodge?'

'What of it?' he demanded, his irritation growing. Sarah noted that he had not answered the question.

'The most dreadful calamity. The reason she mentioned it was that there was a terrible fire overnight. They woke to the sight of smoke. The house is ruined. I had hoped word might already have reached you, so that I would not be the one to bring such news, but alas it does not appear to be the case.'

'I had heard no word.'

She noted that he did not ask after the welfare of his uncle.

'I realise this must be particularly distressing as you were to inherit this house, were you not? Though Miss Grindlay said it was in a state of some disrepair and would not be all you once hoped.'

She could see cogs whirring behind his eyes. Raven had warned her that Beattie would not answer questions of a housemaid, so she had considered her strategy accordingly. The bait in her trap was to offer Beattie a lie that would extricate him from a previous deceit, one she believed he was already laying the groundwork to escape. Tales of the house's disrepair and his uncle's illness were a means of preparing the path to tell Mina there would be no house to inherit, from an uncle who would die before she could meet him. If it turned out there was indeed a house in the area that had been so devastated, inhabited by a single elderly gentleman to boot, then this would solve the problem for him.

'Indeed. This is distressing news. You describe the place I know so well. Canaan Bank is lost.'

Sarah suppressed a smile of satisfaction. By naming the house, he had committed himself. She had him.

'I must say, Dr Beattie, I am troubled that you have not enquired as to the welfare of your uncle.'

Beattie was unfazed in his response. His answer was calmly logical, and for that, betrayed him all the more.

'I assume he was not a casualty, otherwise you would have led with his demise.'

'Or is it not that you have no such concerns because you have no such uncle? There was no house named Canaan Bank, and no fire either. I made it up – as did you. I would know why.'

Beattie appeared frozen for a moment, his expression fixed like one of Miss Mann's calotypes. He blinked once then gave his answer, his nose wrinkling in distaste.

'I cannot think what possessed you to undertake this charade, Miss Fisher, but I knew you were making it up from the moment you walked in here. Which is why I indulged your silly parlour games in order to see where this impertinence might lead. And the answer is that it will lead to the street. I will see you dismissed without character.'

As a threat Sarah had lived under for some time, it held far less fear than Beattie intended. Sarah met his eye brazenly.

'I suspect Dr Simpson might take a different view, unless you can produce this uncle of yours and the house he lives in. I have consulted the parish register and there is no record of a Charles Latimer. I have been also to the Post Office, where I verified that nobody by that name lives in the city even now. Why are you deceiving Miss Grindlay, Dr Beattie?'

FIFTY-SIX

he carriage bucked and rattled, travelling faster than it ever had before, faster than it was designed for, in fact. Raven heard crack after crack of the reins, Flint's man showing no restraint as he urged on the horses, giving little consideration to the growing dark and fog. Many an unwary pedestrian had found themselves in need of Syme's ministrations after straying into the path of a carriage when visibility was this bad, but at such speed it was unlikely any unfortunates would survive long enough to face the further ordeal of surgery.

Each corner threatened to tip the brougham, though it never quite came to that; more's the pity, Raven thought, as it might have offered the opportunity to crawl from the wreckage and flee. He tried to estimate the damage should he throw himself from the carriage in order to escape, but it was as though his captors had anticipated such a manoeuvre. They were seated tight on either side of him, wedging him in place. One of them bore a scar from his forehead to his chin, as from a sword blow. The other was distinguished by a goitre so pronounced that he looked like a toad. They had said little, and Raven less.

He saw his foolishness now. He had come to believe he merely had to keep evading Gargantua and the Weasel, and had reserved his vigilance for his ventures south of Princes Street, as though the New Town was some protected kingdom beyond Flint's reach. They had been lying in wait, apprehending him as soon as he stepped outside the door to 52 Queen Street. They had asked questions and tracked him down, and now he was being taken to his doom, a fate he had long tempted.

You have the devil in you.

He thought of the recklessness with which he had regarded his debt. He feared men such as Flint, but that did not leaven the contempt in which he held them, and sometimes the former was over-ruled by the latter. It satisfied that perverse and angry part of himself to defy them. Thus he had not merely evaded making repayment, but had insulted Flint in the way he resisted, and even injured his men.

As though mocking him, Dr Simpson's bag sat upon the bench opposite, a totem of the future he dreamed for himself and which he would not live to see. It had been at the coachman's behest that he leave it in the brougham between trips, Angus having too frequently been forced to double back mid-journey because Simpson had forgotten it in his haste to reach an urgent case.

Raven found it difficult to make out the buildings clearly in the gloom, but his sense of direction told him they were in Fountainbridge, on the outskirts of the Old Town. Tellingly, the carriage pulled up not in front of a building, but at the rear, where he was bundled out of the coach and marched into a back court, gripped either side by Scar and Toad.

The Weasel came scurrying from the close at the back of the building in response to the coach's arrival. He gazed upon Raven with an ugly mix of anger and confusion at him being delivered thus. Raven wondered why he would seem surprised.

The Weasel was followed by a frightened young woman sporting the beginnings of a black eye, the skin around her right orbit red and swollen with a small amount of conjunctival haemorrhage. She looked drained and pale, with blood smeared about her clothes. Raven could barely guess at her role here, and wondered at the whereabouts of Gargantua.

The Weasel strode across and punched Raven hard in the stomach but was pushed back by Toad.

'What the devil are you doing? This is Dr Simpson, whom Flint bid us fetch.'

'No, it isn't,' Weasel replied. 'This is Will Raven, the whelp who near blinded me and who yet owes Flint two guineas.'

'I assure you it is Simpson. Flint told us he lives at 52 Queen Street and is to be recognised by his black sealskin coat. We saw him leaving that very house dressed thus.'

'And I'm telling you this one might be wearing his coat, but that's as close as he will ever get to being Dr Simpson.'

At that moment, out strode the man to whom Raven owed the debt: Callum Flint himself. He was as Raven remembered: not the biggest of men, but lean and wiry, quick of mind and quick of movement. The build of a pugilist and the brain of a schemer.

He looked unlikely to be in a forgiving mood, as rather improbably, his nose was bleeding, the blood still dripping onto an already damp shirt. Some altercation had recently taken place. Raven could hear screaming from somewhere within, no doubt retribution being meted out to whomever had dealt the blow.

'What in the name of God is this wee streak of piss doing here?' he demanded. 'Where is Simpson?'

The Weasel wore a look of satisfaction, enjoying the moment his colleagues had their mistake confirmed. It was like an overture for the symphony of vengeance with which he was about to indulge himself.

Flint wiped the blood from his nose with his sleeve. He had an overwrought look about him, a man at the end of his tether. A man in need of an outlet for his frustrations.

'They lifted this skitter by mistake,' Weasel said. 'He owes you two guineas and me a debt of another kind.'

Flint looked at Raven with sparing regard, as though his true thoughts were somewhere else.

'Do you have the two guineas?' he asked.

Raven could not speak to answer, such was his fear.

He heard another scream, thinking for a moment it was a foretaste of his own. Then he realised it was a woman's scream, and deduced what was going on.

'Mr Flint, you sent for Dr Simpson. Is your wife in labour?'

'Aye,' said the young girl with the black eye, hurried and imploring. 'She is, these fourteen hours. Blind and insane in her agonies. Lashing out at those who would try to assist her.'

'I can help.'

'What know you of such things?' Flint demanded.

'I am Dr Simpson's assistant. A man midwife.'

'I want the professor, not his student.'

'But I am here now, and Dr Simpson yet at Queen Street.'

At that moment, there came another scream from inside the building.

'Bring him forth,' Flint decided.

'I need the bag that sits inside the carriage,' Raven said.

'Fetch it,' Flint commanded Scar. 'And see to it that this time you don't bring a hat or a horse-turd by mistake.'

Raven was escorted into the building and led to a room on the first floor, where he was confronted by a scene that immediately brought to mind the Simpsons' dining room on the night of the chloroform discovery. Several pieces of furniture were upturned and a ewer and basin were in pieces upon the floor. The smell was reminiscent of a tavern at the end of a busy night, a noxious mix of stale alcohol fumes combined with various bodily odours and the very distinct tang of blood.

Flint's wife was being forcibly held in the bed by a number of persons including Peg and Gargantua. They were all in a state of dishevelment and perspiring almost as much as the patient herself. Gargantua looked at Raven with confusion and growing rage, but did not abandon his post.

Among those around the bed was a midwife, sporting a bruise to her cheek. She looked upon Raven with almost as much disdain as the giant. Midwives had little love for their male competitors, and that she was being asked to defer to one as young as him would be all the more galling. That said, like everyone else present herein, she looked desperate. This was one occasion where Raven felt sure he couldn't make the situation any worse. However, his only chance to avoid being murdered was if he could make it better.

'Tell me what has gone on and make it quick,' he said, his commanding tone a means of disguising his fear.

'The membranes ruptured in the early hours of this morning and I have been dosing Mrs Flint regularly with brandy and water,' the midwife said.

The woman was writhing and thrashing, trying to free the arm the midwife clutched.

'However, she became delirious and increasingly restless. I administered several doses of laudanum but to no avail; her delirium only worsened, and as you can see, she became most violent in her agonies. If you believe *you* can restrain her where all of us have failed, then I would welcome the chance to watch you attempt it.'

With that she let go of the arm she was holding, all the better for Mrs Flint to lash out at Raven with it, and stepped clear of the bed.

Raven delved into Dr Simpson's bag, struggling initially to see into it in the dim gaslight. For a heart-stopping moment he could not find the bottle he sought, but then there it was.

Raven put about twenty drops of the chloroform onto a pocket handkerchief, which he rolled into a cone shape as he had been taught. Mrs Flint bucked and screamed, swiping an arm at him as he approached. Raven blocked the blow with his forearm and held the moistened handkerchief about an inch from her face before bringing it closer until it covered her nose and mouth. Within about a minute, her writhing ceased and her attendants were able to release their hold of her, though they appeared wary that she might resume.

'He has poisoned her!' the midwife cried. 'Mr Flint, this man has murdered your wife!'

'This is chloroform, a new drug,' Raven retorted, looking Flint in the eye. 'She will sleep and feel no pain until I revive her.'

With the patient now at rest, Raven was able to perform an examination, upon which he ascertained the position of the infant and the reason for the lack of progress. He felt a knot tighten inside him. He had been wrong in his impression when he first entered the room: there was a way he could make the situation worse, if only for himself.

His examination had identified not the head of the infant in the birth canal but its arm. The mother and baby could both die here. He had administered chloroform, and though it would not be what killed her, if Mrs Flint never regained consciousness, he would be blamed. The midwife would make sure if it.

Raven could not afford to think what would happen after that.

He would have to turn the child in the womb before he could attempt to deliver it, a manoeuvre he had never performed. If he failed, he would certainly be killed. Even if he succeeded, his fate was far from certain.

Raven closed his eyes a moment and took himself from this place. Not far, perhaps a little more than a mile, to a room above the Canongate: the first case he had visited in the company of Dr Simpson. He pictured the diagram the professor had sketched on a sheet of paper upon a wax-spattered table in that hot and foetid room. *The whole child can be considered to be cone-shaped, the apex or narrowest part being the feet. The skull can also be thought of as a cone, the narrowest part of which is the base.*

Raven took a breath and began. His hand passed easily into the uterus and found the infant's knee without difficulty. From there he found both feet and pulled them down, firmly but gently. The chloroform had relaxed the maternal muscles and the delivery was completed some five minutes later; a male child, born alive, although the arm which had been residing in the birth canal for some considerable time was almost black in colour.

The placenta followed shortly after the child, and there was little bleeding. The child was swaddled by the girl with the black eye, whose name turned out to be Morag.

Flint took the baby from her, holding his son in his arms quite jealously.

His wife awoke shortly after, her face a study in disorientation and confusion, as though rousing from a dream. Flint offered her the child, which she regarded with disbelief for a moment before hugging it to her breast.

'I thought myself in the throes of death,' she said. 'Yet here is the bonniest wee thing. How can this be so?'

'It was the young doctor, ma'am,' said Morag.

Flint walked Raven out to the back court, Peg and Gargantua at their backs. The Weasel, the Toad and Scar awaited, accompanied by the man who had so terrifyingly driven the horses. He was a gaunt and ancient thing, looking like his bones ought to have crumbled from the shaking. Evidently he was made of sterner stuff than he appeared, inside and out.

The Weasel was sharpening his knife by dragging it across the stone of the building, eyeing Raven with a purposeful stare. They were all five at their boss's command, which Raven was also waiting for, upon tenterhooks.

'I remember you now,' Flint said. 'When you came to me for money, you said you might not be able to pay it back swiftly, but that you were a man of some prospects. I can see that to be true. That stuff you used was quite miraculous. What was it called again?'

'Chloroform,' Raven replied.

'Where might a man procure this wondrous liquid?'

'From Duncan and Flockhart, on Princes Street.'

'Hmm,' Flint mused. 'A business such as that is liable to take note of who is purchasing their wares. Might one acquire it otherwise? Through an intermediary, perhaps?'

Raven could see where this might lead, but was in no position to refuse.

'Perhaps.'

The Weasel continued to scrape his blade, impatience writ upon his face as he became concerned that the evening might not reach the conclusion for which he hoped.

'Put that damned knife away,' Flint commanded, as though irritated by the sound.

The Weasel complied with a sigh.

'Mr Raven here is to go about his business unmolested from here on,' Flint announced to the ragged assembly. 'I am the one in *his* debt tonight.'

'He's still in mine,' the Weasel protested. 'He near took my sight.'

'You seem able to see well enough,' Raven retorted.

'Aye,' Flint mused. 'I gather you bested this pair single-handed a wee while back.'

'He blinded me with a powder,' Gargantua grumbled.

'Exactly,' said Flint. 'You strike me as a man of some resource and gumption. I wonder if in lieu of your debt, you and I might reach an understanding.'

Flint looked him in the eye. Raven knew he was doing a deal with the devil, but it was better than having the devil on his back.

'We might.'

'And is there something I can offer you, by way of thanks?'

Raven was about to politely refuse, not wishing to delay his departure, when it occurred to him that this was a man with an ear to the underbelly of the city, and many eyes reporting back to him.

'Only information. There is someone I seek. Perhaps you might get word to me if you or your men should encounter her.'

'A woman? Who?'

'She is a French midwife who goes by the name of—'

'Madame Anchou,' said the Toad. 'Sells pills and potions, at quite a cost.'

'Aye,' said Scar with a chuckle. 'He bought one from her that was supposed to help him stand proud, if you take my meaning. Suffers from brewer's droop.'

'Didn't bloody work, did it?' the Toad moaned bitterly.

'What did you expect?' asked Scar. 'There isn't a potion known to Merlin could make a man's cock stand tall at the prospect of any woman who would have you.'

'Where did you see her?' Raven demanded, his urgency cutting through the growing levity.

'In a tavern off the Canongate. I was given her name by a Mrs Peake, runs a whorehouse nearby.'

'What do you remember of her?'

'Not much. It was dark and she had on a cape and a hood. I recall that she had a smell about her, an exotic scent. So strong it would have choked you.'

Raven felt his skin prickle, cold even beneath Dr Simpson's troublesome coat.

'What was it like, this scent?'

'Oranges.'

FIFTY-SEVEN

eattie now had a thunderous look on his face. This was when Sarah expected to be shown the door, amidst a pompous tirade about impropriety and further insistence that he would see her sacked.

Instead, a sudden calmness seemed to come upon him. A transformation. He sat back in his chair, holding open his hands in a placatory gesture.

'Miss Fisher, I owe you an apology. You are correct. All is indeed not as it would appear.' He got to his feet, his expression sincere. 'I would ask of you the courtesy of allowing me to explain. And by way of contrition, let me offer you some tea, that we might take it together while you hear me out.'

Sarah stood up too, almost by reflex. 'Allow me to assist you then, sir.'

'No, please. The kettle is not long boiled in the grate, and you have served me often enough. It is right and fitting that I should reciprocate for once.'

Sarah knew not to push the issue. She watched him leave the room, then made use of the brief time he was absent to step quietly across the hall and take a closer look at his study.

She saw anatomy specimens arrayed in jars upon shelves against the wall, reflected gaslight glinting in the glass. There were examples of every organ preserved in clear fluid: hearts, lungs, kidneys, even a brain. Sarah could well imagine how this sight might unnerve many an unwary visitor, but as someone used to the ways of medical men, she did not regard it as out of the ordinary. That said, something struck her as unusual about the specimens, though she could not from such a brief glimpse discern what it was. It gave her a vague sense of unease, but that was as nothing compared to the shock of seeing the pair of kid gloves that were lying upon his desk.

Sarah returned to the drawing room in time for Beattie's reappearance bearing the promised tea on a tray. He placed it down on the low table, whereupon it was made clear that he was unused to serving anyone. She noticed that the cups were not matching and that the tea was already poured.

'Thank you,' she said. 'It is such an unaccustomed honour to be waited upon by a gentleman. Might I then be so bold as to trouble you for a fancy or even a biscuit?'

Beattie looked annoyed with himself at this oversight.

'Of course. I bought scones this morning, if that would suffice.'

He returned presently with a solitary scone on a plate. He had forgotten to bring a knife or butter, but she was content with what was offered.

'How did you come to be in Dr Simpson's service?' he asked.

Sarah answered briefly, sipping from her cup. The tea was passable, but far from the finest.

'It is a most unusual household, is it not?' Beattie went on. 'What strange sights you must have seen there.'

For a man who normally talked exclusively about himself and his ambitions, this was a remarkable level of interest to be showing in anyone else, far less a housemaid. It was almost as though he was waiting for something. Perhaps he thought that if he stalled her long enough, she would forget about her own questions. She would put him straight on that.

'Dr Beattie, you promised me an explanation. I wish to know

why you lied to Miss Grindlay and to Dr Simpson about having this uncle. Because if you are prepared to lie about that, one must wonder what else you might be lying about.'

With that, she drained her cup, thus underlining that the niceties were over.

Beattie watched her place it down upon the saucer, at which point she was sure she detected another transformation. He seemed more himself again, confident and haughty.

'I asked about your service, Miss Fisher, because I hoped you would understand that opportunities are not always easy to come by. Sometimes they must be manufactured. People can be encouraged to believe in something, that they may have confidence in it. I wished them to have confidence in me.'

He took a drink from his own cup.

'You are correct. I have no uncle and no house to inherit. All that I have, I have made for myself. My background is of no real relevance. It is my prospects and my future that are important, and I will have a great future. Mina is very lucky that she will share it.'

'You are only interested in her for the connection to Dr Simpson such a marriage would afford, are you not?'

'Let us be realistic. Mina's only hope of a husband was someone seeking association with Dr Simpson. She is fortunate that it should be me. In the field of my profession, my gifts are only matched by my ambitions.'

He was finally showing the true face she suspected, and he clearly knew that he had nothing to fear from such candour. Not from this housemaid before him.

'On the subject of gifts, Dr Beattie, I saw you purchase a pair of kid gloves at Kennington and Jenner's. I assumed them wrapped as a present intended for Miss Grindlay, and yet I spied them open and worn in your study. Do you have another woman?'

'I have many women. One would imagine Mina ought to be realistic enough to understand the nature of the match. But I will own that those gloves do belong to one who is particularly dear to me.'

He wore an odd smile, one that Sarah found unsettling.

'You were prying around my study, then,' he went on, standing up once more. 'Perhaps you should come and pry a little closer. For I have something there that I would like you to see.'

Beattie took hold of her arm and pulled her roughly to her feet, leading her from the room with a tight grip. He hauled her into the study, where he stood her next to the table upon which the gloves lay.

'I am not the only one disguising their true intentions. You and young Raven are secretly in league, are you not?'

Sarah said nothing. She was looking for how she might flee, but Beattie stood in the doorway.

'Have a look in that press, there by the window.'

Sarah approached it, her heart beating a tattoo. Even before opening the door, she knew what she would find inside.

Hanging before her in the cupboard was the French midwife's robe.

'Have you answers enough now?' Beattie asked, his tone distressingly calm.

She stared at the garment, contemplating all of its implications.

'The gloves were for you. You are Madame Anchou. You murdered Rose Campbell because she discovered this.'

'Like you, she saw things she should not have. At least in her case, she was not spying. I thought her asleep and she witnessed me take on my disguise.'

Sarah turned to face him. 'Why are you telling me such things? Why would you show me this?'

'I'm sure even a housemaid must have the wit to work that out.'

Sarah swallowed, her mouth dry and her voice failing. 'Do you intend to kill me, Dr Beattie?'

'No, Miss Fisher, I do not *intend* to kill you. I killed you two minutes ago, when you drank your tea.'

aven clung to the inside of the door as the brougham took another tight corner. His heart leapt as he felt the wheels on one side actually leave the ground, but he suppressed the urge to tell the skeletal coachman to slow down. Shorn of the weight of two passengers, he was driving the horses even faster upon the return journey, and Raven had no wish to interfere with that.

Sarah's instincts had been right all along. She had talked of a whiff of deceit, but it was a stench, covered up by bergamot and sandalwood. It was not Sheldrake, but Beattie who was the French midwife, Beattie who had recognised Raven from a distance as he waited on the dockside, Beattie who had killed Spiers for fear that the landlord might spill his secret. And Beattie to whom Sarah was headed to confront this night, alone and with no notion of just how dangerous he was.

Raven had deduced all of this in a twinkling the moment that overpowering scent was described. He saw beneath the veil Beattie had cast about himself and understood what had been before him since the beginning. That calm he exhibited in the face of suffering was not due to knowing true sorrow. It was because he genuinely felt nothing. He did not care about the patients. He did not care about anyone. That equanimity, that assuredness, it was a detachment from human emotion.

Raven thought back to when Beattie told him about his lamented Julia, his one true love who died the day before their wedding. What a look of anger had preceded this revelation, an outraged fury that briefly surfaced at having been challenged. Beattie had then composed himself and responded with a tale so tragic, so poignant, and so tailored to assuage Raven's suspicions.

Raven recalled the pause after he asked for her name. Beattie had needed a moment to make one up.

Suddenly every remembered conversation seemed to reveal a hidden truth.

It is always wise to learn as much as you can about the great names in your field, in case fate should throw you into their company.

Beattie boasted how he had researched Simpson's background in depth. Did he know all along about the unmarried sister-in-law who might provide a route into Simpson's family and his name? Was this in his plans even as he sent that blood-smeared note calling for Simpson's assistance?

Raven understood now how adept Beattie was at playing a part. He could pretend to be genuinely interested in Mina, just as he could pretend to be protecting Raven from the consequences of Caroline Graseby's death. Raven had been unable to see how she could have died from the ether. It was clear now that it was likely something Beattie did that killed her. He had killed Graseby and he had killed so many others: some he perhaps hadn't meant to and some he certainly did – those whose on-going existence threatened to expose him.

Raven had raced without hesitation from Flint's yard to the brougham, urging they proceed with all haste, until the coachman asked where they were bound. That was when he realised he did not know where Beattie lived.

He leapt from the carriage even before it had come to a halt outside No. 52, racing across the pavement and throwing open the door. He found Jarvis in the hallway, Mrs Lyndsay standing beside him. Her face was ruddy, and not merely from the heat of the stove. She looked furious.

'Where is Dr Simpson?' Raven demanded.

'He is gone with Angus to fetch McLevy,' Jarvis answered. 'His coach and horses were stolen – with you in it, I believe. They hailed a hansom and set off for the High Street and the police office. Where have you been? Why are you wearing Dr Simpson's coat? And do you know what is become of Miss Fisher? She has not returned for dinner duties.'

'Nor ought she to return now,' Mrs Lyndsay added, 'for if she does, she will find no tasks awaiting her. She is gone without leave and it is the last I will tolerate. The girl can consider herself dismissed.'

He took the stairs three at a time in a rapid ascent towards Dr Simpson's study. He knew there had been correspondence between Beattie and the professor, from which his place of residence might be ascertained. He knew also that Mina's own letters had been Sarah's source, but there were any number of subjects he did not wish to broach with Miss Grindlay in order to procure this information.

Simpson's desk was in its usual state of chaos, covered in so many sheets of paper that it resembled the floor of a white-treed forest in late autumn. Raven rifled through it, separating technical notes from correspondence and discarding items he had checked by dropping them to the floor. He soon happened upon what he required: a letter from Beattie formally proposing his marriage to Mina. There it was: Shrub Hill, just beyond the edges of the New Town.

Raven's eyes had no sooner lifted the letter than he noticed Simpson's case journal beneath it. It was open at a recent entry concerning a visit to a house on Fettes Row, the chloroform-assisted birth of a daughter to a Mrs Fiona McDonald. Simpson kept detailed notes of all his visits in this volume, and that would include the case at Danube Street about which he was sworn to secrecy.

He was aware time was wasting but he had to know, especially in light of what he had now discovered about Beattie. He flipped the pages frantically until he found the entry, made only hours before that fateful gathering in the room downstairs.

Raven felt a lurching in his gut as he confirmed that the procedure at which he assisted had in fact been an attempted abortion. But that was nothing compared to what he felt as he read on. Rather than having difficulty in becoming pregnant, Caroline Graseby's problem had been quite the opposite. She *was* pregnant, but the dates of an extended business trip to America quite conspicuously precluded her husband being the father. 'Inconvenient evidence of indiscretions' was how Simpson delicately put it. Terrified of the consequences, Mrs Graseby had sought the means to correct her condition.

According to Simpson's notes – which mercifully did not mention Raven's name – the individual who carried out the procedure was a Dr John Mors. It was an alias, and one of the unfamiliar names that had appeared in Duncan and Flockhart's ledger. Graseby had called him Johnnie, and Beattie had instructed Raven similarly to call him only John. He had claimed this informality put the nervous Graseby at ease, but now Raven understood that it was to prevent them each learning that the other knew him by a different surname.

Raven recalled the easy manner with which Beattie and Graseby had sat together, and the pressure he was putting on her to submit to the procedure. He suddenly had a notion that Beattie had been attempting to abort his own child.

However, none of these things was yet the most shocking. Simpson had been able to discover all this from the patient herself, for Caroline Graseby was not dead.

FIFTY-NINE

aven ran out onto the pavement, where he found that his ancient coachman had vanished. Perhaps they had passed a comfortable-looking cemetery on the return journey and he had gone there to take up residence. Raven looked left and right in the hope that he might find Dr Simpson and Angus hurrying back. Instead he merely saw darkness and fog.

Having no notion of how to drive horses or to ride one, he had little option but to run. He took off along Queen Street, heading east at a pace he estimated he could maintain for the entire journey. Shrub Hill was almost the distance he had run from Professor Gregory's lab after discovering the dead rabbits. Recalling that occasion, he wondered whether once again he might be wrong about the danger, just as it transpired that Sarah had mislaid the deadly vial. Beattie would have no reason to suspect Sarah's queries on Mina's behalf indicated any inkling of his greater secret, so perhaps at most he would send her away with a scolding for doubting his word, and for her insolence in pursuing those doubts.

After all, Sarah *had* no inkling. If she did, she would never have gone there.

But as he ran, he saw how Beattie might indeed suspect. He

had recognised Raven on the dock outside the King's Wark and understood that Raven was looking into these matters. Beattie had fled, and then doubled back to kill Spiers. Had he also seen Sarah, and deduced she was the housemaid who sought Madame Anchou's services in order to draw her out?

Raven cut around the back of Hope Crescent, sacrificing street light for the ability to approach Beattie's cottage from the rear. It would not do to present himself at the front door, as Beattie already knew Raven was a threat. He would have to take him by surprise.

He crept quietly into the grounds, picking his path carefully in the sparing glow of light from a rear window. He saw no shadow, no flicker of movement from within, and heard no voices. The sound of argument would have been a welcome one.

Raven drew closer, crouched beneath the sill, then slowly raised himself up to look inside. All thoughts of stealth and strategy flew from his mind as he peered through the glass and saw Sarah's body lying on the floor.

He ran directly to the back door, ready to break it down if he had to. It was not locked. He charged inside with no thought for quiet, passing through a kitchen where he caught a glimpse of a mortar and pestle next to the kettle, fine powder dusting the marble's rim.

From the hall he could see Sarah's arm outstretched where she lay on the floor of Beattie's study. Raven felt propelled towards her as though driven by a hand at his back. As he neared the doorway, he was felled by an explosion of light and pain. Something solid and heavy struck him across the face, the full force of its swing added to the weight of his own momentum.

He reeled from the impact, blind and dazed, his legs weakened beneath him. Raven caught a flashing glimpse of Beattie clutching a poker or a stave. Further blows rained without mercy, one to the base of the spine, another to the back of his legs, another smashing down upon his head. He collapsed face-first to the floor, where still another strike to his side left him barely able to breathe. He was helpless.

Beattie knelt on his back and began securing his wrists with twine. He did so tightly and expertly, in a way that told Raven he was not the first person to be bound by this man.

He tried to raise his head, but as he did so, blood ran from his scalp into his right eye. Through his left he could see Sarah lying on the carpet a few feet across the room. She was utterly still. No twine had been necessary for her.

He would have cried then, but he did not have the breath.

Above her body, he saw shelves upon shelves of anatomy specimens ranged in jars, dominating the room. Even in his damaged state, something about the collection struck Raven as strange, though it took him a moment to grasp what was wrong with them.

The answer was: nothing.

Most medical men kept specimens of diseased organs as well as healthy ones, illustrative of unusual and damaging conditions. Beattie's were all perfectly healthy, utterly normal.

'You killed them,' Raven said, finding a voice.

'Killed who?' Beattie asked, as though irritated by the query.

'So many. The women who took your pills. You gave them a slow and painful death, and you cared not. The women you operated on for abortions died just as slowly. You killed them too.'

Raven glanced across the room once more, some part of him still hoping he would see the movement that would prove him wrong. It did not come.

'And you killed Sarah.'

'Quite,' Beattie replied, as though it were a mere detail.

Raven struggled to find his voice through anger and grief. 'My God, man. The only woman you *didn't* kill was Graseby, yet you told me I had. Did you think I would never find out?'

'As you suggest, I cared not. But I knew that believing it

would make you most obedient, almost as obsequious as you are towards that bombastic and self-regarding prig you work for.'

'Self-regarding? You murdered Sarah, Rose Campbell and Spiers, merely to silence them.'

'Their sacrifice is unfortunate, but they forced my hand. I am on the cusp of remarkable things that will bring untold benefits. For a housemaid or a publican to have stopped my work would have been a disaster.'

Beattie satisfied himself that the bonds around Raven's wrists were tight and began binding his ankles.

'You, by contrast, will not be a great loss. You would not have made a good doctor, Raven. You let sentiment hold you back: sentiment and sympathy. To truly succeed, you must set the patients apart from yourself, and I saw no evidence you could do that, which is why you would never have been anything more than a nurse.'

'Set them apart? You use them as subjects for experiment. You poisoned those women. Was it not enough to profit from their desperation by selling them a useless pill at exorbitant cost? Did you have to give them a painful death so that they did not come looking for their money back?'

'That was not my intention. Again, you do not have any understanding. These were necessary sacrifices on the path to progress. I sought to get the measure right so that it might bring on premature labour without harming the mother. Imagine what a boon it will be when I perfect a safe and effective means to deal with the unwanted fruits of passion, to say nothing of a preventative check on the relentless spawning of the poor.'

Beattie stood up straight, standing over Raven as he lectured him. He always did love the sound of his own voice. Raven was keen to keep him talking, as his only hope of salvation lay in Simpson and McLevy getting his message via Jarvis and hurrying here in response.

'I sold my remedy in good faith, Raven. If the pills did not get the desired result, I offered the operation. There were many who took formulations of my drug and, though it did not have the desired effect, they did survive to request the procedure.'

'Which was when you killed them with your ham-fisted butchery.'

'How else is one to learn but practise? And it is vital to perfect a technique before offering it to the wealthy ladies of the New Town. So who better to learn on than whores and housemaids, as the former will be buried unmarked and the latter buried unmourned?'

'What about Graseby? Your technique was not perfected when you operated on her, for I know you have killed others since.'

'That was something of an emergency. Her husband was apt to cause trouble so I had to act, and I knew that if she died, then either way it solved my problem.'

'So the child was yours. You are an abomination, Beattie. *Primum non nocere*. Do you remember quoting those words to me? You say I am held back by sentiment and sympathy, but what is our purpose if not to alleviate suffering? To lengthen out human existence, not to curtail it? And to do those things, a doctor must not be apart from his patients, but one with them.'

Beattie sneered, ugly and yet amused. 'You sound like your mentor: encumbered by emotion to the point of being unmanned. Do you think posterity will remember him just because he spared a few women an everyday and natural pain? I will grant you his chloroform has proven useful, but in the grander scheme, suffering has an important purpose, Raven. It is necessary. As is sacrifice.'

Raven swallowed, the fear gripping him as surely as the bonds. Beattie had said all he wished to, and was preparing for action.

'What do you mean to do?'

'Young Dr Duncan was right, though he spoke in jest. A footnote might yet be made of you in medical history. You will not be a doctor, but you will make a contribution as the subject of experiment.'

Raven's eye was immediately drawn to the jars. He felt a growing panic, manifest in a struggle against his bonds, but his hands and feet were securely tied.

'No, no, you misunderstand,' Beattie told him. 'The late Miss Fisher will fulfil that purpose adequately, for which I am grateful to her. Even with the Anatomy Act, cadavers for dissection are not so easy to come by. Whereas you, Raven, will provide me with something far more valuable: the opportunity to practise multiple surgical techniques on a live patient.'

He felt rough hands around his shoulders as Beattie began to drag him from the study.

'I warn you,' Raven said breathlessly. 'You are already undone. When I left, Simpson had gone to fetch the policeman McLevy. I have left word for them to come to this address.'

'Yet they do not arrive. But thank you for the warning: I shall extinguish the lights, so that if they do visit this house, they shall find me not at home. For the only lamps I burn will be down in my cellar, illuminating our work together.'

Raven saw the inescapable truth of it, and had no play left but to cry 'Murder!'

Even as he shouted, he could tell his voice would not carry beyond the house. Nonetheless, Beattie stopped and crouched over him once again in order to stuff a handkerchief into his mouth.

This is how it ends, Raven thought. This is how it ends, as it was always destined to do. It was where his path began: with two bodies lying on a floor, one man and one woman. In the beginning, the man was dead, the woman alive, though scared and bleeding. At the end, it was the woman who was slain and the man bloodied but breathing – though only for now.

Where it began: in his mother's kitchen, watching his father beat and kick her, oblivious of the blood and the screams, too drunk and blind in his rage to see that he would soon kill her.

Too drunk and blind to see his son approach from behind, clutching a candlestick, its round, heavy base to the top.

He had swung it only once, to the back of his father's head. He meant only to stop him, but his blow was truer than intended.

You have the devil in you, she always said.

And in that moment, the devil claimed him.

Raven set out upon a mission to redeem himself, to become a doctor: to heal, to save, to atone. It was one of many fool's errands in his life, for there was no redemption: only the twisting path that inevitably led him here to his final damnation.

He heard a whipping sound, something cutting through the air.

Beattie stopped. He let go of Raven, his eyes bulging as he clutched between his legs, a crippling, uncomprehending agony on his face.

He dropped to his knees, revealing Sarah behind him. She stood with a poker gripped in both hands, fire in her eyes.

'I also have the wit to know that a preening onanist who regards himself a god does not gladly wait upon a housemaid,' she said.

As these words met Beattie's ears, the poker whipped through the air again, this time connecting with his skull.

SIXTY

t was tea that proved her salvation.

This most mundane of tasks had insultingly come to define her everyday life: an endless ritual of making and serving hot refreshments, but loath as Sarah might be to admit it, it had also saved her life.

Miss Fisher, I owe you an apology.

Beattie's manner had changed so suddenly. His look of gathering anger had vanished in an instant, replaced by a solicitude that was supposed to reassure her, but which in fact provoked an impulse to flee. She felt an acute sense of impending peril, an instinct of fear more profound than she had ever known.

She might have dismissed this as merely an accumulation of her anxiety in confronting Beattie about his lies, but that he meant her harm was in no doubt when a moment later he offered to make her tea. A man of his character did not make tea for anyone, least of all a housemaid.

In that moment Sarah understood that he meant to poison her, and from such a horrific realisation she began to understand far more than that. But to be absolutely sure, she offered to join him in the kitchen. She knew not to push the issue, for if she did not make it easy for him to carry out his plan, he would surely improvise another.

Though her instinct was to run, she feared she would be caught, and at that point her only advantage would be gone: that he did not realise she knew what he was about. Had he locked the front door? She could not remember. Even if it was open, he would be faster, and he would certainly be more powerful. She would have to choose her moment, when he believed he had already dealt with her.

While Beattie busied himself preparing her death, she seized the opportunity to search his study. Something unsettled her about his anatomy specimens, but the thing that most set her mind racing was the sight of the black gloves. It all fell into place when she saw those. She knew who had been wearing them and why. She knew that Beattie was Madame Anchou.

He brought the tea in already poured, which was quite wrong. This was because there was something slipped into one of the cups: cups that did not match – also quite wrong – so that he knew which one to offer her, and also an insurance against her having guessed his intention and swapping them around amidst distraction.

Steeling herself to hide her fear, she had asked him for a biscuit. As soon as he left the room, she emptied her tea into an earthenware vase, replenishing it from the pot before Beattie returned.

His conduct had been utterly transparent after that. He was stalling for time, avoiding giving anything away until he was certain of her fate. As anticipated, his manner changed again as soon as she had drained her cup.

After that, it was a question of choosing her moment to feign the effects. To assist with this, she had to know what he thought he had given her.

She clutched her stomach in reflexive response. 'Strychnine?'

Beattie wore a patronising smile. 'Yes, I gather you have been reading Christison. Not, I imagine, that you have understood much of it, but be reassured that no, I have not used *nux vomica*. It is my intention to dissect you, and I don't wish to have to wait so long for the rigid contortions to loosen. No, I have given you prussic acid. It is a narcotic poison, swift and painless. Believe me, I would have done the same for Rose had it been to hand. I do not believe in unnecessary cruelty, Miss Fisher. I am not a monster.'

Prussic acid. She knew it from her reading. Symptoms commenced within two minutes and it caused death within ten. She also knew that unlike strychnine, prussic acid was detectable after death, but this would be of significance only if a body was found.

Sarah looked at the jars and understood Beattie's full intentions.

Her legs had gone from under her shortly after that. She fell to the floor, breathing slowly at first, then gasping deeply for a while before lying absolutely still. Beattie did not check her pulse, which would have easily betrayed her, for it was pounding. He seemed absolutely confident about the poison, which made her wonder whether it wasn't the first time he had done this.

Shortly after, she heard the back door open followed by footsteps from the kitchen. She dared open her eyes just a little, and almost cried out in warning to whoever approached when she saw Beattie swing back with a wooden stave, but it was already too late. She would only get one chance to act, and she had to make it count.

Sarah untied Raven and together they fastened the twine around Beattie, who was beginning to rouse. He and Raven were both bleeding, but her healing instinct only applied to one of them. In the case of Beattie, she merely wished she had hit him more than twice.

From outside, she heard the sound of horseshoes on cobbles.

'Simpson,' said Raven.

So he had not been lying in desperation when he told Beattie he had left word for the professor to come here.

Dr Simpson swept in through the front door. His expression of irritation and curiosity turned to one of confusion and dismay as he took in the scene that greeted him: his housemaid in another man's home after dark, his apprentice bruised and bleeding, and both of them standing over the trussed-up figure of his sister-in-law's betrothed.

'I have one or two wee questions, laddie,' he said quietly.

Raven told Simpson all.

Sarah had seldom seen the professor angry. It was a slow process, like clouds rolling over the Pentlands, thickening and darkening, gradually portending the storm to come. He looked down with fury and disgust upon Beattie, who was in turn eyeing the group standing over him with a calm that unnerved Sarah.

'Where is McLevy?' Raven asked.

'He went away as soon as we returned and found my brougham back in its right place. I offered him a drink for his trouble, but he had a matter to return to. I entered the house to find Jarvis beside himself, and that is not a sight one sees every day.'

'We must fetch him back again,' Raven insisted. 'Tell him what has transpired. And then this diabolical specimen will surely hang.'

Beattie snorted. 'This gentleman and physician surely will not,' he said, an arrogant confidence about him despite his predicament. 'For you have proof of nothing. What can you present? A robe that you claim I wore in order to disguise myself as a French midwife? How preposterous do you think that will sound?'

'You murdered Spiers and Rose Campbell,' Raven retorted. 'You dealt in poison. You killed we know not how many women.'

Beattie shrugged, as though this were all a trying inconvenience for him. 'Again, you have no proof.'

Sarah wanted to hit him with the poker again, but there was something worse than his manner. He might be right. Strychnine could not be tested for. It left no detectable trace. There was no evidence Beattie carried out the fatal abortions, as the only witnesses were dead, and those who survived would not come forward to admit their own crimes.

'We will search this place and find your pills,' Raven told him.

'And how would you prove my intention in concocting them was other than noble? How would you even prove what the pills might do? Or perhaps you could volunteer to take one in court, Mr Raven, in order to demonstrate your hypothesis. That is a trial I would be happy to attend.'

Sarah felt like the solid ground beneath her was turning into mud. Raven sensed it too. They both looked to the professor, who always had wisdom, always had answers.

Dr Simpson led them from the study and into the hall, away from where Beattie might hear.

'This is unthinkable,' Raven said. 'Surely he will not walk away from this, and escape justice as he describes?'

'I cannot say for sure,' the professor replied. 'It is the case that what you know and what you can prove are often two entirely different matters, and the court of law can be a harsh place to see that difference demonstrated. But there is another consideration.'

Sarah noted the unusually troubled expression upon Dr Simpson's features, and she guessed what it was before he could voice it himself.

'Such a trial would crush Miss Grindlay,' she said.

'Indeed, Sarah. Imagine Mina's anguish should all of this be made a public spectacle. Not merely for the world to know how she was used and deceived, but to think that she set her heart at this vile creature.'

Raven looked withered and pale in his incredulity, as though the last of his hope was draining from him.

'You cannot be suggesting we ignore what we know simply in order to spare Mina.'

'I could not spare Mina such hurt were it to stand in the way of justice, but nor would I put her through it when the risk is that a murderer will walk free at the end of it anyway. But you are right: we cannot ignore what we know, for a man such as Beattie will surely repeat his crimes. That would be, as you say, unthinkable.'

'So what should we do?'

The professor looked at the wretched figure lying upon the floor of the study, gazing at him a long time. He then glanced at the array of jars, containing so many specimens of untold provenance. There was a look of resolve upon his face, an expression of stony determination.

'The course we must take is also unthinkable,' he said. 'And as such its sin will bind we three, a burden we each will have to carry for the rest of our days. Nonetheless, this duty has fallen to us and we are left with no other choice.'

Dr Simpson put a hand on Sarah's shoulder, his voice low. 'Go to the carriage,' he instructed. 'Fetch me my bag. Raven, you will help me carry him to the cellar.'

SIXTY-ONE

o human being ever comes into the world but another human being is literally stretched on the rack for hours or days.' These words of John Stuart Mill came to Raven's mind as he toiled in a cramped attic above the Lawnmarket. He was no great reader of philosophical tracts, not having the time, so presumably he had heard the quote cited by the professor, or by one of the visiting dignitaries at Queen Street. Raven might be sweating from his efforts, though the room was cold, but he knew the woman lying before him had already given so much more before he arrived to assist.

His perspiration was not entirely down to his physical exertions, but as much from his anxiety that there should be no mishap. Simpson had entrusted him to deal with the case on his own, not deeming it sufficiently challenging to haul himself away from a particularly busy morning clinic. Raven was dispatched in his stead, having been told: 'You felt able enough to administer ether unsupervised.' How typical of Simpson that his words should be simultaneously a reassurance and an admonishment.

Raven pulled down hard on the forceps as the uterus contracted again. He almost laughed with relief as he felt movement of the infant's head in response to his efforts, while before him the patient slept on despite his less than tender manipulations. In addition to relieving her pain, which had been considerable, the chloroform had worked its usual magic in relaxing the maternal passages, allowing Raven to apply the forceps blades with ease. The insensibility of the patient also allowed him to dispense with the modesty blanket that pointlessly impeded his view. Draping such a thing was akin to asking a surgeon to operate in the dark. He wondered what Syme would make of such a request.

Another contraction and the head emerged, followed by the trunk and possibly a gallon of amniotic fluid, which rapidly filled his shoes. Raven cared not at all, as he had just performed his first forceps delivery – with a pair of Simpson's forceps, of course – and it appeared as though both mother and child were going to survive it.

'A wee lassie,' the mother said upon waking shortly after, tearful in her gratitude as the baby was placed in her waiting arms. 'Dear heavens, you're so bonny,' she told her daughter.

A little later, having packed away his instruments, Raven bade his patient farewell and made for the door, his feet squelching quietly in his sodden shoes. His exit was impeded by the arrival of the patient's husband, who shook Raven's hand vigorously before reaching into his pocket.

Raven's financial situation had improved of late, sufficient that he would not need to borrow from his mother for a while, and therefore she would not need to humble herself before his miserable uncle. In order to conceal what they had done with John Beattie, it had been necessary to give the impression that he had fled his home. This they had achieved by packing up certain of his clothes and belongings in a trunk and quietly disposing of them. Though he did not say as much to Simpson, Raven had privately decided that it would create a more convincing picture if it appeared such a fugitive had not left any cash behind.

It was just a pity this windfall had not come a day sooner, as he could have comfortably paid off Flint even after giving half to Sarah. Flint had, of course, forgiven Raven's debt, but he feared the new terms he was on with the man might prove far more onerous in the long run.

The smiling new father pressed a clutch of coins into his palm. It was the first money he had earned as a medical practitioner, and he thought with some pride that he had earned it well.

Raven looked around the attic room in which he had spent the last couple of hours – a few bits of furniture, no coal for the fire – and came to a remarkably easy decision, one that would have been unthinkable a few weeks before.

'Naw, naw,' he said. 'Away with ye.'

SIXTY-TWO

arah was tarrying in the professor's study when the bell rang, an unwelcome but inevitable interruption to a moment of tranquillity. It reverberated all the louder because the house was unusually quiet, the insistent peals rattling back and forth off the walls of empty hallways. The morning clinic was over, all of the visitors dispatched with poultices and prescriptions. Dr Simpson was on his way to Musselburgh to see a patient, Raven was out on a house call, Mrs Simpson had taken the children to visit a friend in Trinity, and of course Miss Grindlay remained confined in her room.

Poor Mina had not emerged in days. She was distraught and inconsolable over the news that her intended husband had absconded, having been unmasked as a fraud. She was told that he lied about his uncle and the fine house in Canaan Lands, that his intentions towards her were insincere and that his name was probably not even John Beattie.

'We may never know who he truly was,' Dr Simpson had informed his weeping sister-in-law, but it was the knowledge of *what* he truly was that she had to be protected from. Sarah did not like to think what it would do to Mina if she were to learn this, and still less what had really happened to him at the hands of three people who lived with her under the same roof.

The bell sounded a second time. Sarah sighed and was about to head for the door when she remembered that she didn't have to respond. Though she knew Jarvis was out on an errand, the new girl had started yesterday, so she could let her jump to it instead.

With a smile she resumed the task of restocking the medicine cabinet, arranging the bottles in neat rows, labels to the front. She took a satisfaction from their careful organisation and from her understanding of their names, regarding the medicines as tokens of her new responsibilities.

Dr Simpson had taken on a second housemaid in order to free more of Sarah's time for assisting with clinics and other related matters. This had come about as a result of her informing the professor that she intended to hand in her notice so that she might seek her living as a nurse at the Royal Infirmary.

'Why ever would you want to do that, Sarah?' he asked, looking not merely surprised but, she would have to admit, a little hurt.

'Through my duties here, I have felt privileged to assist in the care of patients and would prefer a position that allowed me to dedicate more of my time to that.'

'That strikes me as a terrible waste. As a nurse at the Infirmary, you will spend most of your time washing floors and emptying bedpans. A bright girl like you will learn a great deal more if you simply remain here.'

'But what is the point of learning that which I cannot put into practice? I could accumulate more knowledge than any man in Edinburgh, but my status would be that of the best-read housemaid in the city.'

Passion drove her words, but she feared she had been injudicious in venting her frustrations to Dr Simpson in such an unguarded manner. The professor had merely nodded, however.

'It may not always be thus,' he said softly. 'And if things are ever to be different, it will take women like you to change them.'

SIXTY-THREE

e feels the lurching again as he lies in the dark, a sensation he cannot make sense of. It is dizziness, perhaps, like when he has drunk too much wine. There are cries from without, shouts of men, like labourers working a job. They are oddly muted, though, no sense of echo from the walls of buildings.

He can open his eyes now, he discovers. He has memory of being unable to before. He thinks he was blindfolded. He can see little nonetheless. The room is almost completely in darkness. His hands remain bound together, but his feet are free.

There is a dreadful smell, sharp and choking, and he is aware of a dampness next to his cheek. It is vomit, his own. He remembers nausea, but not the action of being sick. Consciousness has been an occasional visitor of late but not a fast friend. He recalls a blurry semi-waking state, feelings of disorientation, not assisted by his being able to see nothing. Exhaustion despite never being fully awake. Sleep coming as a mercy.

He does not know how long he has lain here. He puts his bound hands to his face and feels the growth. He estimates it has been at least three days since last he shaved.

Slowly come the memories, incrementally into focus like he is minutely twisting the lens on a microscope.

Being dragged to the cellar. Lying there on his own operating table, bound and strapped to it, unable to move. Lacking any sense of time, long fearful seconds turning into minutes turning into hours. Wetting his trousers for there was no option to relieve himself any other way.

Raven and Simpson returning. Neither of them speaking. Raven forming the cone of a handkerchief, dripping the chloroform. Then oblivion. Then this dark chamber, its whereabouts unknown.

He sits up and promptly cracks his head on something. At first he thinks the ceiling must be low, but his hands discern there is a bunk above. There is no window, no lamp, and he cannot see to find a door.

Tentatively he puts his feet over the side and slowly stands up straight. He hits his head again, for the ceiling is indeed low.

He advances, hands extended until they meet a surface. He is lucky, he thinks, for his fingers are touching wood. It is the door. Now he must find its handle.

He cannot. He searches with his hands, and discovers that all around him is wood. What manner of chamber is this? Is he in the country, the forest?

He balls his fists and begins to pound on the wall, shouting to be let out.

Shortly after that, he hears footsteps. Light spills in, dazzling his unaccustomed eyes as a door is pulled open perpendicular to where he had sought it. There are strong hands about him and he is hauled down a corridor. Even here, all around him is wood. The men hauling him along are in uniform. Soldiers. Has he been taken to Edinburgh Castle?

As he ascends a narrow staircase, he hears more shouts of men and once more feels the lurching sensation. With a burning fury, he understands.

He hears the slap of the waves against a hull, feels the stinging cold as he steps onto the deck.

All around is water, horizon to horizon.

He is presented to a bearded gentleman, by his uniform clearly a man of some rank.

'Good morning,' he says. 'I am Captain Douglas Strang.'

'Where am I?'

'You are aboard the Royal Navy survey vessel HMS *Fearless*, bound for South America on an extended mission of coastline cartography.'

'How long are we from Leith? You must turn around at once!'

Strang laughs. 'We will not be turning around for some time. Perhaps never, in fact, as we may be circumnavigating dependent upon further orders. Our commission is for three years, initially.'

Beattie feels his legs weaken, and not from the sea.

'Captain James Petrie volunteered your services as ship's surgeon. His brother-in-law, Dr Simpson, intimated that you had problems regarding your conduct with women, so I am sure it will come as some relief to know that you will not be in the company of one so long as you remain under my command.'

'This is illegal. This is press-ganging!'

'Captain Petrie did forewarn that you may not be satisfied with the arrangement, so we came to an understanding. I am obliged to offer an alternative should you decide you do not wish to take up the post.'

'And what is this alternative?'

'We drop you over the side. Your choice, Dr Beattie.'

ACKNOWLEDGEMENTS

armest thanks to:
    Sophie Scard, Caroline Dawnay and Charles Walker at United Agents.

    Francis Bickmore, Jamie Byng, Jenny Fry, Andrea Joyce, Becca Nice, Vicki Watson and all at Canongate. Their passion and enthusiasm for this book has been overwhelming.

Professor Malcolm Nicolson at the Centre for the History of Medicine, University of Glasgow, whose MSc course led to the material upon which this book is based.

Moniack Mhor, Scotland's Creative Writing Centre. Their course on historical fiction was an inspiration.

The National Library of Scotland, whose digitised town plans and Post Office directories provided an invaluable resource.

And of course to Jack, for listening without complaint to long-winded tales of the nineteenth century; and to Natalie for her indefatigable enthusiasm for this project from its inception.

TURN THE PAGE FOR THE FIRST
CHAPTER OF

THE ART OF DYING

THE NEXT IN THE GRIPPING
RAVEN AND FISHER MYSTERY
SERIES

PROLOGUE

here is not a woman in this realm who does not understand what it is to be afraid. No, not even she who reigns over us, for she was not born sovereign. She was born a girl, and that is why I can be sure that even she has known the fear and the helplessness of being subject to man's dominion. Every woman has felt the fear that derives from her own weakness before men whose greater power derives from a stature that is not merely physical.

Many men have held power over me. They were not great men. Oftentimes they were not even strong men. For in this world, you need be neither of those things to exercise your will upon the weak and helpless. Or at least upon those who have come to believe that they are weak and helpless.

In my life I have learned much about treachery and deceit, but surely the cowardliest trick of all is that of persuading someone that they have no power when you know the opposite to be true.

In order to survive, it is thus vital that a woman should learn to assuage her fear; she must recognise and harness her power. But this must be done with subtlety. Without intimidation. Without overt threat. It is the lot of remarkable women that the world will not know our names: that we might not take the true plaudits for our achievements, though they outstrip the deeds of men.

We must exercise our power unseen. As women we may not venture forth alone beyond the dusk, but I do not speak of time when I suggest that we must operate in the twilight. I speak of the interstices, the places in between darkness and light, the blind spots in men's vision.

You wish to know how I could have done what I did, how I could have taken so many lives without arousing the merest suspicion. The answer lies within yourselves. It is easy to hide in the plain sight of those who do not consider your presence worthy of notice.

1849

BERLIN

ONE

e could feel warm blood upon his face. He could see blood upon steel, upon cloth, upon the walls and upon the ground. But what mattered was that blood still pumped beneath his breast.

Will Raven caught his breath and steadied himself. He heard footsteps slapping the flagstones as his assailants disappeared into the darkness of the winding passage, the sound slightly muffled by the shot still ringing in his ears. There were sweet smells on the breeze, a bakery preparing its pastries for the morning's sale. Such warmth in the night air had seduced him into dropping his guard. He would not have walked so freely under darkness in Edinburgh, where even on the most drunken night he remained soberly alert to what might lie around every corner. Here in Prussia that vigilance had become distracted by how different the place felt.

They had been attacked as they walked down Konigstrasse, a broad avenue leading from the expanse of Alexanderplatz across the Spree to the Konigliche Schloss. A castle in the centre of the city was at once a reminder of where he had come from and a stark illustration of his distance from it. With its striking green cupola and rigid geometry, it was hard to imagine a more vivid contrast to the grim barracks atop the old volcano at the end of the High Street back home. But even here, the widest avenues were still transected by dark and narrow passageways, and it appeared that what lurked there was the same the world over.

Three masked men had set upon them, emerging from the shadows where they had lain in wait. One of them demanded money. His German had been strangely accented but the instruction was clear enough. However, one of his comrades had evidently decided it would be easier to raid the pockets of the dead. A pistol was drawn and everything thereafter was a blur.

Fate had turned upon a single stroke of a knife. Few surgeons could boast of such an outcome. This thought passed in a fleeting moment of relief before he was overtaken by a terrifying new fear: that there would be yet a greater price to pay for cheating his destiny.

Raven was a man haunted by the premonition that he would die by violent hands in just such a dark and squalid alley. It was a vision born in Edinburgh on a cold, wet night in 1847, two years before, when he believed he was about to meet his end. He had survived, but the vision had haunted him ever since; not so much out of a fear of death, but of not having made something of his life. He worried that it was a path he was fitted for: that his high aspirations were mere delusion, and that in his essence he was the kind of man who *would* end up dead in an alley.

He turned and looked to the mouth of the passage. He could see Henry slumped against the wall, half visible beneath the light of a street lamp. It felt like the report was still bouncing back and forth between the walls, but really it was just bouncing around inside his skull. His memory of the last few moments was a blur. He recalled the familiar crunch of fist upon bone, Henry being spun by a punch and his head striking the wall. The raising of a pistol; Raven lunging to deflect the arm that held it. A gunshot. Then they had run, and Raven had chased.

Raven hurried to his fallen friend and crouched before him. He lifted his chin to look at his face, upon which blood was running in streams. Happily, his eyes were open, though not exhibiting their usual focused scrutiny.

'Where are they?' Henry asked.

'Fled. Are you hurt? Your face is bloody.'

'I could say the same. This is just a scalp wound. They bleed out of all proportion. Think I struck my leg on something on the way down, though. That hurts more. What about the ladies?'

Raven looked down the street, where he saw Liselotte and Gabriela by a fountain on Schlossplatz. He had yelled at them to run when the attack started, but they hadn't got far. These things were always over far quicker than one realised. Events that seem an hour's battle pass in the blink of an eye to those merely observing. They had stopped and were looking back towards where Henry had fallen.

Raven attempted to help him to his feet, at which point Henry howled.

'Gods!'

They both looked down, seeing a glistening darkness on Henry's thigh. Instinctively Raven put a hand to it, whereupon Henry howled twice as loud.

'I think you've been shot.'

Henry's expression was a mixture of pain and confusion.

'How did he manage to shoot me in the front of the thigh? I had my back to him and was in the process of bouncing face-first off the wall when he pulled the trigger.'

'An unfortunate ricochet,' Raven replied, conscious that it could have been so much worse. He was sure the coward holding the pistol had been aiming for Gabriela when Raven grabbed his arm.

Liselotte and Gabriela had hurried back to assist, concern on both their faces.

'We heard the shot,' Gabriela said. 'Which of you was hit?'

Raven looked at her quizzically, thinking the answer obvious: the one who is bleeding. Then he put a hand to his face. There was blood spattered upon it, and all over the sleeve of his right arm.

'This is Henry's,' he told her. Not entirely the truth, nor entirely a lie. 'He was struck in the leg.'

'We must get him to a surgeon,' Liselotte said, urgency in her tone.

'I *am* a surgeon,' Henry reminded her. 'Just get me back to Schloss Wolfburg and I can assess the damage.'

Raven ripped off the bloodied sleeve of his shirt and tied it tight around Henry's thigh to staunch the flow. With support on either side he was able to hobble on one leg. They were not far from the apartments they shared on Jagerstrasse.

They had been on their way back there when they were set upon. Perhaps they had been assumed to be rich travellers from overseas. If so, Raven would accept it as a compliment that someone thought he looked sufficiently respectable, but though they were travellers from overseas, he and Henry were anything but rich. They were studying at the Charité Hospital and had been there for two months, following a stay in Leipzig. Before that they had been in London, Paris and Vienna.

Raven opened the door to the apartments and began lighting the lamps as Liselotte and Gabriela helped Henry inside.

'Get him to the bedroom,' Liselotte urged.

'Words spoken with a familiar insistence,' Raven said with measured impropriety.

Liselotte tutted. She had been around them long enough not to expect better.

In truth, after what had just happened, Raven wasn't feeling inclined to give rein to his impish nature, but he wished to keep his friend's spirits up.

'No,' Henry objected. 'The light is better here. And I need to sit up.'

They helped him to a couch by the fireplace in the central room.

'Bring in all the lamps.'

Henry let out an agonised moan as Raven pulled off his trousers, the pain starting to overwhelm him. Shock and urgency had muffled the worst of it at first, but now he was being spared nothing.

Henry examined the wound, probing with delicate fingers. He looked at Raven, who was holding a lamp over his thigh.

'The ball did not go through. It's not deep but it's stuck in there.'

He was wincing with every word. Sweating. Raven knew what was coming; had known since they discovered the wound.

'I'm afraid I'm going to have to ask you to oblige me, old friend.'

'Ah, but what is it your esteemed Professor Syme maintains? Obstetricians ought not to be carrying out surgery.'

'And how does your esteemed Professor Simpson counter? We are all licentiates of the Royal College of Surgeons, are we not?'

'Very well. It would appear that I have little choice in the matter.'

Henry lay back upon the couch, resting his head, then let out another groan.

'What? I haven't even started yet.'

'I just remembered I left my instruments at the hospital. Do you have your own?'

Raven masked his feelings with a smile as he patted the pocket of his coat, inside which sat his knife.

'And more importantly, do you have chloroform?'

'No. You'll just have to tolerate it.'

Raven was echoing the words Henry once used when he had been called upon to stitch Raven's cheek. His hand went to the scar as he spoke, by way of reminding him. Henry looked despondent.

'I jest,' Raven said. 'Gabriela, would you fetch my bag from the bedroom?'

'Thank you,' said Henry. 'It's not so much for the pain, as to spare me the greater agony of witnessing your ham-fisted butchery upon my leg.'

'Oh, don't be so precious. You have another.'

Raven pulled the knife from his pocket. Henry's eyes were immediately drawn to the blade, noticing that it was blood-smeared. Raven hoped that in his delirium he did not think to wonder how.

'I hope you're going to wash that thing first. Remember Semmelweis.'

Henry was referring to a doctor he had spoken to in Vienna. Semmelweis had published a paper examining the far higher death rate of maternity patients on a ward staffed by medical students compared to one staffed by midwives. He maintained that this was because the students were coming directly from the dissection room without washing their hands, postulating that morbid material was being transferred from the students to the patients. When he made the students wash their hands in chlorinated water, the death rate went down. Despite this, Semmelweis was having difficulty convincing his colleagues that he was right and was venting his frustrations at anyone who would listen. Henry had proven a sympathetic ear.

Raven did not need to be lectured on this subject. For years Simpson had been teaching his students that puerperal fever was a disease transmitted from one patient to another via the attending doctor or midwife.

He bade Liselotte fill some jugs with water and tear up some sheets to make bandages. While she obliged, Raven prepared the chloroform, asking Gabriela to pay close attention in case he required her to administer more while he worked on Henry's leg.

Raven shaped a small piece of muslin into a cone and proceeded to carefully angle the bottle so that the liquid fell onto the cloth in small drips. He could not help but think of how Dr Simpson's discovery had preceded him on all his travels. Chloroform was transforming surgery, its use spreading fast. In London he had heard John Snow lecture on the importance of precision and control in the dosage. Raven had then witnessed him demonstrate his vaporiser device, invented for the purpose of administering a quantifiable amount of chloroform. Tonight in Berlin he would be relying on an untrained assistant dropping the liquid from a bottle in poor light, and all of them half drunk.

'The drops must be small,' he stressed to Gabriela. 'So that he does not inhale too much.'

'Right now I'm concerned with inhaling too little.'

Raven held the cone above Henry's face.

'And take care not to let it touch his skin. It is an irritant and apt to leave a mark.'

'Much like yourself,' Henry added pointedly. He was of the belief that Raven had a gift for attracting trouble.

'I had no role in bringing down those men upon us.'

'And once again, here I am, in your company in the bloody aftermath of a fight.'

'Maybe you are the one who courts mayhem and you are merely fortunate to have me on hand to assist. Have you thought of it that way?'

'Not once. But often have I said you'd be the death of me.'

Raven searched his memory.

'You have never once said that.'

'No,' he admitted, 'but I must have thought it. So please prove me wrong. And don't forget to wash the knife.'

Raven dripped more chloroform into the cone and bade Gabriela hold the muslin while he poured water over the blade. He watched the blood dilute and run from the steel, trickling into the dish he had placed below.

He thought of something Gabriela had told him about her former home in Madrid. She had grown up in a place called Lavapies. It was at the foot of a hill, where the rainwater from the city had flowed down its carefully maintained gutters for centuries. People would wash their feet there, hence the name.

Unfortunately, there was only so much that mere water could wash away.

Raven cleared his mind, hoping the wine he had imbibed served to steady his nerve rather than tremble his hand. He tentatively touched the area around the wound. Then with the lack of a response from Henry confirming that he was unconscious, he was able to feel for the hard lump where the ball was lodged.

Upon his instruction, Liselotte drizzled water from a cloth to gently wash the blood away as Raven made a small incision. Mercifully, the shot had not struck any of the major blood vessels, though it had been perilously close to the femoral artery. The difference between life and death on this occasion was less than half an inch.

Raven tugged the ball free with a pair of tongs. He was about to discard it but decided that Henry might like it as a memento.

Liselotte drizzled more water to clean out the wound, her face intent upon the task.

The blood and water were soaking into the fabric beneath Henry as Raven commenced his suturing. He tried not to think what their terrifying landlord, Herr Wolfburg, would make of the staining to his couch.

Henry came to a short while later, blinking and groaning. Gabriela looked to Raven, ready with more chloroform, but Henry was awake enough to refuse her.

'Thank you, my dear, but I am impatient to survey Raven's handiwork.' He grimaced. 'Gods, it looks like a pigskin football.'

Then he offered Raven a smile.

'I jest. Neatly done, old friend. You have my gratitude. Now, if you don't consider it rude after your considerable endeavours, it is my firm intention to lapse into unconsciousness, which will not require the assistance of your chloroform. If it turns out I am not dead in the morning, please do make sure I am roused by eight. Langenbeck is giving a lecture on battlefield amputations at nine and I do not wish to miss it.'

'Full of twists and turns'
EVENING STANDARD

'Gripping'
SUNDAY EXPRESS

THE ART OF DYING

'Victorian Edinburgh comes
vividly alive – and it's a world of pain'
VAL McDERMID

AMBROSE PARRY

'Brilliantly conceived, fiendishly plotted and
immaculately realised' Mick Herron

CANON∥GATE

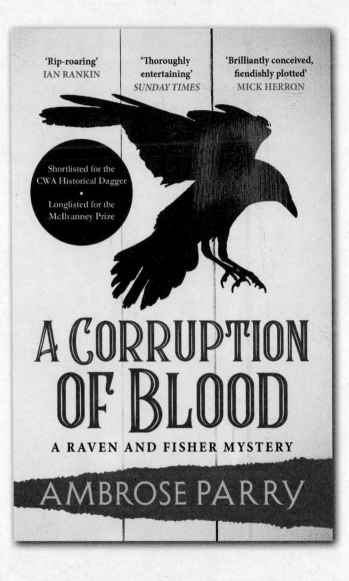

'Rip-roaring'
IAN RANKIN

'Thoroughly
entertaining'
SUNDAY TIMES

'Brilliantly conceived,
fiendishly plotted'
MICK HERRON

Shortlisted for the
CWA Historical Dagger
•
Longlisted for the
McIlvanney Prize

A CORRUPTION OF BLOOD

A RAVEN AND FISHER MYSTERY

AMBROSE PARRY

'The immersive world of Ambrose Parry just gets
better and better' Jess Kidd

CANON GATE